James Philip

———

The Mountains of the Moon

[The Gulf War of 1964: Part II]

———

Timeline 10/27/62 – BOOK EIGHT

Cover concept by James Philip
Graphic Design by Beastleigh Web Design

————————

The Timeline 10/27/62 Series

Main Series

Book 1: Operation Anadyr
Book 2: Love is Strange
Book 3: The Pillars of Hercules
Book 4: Red Dawn
Book 5: The Burning Time
Book 6: Tales of Brave Ulysses
Book 7: A Line in the Sand
Book 8: The Mountains of the Moon
Book 9: All Along the Watchtower
Book 10: Crow on the Cradle
Book 11: 1966 & All That

A Standalone Timeline 10/27/62 Novel

Football in the Ruins – The World Cup of 1966

USA Series

Book 1: Aftermath
Book 2: California Dreaming
Book 3: The Great Society
Book 4: Ask Not of Your Country
Book 5: The American Dream

Australia Series

Book 1: Cricket on the Beach
Book 2: Operation Manna

————————

Check out the Timeline 10/27/62 website at
www.thetimelinesaga.com

Chapter 1

Friday 5th June 1964
HMAS Anzac, Shatt al-Arab, 33 miles South of Abadan

Commander Stephen Turnbull eyed the low, hazy coast to the north-west as it was imperceptibly swallowed by the gathering dusk. In these latitudes night fell like a veil in minutes. A mile astern the big dark silhouette of HMAS Sydney – the former aircraft carrier converted into a fast transport - was already just a vague, blackening outline against the velvet cloth of the warm, still evening and her smaller attendant minesweeping companions invisible. In a few minutes the only thing which would tell a mariner that he was not steaming across a great ocean far from land, was the slowly surging tidal current of the Arvand River – fed by the great press of fresh water flooding down to the Persian Gulf from the confluence of the Tigris *and* the Euphrates at al-Qurnah above Basra - and the narrowing of the deep water channel to the north as it carved through the endless sandbanks and treacherous shoals at the mouth of the Shatt al-Arab.

Her Majesty's Australian Ship Anzac was closed up at battle stations, running without and lights other than a single hooded stern lamp, sounding her way up river, searching for the deepest water. Over geological time the Shatt al-Arab had moved east and west along the northern shore of the Persian Gulf, and every year it deposited millions of tons of new silt, moved old sandbanks, cut a myriad of unsuspected channels to the sea, and closed others. No chart was to be trusted a year after it was drawn and the shifting 'navigation', twenty-five to fifty feet deep most of the thirty-three miles from the Gulf to Abadan and up to thirty feet deep as far north as Basra moved seasonally. It was for this reason that the border between Iraq and Iran south of Basra and Khorramshahr followed the middle of the 'deep water channel', rather than the middle of the Arvand River.

At fifty-six Stephen Turnbull was the old man of the Royal Australian Navy contingent in the Gulf. He had been on the Reserve List eight years – running the family sheep farm in the New South Wales outback – before the October War; the senior substantive commander on the Navy List, his promotion dating back to February 1943. He had been one of the few survivors of the doomed ABDA – Australian, British, Dutch and American – squadron destroyed by the Imperial Japanese Navy in the Battle of the Java Sea in early 1942, ended the Pacific War in command of a fleet destroyer in Tokyo Bay, and before his 'retirement' had commanded one of Anzac's sisters during the Korean War. He had honestly believed he had come ashore for good in 1954; and to his astonishment never really missed the sea.

He would not have returned to the sea at all if his wife and youngest son had not been in London on the night of the war. He had married Hermione in 1940, both their daughters, Daphne and Janet having been born during the 1945 war and their son Donald in late

1946. Hermione had emigrated to Australia in 1936 with her first husband, Dan. She was from Sheffield, England and the newlyweds had moved to the other side of the World in search of work and a better life. Dan had died in a dockyard accident and Hermione had – like a perfect English rose – brightened Stephen Turnbull's life from *that* moment on *that* day in December 1939 that he had first set eyes upon her.

They had talked about 'taking six months out' to go back to the old country for twenty years, but never quite got around to it. With Daphne recently married, with Janet in the second year of her nursing training in Melbourne, and Stephen unable to find anybody he trusted to manage the family farm for such a long absence, in the end Hermione had taken Donald on 'the trip of a lifetime back to the old country' in September 1962 to meet her maternal grandmother and her surviving aunts, uncles and cousins. The commanding officer of HMAS Anzac, at that time still an outback sheep farmer, had planned to fly to Europe to join his wife and son for the last weeks of their stay in England in late January 1963. And then the World had gone mad.

The Navy had tried to promote him Commodore; to stick him behind a desk in the Navy Department in Canberra, or at the rapidly expanding base at Williamstown in Victoria. He would have none of it, had demanded a sea command and eventually he had been reunited with Anzac, a ship he had last seen a decade before in the Korean War during the blockade of Wonsan.

At the time he assumed command the Battle class destroyer with the proudest name in the Service had been in a sorry state. When he first walked up the gangplank she was in dry dock, undergoing a 'wholesale restoration'. In 1961 the Royal Australian Navy – RAN - had decided, in its wisdom, that it no longer needed its 'Battles'; the age of the big gun ship was over and consequently Anzac had been converted into a 'training ship'. Half her main battery had been removed, her torpedo tubes and most of her anti-aircraft cannons sent ashore and the Williamstown Naval Dockyard at Melbourne, where she had been built, had quite literally, been attempting to restore Anzac to her original glory. Inevitably, the addition of modern electronic equipment, updated gunnery and air search radars – the latter relatively high above the waterline - had meant top weight had had to be reduced elsewhere; so Anzac had lost both of her two quadruple 21-inch torpedo launchers, and but for much acrimonious argy-bargy with the idiots at the Design Office, she would also have lost half of her dozen 40-millimetre Bofors anti-aircraft guns.

At one stage everything had been put on hold while the RAN considered the viability and the desirability of modernising both Anzac and the Tobruk along the same lines as their British sisters Agincourt, Barrosa, Corunna, Aisne, Oudenarde and Talavera. Every time that Stephen Turnbull went ashore or viewed his command from a distance, he breathed a sigh of heartfelt relief that the 'clowns' at the Defence Ministry in Canberra had vetoed that particular option. It beggared his imagination that any naval architect would even contemplate bastardising such an intrinsically *perfect* fighting machine in such a cold-hearted way. The Battles were a marvellous combination of firepower, sea-keeping and well, *elegance*; superbly balanced expressions of the final word on conventional – gunship – fleet destroyer form and function.

But what did he know?

Other that was, than that there was little or no honour in fighting it out with one's enemies tens or hundreds of miles away via electronic links at the push of a button with sophisticated guided missiles?

In the gathering darkness of HMAS Anzac's open bridge Stephen Turnbull chuckled almost, but not quite to himself. Anzac's Clydebank-built British sister, HMS Talavera had had her famous day only *after* she had had all the modernity shot to pieces or stripped out of her in Malta; her magnificent finest hour had been as an old-fashioned gunship destroyer.

Now as Anzac edged cautiously into the mouth of the Shatt al-Arab he was thankful that he had four quick firing 4.5-inch 45-calibre Mark V guns and a dozen 40-millimetre Bofors cannons at his command. He had no need of fancy – probably unreliable - surface-to-air missiles like the GWS Sea Cats carried by many British ships; the work upon which he was engaged was only ever likely to call for shot and shell.

Anzac and the Ton class minesweepers Essington and Tariton, were escorting the Sydney on her latest 'run' up to Abadan. This time she was carrying five Centurion Mark IIs, a company of Royal Marines and a whole ammunition dump of ordnance of every description. Previous runs 'up river' to Abadan Island on the right bank of the Arvand River some 30 miles below Basra had been in daylight; tonight was both a resupply mission and an operational rehearsal – albeit on a small scale – in preparation for Operation Cold Harbour. Anzac in the lead with the much smaller minesweepers bringing up the rear was steering a slow meandering northerly course across the *probable* deep water channel to establish if, or how much it had moved in recent weeks.

"Ten feet under the keel, sir," Anzac's bridge repeater called, relaying the report from the sonar room.

"Right full rudder!" Stephen Turnbull ordered quietly.

The destroyer drew nearly fifteen feet fully loaded; this evening she was drawing fourteen feet forward, and a few inches less at the stern. The bottom had shelved from fifty feet to less than twenty-five in a handful of seconds even though Anzac was barely making steerage way in the turbulent muddy water of the river mouth.

"Signal Sydney to steer to a cable to starboard!"

Some years a treacherous shallow bar formed across the mouth of the Shatt al-Arab, threatening to temporarily close the waterway to big ships. The draught of the fifteen thousand ton former aircraft carrier astern of the Anzac was twenty-five feet. Before the October War limited dredging exercises had been carried out on the approaches to Abadan, and around Basra, enabling ten thousand ton tankers to navigate in relative safety as far as the refinery jetties at Abadan, and smaller steamers all the way up to Basra. The trouble was that 'before the war' was another age and no dredging had taken place since October 1962. It was one thing for hydrologists to blithely assert that all the dredging had ever achieved 'was to move the sandbanks around', another entirely to guide a lump of a ship like the Sydney safely up river in pitch darkness.

"Twenty feet under the keel, sir!"

"Wheel amidships. Steady on three-five-zero!"

In the west the sun had set. Briefly, its afterglow traced the black line of the coast of the Faw Peninsula. This far south the land on the Iraqi side of the Shatt al-Arab was marsh and desert, a delta wilderness untrammelled by modern asphalt roads. In this part of the Gulf everybody went everywhere by boat, and even in the burning heat of summer the main waterways never dried up. One road, from Basra ran down the extreme western edge of the marshes to the port of Umm Qasr, otherwise the Faw Peninsula was a watery estuarine world populated by the Marsh Arabs; who lived on their boats, or in the dunes or in houses on platforms raised above the seasonal floods on stilts. Umm Qasr was more accessible than Basra, via year round deep water channels north of Warbah Island or by the channels between that island and Bubiyan Island to the south. In a saner age Umm Qasr would eventually have become Iraq's gateway to the World.

When the Soviet High Command looked at southern Iraq it would see that Basra might be the key to Abadan, and the anchor for a drive east into Iran across the plains below the foothills of the Zagros Mountains; but Umm Qasr would be its long-term warm water port, and the key staging post for its future southward expansion into Kuwait and Saudi Arabia.

Nobody had updated any of the navigation charts for the northern Persian Gulf since before the October War. Apart from the tankers feeling their way up to Abadan, and occasional visits by warships, there were only small boats on the Arvand River.

Umm Qasr had been closed to international shipping since the previous year's coup in Baghdad. The ABNZ – Australian, British and New Zealand - Persian Gulf Squadron needed to re-establish the limits to navigation not just up to Abadan but beyond it to Basra in the east, and to Umm Qasr in the west. And it *needed* to do it *now* so that detailed planning could be undertaken for Operation Cold Harbour.

If and when Commonwealth ground forces - with or without its Iranian friends in the Abadan sector and possible Egyptian and Saudi 'allies' in Kuwait and Arabia along the southern border of Basra Province - ever came to grips with the Red Army they were going to *need* all the help that the RAF and the Royal Navy could give them. Therefore, Rear Admiral Nicholas Davey, the man in charge of the ABNZ Persian Gulf Squadron badly *needed* to know the limits of navigation on the Shatt al-Arab and the approaches to Umm Qasr.

'I want to know how far up river I can take my cruisers, Tiger, Royalist and the rest of my gun line," the Squadron Commander had explained to Turnbull over beers in the wardroom of the flagship four days ago. 'The Moon will be on the wane in a few days. As soon as Sydney is loaded for another run up to Abadan I want you to 'ping' as far up the Arvand River as you can get without actually drawing the fire of the Basra garrison. Don't poke the wasps' nest too hard but bring me back a chart with the *current* deep channel.'

The two men were unlikely kindred spirits; both had carved their own path in life without reference to, or a great deal of respect for the normal proprieties of their respective services. Davey had *got away with it* because he had never entertained ambitions of high command, and to a degree, because he enjoyed the firm friendship and indirectly, the patronage of Julian Christopher. Davey and the late 'Defender of Malta' had raced America's Cup contenders between the First and Second World Wars, two whole decades before the name 'Christopher' had become synonymous with British Bulldog grit, determination and outrageous courage in the brave new post-October War World. Davey had commanded the 7th Destroyer Squadron at Malta at the time of the February nuclear strikes, his ship, HMS Weapon and Peter Christopher's *Talavera* – a name now emblazoned across the Commonwealth as an immutable symbol of the best of the old World and the modern Royal Navy – had recklessly steered under the stern of the burning American super carrier USS Enterprise to fight her fires and more than likely, saved the great ship that day.

Later Davey had commanded the 23rd Support Group off Cyprus during Operation Grantham, the successful retaking of that island from the Red Dawn horde. He had been the obvious man to send to the Gulf where élan and a cavalier disregard for 'the facts on the ground' were more important than the 'steadiness' and 'reliability' that the Royal Navy usually preferred in its flag officers. Moreover, Davey was one of those men who had an innate capacity to get on with everybody. In swiftly and successfully melding his rag tag ABNZ 'flotilla' into a fighting force which was significantly more than the sum of its old-fashioned, disparate parts, it was very hard to see how any other man could have achieved so much so swiftly as 'Nick' Davey.

'I've been wanting to meet you for ages, Commander Turnbull,' the gregarious, somewhat portly Squadron Commander had declared, smiling broadly and sticking out a meaty right hand to welcome the captain of HMAS Anzac three days after the Australian had tweaked the beard of Davey's counterpart onboard the USS Kitty Hawk, the flagship of the US Navy's immensely powerful Carrier Division Seven.

Turnbull had steamed Anzac straight into the great American fleet and manoeuvred around the big carrier at high speed, somewhat over-playing the brief Davey had given him. Specifically, he had 'ordered' the US Navy to stop broadcasting operationally sensitive operation about ABNZ's activities in the Gulf and instructed Carrier Division Seven's C-in-C to stand ready to receive the arrival of his own admiral. Then he had deliberately steered Anzac between the USS Kitty Hawk's anxiously circling escorts until Davey's helicopter had landed on the carrier's deck.

Turnbull had been anticipating a dressing down for 'over-egging his hand' and gone onboard HMS Tiger grim-faced and ready to stand, and if necessary, to fight his corner.

'Julian Christopher spoke very highly of you,' the Englishman had informed him in a tone which indicated that that was good enough for him! 'I'd ask for you to be promoted Captain 'D' of ABNZ destroyers but you'd only make a scene,' he had added ruefully, 'so we shall not go down that road. However, when things start to get *sticky* Anzac *will* be at the head of the line.'

Until that day Stephen Turnbull had had no idea exactly how Nelsonian the Royal Navy had become in the last eighteen months. The Royal Navy had saved the old country by mounting Operation Manna from the other side of the World and fought a latter-day Battle of Trafalgar at the end of last year against Generalissimo Franco's old-fashioned Spanish Air Force. It had secured the Central Mediterranean, along the way fighting a savage inshore battle to capture the key island of Lampedusa, become embroiled in a brutal war of attrition with Red Dawn in the east, lost and later pulled out all the stops to recover Cyprus from that blight upon humanity. Recently, it had begun to wage a submarine war against the Argentine in the South Atlantic; now it was planning to fight a new, seemingly hopeless, campaign in the Persian Gulf. To paraphrase the words of one famous admiral: '*It takes three years to build a ship. It takes three hundred years to build a tradition; the Navy will continue to fight!*'

In keeping with this mantra, the spirit of the Talavera and the Yarmouth at the Battle of Malta in early April would outlive the broken corporeal hulls of both ships for another three hundred years, possibly forever. It was hardly any wonder that the powers that be in Oxford had sent Peter Christopher, the man of the moment in the fight at Lampedusa, Nick Davey's right-hand man in the fight to save the Enterprise, and *the* hero of the Battle of Malta to the United States. The Royal Navy had found its new talisman and exemplar and only errant fools would allow a man like that to place himself in harm's way again so soon.

The darkness was Stygian in the hours before the Moon rose.

There was only the muted roar of the blowers, the soft vibration of the ship, and a very nearly imperceptible motion as it pressed up river against the seaward flow. The waters under Anzac's keel had flooded down all the way from the mountains of Kurdistan and Iran, fresh water mingling with salt as the tide began to flood the lower reaches of the Shatt al-Arab. Anzac, Sydney and the trailing minesweepers might have been alone, unseen in the night.

"Ten feet under the keel, sir."

Then. "FIVE FEET UNDER THE KEEL..."

Anzac's sharp stem juddered on the sandy bottom.

The ship, making revolutions for eight knots but travelling at only three or four against the flood of the Arvand River; lurched to a halt in the water.

Chapter 2

Friday 5th June 1964
Heliopolis Presidential Palace, Cairo, Egypt

From the roof of the Presidential Palace in the heart of Cairo the fires burning in the near distance, the flash and bark of the 100-millimetre rifles of the Soviet-supplied T54s in the streets, the rattle of machine-gun fire and the foul taint of oily, metallic smoke spoke to the utter madness of the hour.

"Your Excellency," pleaded the Head of the Presidential Guard, "we cannot stay here. It is too dangerous. It is only a matter of time before the rebels concentrate their fire directly on this place!"

The President of Egypt had no intention of cowering in a bunker while others fought for the future of his country; but for the moment Gamal Abdul Nasser was too angry to slap the man down for his presumption.

There had been other 'palace coups' before now, each arising out of the febrile, ever shifting background noise of ideological dissent, religious manoeuvring and the unbridled ambition of mainly, middle-ranking army officers. In a young, revolutionary state such things were to be expected but *this* uprising was different; both in terms of its timing and its ferocity. Worse, whereas usually the locus of a rebellion was within a particular section of the officer corps or a disaffected divisional staff, tonight elements of several formations had apparently acted in concert. Notwithstanding that he and his deputy, Anwar el Sadat had been aware that something was in the wind, the scale and the expert co-ordination of the *putsch* had come as a total surprise. It was likely, probable in fact that some of the troops he had stationed in advance at key locations around the city – the radio and television station, the Army and the Air Force headquarters, and protecting government ministries – were disloyal, and that others, in the confusion of the moment, were fighting on the rebels' side because they had no idea who was actually fighting whom.

Bullets whistled randomly through the air, clattering and ricocheting, exhausted on the roof around the President and his small group of trusted lieutenants. The searing heat of the summer day had turned to coolness, although somebody accustomed to northern climes would still have regarded the ambient temperature as balmy.

All of the men around Nasser were of the Nubian Desert; hard men from the south, Upper Egyptians, personally selected by Sadat.

"We will defend the Presidential Palace," Nasser decided, his measured tones belying the incandescent rage burning deep in his soul.

This was the doing of his former Soviet paymasters!

The doing of those bastards in Chelyabinsk whom his British *friends* had warned him would do their best to sow chaos in the lands of their enemies ahead of the Red Army's decampment south from

Baghdad!

Smoke and mirrors!

Such was the unvarying principle of warfare drummed into his young officers by those duplicitous Soviet *advisers* who had infested his Army and Air Force as part of the deal to supply tanks and fighter aircraft in the fifties.

War is not just fought at the front but in the homeland of one's enemy. War is not simply waged by or against armies, air forces and navies but by one people against another at every level of both societies; industrially, politically by whatever means are to hand. There are no non-combatants in war and every citizen of every country involved is a *military* target. Pragmatically, sneaking around behind an enemy and stabbing him in the back was a much more efficient way of waging war than mounting a full frontal assault against his main defences!

But Nasser had known all this long before he treated with the British.

The risk had seemed calculated; the prize great and the internal threats to his regime *manageable.* Nevertheless, only two brigades of the Divisions he had 'promised' the British had so far begun to move down to Suez to 'prepare' for embarkation for the journey by sea around the Arabian Peninsula to Dammam and Kuwait City, or in extremis, Abadan Island. The other two brigades of the 1st and 3rd Armoured Divisions, one at full strength and the other in reserve had been held back in Sinai and around the capital. The 2nd Armoured Division had already deployed its assault brigade, the 3rd, west of the Delta ahead of the planned push into Cyrenaica to seize eastern Libya and the key port of Tobruk. Once Tobruk was in Egyptian hands then the resupply of a substantial armoured force in Libya could be contemplated and the conquest of the rest of the potentially oil-rich country would proceed. Given the fragmented, ramshackle condition of the old Italian colony, which was essentially governed by feuding tribes and the dissolute remnants of the former colonial army of occupation, the planned 'Libyan Campaign' presented few military 'terrors' and ought to have been over and done with long before the autumn...

Nasser realised he was allowing his mind to walk in places disconnected from the crisis of the moment. Standing on the roof of his embattled Presidential Palace it was too easy to forget that the grandeur of his surroundings and the prestige of his position counted for nothing in this hour of trial. As if to remind him of the dangers of hubris the building flinched beneath his feet as another 100-millimetre round crashed into the river facade of the former Heliopolis Palace *Hotel.* White hot tracer rounds curved lazily across the sky in the east, and another heavy calibre high explosive round exploded somewhere inside the Presidential Palace with a crunching 'WUMPH!'

Nasser drew a scintilla of comfort from the fact that one of the things which had so strongly recommended the great, dilapidated pre-Great War hotel for its current role had been its monumental architecture. Parts of the huge complex were built like a medieval castle and beneath it all lay a warren of subterranean bunkers serviced by a narrow gauge railway running the whole length of the building.

If the Presidential Guard stayed loyal nothing short of a corridor by corridor, room by room bloodbath costing the traitors hundreds, perhaps thousands of casualties was going to prise the Heliopolis Palace from *his* hands.

"Leave men on the roof to act as spotters," Nasser commanded. "The rest of you come with me to the Command Room."

There was smoke from the small fires burning in rooms on the river side of the building, and the air was full of pulverized brick dust as Nasser led the phalanx of heavily armed troops down into the bowels of the old hotel.

General Mohamed Abdel Hakim Amer, the forty-four year old Chief of Staff of the Egyptian Armed Forces straightened to a semblance of attention as his leader marched into the dimly lit basement at the heart of the Heliopolis Palace. Problematically, since the headquarters of the Army and of the other armed services were located nearby, little treasure had been invested in command and control facilities within the Presidential Palace other than in the installation of modern communications equipment, including systems for scrambling telephone and wireless links.

Amer and a small cadre of loyal officers and men had rushed to the Presidential Palace as soon as it became clear that the rebels had either seized the Army headquarters building, or that it had fallen to traitors within it. Amer was a tall, lean man who had been born in the Al Minya Governate of Upper Egypt. He had graduated from the Cairo Military Academy in 1938 and played a prominent role in the overthrow of King Farouk in 1952. Subsequently, Nasser had promoted him four ranks in installing him as Chief of Staff in 1956; and soon thereafter he had had the thankless task of commanding Egyptian forces against the better equipped French and British invaders during the Suez War. In the aftermath of *that* war Amer had railed against Nasser for provoking an 'unnecessary war' and for attempting to blame the military – him actually – for the shortcomings in the Egyptian military exposed by it. Nevertheless, Amer had survived and following the nuclear strike on Ismailia in February, Nasser had nominated Amer as 'Second Vice-President' after Sadat because notwithstanding Amer's proven limitations as a military high commander, he was nothing if not a staunch regime loyalist.

"We think Sadat is still holding out at the radio station," Amer reported, saluting cursorily. "I think we have a situation where several units are inadvertently fighting on the 'wrong side', Mr President," he added, infuriated.

"Who do we know is *loyal*, Hakim," Nasser asked brusquely, joining the Chief of Staff at the hurriedly populated map table in the middle of the claustrophobic makeshift command centre.

"Well," the other man hesitated. "Most of 2nd Armoured, pretty much all of 8th Mechanized and from the lack of incoming indirect fire I'd guess that practically all the local artillery commanders are *loyal*."

The building shook from two rapid impacts.

"What about the Air Force?"

"Those bastards are probably waiting to see what happens!" General Amer grunted disgustedly.

Gamal Abdul Nasser stood tall, puffed out his chest.

"Get me Air Marshal Mahmoud on the scrambler."

Amer raised an eyebrow.

Nasser scowled: "Tell his staff that if he doesn't come to the phone I'll have him publicly fed to the bloody Nile crocodiles!"

An orderly brought the President of Egypt dusty coffee as he waited in an anti-room. Periodically, more relatively small calibre shells crashed into the monumental brick and stonework high above his head. It worried Nasser that there was as yet no direct word from Sadat at the radio station.

"Profound apologies for my brief unavailability, Mr President," the Chief of Staff of the Egyptian Air Force apologised through the swooping and dipping attenuation, clicking and crackling of the scrambled line between the Presidential Palace and the Air Ministry building less than a block away. "We had a few local *problems* that needed to be resolved in the headquarters."

Mohamed Sedky Mahmoud had held the rank of Wing-Commander at the time of the 1952 revolution when, aged thirty-eight, he had been appointed Chief of Staff of the then small and antiquated Egyptian Air Force. Born in the Dakahlia region of the delta he had been the first *Egyptian* Instructor in the Air Force on his graduation from the Abu Swair Aviation School in 1936, and the first *native* Chief Instructor in 1944. At the time of the overthrow of King Farouk he had commanded the Almaza Air Base. Like Amer he had faced – albeit more muted – criticism after the Suez War but survived not because of any outstanding qualities of leadership or strategic or tactical acuity but because he was *loyal*.

Or at least he had been *loyal* up until now.

"Do you have command of the Air Force?" Nasser demanded.

"Yes, Mister President."

"How soon can you bomb the counter-revolutionary traitors attacking the Presidential Palace?"

Several seconds ticked by very slowly before the other man responded.

"My pilots are not accomplished night fliers, Mister President. Precision cannot be guaranteed..."

"General Amer will provide you with map references which are to be suppressed. If you have to knock down whole districts to get these bastards, so be it!"

"Yes, sir!"

Chapter 3

Friday 5th June 1964
Blenheim Palace, Woodstock, Oxfordshire

Queen Elizabeth the Second, by the Grace of God, of Great Britain, Ireland and the British Dominions beyond the Seas Queen, and Defender of the Faith, had been informed within minutes of the deeply troubling – 'troubling' because one used the word 'disastrous' very advisedly these days – news from Parliament in the Great Hall of Kings College. Thereafter, she had asked the Cabinet Secretary, Sir Henry Tomlinson to briefly reiterate what *he* understood *her* constitutional position to be given that the governance of the United Kingdom, its overseas dependencies and territories was still, strictly speaking, being conducted under the remit of the pre-War Emergency Acts, and certain 'piecemeal' amendments hurriedly enacted in the months since.

She had spoken to Sir Henry Tomlinson first because he was the greying éminence grise actually running the machinery of government which underpinned the Unity Administration of the United Kingdom. While the *constitutional* niceties had to be observed – at least in the letter – in the unfortunate circumstances of this brave new age this was no time to shilly-shally around the 'facts on the ground'. Figuratively speaking, although the fires were presently being set all around 'Rome' she was not about to start fiddling!

Awaiting the arrival of the Prime Minister the Queen had been deep in conversation with her consort, Prince Philip and with the man who had been her Private Secretary since the beginning of her reign. Fifty-three year old Lieutenant Colonel Sir Michael Edward Adeane had been seriously wounded in the attack on Balmoral in December, the regicidal attack in which her husband had been critically injured and her three year old son Andrew, killed. Robbed of the support of both her husband and of her trusted Private Secretary in the weeks after that attack, looking back she hardly knew how she had carried on. Thankfully, Sir Michael had been restored to his duties and been at her side and by her shoulder since late March, and her consort, Prince Philip, the Duke of Edinburgh had since re-joined her at Woodstock more recently. Consequently, despite the ongoing physical 'discomfort' caused to her by the IRA's 'failed' attempt on her life at RAF Brize Norton in April, she now felt herself able to withstand *any* shock. Even the *shock* of being reminded, in the most unambiguous fashion, that the House of Commons was self-evidently partly comprised of an over-large gang of idiots who seemed intent on stabbing the country, and its fighting men in the back in pursuit of their own selfish advancement.

Although of course, constitutionally speaking, it was not her proper place to say as much in public.

The discussion in the Library of the great old mansion gifted by a grateful nation to John Churchill, First Duke of Marlborough in which Great Britain's incomparable wartime leader, Winston Churchill had been born in 1874, was conducted in sober, considered tones other than when Prince Phillip – a man whose views on the conduct of international affairs had been hugely influenced by his early career in the wardrooms of naval vessels in his wife's father's Navy – made plain his fulminating frustration with the 'bloody lefties' and 'faint hearts' in Oxford in middlingly pungent terms.

Sir Michael Adeane rode out these effusions of angst with the practiced charm and dignity of a master diplomat as befitted a man who had, quite literally, been born into Imperial, and now Royal service. This was hardly to be wondered at given that he was the maternal grandson of Lord Stamfordham, Private Secretary to Queen Victoria from 1895 to that monarch's death in 1901, at which time he had then become secretary to the Prince of Wales, Duke of York and Cornwall, and later to King George V. It had been Lord Stamfordham who had advised the King – the Queen's grandfather - to change the family name from Saxe-Gotha-Coburg to Windsor during the First World War, and to decisively abjure the temptation to offer Tsar Nicholas II and his family sanctuary in England after the Russian Revolution. Stamfordham had died at the age of eighty-one in March 1931 while still in the service of George V.

Sir Michael had been educated at Eton and graduated from Magdalene College, Cambridge in 1934 before serving as aide-de-camp to two successive Governor Generals of Canada - Vere Brabazon Ponsonby, 9th Earl of Bessborough, and Lord Tweedmuir, a man better known to his avid readers as the author John Buchan – before returning home in 1936. Subsequent to his war service he had become Assistant Private Secretary to the Queen's father, King George VI, before being promoted on that monarch's death to his present post.

"I believe that Sir Henry is correct in his analysis of the essentials of the current *situation*, Ma'am," the Queen's Private Secretary remarked solemnly. "Clearly there is a constitutional 'grey area' between the arrangements pre-war, the practical implementation of the War Emergency Acts, particularly those amendments enacted *de jure* by the former Interim Emergency Administration of the United Kingdom under Mr Heath's leadership, but I think that the salient *facts* of the matter are relatively straightforward."

The Queen and her husband listened patiently.

In his role as her Private Secretary Sir Michael ran the Royal Household, responsible directly only to her person. He dealt on a day to day basis with government departments, and liaised constantly with the Cabinet Office and the Prime Minister's Private Office – in pre-October War days separate departments but latterly indistinguishable other than that Sir Henry Tomlinson was, strictly speaking, the Head of the Home Civil Service and as Cabinet Secretary, theoretically separate from the Prime Minister's 'private' office – and when appropriate, with foreign ambassadors and Commonwealth high commissioners. Sir Michael's role was one of oiling the wheels of governance, of seamlessly enabling communication and intercourse between the upper echelons of the machinery of state; and the Queen who was the constitutional, but non-executive head of that State. Sir Michael discharged his duties with peerless grace and efficiency.

"Under the provisions of the various War Emergency Acts Parliament, specifically, the House of Commons sits in an advisory *not* an executive capacity. The question of whether the Prime Minister, and or the Unity Administration of the United Kingdom may, or may not, have subsequently made a decision inter alia, that the 'Parliamentary system' should be in some sense 'fully restored' does not alter the *fact* that under the said War Emergency Acts Parliament sits *only* at the convenience of the 'executive' of *Your* government 'governing' under the 'Royal Seal'. Specifically, that is the 'Great Seal of the Realm'. Therefore, under the powers invested in the Crown, and the executive, or Government entrusted by the Crown in *Your Person*, Ma'am, the situation is that while the Commons is perfectly entitled to express its confidence or otherwise in '*Your* Government', its 'expression' is *only* that. No more or no less. Therefore, it follows that under the letter of the law the Prime Minister is free to disregard the will of Parliament. In fact given the current exigencies under which the nation and the Commonwealth labour, an expression of 'no confidence' in Her Majesty's Government by members of the Commons, if not couched in the most emollient of terms, might reasonably in some circumstances be regarded as *treasonous*."

Prince Phillip snorted.

"Personally, I'd lock up the whole crowd of them!"

Sir Michael Adeane smiled thinly.

"Quite, sir," he concurred without actually agreeing or disagreeing with the Duke of Edinburgh's proposition. "However, I believe that there is a more important consideration. Sir Henry Tomlinson is correct, in my opinion, to caution that whatever action is taken in this matter we must be mindful that without the implicit active participation and whole-hearted support of the Chiefs of Staff, the United Kingdom is at this time ungovernable."

"If David Luce was still alive we'd know exactly where we stood with the Chiefs!" Prince Phillip observed, sadly.

"What is your feeling on this matter, Sir Michael?" The Queen asked her private Secretary. Her voice was very quiet, a little distracted as if her thoughts were far away.

Her distraction had nothing to do with any wooliness of thinking; rather more to do with the nightmare prospect of a vacuum of power at the very nexus of the half-broken realm over which she reigned.

Neither the post-cataclysm United Kingdom Interim Emergency Administration, nor its more inclusive successor the Unity Administration of the United Kingdom, could have been brought into being or made to function in any meaningful way without bending the *unwritten* British constitution – virtually to destruction - in hitherto untested ways; or without her explicit ongoing consent to the *experiment*.

The post-October War governance of the United Kingdom had been a conspiracy between the political parties, the armed forces and the crown, a ramshackle three-legged construct liable to be undermined at any time. The Queen had had her doubts about the wisdom of reinstituting Parliament – a Parliament that the war had made intrinsically unrepresentative because it was so obviously replete with Members who spoke for now non-existent or wrecked, depopulated 'rotten' boroughs – and giving a premature national platform for malcontents and dissenters who wanted to refight old battles pertinent only to the affairs of a World which no longer existed.

"My understanding is that the Chiefs of Staff stand squarely behind *you*, Ma'am." Sir Michael Adeane sighed. "Moreover, Sir Henry Tomlinson detects no sign that the Chiefs of Staff are remotely interested in taking upon themselves the heinous burden of national government at this time. While the Chiefs of Staff entertain a range of views concerning how best to 'deal with' the Americans, and around the resources available to and the prioritisation of military needs over those of the civilian population, broadly speaking it is Sir Henry's judgement, and my own from conversations I have had with senior people close to the Chief of the Defence Staff is that *Mrs Thatcher's* administration retains the *conditional* backing of the Chiefs of Staff. Mrs Thatcher for all her relative youth and lack of experience in government retains the support of the Chiefs of Staff on two counts. One, she generally listens to what they say to her; and two, when she makes a decision she usually sticks to it. This said, Ma'am," he went on, "the sad death of Mr Macleod, the man around whom a substantial part of the Conservative Party might, reasonably, have been expected to coalesce at a time like this, somewhat muddies the political waters around the Prime Minister."

Prince Philip rose slowly and very painfully to his feet to stand behind his wife.

"What you are saying is that now Mr Macleod is gone half-a-dozen of the other Tory bigwigs will start jockeying to undermine and eventually replace the lady?"

"Yes," Sir Michael Adeane admitted sadly. "Very much in the undignified manner of sharks smelling blood in the water, I suspect."

The monarch's consort placed his hand gently on the Queen's shoulder, and she half-raised her face to meet his stoic grimace. They were both still 'crocked'; twin metaphors for the state of the nation. She was just out of plaster, limping like a steeplechaser with a strained fetlock, he was hobbled like a knight in armour trudging across a water-logged ploughed field.

Sir Michael Adeane cleared his throat respectfully.

"Of course," he remarked gently, "much depends upon the Prime Minister's appetite for the fray."

"Quite," the Queen murmured.

In Oxford the factions in each political party and grouping would be gathering to rake through the runes of today's Parliamentary debacle; fomenting plots and coups, manoeuvring for advantage, attempting to make pacts, and form transitory conspiratorial alliances. It was disgraceful but politics had ever been thus.

"What will the Commonwealth make of this?" The Queen asked. While the question was voiced rhetorically it was anything but rhetorical. With Margaret Thatcher at the helm the United Kingdom's allies and friends had known where they stood; beneath the RAF's umbrella of V-Bombers, their sea lanes protected by the Royal Navy, their soldiers standing shoulder to shoulder with British Tommies who were not about to take a single backward step But with a new government? With the Angry Widow gone?

"Both the Australian and the New Zealand High Commissioners have requested audiences with you tomorrow morning, Ma'am," Sir Michael Adeane informed his monarch.

At this point the Queen's Private Secretary broke off.

A lady in waiting entered the room. "The Prime Minister, Ma'am!" A young woman with an unaffectedly plummy voice – as befitted the second daughter of an Earl – declared, bowing her head before and after she had made her announcement.

Sir Michael Adeane stood up and Prince Philip, grasping his walking stick moved to his wife's right so that he could offer her his free hand as she rose tentatively to her feet. They joked a lot about how they were two 'old crocks', like the country, battered and bruised but in absolutely no way bowed by the vicissitudes of the recent months.

Margaret Thatcher's face was impassive.

For all that she looked very tired she was also *younger* than she had seemed the last time she had visited Blenheim Palace only a few days ago. Then she had had the weight of the world on her shoulders; she had been alone and harried from all sides and worried about her trip to Cape Cod to confront Jack Kennedy in his lair. This evening she was herself again. Her war paint was perfectly applied, not one hair was out of place on her painstakingly coiffured head, and her trousseau, a blue two piece no doubt acquired for her at Bloomingdales in New York by Lady Patricia Harding-Grayson, artfully complemented the steely blue in her eyes. A neat black handbag hung from the crook of her left elbow. Her shoes were half-heeled, fashionable but sensible, buffed to a fierce shine.

During the brief civilities of the formal welcome the Queen found herself reflecting that in the decade and more that she had been on the throne that she must have met dozens of movie stars, princesses and famous women, not one of whom had half the personal magnetism of sheer force of presence of the woman who had been *her* Prime Minister for the last six months.

It infuriated her that those hidebound Parliamentary buffoons and dimwits – the vast majority of whom were men of a certain age, class and education, regardless of their current political loyalties or creeds – had stabbed Margaret Thatcher in the back in the nation's hour of greatest peril!

Chapter 4

Lieutenant-Commander Francis Barrington would not have believed it if he had not seen it with his own eyes. After he had sunk the French destroyers Surcouf and Cassard, the latter with a heavyweight Mark VIII torpedo fired at two thousand yards from HMS Alliance's stern tubes; *absolutely nothing else had happened* until – several hours later – as it was getting dark and then, and only then had a procession of small boats – the largest some kind of trawler with an Oerlikon cannon mounted on its stern – apologetically straggled out and begun belatedly looking for survivors with searchlights blazing. By then most of the men in the water would have been long dead.

Hanging around the scene of the crime had been a calculated risk but nothing he had learned about the French squadron based at Ajaccio in the last few days had given him any reason to think it posed a significant threat to Alliance, or for that matter, any other British submarine operating in these waters. And besides, his torpedo tubes were reloaded and he was hoping that if he loitered in the vicinity of the Gulf of Ajaccio, sooner or later other big ships bottled up in harbour would attempt to escape, or fresh targets would arrive from elsewhere.

Alliance had her snorkel – 'snork' or 'snort' in submariner's parlance – up and was running dead slow on her diesels recharging her batteries just in case more 'trade' obligingly turned up in the area.

Raising the *snork* this close to shore would have been inviting trouble off a Royal Navy base in time of war, and definitely not the sort of thing one would have contemplated if one thought there were any Soviet submarines, or surface units anywhere within a twenty mile radius of one's position. However, this close inshore, given the vagaries of sonar and the water column hereabouts in the Western Mediterranean unless somebody actually spotted the snorkel by chance – unlikely because it was a dark, cloudy night and the sinking of the two destroyers had seemingly driven away every craft other than those comprising the motley flotilla of small boats pulling bodies out of the sea over ten miles away – Alliance was safe enough. More to the point Barrington was unwilling to voluntarily vacate such an excellent 'ambush' locale.

The submarine game was a waiting game and lately, he had discovered, much to his own surprise, that he was very, very good at playing it.

Every half-an-hour or so he raised the attack periscope for about twenty seconds; twenty seconds was amply sufficient time to complete a single quick sweep around the horizon. Either Barrington or his second-in-command, Lieutenant Michael Philpott would do the honours.

At 22:08 hours – the scope went up twice an hour but at twenty-five and thirty-five minute intervals, *never* on the hour or the actual half-hour – it was twenty-four year old Philpott's 'turn'.

"Bloody Hell!" He muttered. "You need to look at this, skipper!"

Francis Barrington disagreed.

He liked his executive officer and was confident that he one day he would be an accomplished captain of one of Her Majesty's Submarines. Presently, however, he was something of a rough diamond with one too many rough edges needing to be cut to size.

He half-smiled a grim smile.

"Belay that, Number One," he said gently. "Scope down please!"

Barrington waited patiently.

"What did you see, Michael?" He asked in that paternal, friendly way he preferred to employ when trying to convey important matters to his subordinates. He was abysmal at shouting at people and besides, he honestly did not believe that shouting did a lot of good in the long run. Likewise, other than in a life or death situation he would not dream of in any way slighting or belittling one of his officers in front of his men. Moreover, in this case it would have been a waste of time because Michael Philpott was already realising the error of his ways.

He had been the man at the attack periscope. He had seen what he had seen and he had delayed firstly, communicating what he had seen; and secondly, taking action. He was starting to wear a hangdog look.

"There's a huge firework display going on somewhere beyond Parata Point, sir. Possible big explosions and a lot of what looks like light AA fire hosing all over the sky."

The older man thought for a moment.

"No nearby surface contacts?"

"Er, no, sir."

Barrington sighed, resisted the temptation to 'air' the attack periscope for a ten second 'look' at the situation.

"Right," he decided, speaking as if he was taking his executive officer into his personal confidence. "We'll drop the *snork* and sit at a hundred feet for an hour or so before we head south. We'll stand off the mouth of the Gulf of Ajaccio to get a straight line look at whatever is going on in Ajaccio, Number One."

Ninety minutes later and some five miles off the broad entrance to the Gulf of Ajaccio, Barrington could see fires burning in the distant port, or rather the glow of big fires painted on the underside of the clouds above Ajaccio. Evidently, it seemed that somebody in England had not been satisfied with just sinking of a couple of destroyers; either that or the RAF had felt a little left out and joined in the fun. Briefly, he considered taking Alliance into the wide bay south of the burning town but quickly talked himself out of it. His job had been done, very well done, and risking stooging around any longer was asking for the sort of trouble that neither he, nor his boat needed.

In any event the order from Malta to make his best underwater speed to a new patrol area was received at 23:57 hours.

Alliance was to take up station off Rosas, a small coastal town and port in the extreme north eastern corner of Catalonian Spain very nearly within touching distance of the French border.

Francis Barrington had quirked an involuntary grin when he read the decoded plain text.

'Rosas', now there was a name to play with. He had read all of C.S. Forester's *Hornblower stories*, positively lived and breathed the career of Horatio Hornblower. *Rosas* was where Hornblower had fought HMS Sutherland to the death against four French ships of her own size and weight of broadside in '*A Ship of the Line*'. The story had ended with the Sutherland sinking in Rosas harbour surrounded by the dismasted, crippled hulks of her four foes with the hero of the piece about to fall into French hands; a cliff-hanger marvellously resolved in the sequel '*Flying Colours*' published in 1938.

Back in 1942 the captain of HMS Alliance had imagined, falsely, that he was destined to live that dream in another, different war when he was posted as an RNVR – Royal Navy Volunteer Reserve – freshly minted sub-lieutenant to Malta in 1942. That had been a nightmare experience. The constant bombing, the dreadful attrition against the Italian Navy in the fatal waters around the Maltese Archipelago, the drip, drip, drip of boats lost and friends consumed in that war. He had been a very young man, in many ways younger even than his years with no real experience of the world, people or of anything much in particular. Looking back his wartime experience in the Mediterranean had been a bewildering melange of terrors and blunders that he had been outrageously lucky to survive. He had believed he had left all that behind him and that his seagoing days were long over; and then the cataclysm had fallen and *that* unexpected letter had arrived calling him back from the wilderness. Suddenly, a life unfulfilled had acquired new meaning.

Now in a few days' time he would be steering Alliance into the same waters sailed by his younger self's Georgian hero.

Oh, to be the captain of a 74-gun ship of the line in Nelson's Navy! To place one's ship alongside another and do battle like men of yore! Oh, to fight with steel and blood and iron, not Torpex, at ranges far too far apart to be able to see one's enemy's eyes...

It was all nonsense, of course.

People said that one in four, possibly as many as one in three of the population of the planet had perished in the October War or from the sickness and famines in its aftermath. Hundreds of millions had died or were suffering still, and all Francis Barrington, RN (Reserve) could think about was aping his fictional role model!

How ridiculous was that?

Barrington had gone to his cabin to decrypt the sensitive part of the communication from Flag Office Submarines, Malta. Now he returned to the control room.

The boat was still running *quiet* as she crept out to sea to the west of Corsica like a thief in the night, seeking sea room before the dawn when she would run north west at eleven knots on her diesels with the snork up.

"We have new orders," Barrington announced, unable to eradicate a certain quiet pleasure from his voice. "We are congratulated for our good work in these parts and are required to make ourselves scarce. Pronto!" He smiled and made eye contacts around the compartment. "Further, we are to make best underwater speed to a new patrol area off the Spanish coast north of Barcelona. Specifically, we are to watch and report on shipping movements in, around and out of the Spanish port of Rosas, before proceeding north to stand off Perpignan. That is all. I will let you all know if I receive any further clarification of our orders. You may pass on what I have said to other crew members."

Barrington joined Michael Philpott at the plot table.

The younger man opened his mouth to apologise for his earlier inadvertent lapse at the attack periscope.

Barrington chuckled, raised a hand to pat his shoulder.

"Live and learn, Michael," he said quietly. "That's the ticket." A wayward thought crossed his mind. "I suppose that after the excitement of earlier today we ought to see if we've got a Jolly Roger in our signals locker, what?"

Chapter 5

Saturday 6th June 1964
Dammam, Saudi Arabia

Fifty-one year old Major General Thomas Daly's aircraft had landed thirty minutes before the first giant explosion within the sprawling US War Stores Depot in the desert west of Dammam.

The commander designate of all Australian and New Zealand ground troops in the Middle East might have been forgiven for thinking the gods were against him as he clambered out of his car, surveyed the debris-strewn quayside and contemplated the still burning warehouses adjacent to where the Royal Fleet Auxiliary Ammunition Ship Retainer had been moored twenty-four hours ago. The bow and stern of the ship, fire scorched and twisted almost out of all recognition stuck out of the water at unnatural angles, and tens of tons of ordnance, fixed naval and tank rounds and shells mostly, lay in the tangled steel and shattered brickwork...*everywhere.*

"You must be Tom Daly!" Called a comfortably proportioned naval officer who, even at a distance; was clearly of a similar vintage to the newcomer. Several predominantly youthful staffers followed in the other man's wake as he approached the Australian.

"I'm Nick Davey. Flag Officer, ABNZ Persian Gulf Squadron, presumably on account of my many and egregious sins committed in a former life," the Englishman declared cheerfully. "Dear, dear," he tutted, "this is a bit of a mess, isn't it?"

The two men shook hands, taking the measure of each other.

The Australian's gaze shifted to the small, sinewy, scarred man of indeterminate middle years standing beside Davey with a holstered Webley revolver on his waist band.

"This is Fleet Chief Petty Officer McCann," the Englishman declared. "VC!" This he added with a barely suppressed chortle of delight.

"Mister McCann," Daly saluted cursorily and stuck out his right hand.

Nevil 'Spider' McCann was still not reconciled to his new rank – one specially made up for him by the First Sea Lord, Sir Varyl Begg – or to the notoriety that was the fate of all holders of the Victoria Cross. His days on HMS Talavera had been among the happiest days of his life and secretly, he yearned to be back on the old Battle class destroyer; but Talavera was gone, her survivors scattered to the winds and as his late wife had often observed 'the Devil always makes work for idle hands', so once he discovered Peter Christopher was being sent to America he had put in a request to be reassigned to sea duty. Shortly thereafter, he had found himself on the aircraft carrying Rear Admiral Davey to South Africa to join HMS Tiger on her passage around the Cape to the Persian Gulf.

"After that business at Malta," Daly inquired as she shook the smaller man's hand, "I'd have thought you'd earned a good rest ashore, Mister McCann?"

"I lost my wife on the night of the war, sir," the former Bantamweight boxing champion of the Mediterranean Fleet explained respectfully. "There's nothing to keep me in England. Admiral Davey was so kind as to request my services on Tiger, sir."

Daly and the two Englishmen fell into slow step.

The Australian had not canvassed for, nor expected to be sent to the Middle East. He had thought his fighting days were over after Korea. A native of Ballarat in Victoria he had attended the Duntroon Royal Military College in the Australian Capital Territories before being commissioned into the Light Horse Regiment. In the late thirties he had served in the British Army on the North West Frontier in India, and thereafter 'enjoyed' a crowded and varied career during World War II. Rising to Brigade Major of the 18th Brigade at Tobruk he later attended staff school at Haifa in Palestine preparatory to joining the 5th Division in New Guinea as Senior Staff Officer. By the end of that war he commanded the 2/10th Battalion in the invasion of Balikpapan in Borneo, earning a Distinguished Service Order. Post war he had had spells at the Joint Services Staff College in the United Kingdom, during which he had met and married his wife, Heather. Back in Australia he had been posted to Duntroon and in 1952 gone to Korea to take command of the 28th Commonwealth Brigade, becoming the first Australian to command a combined Australian-British infantry formation in that conflict. But all that seemed an awfully long time ago and a long succession of staff jobs since had not been the ideal preparation to lead men in what seemed likely to be an extremely bloody campaign.

"Sabotage, we think," Nick Davey offered, looking around at the destruction as smoke billowed across the dockside. "At the time this was going on there were several attempted assassinations in Riyadh according to our Saudi hosts. Cairo is in flames, they say. My intelligence people think all the trouble was caused by Soviet 'sleeper agents'. They may be right; first time for everything, what!"

"We must have lost a lot of ordnance, Admiral?"

"I'm told most of the AP rounds for your Centurions were offloaded or sitting on the quayside ready for transport north. Retainer was making ready to cross deck reloads onto my frigates and destroyers. Most of my ships have half-empty magazines." Nothing in Davey's manner gave Daly the impression that this was remotely troubling him. "Never mind! Worse things happen at sea, what!"

Spider McCann had hung back a few feet so that the two commanders could converse confidentially. The officers could get on with their chit chat and he would watch their backs in the meantime. The wreckage all around him told him everything he needed to know about how 'safe' the ships and the men of the ABNZ Squadron were in this particular harbour. That was why whenever *his* Admiral went ashore he had plenty of *his* men – armed to the teeth - loitering in the vicinity.

"If you say so, Admiral..."

"Nick, old man. Please call me Nick. I've never been one to stand on ceremony and I'm far too old to change my ways now."

"Tom," the Australian volunteered in exchange, trying to conceal how taken aback he was. Even in this day and age most British officers of his acquaintance were sticklers for their 'prerogatives', rights and ranks. Even though he and Davey were of equivalent seniority in their respective services, it was unsettling to encounter a man so obviously unconcerned with the old 'proprieties'. "It is good to meet you, Nick."

The Englishman waved around at the scene of devastation.

"If the bastards think this will make us pack up and go home they've got another thing coming, Tom!"

Chapter 6

Saturday 6th June 1964
HMAS Anzac, Shatt al-Arab

The pre-war navigable channel had not so much shifted as split into two distinct openings at the margins where the Arvand River flowed into the Persian Gulf. HMAS Anzac had grounded twice before Commander Stephen Turnbull had called forward the smaller, shallower draught Ton class minesweepers HMS Essington and HMS Tariton to lead his ship, drawing fourteen feet, and the bigger HMAS Sydney with a draught of twenty-five feet up river. The two deep water channels merged about five miles upstream where, it was discovered the 'navigation' had shifted some fifty to a hundred yards closer to the western shore of the Faw Peninsula than it had been the previous occasion Turnbull had taken Anzac up to Abadan some three weeks ago.

This had prompted dark premonitions that it might be problematic to bring Sydney, the former aircraft carrier now operating as a fast transport ship, alongside the unloading jetties at Abadan. When the Red Army arrived in Basra Province the garrison at Abadan was going to need every tank, round of ammunition and all the reinforcing Commandoes that Sydney was bringing up river. However, as dawn broke over the grey, churning waters of the great waterway of the ancient Mesopotamian world Anzac's constantly pinging sonar was consistently indicating fifteen to twenty feet under her bow as he accepted the TBS – 'talk between ships' – handset from the bridge speaker.

"Anzac speaking," he drawled, squinting into the brilliant sunshine bathing the bridge. Just an hour after full dawn it was getting hot, very hot even for a man acclimatised to the dry, fiery heat of the New South Wales outback.

A mile down river the Sydney was idling in the mainstream, treading water awaiting the arrival of a pilot to con her inshore.

Silvery towers rose above the metallic sprawl of the refineries spread across Abadan Island less than a mile away, as Stephen Turnbull surveyed the approach to the oiling piers and wharves. Tanker skippers had been the only westerners who really understood the moods of the Shatt al-Arab, where to find deep water and how to keep out of trouble but the river had been closed to civilian traffic for over a month now. It was only a matter of time before the Red Air Force – whether by design or error – attacked Abadan or began to prey on shipping on the Arvand River.

Since the Soviet invasion of Iran much of the Abadan complex had been shut down; and the tankers had diverted to Dammam-Dhahran where the Saudis had been only too keen to accept - probably worthless - *notes of credit* issued by the Unity Administration of the United Kingdom.

They said there were hundreds of tons, perhaps, thousands of tons of gold, silver, platinum and other rare, and in current times hugely precious metals buried under the ruins of London; that the Army had moved in to guard the vaults of the Bank of England from looters. They said that millions of diamonds and gems of every description were in 'sealed off' subterranean safe rooms; that the wealth of the old Empire was waiting to be unlocked to pay for the rebuilding of a new, garden city London. But talk was cheap and the rumour mill insatiable; to the best of his knowledge there was very little of any substance to lend any real value to the *notes of credit* buying every drop of the Middle Eastern crude oil that now reached British ports.

"My intention is to hold station in mid-stream or in the general vicinity while Sydney docks and unloads," Stephen Turnbull said, trying not to sound overly tongue-in-cheek. The Soviets would be listening to every word spoken over the unscrambled VHF link; the Russians were not the only ones who dealt in 'smoke and mirrors' tricks. "Please send me a pilot boat. I may need to move a mile or two up river to anchor overnight. Anzac Out."

Actually, what he had in mind was taking the Anzac, Essington and the Tariton up beyond Khorramshahr, and if possible, all the way to the outskirts of Basra where before the war an ugly industrial area had been spreading along the eastern bank of the river opposite the old city. This industrial' area was home to hundreds of workshops, the river's eastern bank was where fishing boats were hauled out of the water for repair, and nets were dried and patched. In the warren of small factories, some of which were built right on top of the Iraq-Iran border, lay the real 'industry' of Iraq. The whole district had been evacuated after the abortive Iraqi armoured incursion into Iran north of Khorramshahr. If it remained deserted it might be possible to steam right up to Basra. But that was looking too far ahead. Turnbull's mission was firstly, to see if the Arvand River was navigable south of Basra in this season – it ought to be even though he winter melt waters from the far north were exhausted and the level of the river was falling towards its annual low - and; secondly, to look for trouble.

Trouble came in many forms in these regions and Turnbull had been given carte blanch to 'look for it'. Current intelligence was that in the aftermath of recent heavy Red Air Force bombing raids the Iraqi forces in Basra Province were melting away into the civilian population, that large quantities of equipment had been abandoned or sabotaged and that many areas of Basra had become self-governing 'communes' violently defending their boundaries. A consequence of the military and civil breakdown of order was that refugees were flooding out of the city into the marshes, down towards Kuwaiti territory, and attempting to cross the Arvand River into Iran.

Stephen Turnbull had consciously put the bad news from Dammam to the back of his mind; filed it away for future reference because it had no bearing on his immediate mission.

HMS Tiger, Rear Admiral Davey's flagship had broadcast a general alert to all ships reporting explosions at the Dammam-Dhahran United States War Stores Depot, a subsequent 'large' explosion onboard the Royal Fleet Auxiliary Ammunition Ship Retainer and that 'civilian unrest' was currently denying ABNZ ships 'routine' access to the port facilities of Tarout Bay. However, other than to maintain a heightened state of alert 'all current evolutions are to continue as planned'; which was exactly what the commanding officer of HMAS Anzac intended to do!

Stephen Turnbull handed back the receiver.

He turned to the officer of the watch, a red-headed Queenslander. The kid was thirteen years younger than Turnbull had been that day in February 1942 when he had watched HMS Exeter, the heroine of the Battle of the River Plate run down in a desperate stern chase by a squadron of Japanese heavy cruisers, and shot to pieces. With her battle flag streaming through the flames and smoke the great ship had fought like a lion until, in the end, she was overwhelmed. Exeter had sent away her escorts; they had fled for their lives and most had perished, either in a deluge of hideously accurate long-range naval gunfire or dive bombed and torpedoed by Japanese Navy aircraft that had owned the skies...

"The ship will remain at Air Defence Condition One," Turnbull ordered, breaking from the circle of his memories. "Tell the galley to bring food and drink to the men at their stations."

The Royal Australian Navy's priorities for much of the last year had been supporting ongoing British operations against insurgents in Borneo – essentially, safeguarding the oilfields of Brunei, vital to the Australasian economy – and general peacekeeping in Indonesian waters, maintaining a presence at Singapore and Hong Kong, and in assisting in the preparations for the Operation Manna convoys. Thus, although Anzac had been released from dockyard hands around the time of the Battle of Washington in December, due to manpower shortages it had not been practical to run trials or to commission her until February.

On the day that the destroyer and her similarly repaired and restored sister, HMAS Tobruk, were ordered to the Persian Gulf neither ship had been fully crewed or in any way ready for sea. Anzac and Tobruk both had a 'list' complement of three hundred and twenty men but had departed respectively sixty-seven and fifty-three men short, necessitating stops at Adelaide and Perth to take onboard volunteers, merchant seamen, reservists and between them, over forty cadets before leaving Australian waters.

It had been a strange crossing of the Indian Ocean; an unlikely passage given the history of the two repaired and partially rebuilt sister ships. In September 1960, shortly before Anzac had been scheduled to go into dock to be converted to a training ship, she and Tobruk had been conducting live firing gunnery exercises off Jervis Bay on the New South Wales coast. Normally, it was customary for the vessels carrying out such 'exercises' to apply a six degree offset in all their fire control solutions; but on this occasion - due to an unidentified mechanical malfunction over which two of Anzac's crew were later prosecuted – Anzac had inadvertently fired *directly* on Tobruk and hit her, causing several casualties and such extensive damage that, at the time, it was considered uneconomical to repair the ship.

Prior to the October War Anzac had been converted into a non-operational trainings ship stripped of much of her armament; and Tobruk had been mothballed in a damaged condition in reserve in October 1960 at Sydney. The October War had called both ships back into service and the Soviet invasion of Iran and Iraq had sent them racing to the Persian Gulf. Two proud ships with names that invoked the gallantry and sacrifice of earlier generations of Australians in the cause of freedom were back in harness, steaming towards the sound of the guns.

The two destroyers had moved across an empty, silent ocean, making first for Colombo in Ceylon to refuel and re-provision, to collect British code books and to escort several merchantmen carrying equipment and general supplies for the forces already in the Persian Gulf.

Turnbull – by fifteen years the senior of two ships' captains - had worked both Anzac's and Tobruk's green crews hard all the way from Victoria to Abadan. Two-thirds of his people had never been at sea for more than a few days at a time, three-quarters had no experience of combat and both ships were officered in the main by short-commission men or reservists, or boys just out of HMAS Creswell, the Royal Australian Navy College.

Anzac was idling in the main channel.

To the north the great river began to sweep to the west in a huge, shallow bend up to the mouth of the Karun River and Khorramshahr in the east, towards Basra on the western shore another thirty miles upstream.

Stephen Turnbull smiled to himself, vented a quiet ruminative snort.

Nobody at HMAS Creswell had mentioned that one day he might be asked to take a three thousand ton fleet destroyer more than sixty miles up a river 'looking for trouble'; but then he seriously doubted if any of the instructors at the College had ever envisaged any kind of World remotely like the one in which he now lived.

Turnbull had been his father's bane as a young man; and but for the Navy he might have become a wastrel, a drifter whose life never amounted to what his World War II American friends would have termed 'a mess of beans'. The day he had scraped into HMAS Creswell had been the making of him as a man, an officer and he liked to think, as a human being. Those now long ago days still spoke to him, providing a wealth of memories to sustain and to fortify him. He had discovered himself and God at the College and been, broadly speaking, at peace with both ever since.

He had passed through HMAS Creswell in the late 1920s, before drastic cuts to the Navy budget during the Great Depression resulted in the establishment moved from its original Jervis Bay home, to HMAS Cerberus on the Mornington Peninsula south of Melbourne. The College had only moved back to New South Wales as recently as 1958, from whence a slew of newly trained and partly-trained fresh-faced members of the crews of the Anzac and the Tobruk had been plucked that spring; 'plucked' as in the sense of babies having been 'snatched from their cradles'.

Turnbull had run his crew ragged in the last two months knowing that in the heat of battle training and mental preparation was *everything*. Essential to that psychological adjustment was a blanket acceptance that war was not a thing that touched a man now and then. War was a constant; terrible things could happen at any time and exhaustion was no excuse for letting one's guard down for a single moment.

A man had plenty of time to sleep when he was dead.

Stephen Turnbull scanned the immediate horizon. Hemmed in by the river banks – the nearest approximately five hundred yards to starboard – he felt the normal mariner's claustrophobic disquiet. Above Abadan the Arvand River began to narrow. Here at Abadan it was three-quarters of a mile across, the deep water channel one to two hundred yards wide, in most places broad enough for a ship of Anzac's size – nearly three hundred and eighty feet in length and forty-one on the beam – to turn freely, and to afford some small leeway in which to manoeuvre. Up beyond Khorramshahr, well, that was the question!

He would have much preferred to have investigated it in the dark of the night. However, shepherding the Sydney through the shoals had taken longer than anticipated. Night or day, he had a job to do. The ABNZ Squadron 'owned' the Shatt al-Arab and the approaches to Umm Qasr in the west, and it was important that the Soviets and the Iraqis – those who had yet to run away – understood as much.

Stephen Turnbull went to the navigation plot.

He pondered Anzac's erratic track up river, grimaced.

"Right, gentlemen," he chuckled lowly, 'I want to anchor opposite Khorramshahr around noon. Let's get about our business."

Chapter 7

Saturday 6th June 1964
Oak Hill, Wethersfield, Connecticut

The forty-four year old former Soviet Ambassador to the United States of America, Anatoly Fyodorovich Dobrynin, had first been brought to the old wood-framed house built into the side of a wooded hill over a year ago.

Dobrynin had become a diplomat at the age of twenty-six in 1946 after an early career working for the Yakolev Design Bureau. Having previously been head of the Soviet Foreign Ministry's America Department, he had arrived in the Washington Embassy in March 1962 - mercifully unaware - that his principals in Moscow had already acquired a collective death wish.

In retrospect he had concluded that the Cuban Missiles Crisis had been badly handled by *everybody*; not least the USSR's two representatives to the United Nations whose hands had been tied behind their backs by Khrushchev's ill-judged blustering brinkmanship.

Dobrynin had met with the late Secretary of State Dean Rusk several times last autumn at Oak Hill. It had been clear to Dobrynin that Rusk entertained worrisome doubts as to the 'completeness' of his country's victory in the Cuban Missiles War, and unlike the majority of other senior cabinet members in the Administration he was greatly exercised by the viral spread of pre-war Soviet backed 'freedom movements' throughout Sub-Saharan Africa and in South East Asia. Rusk had hardly been the most flamboyant or the most spectacular member of President Kennedy's new Camelot; but he had been one of the most diligent and, in retrospect, among the wisest of White House insiders.

Rusk had been exploring ways to mitigate the resentment caused by the brazen 'bootlegging' and 'piracy' of US banks and corporations in – among other places - Nigeria, the Gold Coast, Congo, Namibia, Mozambique and Rhodesia in Africa, and Malaysia, Thailand, Vietnam and throughout the Indonesian archipelago in the Far East, by seeking to engage surviving Soviet overseas 'legations' in those countries in an 'ongoing dialogue'. Although nothing concrete had come of their 'dialogues' before Rusk's death, Dobrynin had enjoyed his regular trips to Connecticut.

Those 'trips' had ceased after the Battle of Washington. Instead, he had been interviewed by crassly hostile representatives of the Federal Bureau of Investigation, and at one point, threatened with prosecution for espionage and plotting to overthrow the US Government.

Intriguingly, three weeks ago he had been visited in New York, by the daughter of the owner of Oak Hill. Gretchen Betancourt-Brenckmann was a striking young woman increasingly in the public eye in her role as the lead defence attorney of the ring leaders of last December's insurrection.

She was a most remarkable young woman...

Initially, Dobrynin had dealt with the FBI's threats and the decidedly non-confrontational inquiries of the strikingly attractive, much vilified lawyer in the same, unflappable fashion in which he had parried Dean Rusk's overtures. In the same way that he had no inclination to assist the US authorities in undermining legitimate freedom movements across the globe; he had no intention of co-operating with internal witch hunts. However, although it was unclear exactly whom Gretchen Betancourt-Brenckmann represented, she had brought with her an invitation to re-visit Oak Hill for the purpose of exploring the possibilities of resuming an 'adult' bilateral 'conversation' between 'interested parties', and Dobrynin had drawn the obvious conclusion that somebody in the US Government wanted to 'talk turkey' rather than bluster and posture for public effect. Vitally, the young woman had assured Dobrynin that if he attended 'talks' at Oak Hill that 'confidentiality' would be 'guaranteed'.

Oak Hill belonged to Claude Betancourt, the secretive, shadowy figure who had once been Joseph Kennedy's, the President's late father's, attorney. Latterly, so far as Dobrynin could establish, Betancourt had become the eminence grise behind President Kennedy's re-election campaign. Legend had it that he was the only man in America who had more dirt on the Kennedy family than J. Edgar Hoover, although Dobrynin doubted that he was quite the Machiavellian 'power behind the throne' that some Democratic Party insiders claimed. Notwithstanding, he was immensely wealthy, undoubtedly influential and while the Kennedy Administration survived, lurching from one crisis to another like a drunken man on a tightrope, Claude Betancourt was the only 'fixer' in the game.

Dobrynin stepped out of the car, a 1962 Chrysler, flanked by his Secret Service bodyguards. Marine Corps sentries armed with M-16 assault rifles had manned the gate at the bottom of the hill leading up to Oak Hill.

"Welcome back to Oak Hill, Ambassador," declared the stern matronly middle aged woman who greeted the Russian on the porch.

"It is good to see you again, Mrs Nordstrom," Dobrynin smiled. He had used his time since the war under virtual house arrest in New York productively, honing his English and learning everything he could about his strange, somewhat conflicted hosts. "If you will forgive my impertinence, may I observe that you look well?"

"Well," Mrs Nordstrom - with her husband for over three decades the 'keepers' of Oak Hill for the Betancourt family - was not accustomed to unsolicited pleasantries. She hesitated, smiled an unlikely smile and lowered her eyes. "Thank you for saying so, Ambassador."

"Is Mr Nordstrom well?"

"He has a bad chest. He is in hospital in Wethersfield, presently. He hopes to be home in a day or two."

"Please be sure to send him my kind regards and my best wishes for his prompt recovery."

"I will, Ambassador."

The Betancourt family summer 'weekend' retreat – as befitted a country hideaway where senior Democrats all the way back to FDR's time had secretly met in conclave to foment forthcoming plots and coups - was a large, much modernised old six bedroom colonial style house dating from the middle of the last century. Walking into the lobby of the house was like walking into something out of another age. There were polished boards underfoot, ancient gas light fittings now glowing with electric bulbs, big portraits in coarse oils on the walls, and the stuffed head of an Elk; just one of a dozen mounted animal heads on the wall. In places the low oaken frames of the house might easily brain a tall man if he stood up too quickly.

"I had the honour to meet Mr Betancourt's daughter in New York recently," Dobrynin told Mrs Nordstrom as the woman ushered him deeper into the house. "She seemed very much recovered from her injuries. Unfortunately, I was unable to materially assist her with her present cases."

Claude Betancourt's daughter had put out a press release explaining away her meeting with Dobrynin as an attempt to depose the diplomat on the subject of the Soviet Union's alleged involvement with the failed December coup.

"Gretchen stayed with us in the spring while she was convalescing," the woman re-joined, her voice swelling with obvious maternal pride.

Dobrynin tried hard not to broadcast his displeasure to find the USSR's sixty-two year old former Representative to the United Nations, Valerian Alexandrovich Zorin standing in the picture window of the lounge in which he and Dean Rusk had conferred the previous year.

The two Russians had not met since before the Cuban Missiles War; Zorin and his co-representative - Platon Dmitriejevitsj Morozov – had been held under house arrest in the old Soviet UN legation building in New York, while Dobrynin and his staff had been transferred to a compound in Maryland thirty miles outside Washington last August. Morozov had succumbed, already broken-hearted, to the second wave of influenza which had swept through Manhattan earlier that year. The Americans characterized every new wave of the 'plague' which washed periodically across the northern states as 'flu' or 'influenza' but nobody really knew what it actually was, or when it was likely to return again. Dobrynin himself had been laid low that spring, when several older members of his staff had died.

Back in March 1962 Zorin had viewed Dobrynin as an upstart; he had been a member of the Party almost as long as the younger man had been alive. He was old school, a product of the hardest days, a survivor of the purges and the Great Patriotic War, a man who had ridden out the Stalin years and come to an accommodation with the Khrushchev regime. When Zorin had been Ambassador in Prague in 1948 Stalin had ordered him to organise the coup d'état that toppled the last democratically elected post-1945 government. Shortly afterwards, the one remaining non-communist member of the Czech cabinet, Jan Masaryk, had conveniently committed suicide. Masaryk's had been a very 'tidy' suicide; of that variety where a man jumps from a great height in the middle of the night in his pyjamas while retaining the presence of mind to shut the window on the way out...

Dobrynin and Zorin shook hands with stiff, cold formality.

"You look well, Comrade Ambassador," he murmured.

"It is good to find you so well also, Comrade Valerian Alexandrovich," Dobrynin replied guardedly, sensing little or none of the prickliness of their previous encounters.

Once upon a time Zorin would have bitterly resented having to yield precedence to an upstart like Dobrynin. However, his own *time* had come and gone. His *moment* had been on Thursday 25th October 1962, two days before the Cuban Missiles War when as the USSR's representative on the Security Council of the United Nations in New York – coincidentally a council meeting he was chairing – he had clashed with Adlai Stevenson.

That day was etched on Zorin's memory as if those events had been burned on his consciousness with a red hot branding iron. In the aftermath of the holocaust he had asked himself time and again if there was anything he could have done to defuse the ticking thermonuclear time bomb that day in New York.

'...*Let me ask you why your Government, your Foreign Minister, deliberately, cynically deceived us about the nuclear build-up in Cuba?*' Adlai Stevenson had demanded with the imperious haughtiness of a Tsarist overlord. '...*I remind you that you didn't deny the existence of these weapons. Instead, we heard that they had suddenly become defensive weapons. But today - again, if I heard you correctly - you now say they don't exist, or that we haven't proved they exist, with another fine flood of rhetorical scorn. All right sir, let me ask you one simple question. Do you, Ambassador Zorin, deny that the USSR has placed and is placing medium and intermediate range missiles and sites in Cuba? Yes or no? Don't wait for the translation: yes or no?*'

The anger of Zorin's immediate rebuttal had been genuine.

'*I am not in an American courtroom, sir, and therefore I do not wish to answer a question that is put to me in the fashion in which a prosecutor does. In due course, sir, you will have your reply. Do not worry.*'

For all that Adlai Stevenson was the darling of the centre-left of the American establishment, a two-time failed Presidential candidate and supposedly the great figurehead of reason in the Cold War imbroglios of the 1950s, Zorin had been anything but in the other man's thrall. He had risen through the ranks at the People's Commissariat for Foreign Affairs to be appointed Ambassador to Czechoslovakia in 1945, where his reward for managing the February 1948 putsch had been the post of Deputy Minister of Foreign Affairs, spells as Ambassador to West Germany and from 1956 his appointment as one of the two permanent Soviet representatives to the

United Nations Security Council.

'...*You are in the court of world opinion right now and you can answer yes or no. You have denied that they exist. I want to know...if I've understood you correctly?*' Adlai Stevenson had blustered.

Zorin had retorted: '*You will have your answer in due course!*'

But it had been the Americans who had given their answer first, raining nuclear fire down upon the Motherland.

"It is good to meet again," the older man observed.

Dobrynin nodded.

"We live in strange times," he offered.

Both men nodded.

Mrs Nordstrom had watched the reunion from the doorway with polite disinterest. Eighteen months ago she had been a rich man's housekeeper and the sometime surrogate aunt and mother figure to that rich man's daughter; a daughter whose own mother had gone off and married a feckless, good for nothing actor when Gretchen was just six years old, and whose step mother had quietly abdicated any 'motherly' duties. Now Gretchen was exactly where she had always wanted to be; at the centre of a firestorm of TV, radio and newspaper controversy, and was newly married to a man who loved her 'just the way she was'; and the former rich man's anonymous housekeeper had become Claude Betancourt's accomplice in facilitating a meeting which might well alter the course of history.

The two Russians realised she was still in the room.

They looked to her.

"The Secretary of State and the Attorney General will be here in thirty minutes, gentlemen," Mrs Nordstrom announced. "May I offer you coffee and light refreshments while you are waiting for them to arrive?"

Chapter 8

Saturday 6th June 1964
Junior Common Room, King's College, Oxford

Margaret Thatcher had asked the Cabinet to convene at ten forty-five that morning, and requested the Chief of the Defence Staff to ensure the attendance of the other two Chiefs of Staff at that time. At that hour she had made no attempt to explain the absence of the Cabinet Secretary, Sir Henry Tomlinson, or the increased military presence in and around King's College. If any of the men or women around the big, polished table that morning thought it remotely odd that her mood was self-evidently one of defiance and her manner almost aggressively purposeful, nobody remarked upon it.

"Thank you all for being here in such good time," the Prime Minister prefaced, slowly making eye contacts all around the table.

To the right of Sir Henry Tomlinson's empty chair sat the Secretary of Defence, William Whitelaw the forty-five year old Conservative Member of Parliament for Penrith and Borders, and the Chancellor of the Exchequer, fifty-four year old Peter Thorneycroft, the man with the unenviable distinction of being the last pre-October War Tory grandee still in the government. Fifty-three year old Barbara Castle, the combative red-headed firebrand of the pre-war Labour left and now the Minister of Labour, had settled beside the Chancellor and had been chatting animatedly with him when the Prime Minister entered the room. The chair at the right hand end of the table was vacant having been brought in after all the other members of the Cabinet had already arrived and taken their places.

Continuing counter-clockwise around the table sat the oldest member of the Cabinet, sixty-five year old Lord Brookeborough – who preferred to be known as Sir Basil Brook – a nephew of Winston Churchill's wartime Chief of the Imperial General Staff, and since 1943 the Prime Minister of Northern Ireland and the *de facto* Secretary of State for the province in the Unity Administration of the United Kingdom, softly drumming his fingers on the table top.

Beside Brooke, Airey Neave, the forty-eight year old MP for Abingdon who had taken on the poisoned chalice of the newly formed Ministry for National Security in April, waited impassively, calmly even though his one-time protégé and close friend, Margaret Thatcher had given him no inkling of what might be in store. Sitting next to him was Alison Munro, the fifty year old senior civil servant who had joined the top table of government upon Neave's assumption of the *Security Brief*, taking over the Ministry of Supply, which was currently in the process of wholly subsuming Energy and Transportation into its responsibilities. This formidable woman – effectively, the nation's 'rationing queen' upon whom the onerous and often impossible demands of the military also fell – was in the process of re-organising the United Kingdom's ramshackle command economy displaying in the process, an indefatigable disregard for vested interests and a pragmatic callousness for the wounded sensibilities of her ministerial colleagues.

The Chiefs of Staff sat in a block opposite the Prime Minister's chair; presumably for mutual support and protection, other members of the Cabinet secretly joked.

Air Marshall Sir Christopher Hartley and the First Sea Lord, Sir Varyl Begg, flanked the elder statesmen, Field Marshall Sir Richard Amyatt Hull. Fifty-one year old Hartley was a big, outdoors loving man. Winchester College and Balliol educated he had taught at Eton before flying night fighters in the Second World War. He had been Air Officer Commanding 12 Group, Fighter Command before the October War.

Sir Varyl Begg was a slighter, more cerebral figure. He had been the gunnery officer of the battleship HMS Warspite at the Battle of Matapan in 1941 when the Mediterranean Fleet sank three Italian cruisers; a brace of them, the *Fiume* and the *Zara* in literally two minutes flat. Later he had commanded the 8th Destroyer Flotilla during the Korean conflict, been in charge of the Naval Contingent at the Coronation of Queen Elizabeth in 1953, and captain of the aircraft carrier HMS Triumph. At the time of the October War he had been slated to take over from Julian Christopher in the Far East in the second half of 1963.

Sir Richard Hull had commanded 12th Infantry brigade and then 26th Armoured Brigade in North Africa in 1943, 1st Armoured Division in Italy in 1944 and 5th Infantry Division in the final throes of the war in North West Europe in the winter of 1944-45.

Christopher Mayhew, the Secretary of State for Health had seated himself a little apart from the First Sea Lord; this morning he was visibly uneasy, and a little morose.

Not so Sir Thomas Harding-Grayson. The former Permanent Secretary of the Foreign Office, which he had headed since the death in the Balmoral atrocity of his predecessor Sir Alec Douglas Home, had mentally 'gamed' the most likely scenarios of what was likely to happen today and he was intensely curious to discover if any of his guesses were remotely close to the mark. Although he had not asked to be elevated to the post of Foreign Secretary back in December, life had been uncommonly *interesting* in the last six months; he claimed no inherent right to the job and if somebody thought they could do it better, good luck to them!

A little out of his place and possibly, his depth, Nicholas Ridley, the thirty-five year old MP for Cirencester and Tewkesbury who was occupying – he imagined temporarily only – the chair of his sadly deceased Secretary of State at the Ministry of Information, Iain Macleod, tried not to broadcast his anxiety.

Like Margaret Thatcher, he had been one of the tranche of MPs elected to the House of Commons for the first time in the 1959 General Election. The second son of a Viscount – his mother was Ursula Lutyens, daughter of the famous architect Sir Edwin Lutyens –

after graduation from Balliol College in 1947 he had soldiered briefly before pursuing a career in civil engineering. He had only been working with Iain Macleod since March that year and although – on their occasional encounters - the Prime Minister had always been very civil to him he had not expected to be invited into this august company on *this* of all days.

The Home Secretary, Roy Jenkins met Ridley's eye and winked conspiratorially. Jenkins had a reputation for being the least cliquish of politicians with a host of old and firm friendships that crossed party lines and a famous willingness to seriously consider all points of view regardless of their political flavour.

At the Home Secretary's right sat the Secretary of State for Scotland. John Scott Maclay was a throwback to a different political age. Educated at Winchester College and Trinity, Cambridge he had rowed in the victorious light blue Eight in the 1927 Boat Race. He was the National Liberal and Conservative MP for West Renfrewshire. In his fifty-ninth year he had enjoyed an uneventful political career in which he had held a number of junior ministerial posts before Harold MacMillan had seemingly 'put him out to grass' by sacking him during the course of the so-called 'Night of the Long Knives' in July 1962, during which 'Supermac' had sacked a third of his Cabinet.

At Margaret Thatcher's left hand sat James Callaghan, the Deputy Prime Minister, Leader of the Labour and Co-operative Party of the United Kingdom, Secretary of State for Wales and MP for Cardiff South East. He was self-evidently weary, his lugubrious good humour absent as he waited for the axe to fall.

All eyes had settled on Margaret Thatcher's face.

"You will know that as is the custom in the wake of an unfavourable vote of confidence in the House of Commons," Margaret Thatcher declared in a business-like tone, "I was granted an audience with Her Majesty the Queen at Blenheim Palace late last evening at which I tendered my resignation and that of my government."

She paused, as if hurriedly rehearsing what she planned to say next.

"While I was with Her Majesty at Woodstock the news from the Persian Gulf was still coming in. And, of course, the confirmation that the Argentine Military Governor of 'the Malvinas'," this she said with a frown of profound distaste, "has seized an unspecified number of hostages from among the civilian population and is threatening to shoot them if the Total Exclusions Zones are not lifted to permit the resupply of his 'forces of occupation' on the *Falkland Islands*."

She took a deep breath.

"In the Mediterranean last night the Royal Navy and the RAF carried out my orders to intercept the French warships responsible for the 'sneak' attack on HMS Hampshire. RAF bombers operating from Gibraltar, Malta and the United Kingdom have successfully carried out attacks designed to neutralise the threat posed by the remainder of the French Corsican Squadron, and to disable its shore establishments at Ajaccio. At the time of my audience with Her

Majesty, I was not in a position to apprise her of the most up to date military situation. This morning I am able to report that one of our submarines sank the two French destroyers believed to be responsible for the cowardly attack on HMS Hampshire, and that the RAF have carried out major retaliatory raids on the port and town of Ajaccio."

A frown began to form on her lips.

"At the time I was at Blenheim Palace it was still unknown whether anybody at the Embassy in Philadelphia had been killed or injured in yesterday's terroristic car bomb attacks on the compound; an attack that the perpetrators seem to have co-ordinated to coincide with President Kennedy's address to Congress demanding that the UAUK lift the 'blockade' on the Irish Republic before he considers laying a 'second Marshall Plan before Congress'."

She nodded acknowledgement to her Chancellor at this juncture. Peter Thorneycroft had briefed every member of the 'political cabinet' individually or in pairs on the rough outline of the proposed 'Fulbright Plan'; not so much a revamped version of the post-1945 Marshall Plan that selflessly pumped something like $13 billion into the war-shattered economy of Western Europe; as a multi-billion dollar cash injection to stabilise the United Kingdom's economic and industrial base while simultaneously revitalising the balance sheets of the half-dozen biggest banks in America. The US taxpayer would never get a cent of the money back but then it was not as if US taxpayers were having to fight America's foreign wars with their husbands and brothers and sons; that responsibility having been comprehensively abdicated by the isolationist proponents of the 'America First' abomination!

"In any event," Margaret Thatcher concluded. "Her Majesty, in receiving my resignation, asked to address Cabinet this morning before she decides how best to ensure that the governance of her Kingdom and its Dominions overseas may best be continued and conducted in the coming days."

This said she rose to her feet.

"Her Majesty will be here presently," she explained and walked out of the old Common Room, her heels clicking rhythmically on the bare boards of the floor.

There was a short delay.

Nobody spoke.

"Her Majesty, Queen Elizabeth!" Barked a Guardsman, presenting arms and crashing his two large booted feet together noisily on the ground.

The proclamation and the sound of other rifles clicking metallically to the 'present' in the hallway outside galvanised and, for some of the ministers, came as a horrible heart-pausing shock.

Chair legs squealed and everybody struggled to their feet.

Queen Elizabeth the Second, by the Grace of God, of Great Britain, Ireland and the British Dominions beyond the Seas Queen, and Defender of the Faith walked slowly, regally into the ancient, somewhat shabby Common Room.

The Queen's expression was forbiddingly stern and she avoided eye contact as she walked stiffly, and a little painfully, down the side of the table. Only the three Service Chiefs and the Cabinet Secretary had had official pre-warning of the Sovereign's intention – or rather, *her expressed implacable will* – to attend this specially convened meeting of the Cabinet of the Unity Administration of the United Kingdom.

The Queen was dressed like the housewife she liked to think she was at home with her family, except that the knee length fawn dress was obviously a pre-war Norman Hartnell creation, her hair was freshly coiffured, and her tan shoes polished to a perfect, high sheen. She wore a dark jacket with a single small glittering pin in the form of a thistle over her heart.

Margaret Thatcher had re-entered the Common Room two steps behind her monarch, her left arm threaded through the crook of Prince Philip, the Duke of Edinburgh's right arm as he tottered valiantly forward, his stick clacking loudly on the floor with every uncertain step.

A giant Welsh Guardsman followed carrying a heavy, high-back chair as if it was no weightier than a matchstick. Sir Henry Tomlinson brought up the rear, waiting by the door to the Common Room until the extra chair had been positioned at the head of the table just behind where the Queen's right hand would be when she was seated.

The Guardsman marched out.

The Cabinet Secretary closed the door and tiptoed to his position by the Prime Minister's right hand.

The Queen paused to gently cajole her consort to: "For goodness sake sit down, Philip!" Before, she herself still standing, turned to give her full and undivided attention to her ministers.

In that moment the sound of a pin dropping on a carpeted floor a hundred yards away would have sounded like the distant eruption of Krakatoa.

Chapter 9

Saturday 6th June 1964
Embassy of the United Kingdom, Bellfield Avenue, Philadelphia

The Pennsylvania National Guardsmen who had been deployed on the streets and in the parkland around the embassy compound the previous day had been replaced with M-48 Patton tanks of the 3rd Marines and troopers of the 101st Airborne Division. M-113 armoured personnel carriers and Philadelphia Police Department cruisers were patrolling the surrounding districts broadcasting that: *By order of the President of the United States of America all demonstrations and public gatherings are hereby forbidden within a one mile radius of the boundaries of the British Embassy compound. Any person breaching this order will be liable to immediate arrest or to be shot on sight.*

Lady Marija Christopher was angry.

Not so much about having had her luncheon with her husband and her friends interrupted yesterday by the two explosions in the road nearby, but by the fact that nobody would let her help with the clearing up. She was three months pregnant, almost; she was *not* ill and she hated sitting around doing nothing when there was work to be done. Once the people who had been hurt by flying glass had been given emergency first aid everybody had started treating her as if she needed to be wrapped in cotton wool!

It was ridiculous!

Even now Sten-gun armed Royal Marines stood guard at the doors.

Just because she and Rosa Hannay had sneaked out and gone with the injured to the hospital, they had both been scolded like naughty children and she had been 'grounded', whatever that meant!

They were to stay in their apartment – fortunately hardly damaged by the bombing – until it was 'safe'.

Marija and her *sister* had been 'locked up' this way all day.

The attack had come without warning.

The first car bomb had blown out most of the windows at the front of the main building; the second had splintered several on the upper floors at the back. Lord Franks, the Ambassador had reported that at least ten National Guardsmen and Philadelphia PD officers had been killed in Bellfield Avenue as well as an unknown number of unfortunate people who were just passing by, or 'demonstrating', as they had every right to do in a 'free country' when the bomb went off. Inside and outside the Embassy at least fifty people had been injured.

"The boys were worried about us, sister," Rosa Hannay reminded her friend diplomatically.

Marija began to pull a face at her *sister* then thought better of it, knowing that Rosa and her husband, Alan, the sweetest man imaginable – apart from her own husband, obviously – had had their first *scene* yesterday. She and *her* Peter had not had that sort of argument, *yet*, but they surely would; all husbands and wives fell out eventually, that was the way of the World.

"I know," Marija agreed, unconsciously brushing her right hand across her abdomen, momentarily putting down the dress she was working on. She had never had her mother's gifts as a seamstress and until now, never really worried about it overmuch. She needed to let out two or three of her dresses without completely ruining them, and in comparison with her work as a nurse and midwife it was horrendously fiddly and complicated work. "Ouch!" She muttered, pricking her finger, *again*.

The young Maltese women sighed at each other.

"What ho!" Lieutenant-Commander Alan Hannay chirped cheerfully as he breezed into the first floor lounge. "It is official, the World has gone mad!" He declared, pausing just long enough to exchange a smile with Rosa before drifting to the window and risking a look out across Wister Park.

"What has happened now?" Marija inquired, actually more worried about inadvertently transferring the tiny drip of blood on the tip of her left ring finger onto the partly unstitched frock she had been 'working on', than hearing the latest bad news.

"We've fallen out with the French."

"Oh." Since she had not realised that the British had ever properly 'fallen in' or *made friends* with the French at any time in the eight hundred and ninety-eight years since the Battle of Hastings in 1066, this hardly qualified as *news*.

"And the Ambassador is considering evacuating all 'non-essential' personnel from Philadelphia. Probably, to the old country's United Nations Mission compound in New York, or to Montreal or Quebec in Canada."

Marija shook her head.

"Would we really be any safer somewhere else, Alan?" Before he could answer she went on. "I mean, back in December the Italian Air Force sank HMS Agincourt a hundred yards away from where my Mama and Papa and me were sitting, the American Air Force dropped very big bombs on Fort Manoel a quarter of a mile away while I was treating injured people on the Gzira waterfront. A couple of months ago Rosa and I hid under a table when shells from those Russian ships Talavera sank were shooting right over the top of Kalkara. Crazy people shot down the airplane that tried to land ahead of the one Peter and me were on at Cheltenham a few days later. Forgetting all about what happened with that crazy man on a motorcycle coming back from the Cathedral that day, do you honestly think we were any safer in Malta or in England than we are here?"

"Yes, but..."

Marija smiled seraphically.

"Peter dreams of rockets to the mountains of the Moon; I want to see California. We should all live our lives while we can. If bad things happen," Marija shrugged, "that was what was meant to be but," another shrug, "in the meantime we live our lives."

Alan Hannay laughed.

"Actually, I think that's pretty much what Peter is saying to the Ambassador right now," he confided.

Alan Hannay was a handsome man in a dapper, boyish sort of way, slightly built and more comfortable in his Navy blues than the civilian suit which he was wearing. He was half-a-head shorter than Marija's husband but then Peter, like his late father, was well over six feet tall, and naturally fairer than Alan Hannay, whose mop of short, still unruly dark hair only accentuated his youthfulness even though he was just eighteen months younger than his friend.

Marija's husband would be twenty-eight in six weeks' time; and most likely he would be the youngest full captain in the Royal Navy for many years to come. Alan Hannay, at just twenty-five, was probably the youngest Lieutenant-Commander in the Service and both men had glittering careers ahead of them if, and it was a big if, that was what they really, really wanted. Marija did not think that was what Alan wanted – *not what he really wanted* – and of the two men he was the natural diplomat and facilitator. Her husband was more the sort of extraordinary, reckless and foolish, man who steered a thin-skinned destroyer within a hundred yards of a shoaling rocky shore to engage a gun battery manned by Red Dawn fanatics, or placed his ship under the stern of a burning nuclear powered aircraft carrier to fight fires beyond the reach of that great ship's crew, or steamed at full speed towards a whole enemy fleet just after he had been ordered to run away!

Marija had married a hero.

To her Peter Christopher had always been a hero; just a different kind of hero to the one he had become lately. She wondered sometimes about the toll having lost so many friends would take on him in the years to come, and took great comfort that he and Alan Hannay were such firm brothers in arms even though they had never met until four months ago. Friendship was like that sometimes, two people seeing a spark in the other the day they meet; like star-crossed lovers except in some ways a much purer thing, uncomplicated by the turmoil of new love, infatuation and its strange urges...

Marija broke from the circle of her thoughts.

Quite apart from being sick every day her thoughts were often preoccupied with longings and *needs*, distractions of the sort a good Catholic wife ought not to be so constantly *exercised* by, especially in her condition.

"No, we must not hide in New York or anywhere else," she said finally, as if that was an end of the matter. If one allowed oneself to live in fear life became a tiny death every day. They owed it to the dead to *live* without fear. They had been sent to America to 'fly the flag', to 'make friends' and to 'influence people' and that was exactly what they were going to do.

Moreover, albeit they had only been in the United States a month Marija and her husband – the denigration of 'Britain' in the papers, on the radio and the television, the assassination attempt and yesterday's bombings excepted – had been as fascinated as they were appalled by what little they had thus far seen of the 'land of the free'. They both yearned to break out of the bubble they were obliged to inhabit in Philadelphia and to discover and experience the 'real America'. They had embarked upon a great adventure and their time in Philadelphia was simply treading water. Notwithstanding the hostility directed at their country – Marija had married an Englishman and was therefore now 'English' as well as 'Maltese' – they had encountered nothing other than personal kindness, courtesy and a strange melange of enthusiastic, unqualified curiosity and acclaim, as if they were movie stars in their short time in Pennsylvania. She and Peter had been feted, applauded, cheered and endlessly photographed on their public appearances; Congressmen and Senators who lined up in the newspapers to heap excoriating scorn on the 'British Empire' and the person of the Prime Minister, whom they seemed to regard as some kind of a witch, had positively drooled over the opportunity to be seen and photographed with the English 'Navy Couples'.

It was all very, very odd.

Last night her husband had, gently and rather sweetly, told her off for 'sneaking off to the hospital' with the wounded; and of course, for spending so much time on her feet. They had also talked about how they felt about continuing their 'American odyssey'.

Peter used such lovely words sometimes...

England was a drab, hungry place presently and little was likely to improve in the coming months. Moreover, whatever Peter said or did nobody was going to send him back to sea any time soon. Their situation was uncomplicated. They were in America, they had been sent to America to 'make friends' and that was what they were going to do.

Marija's husband did not make an appearance until later that afternoon. Alan Hannay had been called into his long meeting with the Charge d'Affaire, Sir Patrick Dean and Lord Franks, the Ambassador. The two wives were sipping tepidly warm weak tea when 'the boys' finally escaped.

Marija noted that her husband and Alan were looking smug in a righteous sort of way. Peter bent and planted a pecking kiss in her hair before dumping himself in the chair beside her.

"Two pieces of news," he announced, trying not to grin too broadly.

Alan Hannay's face cracked into a conspiratorial smile.

"All non-essential Embassy staff *will* be packed off to Camp David," Peter explained. "Apparently the President feels so bad about what happened yesterday, and what with all the anti-British 'nonsense' that's flying around he wants to 'make a point about hospitality and civility to *middle America*', whatever that is."

Marija had hugely enjoyed their recent brief stay in the Catoctin Mountains. Dining with the President and the First Lady, meeting the Kennedy children and generally being treated like visiting royalty already had about it a dreamlike quality in her memory.

"In the meantime," her husband continued, "the four of us and our 'personal staff' will leave for California on Friday morning."

Marija knew there was more, so she waited patiently, her expression quizzical as she met her life partner's gaze.

"While the 'staff' go on ahead to set up the 'mission' in San Francisco," he explained, ever more smugly, "we shall be going down to Huntsville. That's in Alabama..."

"Isn't that where they make the rockets?" Marija teased.

"This is true," Peter Christopher confessed, as if this salient fact was of absolutely no interest to him. "We shall be the guests of NASA, the *National Aeronautics and Space Administration*, staying at accommodation within the 'secure area' created after the troubles in Washington last December."

Marija shook her head, viewed her husband fondly.

By his own admission Peter had joined the Royal Navy not because he wanted to be some latter day Nelson but because he wanted to play with expensive 'gadgets and gizmos'. He had been in seventh heaven onboard HMS Talavera with her complicated radar systems and advanced electronics suite. He had only earned his watch keeper's certificate because 'it is good to have another string to one's bow'; the thing for him was his 'toys', all and all the marvellous, sophisticated 'widgets' the Navy gave him to play with to his heart's content. And then the October War had happened, he had become the unofficial radar and electronic warfare 'expert' of the fleet locked up in Portsmouth by fuel shortages; the man who trained all the other radar men and EWOs – Electronic Warfare Officers – and perambulated around the anchorage 'fixing' old kit and 'modifying and, or commissioning' new equipment. Nobody had been more astonished when he was promoted Lieutenant-Commander shortly before HMS Talavera had departed Fareham Creek on the war cruise that had ended a little over four months later, in the bloody Battle of Malta ten miles off Dragut Point. In those tumultuous months the boy who had joined the Navy, in spite of rather than because of his 'Fighting Admiral' father, to gain access to the marvels of the modern scientific age, had become the Royal Navy's most famous son.

"Men!" Marija murmured, her eyes laughing.

"Men," Rosa Hannay echoed complacently.

The two husbands looked to each other for mutual support, much as schoolboys caught doing something they ought not to be doing will.

Rosa was remembering a conversation she had had with her *sister* the second day of the couples' stay at Camp David. Another guest in the Catoctin Mountains had been Wernher von Braun, the man who had designed the first intercontinental ballistic missile and who, notwithstanding his former credentials as Adolf Hitler's chief rocket scientist was Peter Christopher's boyhood hero.

'Sometimes,' Marija had observed, a little resignedly, 'I honestly think that people are more interested in the mountains of the Moon than they are in sorting out all the problems *down here*.'

Chapter 10

Saturday 6th June 1964
Heliopolis Presidential Palace, Cairo, Egypt

Normally, when there was a coup d'état the drill was for diplomats to keep the lowest possible profile until, literally, the smoke had cleared and it was possible to form a coherent view as to who exactly was now in charge. Other than in cases where HMG – Her Majesty's Government – had actually fomented, managed or otherwise facilitated the coup in question the long-established principle of 'wait and see', had served the Diplomatic Corps well over the centuries. However, every now and then circumstances demanded that HMG was seen to be, hopefully, on the 'winning side' prior to the final outcome of the 'local disturbance' becoming self-evident. This was one such case although many times during the harrowing five mile drive and trek through the streets of eastern Cairo from the British Embassy, located on the Corniche on the banks of the Nile to the government district, Sir Harold Beeley had asked himself if the game was worth the candle.

Although the fifty-five year old bespectacled British Ambassador had been in post since before the October War, he had been excluded from the secret talks which produced the unholy accord – a moderately despicable troops for indeterminate territorial and political 'guarantees' kind of agreement - that the Foreign Secretary had concluded with Nasser's regime, and had been 'considering his position' ever since.

Ambassadors rarely resigned 'on principle'; men given to that sort of 'flightiness' tended not to join the Diplomatic Corps in the first place. Nevertheless, HMG's man in Cairo had felt himself to be so marginalised, and so under-mined in the eyes of his Egyptian hosts that he seriously wondered what purpose his staying in the country served...

Within the Foreign and Colonial Office he was not one of those men who regarded *Sir* Thomas Harding-Grayson as some kind of Prodigal Son returned to the fold, or any kind of diplomatic magician. To the contrary, he regarded the man as a menace and he was convinced that *his* reckless perturbation of the finely balanced post-October 1962 status quo in Cairo had prompted this *madness*.

Whole districts of eastern Cairo had become battlefields; and God alone knew how many people, mainly innocent civilians, men, women and children had been killed and injured in the fighting still raging in streets around the Presidential Palace.

From a distance the magnificent facade of the Heliopolis Palace resembled something out of a 1945 Soviet propaganda film of the Battle of Berlin. The great edifice was half-ruined with its still standing southern aspect scorched by fire and pocked with shell impacts; a pall of evil grey smoke hung over the entire complex and wrecked and burning tanks, armoured personnel carriers and cars blocked all the approach roads. The cadavers of the dead, horribly charred and mutilated lay around the gutted vehicles, more bodies were strewn here and there, forgotten as the battle had ebbed and flowed. The nearest apartment blocks were gaunt, smouldering shells now, and hungry, licking crimson flames roared from the upper storey of the nearby Army Headquarters. Overhead, the scream of jet fighters was an ever-present.

Sir Harold Beeley had not joined the Diplomatic Service until 1946, before the Second World War having pursued an academic career as a research fellow and lecturer at Queen's College Oxford and University College Leicester. Rejected for military service in 1939 on account of his poor eyesight, he had worked with the famous historian Arnold J. Toynbee at Chatham House, and in the Foreign Office's Research Department prior to joining the Preparatory Commission of the United Nations in San Francisco in 1945. Beeley's last appointment prior to joining the Diplomatic Service was as a Secretary to the Anglo-American Commission of Inquiry on Palestine, an experience which had permanently coloured his view of the realities 'on the ground' in the twentieth century Middle East. In his opinion – formed in the immediate aftermath of the Second War – was that the founding of the state of Israel would hopelessly 'complicate' Britain's ongoing relationship with the rest of the region; an opinion which had earned him no little enmity from prominent Zionists and perversely, had stood him in good stead with practically all the other governments in the Middle East ever since. Ironically, his first posting in the Foreign Office was to the Geographical Department responsible for Palestine, making him one of Foreign Secretary Ernest Bevin's key advisors in the negotiation of the Portsmouth Treaty of January 1948, which most observers unfairly concluded was a licence for Israel's neighbours to embark upon a huge land grab as soon as British Forces withdrew from Palestine. Thereafter, Beeley's career had prospered with stints in Copenhagen, Baghdad, Washington DC, and in 1955, his first ambassadorship to Saudi Arabia, where in ignorance of the plans to invade the Suez Canal Zone in late 1956, he had inadvertently put himself in the US State Department's bad books by honestly reporting in routine conversations that Britain had no intentions of intervening in Egypt. By 1958 he was Deputy Head of the British Mission at the United Nations; needless to say his arrival in Cairo in 1961 had raised unhappy eyebrows in Tel Aviv and quiet nods of approval throughout the rest of the Arab World.

The one thing Sir Harold Beeley had thus far never had to do in the service of his country, was to scrabble through the ruins of a city in the middle of a coup d'état with a bodyguard of heavily armed Egyptian policemen and volunteers from the thirty-man Embassy Protection Detail – men of the Warwickshire Regiment - waving large white flags. While it had been possible to drive the first couple of miles in Embassy Land Rovers and police trucks; thereafter, the streets had become impassable, clogged with the detritus of the fighting.

By the time Beeley and his bodyguards stumbled into the Presidential Palace he was filthy, sweating like a pig and on the verge of physical collapse. Inside the building the atmosphere was filled with brick and concrete dust, and the vile stench of burning was all pervasive. Farther within the thick walls of the inner corridors the shooting and the sporadic explosions in the surrounding districts were muffled, distant and the air was cool.

"Get the Ambassador a drink!"

The order came from the lips of Lieutenant Miles Winter, the boyish, seemingly unflappable subaltern in command of the Warwickshires; and remarkably, the least hot and bothered man in the Embassy party.

Sir Harold Beeley greedily drank from a canteen. The water tasted metallic and he felt moisture dribbling down his chin. Slowly, his head cleared and he was able to stand again unaided.

He strained to hear what the Egyptian policemen were saying to their compatriots about his party's sudden arrival at the Heliopolis Palace. He only caught a few of the words, but they were sufficient to convince him that he had not just surrendered himself into the hands of the rebels. The relief must have been palpable on his grime-stained, sweat-streaked face but actually he was beyond caring.

The Ambassador had insisted that his deputy, the Charge d'Affaire remain behind at the Embassy, and permitted only two young unmarried second secretaries to accompany him on this 'hare-brained mission'. He attempted to clean his glasses with a handkerchief, succeeding only in hopelessly smudging them.

"Let me do that, sir," offered one of the Sten-gun toting Warwickshires, a small man who also wore spectacles.

Beeley peered myopically at the soldier as he doused his glasses liberally with water from his canteen and produced a small, apparently clean cloth from his top left battle dress tunic pocket. Presently, the Ambassador perched his spectacles on his nose and for the first time in the last hour gained a relatively uncluttered, unobstructed view of his surroundings.

He thanked the soldier.

"Don't mention it, sir."

An Egyptian Air Force officer with staff tabs on his lapels and a bloodied right arm in a clumsy sling indicated for Sir Harold and his two civilian secretaries to follow him deeper into the palace.

"Please mind where you step, sir," he observed in English so perfect that it would have shamed a BBC announcer. "I'm afraid there will be a lot of cleaning up to do after this is over."

Presently, the wounded staff officer led the Englishmen down into the bowels of the building, along poorly lit passageways for what seemed like many minutes. There were wounded men lying on litters, other soldiers tramping past, and the muttering sound of voices in side rooms. Below ground only the occasional thump of a big explosion resonated.

Gamal Abdul Nasser had donned battledress adorned with the

badges of a Colonel in the Egyptian Army. He stepped towards the British Ambassador and shook his hand.

"This is a bad day, Sir Harold," he remarked in English. "Come to the map table and tell me what you saw on your way from the Embassy to the Heliopolis Palace."

Beeley respectfully suggested that the commander of his 'protection detail' might be better qualified to provide 'useful military intelligence'. There was a short delay while Lieutenant Winter was summoned. The young man snapped to attention before the Egyptian President.

"At your ease, Lieutenant," the Egyptian President said, beckoning the young man to approach the map table in the middle of the commandeered abandoned kitchen which now accommodated the headquarters of the Republic's legitimate government.

Harold Beeley stood at the young officer's shoulder listening as he described the journey from the Nile across the embattled eastern city. Winter's report was matter of fact, keenly observed and obviously of huge interest to *all* of the Egyptian officers gathered at the table. Telephones rang in an adjacent bunker, outside in the passageway there was constant footfall, the clicking and clunking of firearms bumping webbing, and of magazines locking home.

Oh, my God...

The thought hit the British Ambassador like an unexpected blow to the solar plexus.

This coup, this bloodshed, this futile mayhem was always likely to happen if the Egyptian leadership got back into bed with the perfidious former colonial overlords!

Tom Harding-Grayson would have known that; the man had a mind like a bear trap when it came to Realpolitik, a poker player's morals and an astonishingly low opinion of human nature, even for an old Foreign Office hand. No, he could not have known that there *would* be a coup, not for a certainty; just that once the news and the implications of the movement of two armoured divisions to the Persian Gulf broke that the risk of a coup would inevitably *spike*.

Was that what embroiling Nasser in the coming Gulf War was really all about?

No more than a cynical attempt to salt the battlefield?

He had never imaged even Tom Harding-Grayson was that cynical...

But suddenly all the pieces of the jigsaw fitted together.

How did you prevent Egypt – the one major regional military power, more powerful than all the other Arab states put together – from taking advantage of the aftermath of a general war in the Persian Gulf?

Answer: by so comprehensively hobbling it politically and militarily in such a way as to *not* invite the Israelis to undertake a tempting, but in the long-term a disastrously destabilising adventure into the Sinai or elsewhere while the Gulf War raged. The United Kingdom would have made it known to the Israelis that it had made a pact with Nasser. That was a given...

How were the Israelis supposed to know that it was a sham?

Tom Harding-Grayson had offered Nasser the one thing he dreamed of most. He had allowed the Egyptian President a glimpse of a way to begin to unite the Middle East under a single pan-Arab flag; a way to make real the 'string of pearls', Nasser's vision of nations linked under a pan-Arabist banner all the way from the Atlantic to the Alborz Mountains of Iran, and from the Nile Delta to the very Mountains of the Moon in the southern uplands of the wilderness sheltering the source of the Blue Nile. Nasser, given a free hand in the west to secure the Mediterranean flank of the British position in that sea had dared to believe that he, in his lifetime, might be the man who began the historic reconciliation and reconstruction of the great Islamic caliphate of yore.

But now that his own Army had turned on him it would be months, more likely years, before the regional 'superpower', the Egyptian colossus would again be in any condition, let alone inwardly united enough, to again flex its muscles and to assert its ambitions. What little impetus there might previously have once been for some kind of Arab renaissance had been quashed overnight. And in the meantime Tom Harding-Grayson's alternative great design – whatever it was - would be free to unfold unmitigated by the one regional player capable of frustrating his Machiavellian schemes.

It could not be that simple of course...

The big questions was: what other consequences, intended and unintended lay in store as *Sir Thomas* Harding-Grayson's personal *great game* began to play itself out in the coming days, weeks and months.

Chapter 11

Saturday 6th June 1964
Junior Common Room, King's College, Oxford

"Everybody should sit down," the Queen commanded.

She remained standing as the members of *Her* Government settled in their chairs. This occasion put her in mind of a similar crisis back in December when things had looked very nearly as grimly dark as they did today; and although at the time she had hoped and prayed that she would never have to again assert, and thereby endanger her constitutional primacy, she had always feared that one day there would be another, even greater test. When everybody was seated and all eyes were upon her she took a final moment to review what she needed to say, collected her composure and began to speak in a quiet, determined soprano.

"Some of you will recall the last occasion I addressed the Cabinet," she prefaced. "On that occasion my son, Andrew, had just been murdered, my husband," tight-lipped she glanced sidelong to Prince Philip who smiled encouragement, "lay critically injured in a hospital in Edinburgh, and over a hundred brave men of the Black Watch and members of the Royal Household – many of whom I had known all my life - at Balmoral had been killed and terribly hurt by *terrorists*."

The thirty-eight year old mother still grieving for her dead son and for all those who had died in Scotland that awful day late last year, and since on land, sea and air battlefields thousands of miles from home, hesitated, swallowed and raised her head to continue.

"We have all lost so much. We have all lost so many loved ones," she sighed, looked around the table, "and so very many good people close to us. Sometimes I fear that we are in danger of losing sight of who we are and what we are. If it is hard for *we* around this table, *we* the privileged few, to remember the things that really matter I wonder sometimes how hard it must be for those over whom *we* claim the right to rule."

The monarch had ascended to the throne in February 1952 at the age of just twenty-five; at the time there was a mood abroad in the country that her accession had ushered in a new and supposedly glorious 'Elizabethan Age'; a nonsense that in the event turned out to be more cruelly false than anybody imagined possible in the early 1950s. Like the first Elizabeth whose reign was beset by religious strife, war and constantly threatened by the mendacity of the great World superpower of that age, Catholic Spain; the present Queen's *dominion* had initially been marked with a period of national decline, retrenchment and a series of disastrously miscalculated foreign adventures culminating in the Suez fiasco of late 1956. She had been crowned in a crumbling imperial epoch, watched the winds of change blowing down the last bastions of empire and lived through the cataclysm which had – at a conservative estimate – killed between thirteen and fifteen millions of her subjects in England alone in the last nineteen months. Her own extended family had been decimated; her mother and sister, Margaret Rose, had been consumed by the firestorm which destroyed Greater London on the night of the war, and with them many of her senior courtiers and advisors. She and her children had only survived because they had been at Windsor Castle that night, and many, so many of those closest to her who had been spared in October 1962 had been murdered at Balmoral in December.

Somehow, she had contrived not to shed a single public tear until the day of the investiture of the heroes of the Battle of Malta, since then she had cried many times but had sworn never again to do so in front of *Her* people. They needed her to be strong for if she weakened then what hope was there for any of them?

The Queen eased herself into her chair, mindful of the recently healed broken bones from the latest attempted regicide at Brize Norton in April. Her bones might have knitted together again but the flesh and sinew around them was wasted and disturbed yet, and every day she ached like an old woman.

"We have all lost so much," she repeated, "that I fear that there are times when we forget how much we still have. We do the living a great disservice to live in the past, and to waste time wishing that things were not as they are."

The silence was such that the conversation of two passers-by in the quadrangle outside was faintly audible within the ancient common room.

"I have no opinion on the political decisions of *My* Government or upon the direct employment of the military forces available to it. It is however, my prerogative to do whatever is necessary to ensure that *My* kingdom is *governed*," the Queen continued. "Yesterday's events in the House of Commons give me little faith that the House, as presently constituted, shares my preoccupation or is ready, willing and able to assume the profound challenges of the *governance* of our land."

Her voice was hoarse, her throat suddenly dry.

"Might somebody bring me a glass of water please?" She asked.

Sir Henry Tomlinson was half-way to the door before she had finished speaking. There was an awkward interregnum, and then Major Steuart Pringle the Commander of the Prime Minister's Bodyguard entered the room bearing a tray with a single glass upon it, which he laid almost tenderly before his monarch. The glass was a broad, crystal tumbler three-quarters filled with clear liquid. The queen sipped daintily.

"Thank you so much, Sir Steuart," she nodded.

Sir Henry Tomlinson retook his place at Margaret Thatcher's right hand as the Royal Marine departed. The Prime Minister never knew how to address her 'chief minder', whom, strictly speaking, was Sir Steuart, 10th Baron Pringle.

"Oh, that's better," the Queen declared. "Where was I?" She asked rhetorically, gathering her thoughts anew.

Aware that in recent weeks the UAUK was haemorrhaging support in the House of Commons, and that yet another vote of confidence was pending on the Prime Minister's return from the 'Cape Cod Summit' with the Americans, she had spent practically every waking hour of the last few days listening to the opinions of the most learned constitutional lawyers in Christendom, making discreet soundings with the Chiefs of Staff and studying the cables she had received from Ambassadors and the Prime Ministers of Australia, New Zealand and Canada.

As was her custom she had bounced the things she had learned, suspected and feared off her husband. Her consort was no strategist or tactician and he was far too much the bluff former naval officer to be overly politically adroit; but as the son of a fallen royal house – he was Prince Philip of Greece, after all – who had grown up under the wing of that wise old owl, and master-puppeteer Lord Louis Mountbatten, he possessed a hard-headed, pragmatic mind alert to the harsh realities of the real World.

'Uncle Louis' had been her husband's self-appointed 'father' figure, the shrewd guiding hand who had steered him into the orbit of the Windsors before the Second World War when she was still just a very young teenage girl. Uncle Louis had probably hoped that one or other of the two princesses would be swept off their feet by the dashing young Prince in his tailored dress uniform, but the Queen had never resented her 'Uncle's' motives. Of all the ways to make a royal marriage, the old rascal's subterfuge had turned out marvellously well for all concerned and that was a very rare thing in the long unhappy history of dynastic marriages. She had actually been 'swept off her feet' by the dashing young naval lieutenant but that had been later, there had been no impropriety, and many years and a World War had passed before they were properly affianced and eventually wed.

"Yes," she murmured as her thoughts clarified. "Even in the hours since yesterday's sitting in the House of Commons affairs overseas have taken further grave turns for the worse." She was mindful not to make any reference to the fact that the code breakers at the Government Communications headquarters at Cheltenham were no longer able to 'crack' two of the four Soviet *Jericho* codes they had been 'reading' since mid-April, or to inadvertently announce the key – ultra secret – elements of the quid pro quo that Margaret Thatcher had negotiated with President Kennedy at the Cape Cod Summit.

Project *Jericho* was only known to a handful of Cabinet members, and the full scope of the 'Fulbright Plan' only to the Prime Minister, the Foreign Secretary, the Chancellor of the Exchequer, and to Sir Henry Tomlinson because nobody could keep anything secret from that particular wily old fox.

The news of widespread fighting in the streets of Cairo; of the potentially disastrous sabotage of the American War Stores Depot, and the blowing up of the Royal Fleet Auxiliary Ammunition Ship Retainer at Dammam in Saudi Arabia had been new and unexpected body blows overnight. In Iraq the latest GCHQ traffic analysis indicated that elements of several Red Army mechanized formations had finally struck out south from holding areas around Baghdad, and according to the Chief of the Defence Staff 'there are no major coherent Iraqi forces between Baghdad and Basra to inconvenience the enemy's line of march'. The Red Army could be opposite Abadan Island and lodged on the northern shores of the Persian Gulf well before the end of the month.

"Suffice it to say that this moment demands if not national unity, then a national unity of purpose," the Queen declared. "We find ourselves fighting a war on three fronts; three wars not of our choosing but which I believe it is in the national interest to fight. We *must* defend the oil of the Middle East. We *must* uphold the sovereignty of British Crown Dependencies and Overseas territories in the South Atlantic. We *must* respond to unprovoked aggression in the Western Mediterranean. We *are* committed to fighting the Soviets in Iraq and the Persian Gulf. We will *not* bow to Argentine threats and atrocities in the South Atlantic. We will *not* permit the regime in France – whatever its nature – to interfere with the free movement of British and Allied air or sea movements in international airspace and in international waters. It is our policy to meet force with force to protect *our* legitimate national interests."

The words were spoken softly, without heat or angst and as Cabinet members digested what they *thought* but did not entirely *believe* what they had just heard their monarch annunciate, the faces of several ministers were wearing vaguely pole-axed expressions.

"In respect of the War Emergency legislation presently in force in the United Kingdom and Northern Ireland," the Queen prefaced, her voice blankly uncompromising, "Sections 4(paragraphs a, b and d), Section 6(paragraphs b and c), and Section 9(paragraphs b to e, inclusive) as amended on the 12th day of our Lord, February 1963," the monarch went on, "vest in the Head of State, powers that are extra-constitutional in the sense that they grant the sovereign extraordinary, albeit time-limited, freedom to in effect, suspend the constitution."

Barbara Castle made a surprised choking sound, while Roy Jenkins, the Home Secretary raised a hand as if he was a schoolboy in a class room wanting to ask a question. William Whitelaw groaned very loudly.

"The Prime Minister submitted her resignation to me last night," the Queen reported, making no sign that she had heard or in any way registered the ripples of consternation around the Cabinet table. "I must tell you now that I categorically *refused* to countenance it."

The Queen paused a moment, comforted by the knowledge that had he had a gun – Prince Philip, Duke of Edinburgh and Consort par excellence - would now be waving it at the members of *Her* Government.

"Prior to leaving Blenheim Palace I signed a decree proroguing Parliament until such time as a General Election can be held. I give you due warning that I will not grant a writ for such an election until three conditions are substantially met. Firstly, there can be no General Election while our brave fighting men are engaged in a major war in the Persian Gulf. Secondly, a census of Parliamentary constituencies must be conducted at the earliest possible time so that an election may be held that accurately reflects the wishes of the *surviving* population of the kingdom. Thirdly, regardless of the outcome of hostilities in the Gulf, the Mediterranean or in the South Atlantic, robust arrangements must be in place to ensure that *My* people are fed, and that sufficient fuel stocks have been secured to keep *My* people warm in the coming winter."

The monarch sniffed.

"The last British Head of State to suspend Parliament came to a sticky end, I recall." This prompted uneasy mutterings, mostly of shell-shocked amusement. The Queen looked thoughtfully to the three Chiefs of Staff. In this new era no government could rule without the implicit support of the armed forces, likewise, no sovereign could exercise his or her prerogatives without the acquiescence of these three men. "I applauded the initiative to restore *politics as normal* at the earliest practical time but that experiment has failed. If in years to come I lose my head for my temerity, so be it."

Roy Jenkins half rose to his feet.

"Ma'am, I..."

"Any member of Cabinet has the right to raise *concerns* with their monarch in their capacity as members of the *Privy Council*," the Queen reminded him, more tersely than she had planned. "Let me make myself clear. The Prime Minister, the Chiefs of Staff and *this* Cabinet as *presently* constituted enjoys my full confidence."

The silence was instantly oppressive.

"That is all!"

With this Queen Elizabeth the Second, by the Grace of God, of Great Britain, Ireland and the British Dominions beyond the Seas Queen, and Defender of the Faith stood up, and while the senior members of *Her* government struggled to their feet amidst a cacophony of loudly squealing chairs on the wooden floor boards, she walked very slowly and regally out of the Junior Common Room of King's College.

Chapter 12

Sunday 7th June 1964
Inverailort House, Lochaber, Scotland

The Royal Navy Westland Wessex flew up Loch Ailort and cast a long shadow as it squatted down on the lawn between the old house and the road which cut a ribbon of worn tarmac along the eastern side of the sea loch. The hamlet of Lochailort was hidden in the lengthening shadows of the late Highland evening as the last rays of the sun brightly illuminated the big house.

Sir Richard Goldsmith White, the Director General of the Security Services stepped down onto the firm dry turf and shook hands with the Commandant of the 'Inverailort Estate', Martin Furnival Jones. Like 'Dick' White the other man wore a civilian business suit; nobody in the small welcoming committee was in military uniform or openly displaying any kind of weapon. In fact there was nothing visible to a passing motorist, hiker or Red Dawn spy – other than the very occasional visit of a helicopter on a routine Royal Fleet Air Arm 'training flight' - to suggest that Inverailort House was the most secure 'safe' house in the United Kingdom.

Until the events of early April fifty-two year old Martin Furnival Jones had entertained the reasonable expectation of succeeding, in due course, his friend and chief, Sir Roger Hollis as Director General of MI5. However, the affair of the GCHQ code breakers locked up in Her Majesty's Prison Gloucester for attempting to blow the whistle on the numerous shortcomings of that organisation – thereby technically contravening the provisions of Section 2 of the Official Secrets Act as interpreted, somewhat high-handedly and certainly, eccentrically, by a certain cadre of senior officers close to the former DG – combined with the dreadful news from Malta and Iran of new disasters which the 'intelligence' community had singularly failed to predict, had abruptly cut short Hollis's career.

And Furnival Jones's career, also, it seemed.

Dick White would have understood if his old colleague from his own days in the Director General's seat at MI5, vacated back in 1956 when he was transferred to the Secret Intelligence Service (MI6) to become that organ's top man, still felt a little 'tender' about his sudden demotion. One day he had been in the 'board room' of the Security Service (MI5) and the next he was exiled to the Highlands to oversee the camp that accommodated MI5's and MI6's most intractable 'incurables'.

In the jargon of the intelligence community 'incurables' described enemy agents, or one's own agents who had become *problematic*, or particularly high value 'assets' who had come into the hands of the British Intelligence community whom nobody knew what to do with. 'Incurables' could not, under any circumstances, be permitted to mix with the general population, nor could their existence be admitted, axiomatically they had therefore to be kept safely and securely, preferably in a remote place under appropriate guard. Inverailort House was not quite the back of nowhere but in the British Isles it was as near as made no difference.

"This is all very mysterious," Martin Furnival Jones observed as the two men walked up to the main house. Inverailort House – locally some people called it 'Castle' – had been a hunting lodge when the estate came into the hands of the Campbell family in 1828. The Campbells had developed the property with positively loving care and attention until the outbreak of the 1939 war; when it had been requisitioned by the War Office. During that war the estate had hosted the prototype Commando Training School, the Special Operations Executive (SOE), briefly the Army, and then for the second half of the war the Royal Navy, becoming HMS Inverailort. Having been returned to the Campbells after 1945 – minus the majority of its contents, lost in moves to and from storage in Fort William – it had been reclaimed by the government around the time of last year's *unpleasantness* with the Americans. "You're a long way from Oxford, Dick?"

The tall, handsome former golden boy of MI5 was drawn and weary, a little worn down. The whole Red Dawn-*Krasnaya Zarya* farrago had blown up in his face and but for Roger Hollis's own, less than stellar performance and it having very much been on Hollis's watch that the IRA had very nearly murdered the Queen a *second time* inside a little over four months at Brize Norton, it would have been White's head, not Hollis's figuratively on the block.

White's double agent inside Red Dawn, Arkady Pavlovich Rykov had been a triple agent, loyal to the KGB all along, sowing misinformation and uncertainty in his path. In his heart he had suspected as much from the outset; and then the October War had changed everything, he had convinced himself that perhaps Rykov was a man on the run from his enemies. Rachel Piotrowska, the woman he had originally sent to Istanbul to assassinate Rykov had caught up with him in the chaos of the days after the war, heard him babbling in his sleep about Krasnaya Zarya, an organisation White had specifically *not* briefed her about ahead of her mission, and suddenly White, his best and most trusted agent, and the KGB's most feared mad dog killer had been playing a wholly different, terrifyingly high stakes game of poker.

He ought to have known that Rykov, or whoever he was because he had never claimed that the legend of Arkady Pavlovich Rykov was his real name, was too good to be true. If he had known eighteen months ago what he knew now he would have ordered Rachel to cut Rykov's – or rather, the man they knew as Arkady Pavlovich Rykov's – throat while he slept. That he had not issued that order was a thing that would haunt him forever. However, what was done was done. He was the man in charge of the Security Services and he could not afford the luxury of dwelling on his past mistakes.

"I'm not checking up on you, old man," Dick White assured the

Commandant of the Inverailort 'home for incurables'. "I know I can rely on you to run a tight ship without the DG looking over your shoulder all the time."

The two men trudged up the steps to the big house.

"I shouldn't complain," Furnival Jones conceded. "At least I'm not banged up in Government House at Cheltenham like poor old Roger Hollis listening to the bloody planes taking off and landing at all hours of the day and night."

Dick White had always highly regarded Jones. Like himself he was a Cambridge man – Gonville and Caius College – who had come into the secret world via a law career abbreviated by the outbreak of World War II and six years in the Army. There was much to respect in the man's no-nonsense manner and professionalism and sooner or later, political tempers having cooled somewhat in Oxford he planned to bring him back into the mainstream. That said, 'political tempers' were not about to 'cool' any time soon; and for the time being the other man was best kept out of the limelight and Inverailort was pretty much ideal for that.

"Roger will only be asked to remain in Cheltenham until his de-briefing sessions are completed, Martin," Dick White informed his colleague. "Contrary to what you hear people saying he is *not* under house arrest."

"But he will be under observation the rest of his life," the Commandant of Inverailort House retorted mildly.

"Yes, well," the Director General of the Security Services shrugged, "that's the fate that awaits us all, isn't it!"

Inside the house the evidence of the building's World War II occupants was preserved by the stencilled names left untouched on the doors; 'W.R.N.S.', 'SHIP'S OFFICE Typing Pool', 'CAPTAIN'S SECRETARY', each sign still relatively freshly painted as if the ghosts of the naval officers, seamen and WRENS who had worked at Inverailort in that war in 1945 still walked its corridors.

Furnival Jones led his chief upstairs to his office and retrieved a bottle of malt whiskey from a nondescript cabinet by the window. The setting sun blazed into the first floor room as the two former MI5 men clinked glasses.

"Old times and old friends," they choarused.

Both MI5 and MI6 were clubbish institutions, MI5 particularly and both men had been immersed in its culture for more years than they cared to remember. Dick White had run MI5 in the first half of the 1950s like a convivial, somewhat relaxed version of the gentleman's club he had joined in the late 1930s. Hitler's war had introduced a host of new faces but in the higher echelons of the Security Service nothing much had changed; likewise in MI6, the Secret Intelligence Service. In hindsight this was probably what had allowed those unspeakable bastards Philby, Burgess, Maclean and their collaborators Anthony Blunt and John Cairncross to get away with spying for the Soviets for so long. It was likely that Philby, Burgess and Maclean had been killed in Moscow on the night of the October

War, Cairncross had succumbed to illness the last winter and Blunt – despite his protestations that he was a changed and 'loyal' man - was a 'guest' at nearby Arisaig House.

"I trust our friend from Bucharest and her ladyship are bearing up?" Dick White inquired obliquely, allowing the ghost of a smile to flit across his lips if not his grey eyes.

Furnival Jones chuckled.

"I swear the blasted man thinks he owns the place!"

"That's the nature of the beast."

"That's true. Comrade Nicolae and her ladyship are inseparable. I think the little creep is actually quite fond of her and she seems devoted to him. Odd, don't you think? What was left of her family got killed because of him and yet she behaves as if she is his wife?"

Dick White thought about the proposition.

"They went through a lot together," he offered. "Including being shipwrecked, twice." Then it was time for business. "The Americans want to talk to him."

"I thought we were operating an 'at arm's length policy with the Yanks'?"

"Officially. Unofficially, we're back in bed with them. Don't expect them to come charging to our rescue in the Middle East or the South Atlantic, or anywhere else but my orders vis-a-vis co-operation with our 'old friends' in Langley have been...relaxed somewhat."

That was a little disingenuous and Dick White understood that his old friend would see through it. While he had been ordered to turn *Jericho* over to the Americans but it had been made crystal clear that the National Security Agency was going to have to wait a while – weeks or months rather than days - before it received the real 'gold dust'. What had been turned over thus far was merely a small, inconsequential, yet tantalising contractual down payment ahead of the delivery of the first significant tranche of 'Fulbright Plan' aid. The whole thing was a straightforward intelligence for cash deal and it was going to cost the US Government billions. It was all rather crass but then half the country was in ruins and nobody was about to take John Fitzgerald Kennedy's – or any of his friends' – words at face value ever again until the UAUK saw the colour of his money.

If the Yanks wanted *Jericho* – and they did want it, very badly – they were going to have to pay through the nose. The Prime Minister had made an agreement 'in principle' with the President of the United States, but nothing 'of real substance' was going to get handed over until the Chancellor of the Exchequer confirmed receipt of eye watering quantities of dollars in *his* Treasury. The CIA and NSA bigwigs – Dick White's transatlantic opposite numbers – were already chaffing at the bit, under the mistaken impression that business as usual had been resumed. Soon, very soon, they would be incensed that material that they honestly believed they had a right to receive actually had a price, a very stiff price.

Having spent most of the last two decades in bed with his American counterparts, the new 'special relationship' came hard to

Dick White. He had tried to explain to the Prime Minister that the 'US Intelligence Community will feel betrayed' but Mrs Thatcher had swotted away his concerns.

'Then so be it. The wounded feelings of our former allies are the least of my concerns!'

Martin Furnival Jones raised an eyebrow, knowing that he had just been permitted a glimpse of the business being conducted at the 'top table' of his old friend's new National Security Service *club*.

"Relaxed, Dick?" He asked.

"Only 'conditionally', our future relations with the Americans will be on a strictly business basis in future. That comes straight from the Prime Minister's lips," he was informed.

"What about *Jericho*?"

"*Jericho* is bust. But yes, my orders include handing over *Jericho*; but not in any way in a lock, stock and barrel sense." Dick White smiled sardonically. "Albeit little by little."

Furnival Jones whistled.

"What do we get in return?"

"A second Marshall Plan."

"But we're on our own in the Gulf?"

"That's the way it looks." Dick White drained his glass. He had already reported to Airey Neave, his political master that the 'background chatter' coming out of the CIA and the NSA was 'inconsistent' with the agreement the Prime Minister *believed* she had brought back from Hyannis Port. Either the President had sold the Prime Minister a proverbial pup, or the Kennedy Administration was not talking to his counterparts in Langley; neither option boded well for the future. "Let's speak to Comrade Nicolae. I have some news for him."

It was over a month since the Director General of the Security Services had spoken to the former First Deputy Secretary of the Communist Party of Rumania.

Nicolae Ceausescu was sitting in a threadbare armchair in the bedroom at the back of the house he shared with his companion, the Greek-Cypriot woman called Eleni. Eleni was a handsome woman in her forties with straw blond hair and suspicious blue-grey eyes who seemed uncomfortable, overdressed in the garb of a British housewife. Instantly the two men came into the room she pulled up a chair beside Ceausescu and clasped his left hand.

The man had been reading a book; *Greenmantle* by John Buchan.

The one-legged former master of the Rumanian Secret Police and until the Red Air Force wiped Bucharest off the map with a huge city killer thermonuclear bomb the heir apparent to the dictatorship of his country, put down his book and extended his free hand to Dick White.

"Apologies for disturbing you this late in the day, Nicolae," the spymaster grimaced. Although he intensely disliked and mistrusted the prized asset who had fallen unexpectedly into his hands after the Battle of Malta; liking somebody and doing business with them were two entirely separate things, and in common with any *commodity*,

Nicolae Ceausescu needed to be cashed in before time and events eroded his remaining 'book value'.

"I am honoured to be visited at any hour by the Director of British Intelligence, Sir Richard," the man in the chair replied, in English significantly more fluent than had been the case on their last encounter.

"I see you are becoming acquainted with Lord Tweedsmuir's writings?" Dick White parried, wondering if the pale, diminished man in the armchair would understand.

"John Buchan, Lord Tweedsmuir," the other man shrugged, as if disappointed by the small test.

"Your English is much improved, Nicolae?"

Ceausescu nodded.

"Are you both well?" The spymaster inquired solicitously.

"Yes," Eleni replied, as if her mouth was full of pebbles. "Thank you, sir."

"Good. I have news for you, Nicolae."

The man in the chair did not ask if it was good or bad news because he understood that any news brought to him by the chief British spymaster was not going to be all good.

"Your wife and at least two of your children, Zoia and Nicu are being held in the Soviet Union. We think somewhere in the Sverdlovsk area. We have no news of the whereabouts of your eldest son, Valentin. So far as we can ascertain your wife and youngest children are being treated decently."

Nicolae Ceausescu pursed his lips momentarily.

"If the Russians discover that I am alive that will change," he said coldly, without angst. If the KGB did not put bullets in the back of their necks his wife and daughter would be sent to a Red Army 'comfort brigade', his youngest son to a penal battalion, all three to be fucked and worked to death. That was the way of things and there was absolutely nothing he could do about it. His former family were dead to him now. "One day they will discover it. We both know that."

Dick White did not linger on the subject.

"I want you to talk to representatives of the American Central Intelligence Agency and the National Security Agency. They have sent a two-man team to England to de-brief you."

Nicolae Ceausescu snorted softly.

"And if I refuse to talk to the Yankees?"

Dick White was silent.

If the 'special guest' of the Inverailort House for 'Incurables' elected not to play ball then his wife and surviving children's fate would be sealed sooner rather than later. Before the October War Dick White might have blanched at this; not now. The Prime Minister had made an apparently Faustian Pact with the American President, one day – possibly very soon - it might bring her down, but in the meantime the survival of country and its ongoing capacity to wage war in the Middle East and the South Atlantic hung in the balance. Set against that the lives of a middle-aged woman and her teenage children in Sverdlovsk was a price well worth paying for the greater good. Or that at least, was what he told himself no matter how dirty he felt inside.

As he had planned – meticulously scripted, in fact - he began to explain that the Americans wanted to assure themselves that they could trust what Dick White's people were telling them. Conditional disclosure was not enough. Either the intelligence partnership was 'open' in both directions or it was not. The de-briefing of a key current 'asset' like Nicolae Ceausescu was the first acid test of the renewed 'special relationship'.

"What is in it for me?" Ceausescu asked bluntly.

"I'm sure our American allies will make it worth your while, Nicolae. They have much deeper pockets than we do and eventually they will remember that it is in their best interests to attempt to rule the World again."

The one-legged man in the battered arm chair smiled saturninely.

"I will talk to them," he decided. "But not in England. I will talk to them in America."

"America?" Eleni queried urgently, her brow furrowing.

Dick White was astonished when Nicolae Ceausescu looked to the woman and, almost paternally, nodded reassurance to her as if he really cared what she thought. What astonished him most was that he could not tell if Ceausescu meant it or not. The notion that a man like him was actually capable of caring about another human being was almost...*shocking.*

"Yes, my dear," he told Eleni gently. "We are going to America; America, the land of the free."

Chapter 13

Monday 8th June 1964
Corpus Christi College, Oxford

"The Foreign Secretary won't be joining us this evening," James Callaghan announced. "He and the Prime Minister agreed that it would be wise for the implications of the Egyptian-UK Accord to be re-stated in Tel Aviv at the earliest opportunity.

"Tom's in the air at the moment," added Denis Healey, the beetle-browed forty-six year old Member of Parliament for Leeds East whose reintroduction to the top table of British political life had come as something of a rude shock to his colleagues. This despite the fact it had been the worst kept secret in Oxford that Tom Harding-Grayson had brought him into the Foreign Office as his a senior policy advisor – with the full support of the Prime Minister - some weeks ago.

Born in Kent Healey's family had moved to Keighley in the West Riding of Yorkshire when he was five, educated at Bradford Grammar School he had earned an exhibition – a bursary rather than a full scholarship – to Balliol College in 1936. In 1937 he had become a member of the Communist Party of Great Britain (CPGB). It was at Oxford that he had met another grammar school boy, Edward Heath, whom he succeeded as President of the Balliol College Junior Common Room. The two men had become close personal friends in those days and during Healey's long post-October War illnesses, notwithstanding the intolerable burden of his duties, *Ted* Heath had regularly written to Healey, extending an open-ended invitation to join his government 'as soon as your health and constitution permit'.

Very few people who encountered Denis Healey ever made the mistake of underestimating his intellect, or his ambition. In the wilderness years following Labour's defeat in 1951 he had been one of the Party's rising stars and few had doubted that sometime during the decade of the nineteen-sixties he would have challenged for the leadership. Whether he would have fought his way past the late Harold Wilson or George Brown, or Roy Jenkins or Callaghan, the Party's post-October War leader was uncertain, but every other contender would constantly have been looking back over his shoulder to see where he had positioned himself in any future leadership race.

After resigning his membership of the CPGB in 1940, Healey enlisted as a gunner in the Royal Artillery before being commissioned in the Royal Engineers, with whom he saw wide and varied war service in North Africa, Sicily and Italy. In 1944 he was brigade landing officer for the British assault at Anzio. Declining a permanent commission at the rank of lieutenant colonel, Major Healey had demobbed in 1945 and plunged straight into political life. Ironically his espousal of left-wing views in the early part of his career had amplified his voice when it was raised in moderation during the left-right schisms of the long years out of power in the 1950s. Embedded in the fabric of Atlee's and then Gaitskell's leadership as a key foreign policy advisor, Secretary of the International Department of the Labour Party, a long-time councillor at the Royal Institute for International Affairs, the International Institute for Strategic Studies, and a member of the Executive of the Fabian Society, Healey was a main mover behind the Königswinter Conferences initiated in 1950 to promote European post-World War II reconciliation. Among the surviving luminaries in the Party, everybody in the room knew that had he survived the October War fit and able to lead, that the Party might easily have rowed in behind Denis Healey rather than Jim Callaghan.

"What the Hell did we promise Nasser, Denis?" Demanded Barbara Castle the MP for Blackburn, and Secretary of State for Labour in the UAUK; her tone was unusually vexed. "More to the point what other *little* pacts and *arrangements* have *we* made in the Middle East?"

This was the third gathering of the leadership of the Labour Party as the ramifications of last week's 'no confidence vote' continued to reverberate around Oxford. Roy Jenkins, Barbara Castle, Christopher Mayhew and Anthony Crosland viewed each other over the rims of their tea cups; the Secretaries respectively for the Home Office, the Ministry of Labour and the Health Department not quite knowing what to make of the presence of Crosland, a former ally who had left the UAUK in protest that spring.

James Callaghan had no illusions that he had become the leader of his party by overwhelming popular acclaim or intellectual perspicacity. He had been the last fit, standing candidate from the pre-war hierarchy. Other more gifted survivors and men of greater ambition, like Roy Jenkins, Denis Healey or Anthony Crosland had been struck down by illness, or simply unable or unwilling to get to Cheltenham, the emergency seat of government in those terrible first days after the cataclysm.

Denis Healey shrugged, a little disappointed by the clumsiness of Barbara Castle's questions. It was fascinating to be again in the same 'coven' with his old 'friends'; and he welcomed the opportunity to study them afresh and to reassess their strengths and weaknesses.

Margaret Thatcher, presumably prompted by the men behind her personal throne – Airey Neave and Iain Macleod, whose recent sad demise might yet come to be seen as the final nail in the UAUK's coffin – had allocated the major posts in her Cabinet between the Conservative and Labour Parties approximately in proportion to their respective shares of the popular vote in the last General Election, that of 1959.

The labour 'contingent' in the UAUK led by James Callaghan, had originally nominated the posts of the Home, Labour and Health departments in favour respectively of Roy Jenkins, Anthony Crosland and Christopher Mayhew.

Roy Harris Jenkins, the forty-three year old, bespectacled Member of Parliament for Birmingham Stechford, was the son of a Welsh miner who by dint of sheer intellectual acuity and determination had strolled effortlessly through his years at Balliol in the late thirties and the early years of the 1945 war. In the very college halls where the rump Home Office now operated he had enjoyed many of the happiest days of his life. In his student years at Balliol he had formed numerous lifelong friendships, including ones with the late Edward Heath, Denis Healey and Anthony Crosland. At Balliol he had become Secretary and Librarian of the Oxford Union Society, and the Chairman of the Oxford University Socialist Club and embarked on his life in politics; albeit a life rudely interrupted subsequent to achieving a First Class degree in Philosophy, Politics and Economics in 1941, by four years spent in the Royal Artillery.

Nobody doubted that Charles Anthony Raven Crosland, the forty-five year old MP for Grimsby, possessed one of the finest minds in British politics, or that he would eventually have risen high in his Party and in Government regardless of the intervention of the October War. His short-lived Ministry of Labour portfolio had included a brief to explore options for re-creating a new national education system. He had left government in March before making his mark. Much as he liked and respected Crosland, whom he also found at times, wholly infuriating, Denis Healey had interpreted his friend's willingness to quit the fray the moment the going got really tough as the signature of the man. Eloquent and sometimes brilliant; Crosland was not a man gifted with the ability to actually get things done.

Forty-eight year old Christopher Paget Mayhew, the MP for the bombed out 'rotten' constituency of Woolwich East, formerly the seat of his old friend and mentor Ernest Bevin was a pro-Arabist with liberal views that before the October War had sat uncomfortably within the Party. Healey had thought him an odd choice for a cabinet post in such troubled times.

The fifty-three year old MP for Blackburn, Barbara Ann Castle, who had stepped into Anthony Crosland's dilettante shoes at the Ministry of Labour, was an entirely different kind of political animal to Jenkins, Crosland or Mayhew. Like Healey she was much more of a street fighter. She came from a family active in the Independent Labour party in the 1930s; her father, a tax inspector by profession had been the editor of Bradford's socialist newspaper, the *Bradford Pioneer*, while her mother had run a soup kitchen for local miners. Barbara Castle's activism had bloomed first in nearby St Hugh's College, where she had earned a third-class degree in Philosophy, Politics and Economics. Later she had written for *Tribune*, then as now a leading mouthpiece of the left in British politics whose editor, William Mellor - a married man some two decades her senior – she was said to have been having an affair with at the time of his death in 1942. When she married in 1944, she was the housing correspondent of the *Daily Mirror*, the populist broadsheet of moderate socialism. Thereafter, she had been for many years been an unapologetic socialist on the Bevanite wing of the post-war Labour Party, promoting the rapid decolonization of the Empire and vociferously opposing the

South African Apartheid regime.

"We are on dangerous ground, Jim," Roy Jenkins observed. The Home Secretary had arrived nearly twenty minutes late. Men – and women - were meeting in smoky rooms all over Oxford at this hour, most of them talking various flavours of treason as they came to terms with the fact that the majority of the surviving members of the pre-war House of Commons had suddenly been deemed irrelevant to the present political process.

It was the manner of the prorogation of the Commons that bothered the Home Secretary. Members of Parliament had been summarily dismissed; those who held reserve commissions in the armed forces had been ordered to report to their units, others had simply been given rail warrants to enable them to return to their homes. Those not fortunate enough to have a specific job in Oxford had been in effect, sacked.

The Parliamentary gravy train in Oxford had, quite literally, been derailed!

It was all very well for the Prime Minister to declaim to the disbelieving chamber that 'this House has freely passed legislation demanding that everybody should do their bit in return for their rations' but nobody in the House had actually thought any of that *austerity, war economy guff* applied to them, their families, retainers and close associates.

Christopher Mayhew, the Health Minister had offered his resignation to the Prime Minister twenty-four hours ago. Margaret Thatcher had bluntly informed him that 'until such time as Mr Callaghan nominates an acceptable replacement you will remain in post'.

He was still brooding morosely on this exchange.

"Does it matter what we promised the Egyptians?" Denis Healey asked tersely. "Will anybody care in a month or a year or in ten years' time? Look at all the things Churchill promised people during the forty-five war. He got thrown out by the people after VE-Day and Clem Atlee did his level best to start with a clean sheet. Whoever comes after us will do the same thing. That's politics, comrades!"

"Notwithstanding that somewhat quaint overview of historiography," Roy Jenkins observed ruefully, for he was nothing if not the premier scholar in the room, "the question of the legitimacy of the Government and our *right* to be a part of it cannot be ducked. I'd hazard a guess that less than a third of the Party stands behind we five."

Within hours of the prorogation of the House scores of its members had been brought straight back in from the cold, installed in government jobs magically created out of thin air by ministers – such as those in the room – to lessen the pain and to shore up their personal fiefdoms. Many MPs, like Denis Healey, found themselves officially installed in the 'informal' jobs they had already been doing for weeks or months in the chaos of Oxford's 'government enclave'.

In times of strife the last thing one did was leave one's friends, or one's key enemies, to their own devices. For example, Iain Macleod's Conservative Party successor at the Ministry of Information – displaying an unsuspected political dexterity - had offered Michael Foot, the radical leftist leader of the putative Independent Labour Party a job, for example. Foot had of course, politely turned the overture down but not before *everybody* in the city had heard about it. Had Enoch Powell not been so ill – he had collapsed in the street as he left King's College last Friday night - he would surely have been given some kind of oversight role in Army Intelligence, or asked to remain in Oxford to 'review' reports coming over Airey Neave's desk in the Ministry for National Security.

It was actually the mark of a functioning democracy that basically, the political classes by and large looked after each other in the name of 'continuity'. It was one of the unwritten laws of democratic process that helped to ensure the 'peaceful handover' of power when the electorate kicked the legs out from beneath one or other of the parties at election time. That such 'protocols' had survived the cataclysm of October 1962 was perhaps, one of the few hopeful signs for the future...

Denis Healey belatedly decided to answer Barbara Castle's original question.

"We promised the Egyptians a mutual defence pact," he told the room. "However, the mutual defence elements of the pact were only to come into effect *after* hostilities in the Gulf had ended."

Roy Jenkins frowned.

"What exactly did we tell the Israelis?"

Barbara Castle had no time for semantics.

"Well, whatever is going on in Cairo isn't any kind of foreign policy coup!"

Jim Callaghan called the meeting to order.

"We're not here to second guess Nasser and his generals," he reminded his colleagues. "Frankly, what mandate I, *we* enjoyed in the immediate aftermath of the October War is long exhausted. If things go badly in the Persian Gulf or in the South Atlantic, as they may well do in the next few weeks, there will be calls by some on both the right and the left, for an indefinite suspension of politics as normal. Presently, I have the Prime Minister's word that a General Election will be held within ninety days of the end of major hostilities in the Middle East, regardless of the ongoing situation in the South Atlantic. I believe that the Prime Minister is sincere in this commitment, albeit with the reservation that her own position in her Party is as precarious as is mine. In many ways she faces threats that I don't because the pre-war Conservative Party still survives as a coherent political entity, unlike our own beloved Party. Be that as it may be, the question is simple. Do we stay in government with the Tories in the national interest? Or do we wash our hands of our responsibilities?"

Roy Jenkins found the framing of the two related questions inelegant. His was a mind with finely crafted, rounded edges keenly interested in all the possibilities of a given scenario; to reduce such great questions of state to a binary 'yes' or 'no', 'true' or 'false' resolution was to misrepresent and to disrespect the complexity of the proposition.

Barbara Castle spoke first.

"Michael Foot and several of his friends came to my office this afternoon and gave me a pep talk about unilateralism and de-colonialism."

Michael Foot and the feisty MP for Blackburn had been twin stars of the left-wing of the Labour Party in the 1950s. It was no secret that they had remained close since Castle's admittance to the UAUK.

"Michael thinks we ought to 'abandon Abadan', he said it several times, I think because he just likes the sound of the words. '*Abandon Abadan*, forget about the Middle East', he says. He thinks we ought to be sitting around a table talking like 'adults' with the Argentine. Oh, and he still thinks we should scrap all our nuclear weapons. He says we live in a country built on top of a giant coal field, that we don't need Middle Eastern or American oil; that we should use coal to make synthetic oil – like the Germans in the forty-five war – and be independent!"

"It's not a completely nonsensical view," Denis Healey remarked contemptuously. "Not completely! What sort of progress would it be to go back to a Victorian industrial model based on coal?"

"We're not here to rehash old arguments," Jim Callaghan snapped. "I want to know how many of you are behind me. I propose to accept the Prime Minister's terms for a continuance of the UAUK."

The others fell silent.

"Tom Harding-Grayson has indicated that he will remain in the government whatever we decide this evening."

Barbara Castle glanced to her male companions.

"We're all behind you, Jim."

Chapter 14

Wednesday 10th June 1964
Joint Allied Forward Headquarters, Khorramshahr, Iran

Lieutenant General Richard 'Michael' Power Carver returned Major General Mirza Hasan Mostofi al-Mamaleki's salute and shook his deputy's hand. It was their first meeting since the new command arrangements had been authorised by Sir Richard Hull, the Chief of the Defence Staff back in Oxford. Around the two men the shell-damaged complex on the outskirts of Khorramshahr – mostly ruins above ground but an extensive warren of untouched deep bunkers below ground - was a hive of activity as British and Iranian officers methodically went about setting up the new headquarters.

Events had moved quickly after General Jafar Sharif-Zahedi – the Military Governor of Khuzestan Province, which covered the Khorramshahr-Abadan Sector – had mounted a clumsy, piecemeal assault on the eastern perimeter of al-Mamaleki's Third Imperial Armoured Division's sector.

Zahedi and members of his extended family had literally been in bed with the Pahlavi dynasty ever since it came to power in the 1920s. Zahedi, a man with little or no actual 'soldiering' experience had based himself and his entourage in the town of Bandr Mahshahr some thirty miles to the east, and was wholly preoccupied with the idea of 'recovering the jewel of Abadan' rather than defending his country's western borders against the onrushing Red Army tide. It was Al-Mamaleki's point blank refusal to collaborate in this adventure that had prompted the botched attack on his lines; easily repulsed by the 90-millimetres cannons of his American built M-48 Patton tanks, the 84 and 105-millimtre guns of his hull down British built Centurion Is and IIs, and the pre-positioned anti-tank platoons equipped with lethal L2 BAT (Battalion Anti-Tank) 120-millimetre recoilless rifles. In the days since, whole units formerly loyal to the Provisional Government had come across al-Mamaleki's lines under white flags of truce to continue the fight under his banner.

Two months ago *Brigadier* Mirza Hasan Mostofi al-Mamaleki had commanded a Brigade, now he commanded the equivalent of a division-sized force comprising the equivalent of two armoured brigades supported by several battalions of variously mechanised infantry; in total some twenty thousand men and around two hundred tanks, including a hundred British built and supplied Centurions. This force, deployed around Khorramshahr and within Carver's Commonwealth Abadan Defence Area, had been further strengthened by its expansion eastward to take in the supplies and munitions dumps of the units which had 'come over' to al-Mamaleki in the last few days.

Unfortunately, this was the only good news anywhere within Michael Carver's Persian Gulf Command.

"The greater part of the west and south of the Dammam-Dhahran urban area is in ruins," he reported to his friend.

Al-Mamaleki was a tall, handsome, Sandhurst-educated man in his early forties with a lovingly tended moustache in the old luxuriant style, wearing battlefield fatigues cut by his long dead Savile Row tailor specifically designed to draw the eye to his lean, muscular frame. Carver always felt as if he was in the presence of a 'real, fighting soldier' when he was in al-Mamaleki's presence; and very aware that he himself cut a somewhat bookish, scholarly figure in comparison notwithstanding that of the two men he had the vastly greater combat experience.

Carver had been with the 8th Army - XXX Corps - in the Western Desert, served with Montgommery, fought in Tunisia, Sicily, Italy and Germany in Hitler's War and subsequently in several of Britain's unpleasant bush fire colonial wars. A cerebral man who thought deeply about the profession of arms he recognised in his Iranian friend exactly the man he needed to strike the decisive blow, if and when Operation Lightfoot, the plan he had first put to the Chiefs of Staff in Oxford in April was ever to be executed.

The 'great plan' had pre-supposed, if not the active military and logistical support of the Saudi Arabian government, then at least the use of the ports, depots and air base of the Dammam-Dhahran conurbation on the southern shores of the Persian Gulf within reach of the Kuwaiti border.

"The US Air Force War Stores Depot in the desert next to Dammam was completely destroyed," he reported. "Suffice to say the violence of several of the detonations was such that unexploded munitions from that site have been discovered between two and three miles away. There is little doubt that the incident was caused by sabotage. Shortly after the major conflagration in the desert a number of mines, each containing around five hundred pounds of TNT, detonated in the aft magazine of the Ammunition Ship Retainer. There were several sympathetic explosions which had the effect of scattering much of the vessel's remaining cargo, mainly fixed naval rounds of all calibres across the dockyard area and into the harbour. The Retainer was totally destroyed and HMS Triumph, the repair ship moored some two hundred yards forward of the Retainer at the main quay was damaged. Some two hundred Royal Fleet Auxiliary and Royal Navy personnel were killed or seriously injured. Recovery squads are presently retrieving munitions on shore and assessing whether they might still be usable. The harbour is being dredged to make navigation safe and hopefully, to recover further undamaged rounds. I'm reliably informed that shells are 'tough buggers' and that many of the rounds we pull out of the harbour and find on land ought to be 'serviceable'. Regrettably, if one is being realistic most of the ammunition on the Retainer is lost, and therefore some of the ships in Admiral Davey's Squadron are likely to have half-empty magazines by the time the Red Army invests Basra and the Faw Peninsula."

Al-Mamaleki's brow darkened.

"Had all the ANZAC tanks and vehicles been offloaded before the 'incident'?"

Michael Carver nodded.

"Thankfully, yes. Unfortunately, a lot of the 105-millimetre AP and HE rounds were stacked on the quay ahead of transfer to the ANZAC forward depots in Kuwait. Most of the 20-pounder reloads for the Mark I Centurions had already been trucked north. Thankfully, the Sydney had already gone alongside Retainer and embarked some twelve hundred tons of munitions for delivery to Abadan."

Al-Mamaleki nodded, thinking hard. Over half of his Centurions were Mark Is, equipped with the long 20-pounder (84-millimetre) post-Second World War vintage anti-tank rifle; a good weapon but nowhere near as lethal as the much bigger Royal Ordnance L7 52-calibre 105-millimetre gun which equipped his Mark IIs.

"The worst of it," Carver explained, trying not to wear his exasperation on his sleeve, "is that the 'incident' has somewhat unnerved our Saudi hosts. Apparently, there is a vociferous 'peace at any costs' camp within the Royal Family. As you know, we've been dealing with the Defence Minister and the Oil Minister, both of whom have been recalled to Riyadh. In their absence their agents in Dammam are powerless and the civilian authorities have failed to get a grip. Admiral Davey is basically in charge of the military *and* the civilian rescue and salvage operation in the area. Hopefully, the Saudi authorities will get their act together sooner or later. Even more troubling are the developments in Egypt."

"Ah, Egypt," al-Mamaleki groaned. He had never liked the idea of having two Egyptian 'revolutionary' armoured divisions anywhere near, let alone planted on the soil of any country in the Persian Gulf. Now he found himself liking the prospect of having to take on the Red Army with several hundred *fewer* tanks even less appetising.

"Nasser's forces appear to have regained control of most of Cairo but there have been further insurgencies and minor rebellions around Alexandria and Port Said, and elsewhere in the Delta. The formations that were due to embark at Suez for seaborne transit around the Arabian Peninsula to Kuwait City," Michael Carver sighed, "have been ordered back to Cairo."

"What price a second Cannae on the road north of Basra now, my friend?" Al-Mamaleki posed rhetorically.

The Englishman shrugged noncommittally

The Iranian officer grinned knowingly.

"I never trusted that madman Nasser," he confessed.

Michael Carver grimaced. He had never actually believed a single Egyptian tank would ever arrive in the Gulf; or at least, not in time to be transferred to a forward position in Kuwait in any kind of good fighting order. Moreover, he was not so naive to believe than *any* Egyptian tanker could be relied upon to obey *any* command issuing from the mouth of one of their hated former colonial overlords. Privately, he was a little relieved. Better the crews of three score British and ANZAC Centurions than three hundred or three thousand tankers who might as easily turn their guns on his forces as upon to the enemy.

"Nor I, Hasan," Carver admitted guiltily.

Al-Mamaleki shook his head and chuckled lowly.

"What else has gone wrong?" He inquired jovially.

"Apart from the renewal of England's traditional war with the French," Michael Carver quipped wanly, "oddly enough, nothing significant has gone wrong in the last few hours."

Several smaller physical maps had been pieced together to make a giant map of the whole of southern Iraq and western Iran on the end wall of the room the two generals had commandeered for their conference.

"I asked my GSO2 to accompany me up here from Abadan," Carver declared, changing the subject and moving from generalities to specifics in the blink of an eye. "He's got the latest radio traffic analysis. We think we may have got a handle on what Comrade Marshal of the Soviet Union Babadzhanian is up to."

Lieutenant Colonel Hamish Clive – so far as he knew no relation whatsoever to the famous 'Clive' who had conquered most of India single handed – had been 'dragooned' into his current job as General Staff Office 2 (Intelligence) by the simple expedient of his long time mentor Michael Carver asking him to 'sort out the bloody mess in my GSO2 department' the day he stepped off the plane from Malta, where incidentally, he had been 'clearing up after the mess the Russians made at the beginning of April'.

Clive was actually a Royal Engineer who had spent a lot of time over the years on the Staff, but these days a fellow had to turn his hand to whatever needed to be done most urgently. He was a less rotund man than he had been before the October War; nevertheless he was still well-padded and his complexion was never less than ruddy with apparent good health. He had taken over the 'GSO2 Department' with the practical *let's get things sorted out* attitude that characterised his twenty year career in the Army.

Clive wasted no time getting down to business.

"The bad news is that I think the Soviets have got themselves organised. Not before time, it had to happen sooner or later!"

Snatching up a pointer he started jabbing the big composite map on the wall.

"In the north Comrade Babadzhanian has done the sensible thing; namely to garrison Erbil, Mosul and Kirkuk, effectively quarantining the surrounding countryside and stopping the one bit of the Iraqi Army that seems to have taken exception to the invasion – the Kurdish regiments – from making trouble, and thus securing the north-western flank of Army Group South as it wheels to the south through Sulaymaniyah. Soon after the Soviets arrived in that part of the country the RAF mounted a series of raids knocking down bridges and choking communications hubs – towns and city centres – with rubble. They stopped doing that once the Red Air Force established advance bases around Baghdad and began ringing the city with mobile radars and presumably, the latest available surface-to-air missile systems. Give the boys in blue credit where it is due," Clive conceded grudgingly, "they made a real mess of the roads to the south and the existing airfields, depots and fuel storage tanks in central Iraq *before* they disengaged."

Clive stepped back for a moment.

"Babadzhanian has placed a small blocking force west of Baghdad commanding the road from the capital to a place called Abu Graib, and the towns of Falluja and Ramadi. That happens to be the highway that goes all the way across the Syrian Desert to Jordan. We believe that elements of the 4th Mechanised Infantry Division of the Iraqi Army ran away in that direction; clearly, the Russians don't want these chaps mucking about on their open flank as they barrel down to the south."

Al-Mamaleki held up a hand.

"Do we have a feeling for what proportion of the Soviet invasion force has reached Baghdad, Colonel Clive?"

"Perhaps, a third, sir," Michael Carver's GSO2 offered. "As many troops are likely to be strung out between the Iranian border east and north of Sulaymaniyah or engaged in low level operations in the Kurdish north. The rest of Army Group South is still in the Alborz and Zagros Mountains keeping the roads passable and recovering broken down tanks and other vehicles."

"So, the push to the south involves say, two or three armoured corps with what," Al-Mamaleki thought out aloud, "around fifty to sixty thousand effectives and about five hundred tanks?"

"Nearer six or seven hundred, I'd guess, sir. Units are reaching Baghdad piecemeal and the Soviets are re-organising on the hoof, as it were. Equipment and front line troops are being stripped from existing units and reformed into all-arms battle groups before being incorporated into reinforced brigade and divisional formations under the command of Babadzhanian's hardest charging generals."

Al-Mamaleki looked up and met Michael Carver's eye.

He would have sworn his friend was smiling but his facial expression was fixedly inscrutable.

"The most likely scenario is that in true Soviet fashion Babadzhanian has been given a serious hurry up by the arm chair generals back in Chelyabinsk or Sverdlovsk," Clive grinned happily, "and basically, thrown caution to the winds."

Al-Mamaleki knew Carver was smiling now.

The faster the enemy came onto his guns the better.

A few minutes later Michael Carver and Hasan al-Mamaleki stood outside the command complex enjoying the cool desert air.

"If you are amenable," the Englishman prefaced, "I'd like to assign a 'liaison officer' to your Headquarters?"

"Who do you have in mind?"

"Julian Calder. You might remember him from the Staff College at Sandhurst a few years ago?"

"Julian?" The Iranian chuckled. "I should have known he'd be around here somewhere!"

"He's SAS these days. Quite apart from making it easier for you and I to keep in touch I'm sure having a fellow like him around will come in handy," Carver went on. "Sooner or later."

"Sooner or later," his friend agreed.

Chapter 15

Thursday 11th June 1964
Merton College, Oxford, England

Lieutenant Colonel Francis St John Waters, VC, felt more his old self in the brand new uniform which almost but not quite fitted him like a glove. Although the news that his wife wanted a divorce had come as a little bit of a surprise there was, as he always told his men in the field, invariably a silver lining to this as there was to the majority of clouds.

The letter had arrived at his billet in Headington a couple miles walk from the centre of the city, before he had got around to making plans to visit his estranged wife Shirley and *the sprog* up in Sheffield. That would have been a tiresome journey and he had never really gotten on with Eric, his older brother.

Funny old World, what?

This was a thing he had mused upon more than once in the last few days. He had been dreading paying a duty call on Eric's hideaway up on Bradfield Moor overlooking Sheffield, making polite forced conversation with his sibling, his wife and his nine year old son. He had not seen Shirley or the sprog since before the October War and frankly, until the Red Air Force was so good as to give him a free 'lift' home he had not given an awful lot of thought to any kind of reunion.

Shirley had sent a picture of the sprog, Harold, *Harry* with her letter asking for a divorce. The sprog looked well, that was something. The letter had been something of a turn up for the books because Shirley had always been such a pretty, passive never say boo to a goose sort of girl; but apparently she and Eric had been brazenly *'living as man and wife for the last year'*.

What with one thing and another Frank Waters had to admit that he was a tad miffed about it all. It was bad enough Shirley was cuckolding him; without discovering that the chap who was regularly dipping his wick – presumably enthusiastically, as one did - in one's wife's private parts was one's own younger brother! Still, *noblesse oblige* and all that, he did not care to be cast in the role of the pot calling a kettle black; given that he honestly could not remember how many floozies, other men's wives, and miscellaneous dusky-skinned maidens he had dallied with since the last time he had had carnal knowledge of Shirley, he was hardly in any position to confidently seize the moral high ground.

'*Shall I cite Eric as co-respondent?*' His wife had inquired. The matter was pressing; it seemed Eric had knocked up the bloody woman. '*Or can I rely on you to organise that side of things at your end?*'

Dammit! Did the woman not understand that was not how things worked these days? The era when a fellow could hire an obliging private eye to scrape up the dirt on an illicit assignation in a hotel room with a willing tart had ended the day the bloody bombs started dropping!

Resplendent in his new uniform and medal ribbons Frank Waters was vexed to be asked for his ID card, before the Policeman – armed with an ancient Lee Enfield rifle - at the main entrance to Merton College allowed him to pass inside. His marital *difficulties* excepted the one thing which really *irritated* the 'returning hero' – as he had been hailed by the Ministry of Information and the Prime Minister herself, more than once – was that for some reason beyond his ken he had been declared *persona non grata* at his alma mater up in Herefordshire.

He had anticipated being welcomed back into the fold with open arms, positively feted and feasted by his old comrades in arms at Stirling Lines, the Headquarters of the 22nd Special Air Service Regiment. Instead, he had been shunned, sent to Coventry by the SAS as if it was his fault that he had had the temerity to come back to England without *any* of the people he had taken to Iran. How was he to know that the whole bloody Red Army would turn up en masse in the middle of nowhere? And it was not as if he had abandoned the chaps to their fate; dash it all he had been unconscious when he was captured and to this day he had no idea what had happened to his people in that bally air strike on the Russian column they had been hiding in! The bloody Regiment was treating him like he was a leper! Every morning he half-expected to receive three white feathers in the post!

"Ah, Frank," Diana Neave, the wife of the Secretary of State for National Security, said smiling in welcome. She pecked him on the cheek and guided him through into the rooms the Neave family shared at Merton College. "It is lovely to find you looking so well after your recent adventures." The Neave offspring; eighteen year old Marigold, an elfin younger version of her mother, sixteen year old Richard, in a cadet uniform, and ten year old William, bright-eyed and still impressed by aging action heroes like Frank Waters, formed an impromptu respectful reception line before being dismissed by their mother.

Frank Waters had been on more than nodding acquaintance with the Neave's ever since the war – the last 'proper' war, the one with that unspeakable bounder Hitler – when he had first rubbed shoulders with the SOE in 1944 and later, MI6 after he came back from North Africa. Airey Neave had been one of the 'comedians' responsible for sending him to the Balkans. Working with Tito's partisans had been quite the dirtiest business he had ever turned his hand to; but at the time it had all seemed like it was in such a dashed good cause that he had never lost a great deal of sleep over it.

"It's jolly good to be back in the old country, Diana," the SAS man guffawed jovially, spying the stocky figure of his old sparring partner, Airey Neave approaching.

The two men shook hands.

Airey and Diana Neave were practically the only married couple he knew who were, to all intents, actually very happily married. Airey, the old dog, had married Diana not long after he got home back from Colditz Castle in 1942. The couple had both been in intelligence during the forty-five war, Diana working with the Polish Government in exile, and Airey doing whatever he did with SOE and MI6. That must have been problematic for them, never being able to discuss what went on in 'the office' while occasionally bumping into each other in the corridors outside some of the most secret rooms in Whitehall.

It might simply have been because he was at a fairly low ebb at present, what with his own wife playing doctors and nurses with his little brother, his being on the wrong end of a Regimental cold shoulder and generally being at something of a loose end in Oxford; but for the first time in his life he found himself rather envying married couples like Diana and Airey Neave.

Catching himself brooding he snapped out of it.

He would get over this passing *mal de mere* sooner or later and it never did any good feeling sorry for oneself!

"Ah, Frank," Airey Neave grinned conspiratorially. He was a ruddy-faced, witty man whom Frank Waters suspected longed for the old brotherhood of the Second War, to relive the life and death exhilaration of those Colditz days and the long 'home run' back to England. "We're just waiting for one more arrival. Come on through to the dining room. You know Nick Ridley, of course."

The Secretary of State for Information greeted the newcomer warily. The thirty-five year old Member of Parliament for Cirencester and Tewkesbury was still getting his feet under the table at his ministry. Trying to fill the unfillable shoes of the late Iain Macleod would have been hard enough at the best of time. In the wake of the prorogation of the House of Commons and the banishment of all MPs not deemed to be essential to the 'smooth functioning of the war economy and the governance of the state', from their comfortable rooms in Oxford back to their constituencies, or country seats in the case of many Tory back benchers, he had unexpectedly found himself in the middle of a political firestorm; cast in the role of the Unity Administration of the United Kingdom's chief apologist and propagandist at absolutely the worst possible time. The bags under his eyes and the greyness in his face told their own story.

It had not helped that an incorrigible old throwback like Lieutenant Colonel Francis St John Waters, VC, had refused point blank all blandishments to be employed as a walking, talking 'good news story' to lighten the indigestible and distasteful realties of the national crisis that daily oppressed the British people.

"Colonel Waters and I have spoken a couple of times this week," Ridley admitted reluctantly.

Diana Neave pressed a glass into the soldier's hand.

"I'd offer you Sherry but despite the entreaties of our Portuguese allies the Ministry of Supply still hasn't put Jerez Sherry – which the Spanish are desperate to sell to them to earn foreign exchange - high enough on the 'Priority Shipping List', Frank," she apologised.

The SAS man was in no mood to refuse two fingers of extraordinarily palatable Scotch Whiskey.

"These are terrible times, dear lady," he chortled wryly as he raised the glass to his lips.

"I can't get used to you without that dreadful moustache you wore for all those years," Diana Neave confided, her lips quirking with mischief.

This drew a mischievous chortle from the warrior.

"The damned thing made me look like something off a Great War recruiting poster," Frank Waters explained candidly, without confessing that lately he had begun to feel as old as Field Marshall Kitchener - the man on those famous Great War posters - had been when they were printed in 1914 and ever afterwards. Old and somewhat worn, not a condition that he planned to succumb to any time soon. "Is one permitted to inquire the name of the personage for whom we are waiting?"

"Yes. You are allowed to ask. But I'm not allowed to tell you!"

"Ah." The man drew the obvious inference. "Enough said."

Airey Neave had started recounting old war stories when, about twenty minutes later there was a commotion in the corridor and a staccato rapping on the door to the Neave family rooms.

A fierce looking Royal Marine stepped into the lobby, glanced around and stood aside, watchfully fingering his Sten gun.

Frank Water's had not realised he still looked *that* dangerous!

A familiar-looking Royal Marine major entered.

Sir Steuart Pringle nodded acknowledgement to Frank Waters – the men had been on convivial 'nodding' terms for many years – but did not salute. Saluting was a tricky business when one was hefting a Sten gun.

"The room is safe, Ma'am."

Ma'am!

"I was so glad when Airey told me that you would be able to come tonight," Margaret Thatcher told Frank Waters, entering the claustrophobic rooms like a minor deity set upon expelling the moneylenders from the temple.

Inexplicably, the most cynical old soldier in England stood before the Angry Widow bathed in the enthralling radiated warmth of her smile, fixed to the spot by the steely blue in her eyes.

It was a stunning thing to *know*, with utter certainty that in a moment one's life had just changed forever.

And to be so totally at peace with the knowledge.

It was all that Frank Waters could do not to drop his whiskey glass and well...*drool* like an imbecile.

Chapter 16

Thursday 11th June 1964
Habbaniyah Air Base, Anbar Province, Iraq

The Mil Mi-6 heavy-lift helicopter in its drab, mottled desert camouflage swooped down onto the packed mud of the pad behind the hastily piled three metre high earthen anti-blast embankments. The RAF had not attacked any target within fifty kilometres of Baghdad for several days; but the wreckage of gutted buildings and several burned out MiG 17s and 21s on the tarmac close to the muddy waters of Habbaniyah Lake bore testimony to the intensity of the most recent raid. Since then two mobile radar units had been stationed at the airfield and a battery of S-75, variant V-750(13D) high-altitude surface-to-air missiles positioned to protect the former Iraqi Air Base.

It had been S-75s which had shot down Gary Powers's U-2 in 1960, and claimed the first victim of the Cuban Missiles War – Major Rudolf Anderson – on 27th October 1962. During the build-up for Operation Nakazyvat, S-75s had shot down two more American U-2s operating out of Dhahran in Saudi Arabia over-flying southern Russia. The missiles had a range of approximately forty-five kilometres and an effective ceiling of twenty-five thousand metres. Radio-controlled they accelerated to Mach 3.5 and were fitted with a proximity fuse to detonate its two hundred kilogram high explosive fragmentation warhead within a sixty-five metre radius of its target.

Sixty-four year old Defence Minister and Marshal of the Soviet Union Vasily Ivanovich Chuikov stepped down from the cabin of the Mil Mi-6, and ignoring the guard of honour exchanged salutes with the Commander of Army Group South. The most decorated surviving 'Hero of the USSR' was an ugly lump of a man with an evilly cherubic face, and a casual contempt for many of the minor idiocies of the Marxist-Leninist state he had served so valiantly his whole adult life.

Contrastingly, both in appearance and temperament fifty-eight year old Marshal of the Soviet Union Hamazasp Khachaturi Babadzhanian, second only to Chuikov in the monolithic hierarchy of the Red Army, could hardly have seemed more different. He was slighter of build, a thoughtful, brooding man who rarely allowed his impatience with 'the system' to break the surface of his glacial composure. He had earned his reputation as a brilliant exponent of mobile warfare in the cauldron of Kursk and a dozen other savage battles during the Great Patriotic War; and he was the man Nikita Khrushchev had entrusted to crush the Hungarian uprising in 1956. For that he had earned the sobriquet of 'the Butcher of Bucharest' in the West – and even in some corners of the Red Army – but he had had no qualms putting down the Hungarian revolution. A door once opened to chaos and anarchy was impossible to shut again without the shedding of the blood of both the innocent and the guilty.

"Those old women in Chelyabinsk are terrified that bastard

Shelepin will mount a coup against them if I'm out of the city for more than a couple of days!" Chuikov complained cheerfully. "Sometimes I think you have to have bollocks for brains to be a member of the Politburo!"

Babadzhanian's own assessment was that not even Alexander Nikolayevich Shelepin the mendacious First Secretary of the KGB would be *that* reckless at a time like *this*. Shelepin was not the kind of man who liked to leave his finger prints all over the scene of the crime.

"I don't think it is a required qualification, Comrade Marshal," Babadzhanian observed quietly. "But it probably helps."

Chuikov vented a bear-like roar of laughter and for a moment the smaller man was afraid his chief was going to heartily thump him on the back in front of the Red Air Force guard of honour.

Vasily Ivanovich Chuikov had been born into a peasant family at Serebranye Prudy, a village south of Moscow. The eighth of twelve children and the fifth of eight sons he had left school and his home, finding work in a factory making spurs for the Tsar's cavalry in distant St Petersburg. When he was in a reflective mood or had been drinking too much Vodka, Chuikov would proudly – and loudly - remind anybody within his hearing that *all* his brothers had fought in the Civil War which followed the October Revolution. Aged only eighteen and already an officer in the Red Army he had fought against the White Russians in the Ukraine, in 1919 he was made commander of the 40th Regiment of the 5th Army fighting Admiral Kolchak's Tsarist lickspittles in Siberia. Between 1918 and 1920 he was wounded four times, the fourth wound leaving him with fragments embedded in his left arm that after initially leading to paralysis of the limb, had plagued him ever since.

Regardless of his *problems* and *disputes* with Chuikov, some small part of Hamazasp Khachaturi Babadzhanian would always be in awe of him. As the two men marched towards the command tent sheltered within the bomb-damaged base buildings, he could not but be aware that he was walking in the shadow of the man who had commanded the 4th Army in the invasion of Poland 1939, and the 9th Army in the Russo-Finnish War of 1940 when *he* had still been a humble subaltern, no more than a company commander. In 1942 when Babadzhanian had commanded battalions and regiments; Chuikov had commanded, successively 7th Guards Army and 62nd Army on the western bank of the Don River. It was Chuikov who had held Stalingrad, Chuikov who had turned the tide of the whole war, Chuikov who had driven the Nazi invaders all the way back to Berlin, where it had been Chuikov who had personally accepted the surrender of the ruined German capital from General Helmuth Weidling in May 1945.

Inside the command tent the great man extracted a cigarette from a crushed pack and half-a-dozen of Babadzhanian's officers simultaneously attempted to strike matches for the Minister of Defence and Commander-in-Chief of the Red Army. Soon foul-smelling smoke filled the air.

Chuikov coughed asthmatically, looked around and grinned complacently because he was never more at home than in a makeshift field headquarters hundreds of miles away from the next nearest Politburo member.

"How are our 'hard chargers' doing, Comrade Hamazasp Khachaturi?" He inquired as he stood over the map table with his Army Commander.

Babadzhanian tried and failed to suppress a smile.

Major Generals Vladimir Andreyevich Puchkov and Konstantin Yakovlevich Kurochnik were not just 'hard chargers', they were natural born 'hard chargers'. Babadzhanian had known as much about Puchkov for many years.

Puchkov was a man of his own age with a weather-beaten face and a shaven head that exhibited the white, gnarled scars of the day back in 1943 when a single German Tiger tank had knocked out three of the four surviving T-34s of his troop in a clearing in the taiga outside Kursk. His gunner had put a seventy-five millimetre round through the side of the Nazi behemoth but not before the Tiger's eighty-eight millimetre canon had put a solid shot into his tank's engine compartment.

Kurochnik had come to the Army Commander's attention after his brilliantly aggressive handling of his mission in Tehran at the start of Operation Nakazyvat. Since then he had distinguished himself at Urmia in Iranian Azerbaijan, and in ruthlessly subduing the northern cities of Kirkuk and Mosul. Since the Tehran action Babadzhanian had promoted him two ranks and given him command of the spearhead division of the eastern 'push' south.

With his Army Group stretched out along dirt roads all the way back into the Zagros Mountains of Iran, his logistics in turmoil and less than a third of his remaining fighting force in any condition to resume the drive south; Babadzhanian had made the best of a bad deal. High command was not about identifying the best of all possible options in any kind of ideal, perfect world; it was about retaining the initiative and throwing every available tank, man and bullet into supporting whatever one decided was the *least worst choice*.

Such decisions were not, in Hamazasp Khachaturi Babadzhanian's experience as difficult as outsiders, or historians later made them out to be. A week ago he had confronted the dilemma of waiting until everything was in place for an overwhelming southward advance; or of striking immediately before the Iraqi Army – what was left of it – and or the British and their allies got their act together. It was no decision at all. Not even the consideration that if he waited another week or two he would probably be sacked had significantly impacted on his deliberations. The *only* decision was to unleash the two available under-strength tank corps which had coalesced in the Baghdad area as soon as possible.

The terrain between Baghdad and Basra – some four hundred and fifty kilometres as a crow might fly, nearer five hundred and fifty along what passed for roads in this part of the world – was rocky desert, marshland and the variously inundated flood plains of the Tigris and the Euphrates Rivers. There were only two roads, two feasible lines of advance and the country over which his men would be advancing was too poor, barren and frankly, medieval for his armour and mechanised units to attempt to 'live off the land'.

While the idiots back in Chelyabinsk understood none of this; Chuikov understood it perfectly. In fact during the planning of Operation Nakazyvat both men had agreed to minimise highlighting the 'critical constraints' that would inevitably blight large scale mobile operations south of Baghdad. The collective leadership and the rest of the Politburo would have 'wet their breeches' if they had known the half of what awaited the Red Army in the deserts and marshes of southern Iraq.

The only thing that neither man had anticipated was the complete disintegration of the Iraqi state and its armed forces ahead of the Red Army reaching Baghdad. Instead of having to fight a bloody attritional battle for the capital Babadzhanian's tanks had rapidly crushed all resistance; and had it not been for the RAF's precision bombing the taking of the city would have been a straightforward 'police' operation.

The western of the two roads south had been allocated to 3rd Caucasus Tank Army; this line of advance arrowed south to Diwaniyah and Samawah, bypassing Karbala and Najaf. The latest reports showed the leading elements of Vladimir Andreyevich Puchkov's 10th Guards Tank Division forging south of Mahmudiyah, and extending a small blocking force down the road towards Karbala, some fifteen kilometres north of the town of Hillah.

The eastern road belonged to 2nd Siberian Mechanised Army. It followed the western foothills of the Zagros Mountains most of the way down to Numaniyah, Kut and Nasiriyah before merging with the western road south some kilometres north west of Basra. Major General Kurochnik's 19th Guards Tank Division was sixty miles down the road to Numaniyah, retracing the steps of British and Australian Great War campaigns; campaigns steeped in the sort of ignominy and unnecessary wastage that Babadzhanian desperately needed to avoid.

Babadzhanian pointed to Basra and the force symbols on the map east and south east of the city.

"There are reports of fighting between Iranian Army units east of Khorramshahr. We're short on detail, unfortunately. I should imagine that the Iranians are fighting among themselves over Abadan!"

"According to Comrade Shelepin," Chuikov guffawed sceptically, "we can forget about having to deal with the Egyptians. And after the 'accident' at Dammam *his* people on the ground are saying that the British don't have anything left to shoot at us with."

Babadzhanian did not believe that for a moment.

However, he was not about to waste time worrying about it.

The British had ships in the Persian Gulf, a few tanks and aircraft in Saudi Arabia, Kuwait and on Abadan Island; 'a few' being the operative clause. The destruction of the nearest substantial war munitions dump at Dammam was a bonus; likewise the confirmation that there would be no Egyptian reinforcements to factor into his calculations. Presently, the British at Abadan were surrounded by hostile forces; friendless across the Shatt-a-Arab in Iraq, and penned in to the north and east by the Iranians.

Now that he had finally launched his tanks towards Basra it was beginning to look as if, against all odds, that the final part of Phase One of Operation Nakazyvat might actually turn out to be something of a cake walk.

Chapter 17

Lieutenant-Commander Walter Brenckmann junior had studied the CIC – Command Information Centre – *battle plot* and the thick sheaf of sonar and the other reports he had requested over the last forty-eight hours; and he still did not know how the USS Permit (SSN-594) had managed to continuously stalk the flagship at ranges of less than two miles for thirty-three hours on the fifth and sixth of June. Up until five days ago he had regarded the rumours – wardroom scuttlebutt really – about how the British nuclear boat HMS Dreadnought had played cat and mouse with the Enterprise Battle Group in the North Atlantic for almost a week in November and December last year, with what now amounted to entirely unwarranted, ill-advised haughty suspicion.

This was pretty much the way Captain Horace Epes, the Kitty Hawk's commanding officer felt about it too, which was bad news for a recently promoted fleet anti-submarine officer. It happened that two days after the Permit arrived in theatre Walter's chief, Commander Holmes, had been struck down by acute peritonitis; a burst appendix was suspected, leaving Walter to take the flak when the skippers of the ships in the flagship's *anti-submarine* escorts 'ganged up' to blame Kitty Hawk's Air Group for the quote 'deplorable shortcomings in the fleet's anti-submarine readiness'.

Although Walter was a submariner by trade, other than a forty-day training tour on the USS Scorpion he had spent all his sea time on a single Polaris missile boat, the USS Theodore Roosevelt (SSBN-600). SSBNs went to great lengths keeping *away* from *all* shipping, especially warships, and operated most of the time in remote and very deep waters far from customary shipping lanes. SSBNs did not routinely exercise with surface ships, or with other submarines. Consequently, his experience of anti-ship operations, of stalking and or, collecting intelligence on friendly or hostile vessels was limited to shore-based training and familiarization courses and technical sessions. Another critical area in which his expertise was constrained was the breadth of his knowledge regarding the performance and sound characteristics of the latest class of SSNs – the Thresher class – now beginning to join the fleet.

He had mistakenly assumed that the USS Kitty Hawk and her escorts would not have put to sea without having first been supplied with the basic sonar profiles of the Thresher class boats, and at least a rudimentary description of the class's underwater performance parameters.

Walter had first got a feel for how 'secret' the Threshers were at the time Carrier Division Seven was informed that the Permit would be its 'guard SSN' for part of the fleet's time in theatre. It had rapidly become apparent that Walter had known more about the Permit than his chief or anybody else on the Kitty Hawk, simply on account of his having been based at Alameda at the time the Permit was commissioned at the end of May 1962.

The USS Permit had actually been built only fifteen miles away from Alameda at the northern end of San Francisco bay at the Mare Island Naval Shipyard. Lieutenant Commander Robert Blount, Permit's first commanding officer had attended a function at Submarine Squadron 15's base at Alameda around that time. Walter had spoken to him briefly about torpedo maintenance histories, although he could not recollect how they had come to converse on that particularly thorny subject. Among the submariner community in the Bay it was known that Permit's completion had been delayed to allow for modifications connected to the new SUBROC – submarine-launched-rocket - system; for which Permit was to be the designated 'trial boat'.

Like other boats built on the West Coast, Permit would have sailed to Bremerton and worked up in the waters around Puget Sound, before returning to Mare Island to fix all the mainly small, minor things that always broke when a new boat ran its first extended sea trials. After that a boat would go down to the San Diego for an operational shakedown, deep dives and evolutions with surface ships and other nuclear boats during an intensive three to four week period.

The trialling of the SUBROC system and the live firing of several weapons had been scheduled for late 1962 and early 1963; but Walter had no idea whether that had gone ahead as planned or where Permit had been deployed in the nineteen months since the October War. More problematic was the fact that the Thresher class boats were so new that nobody knew what they *sounded* like underwater; and the ships of Carrier Division Seven had taken thirty-three long hours to figure it out.

Before the October War the growing Soviet submarine threat had preoccupied the US Navy much more than the prospect of a global nuclear war. Consequently, anti-submarine warfare had recently been assigned an operational prioritisation not deemed appropriate since 1945. Around the time of the October War it had been known that the Red Navy was building the first of perhaps as many as forty nuclear powered submarines at shipyards in the Arctic, the Baltic and the Far East, in a desperate attempt to catch up with the massive technological lead the USN had established since the launch of the USS Nautilus in 1954. However, it was thought unlikely that more than three or four of the new Soviet 'E' or 'Echo' class nuclear boats had been completed prior to the war, and tacitly assumed that none of the completed boats would have been operational at that time.

This had been part of Walter Brenckmann's pre-tour briefing before he flew out to Japan to join the Kitty Hawk. Given that the Soviets might have had as many as twenty nuclear boats 'in the water' or on building slips, he regarded the headline assessment that 'the Red Navy has no nuclear boats' as a little *complacent* but had had to concede that there was no hard intelligence to indicate that since October 1962 the Soviets had any kind of 'deployable nuclear boat capability'. If the Red Navy had had such a capability surely it would have been employed in the Mediterranean against the British? Or in the Pacific against the build-up of shipping for Operation Manna, or against the Seventh Fleet as its aircraft and ships scoured the Sea of Okhotsk for targets in the aftermath of the war? All the damage assessments he had had access to conclusively proved that whatever capacity the Soviets had once had to build nuclear boats was now wrecked; but that did not mean that perhaps one, or two boats had not survived the war. The example of HMS Dreadnought, ninety percent completed in a graving dock in England on the day of the October War ought to have been the perfect antidote to Navy Department inertia; look what that one – prototype – boat had achieved in its first two war cruises!

In analysing how Permit had crept up on and manoeuvred around, within and under Carrier Division Seven undetected and therefore with impunity for so many hours; Walter had begun to wonder if the Red Navy was really quite as 'beaten' as everybody wanted to believe.

The Black Sea Fleet had supposedly been destroyed in October 1962 yet it had very nearly outflanked the Royal Navy at Malta, and Soviet diesel-electric submarines had been encountered off Cyprus and north of Alexandria, this latter had succeeding in launching a nuclear-tipped torpedo at the British fleet carrier HMS Victorious. Was it really so hard to imagine circumstances in which at least one of the new Soviet Echo class boats under construction at the huge Leninskiy Komsomol Shipyard at Komsomolsk-on-Amur in the Russian Far East, might have survived the war in the way HMS Dreadnought survived an attempted Soviet missile strike on its base?

For the moment it remained just a nagging doubt, something of a side issue and he had not allowed it to distract him in his analysis of what Carrier Group Seven, and he personally, had got wrong in those hours before the Permit was identified and successfully tracked in the vicinity of the fleet.

Most of the thirty-three hours that the USS Permit had made monkeys of Carrier Division Seven's shipboard sonar men, and the crewmen in the air in the Kitty Hawk's Grumman S-2 Tracker anti-submarine aircraft, had been in the middle of a force eight gale in deep water one hundred to two hundred miles off the Indian coast, in regions where tidal and prevailing thermocline conditions were poorly documented.

The stormy weather and the unfamiliar – classified - sonar profile of the Permit had almost certainly contributed to the SSN's ability to remain undetected during those hours. However, Walter Brenckmann had come to the conclusion that what had really kept the Permit from being detected and tracked from the minute she came on station, was that she had got lucky. Everything now indicated that the summer storm, a precursor of the Indian monsoon season and local tidal surges had combined to create a particularly favourable thermocline in the water column of the ocean at a depth of between two and three hundred feet.

A thermocline is a relatively thin – thin in the context of the depth of the ocean at a given geographical location – layer within the water column in which for reasons of salinity, surface disturbance, variations in tidal flows or in ocean current circulation, temperature changes less predictably than it typically would as depth increases. In other words, sea conditions in the period under review appeared to have given rise to a layer of warmer or colder water beneath which the USS Permit was in effect, able to hide from the passive sonar systems onboard the ships of Carrier Division Seven; and when she was eventually detected, she remained elusive for several hours from the late 1940s to early 1950s-vintage active sonar arrays which still equipped most of the ships in the fleet.

"A thermocline?" Captain Epes had queried, clearly dubious. He had never been a submariner and he was reluctant to take at face value what he was being told. Had he not previously been so impressed by everything he had seen and heard about the flagship's Acting Anti-Submarine Warfare Officer in the short time he had been onboard the Kitty Hawk, he might have scoffed. However, the young man was self-evidently organised, methodical, and completely on top of his department, and had presented his case dispassionately with almost lawyerly precision.

"Yes, sir. While one can always make the argument that the sonar men on our ships can perform to a higher standard of competence, I think the thermocline theory is the one that makes the most sense. That, allied to the likelihood that the Permit with its tear drop hull design is presumably significantly more streamlined, more 'slippery' in the water and therefore quieter than previous classes of SSN. Thermocline or not we would have detected Permit within hours of her arrival on station had we had a prior recording of her *sound* profile."

"So you are recommending that I advise Rear Admiral Bringle that we're worrying about nothing?"

"No, sir. Now that Permit is in company with Carrier Division Seven she will be our 'ears' beneath any similar thermocline. Additionally, when sea conditions inhibit the efficiency of the sonar arrays on the smaller escorting vessels in company with the flagship, I recommend active sonar emissions should be employed more aggressively, particularly in deep water." Walter hesitated. "At the risk of being involuntarily impertinent, sir," he went on, "our current operational stance greatly contributed to the problems we encountered locating the Permit, and will continue to hinder our anti-submarine defence. We are operating at a reduced, essentially peacetime level of combat readiness, whereas all *other* naval forces in this theatre are continually operating at a level of readiness only one stage removed from *action stations*, sir."

Captain Epes ran a hand through his cropped hair.

He had been sitting behind his desk in his day cabin as Walter Brenckmann delivered his report.

"There is something else, sir," Walter added.

Captain Epes waited.

"While I am confident that the thermocline theory covers most of the obvious bases, nevertheless," Walter tried very hard not to shrug, "when I started studying the Permit's sound profile I was unable to match it with two other profiles we recorded, possibly at relatively long range during the hours she went undetected. The distortion of a given sound profile can be a consequence of a thermocline effect but it is by no means the only explanation."

"You've lost me, Mr Brenckmann."

Walter swallowed hard.

"I think we actually detected as many as four possible submarine contacts during the thirty-three hour period under review, sir." He explained respectfully. "But I cannot be absolutely, one hundred percent, certain that all four contacts were the Permit."

"Is that in your report?"

"Yes, sir. But only as a technical footnote."

"Very good," Captain Epes nodded. He ruminated for several seconds. "Were we to operate at a higher state of alert for any length of time we might risk sending the wrong message to other parties in the region. We are here as peacekeepers, Mr Brenckmann," he sighed. "One might wish for things to be otherwise. Nevertheless, we live to serve. Your comment is well made and I note it accordingly. Thank you for your work. Write it up and submit it to my secretary. I will pass it on to the Fleet Commander. That will be all."

It was not until Walter Brenckmann returned to his quarters that he started to worry.

I told the Captain that I believed there were other unidentified submarines in contact with Carrier Division Seven before we identified the Permit?

I am sure that was what I just said...

Chapter 18

Thursday 11th June 1964
Merton College, Oxford, England

Lieutenant Colonel Francis St John Waters had been in something of a daze – much as if he had just been coshed over the head in a hand-to-hand training melee in those days when his battered frame was still up to it – most of the evening. Or rather, from the moment *SHE* had walked into the room.

The Margaret Thatcher that he had encountered at Brize Norton on his return to England, and the Prime Minister he had listened to on the radio the day after those useless nonentities in Parliament had attempted to boot her out of office, had been *different*, a little humourless and grimly stoic, and much, much *older*. The woman sitting across Airey and Diana Neave's dinner table from him had shrugged off her weariness, caught her second wind and was passionately determined by the rightness of her cause.

And she had seemed to the jaundiced old SAS man to be the most utterly beautiful woman in Christendom.

The papers got it wrong when they talked about her being a 'blond bombshell'; her perfectly coiffured hair, just touching her shoulders was fair, lightly auburn in a certain light. Her complexion was clear, her eyes steely blue and mesmeric and she broadcast a uniquely marvellous defiance.

Frank Waters was putty in the woman's hands.

That had never happened before.

"Your wife and son survived the war, Colonel Waters?"

"Er, yes…"

Airey Neave had previously laid down the law as soup – some kind of vegetable broth which might have included carrots and a couple of potatoes – was served by an elderly woman who was apparently, the Neave's housekeeper, and Marigold the Neave's eighteen year old daughter.

'We'll have no talk of politics, Margaret,' he had cautioned the Prime Minister as everybody sat down around the table. 'We've all earned an evening without politics!'

Given the state of the country and the impending disaster in the Middle East, Frank Waters personally unconvinced that the political classes in general had 'earned' anything other than a good kick up the posterior. But he had let his old friend's diktat go unchallenged. He was an old enough dog to know that in politics, like war, things went wrong most of the time and that there was not a lot one could do about it except keep one's chin up.

"I must confess that my wife and I have become somewhat estranged, Prime Minister," he had confided.

"The war has a lot to answer for," the woman sympathised.

"I was away over a year before the war," Frank Waters said, hardly recognising his own voice. "Things were on the slide even then. My fault entirely," he went on, thinking *I never say things like that.* "Shirley thought I was dead," he lied, "she's made a new life for herself and young Harry. It is just one of those things. It would be unkind for me to seek to turn their lives upside down again after all this time."

Good God, I actually meant what I just said!

The woman's vaguely topaz gaze had softened and its sole object was the face of the man whose proven courage, moral fortitude and self-sacrifice had suddenly touched an unsuspected chord deep within her soul.

"Yes," she murmured, "the thing is to always make the best of things."

"Quite, Prime Minister," the suddenly tongue-tied SAS man muttered. He felt an unaccustomed heat rising in his face as he contemplated the awful truth of his rampant fascination for the thirty-eight year old widow, in whose hands the fate of the nation rested. It was as if the hunter had just turned prey; the man who had been a predatory womaniser his whole adult life was helpless, literally not knowing what to do next. Except try very hard *not* to grin like a Baboon!

"Nick tells me that you are a very reluctant hero, Colonel Waters?" The Prime Minister demanded, turning to Nicholas Ridley, the UAUK's propagandist in chief.

The *hero* protested half-heartedly: "One tries to keep a low profile in my line of work..."

"Colonel Waters wishes to get back into the thick of things at the earliest opportunity, Prime Minister," Ridley parried.

The old soldier decided to keep his powder dry.

"What is it with you men?" Margaret Thatcher inquired, genuinely peeved. "I recollect we had the same problem with Sir Peter; Admiral Sir Julian Christopher's son. All he wanted to do was get back to sea as soon as possible. As if he had not already been through enough already. I don't know what we'd have done with him if dear Iain," she paused, a tear forming in her eye for a moment as she thought about her lost friend and ally, "if dear Iain Macleod hadn't come up with the idea of sending him to the United States, where," she sniffed, choked momentarily, recovered, "he was absolutely invaluable at the recent Cape Cod Summit with President Kennedy."

"Sir Peter went sailing with the President in the middle of the summit," Airey Neave chuckled. "The two of them got on so famously that the Christophers have been invited to visit the Yanks' 'Space Flight Centre' down in Alabama. Lord Franks, our man in Philadelphia, says Sir Peter and Lady Marija are worth their weight in gold. Perhaps," he speculated mischievously, "a similar diplomatic career awaits you, Frank?"

The SAS man visibly blanched at the suggestion.

It was Margaret Thatcher who rescued him from the hostile cul-de-sac into which he had retreated.

"No. No. No. We can't have you gallivanting off willy-nilly,

Colonel Waters," she decided.

Frank Waters's heart sank; the lady had spoken and that was that.

"We need your wealth of experience at home," the Prime Minister continued. "For example, you are one of the few men in England who has actually met Marshal Babadzhanian and at least one of his senior commanders face to face."

"I met Puchkov," the man admitted guardedly. "He's in charge of 10th Guards Tank Division. He's a real hard case. I can't claim to have passed the time of day with him. The fellow's not a pretty sight; he got bust up a tad getting out of burning T-34 at Kursk back in forty-three. Lightly scorched, too," he added matter of factly. "Vladimir Andreyevich Puchkov. Not quite Rommel re-incarnated but you'd put him in the same league as some of the other chaps we were up against in the Western Desert in the good old days."

"What about this man Babadzhanian?" The Prime Minister pressed him. "Is he some kind of superman. Like Rommel?"

Frank Waters shook his head.

"No. But he's their best man. He'd have been one of their best tankers before the October 1962 unpleasantness, but no, he's no Rommel or Guderian, or Patton for that matter. But then he doesn't have to be. There's nothing to stop him motoring all the way down to the Gulf, is there?"

Frank Waters only belatedly became aware that Airey Neave was giving him a very strange look and that the Prime Minister had gone tight-lipped.

Like an old fool he mistook the writing on the wall.

"The Iraqis will wait until the Russians own the whole shop," he blundered on, "before they start nibbling at the fringes and stealing knick-knacks from the Red Army's depots. Our garrison at Abadan will be up a creek without a paddle, if it isn't already. Eventually, there will be a civil war in Iran now the Shah is gone. With what's going on in Egypt we can forget about Nasser getting involved; as for our 'friends' in Arabia, well, if you'll forgive my bluntness, they'd as soon stab us in the back as fight to save a neighbour whose oil fields are in competition with their own..."

Airey glanced to his wife, then to Margaret Thatcher.

"Frank's just your man for wreaking havoc behind one's enemy's lines," he smiled, "but not always so strong on grand strategy."

"True," the soldier conceded affably. "Pray tell me what I'm missing, oh wise one?" He invited his old friend, grinning broadly.

"I thought you wanted to dive back into the fray, old man?"

Oh, bugger! Frank Waters said silently as the main course – mutton and some kind of cabbage adorned with the ubiquitous turnip - was served. If he had not worked it out for himself already, he now knew that Airey Neave had got his hooks into him. Mistakenly, he had thought the Regiment was being sniffy about his leaving his chaps to their fate in Iran; actually, the chaps back at Stirling Lines had obviously been warned off.

"I'm not a bally desk wallah, old man."

"None of us are as young as we once were, Frank," Diana Neave observed gently.

Nicholas Ridley cleared his throat.

"It has been put to me that in this modern age of film, radio, and television it ought not to be beyond the wit of my Ministry, and the BBC, at some stage in the near future, to bring stories from 'the front' to the 'home front' in hours or days, rather than weeks. I'm thinking of the sort of thing that Barry Lankester is pioneering..."

"Lankester? Isn't he the chap who did that Battle of Malta movie?"

"Yes, practically every man, woman and child in the United Kingdom has now seen that 'movie', and I daresay many tens of millions of people throughout the Commonwealth and in the United States where the big television networks engaged in a most unseemly bidding war for the rights to show it first."

Airey Neave confirmed Frank Waters's worst fears.

"Your fighting days are over, old man. Take it from me, retirement in the Home Counties isn't much fun these days. You can come and work for me, or you can try your hand as a war correspondent with Nick's outfit? What's it to be, Frank?"

The old soldier scowled, said nothing.

He prodded his mutton with his fork; the tired flesh was as unappetising as his prospects and he barely trusted himself to speak.

The Prime Minister cleared her throat daintily.

"Now, now, Airey," she chided mildly. "I'm sure Colonel Waters will need a little time to think things through. He has only recently survived a great ordeal, it is hardly reasonable to expect him to be thrust immediately upon a new course in life."

"I am quite recovered, Prime Minister," Frank Waters objected feebly.

"That is most gratifying to hear, Colonel," Margaret Thatcher cooed.

The lady is flirting with me!

No, I must be imagining it.

Stop grinning like a Baboon, man!

"It takes more than a week or two in a KGB dungeon to knock a chap off his stride, *dear lady!*"

Oh, no! I didn't just say that, did I?

However, the Prime Minister was smiling benignly.

"Well, in that case," she declared. "There's no reason for you not to be on the first plane leaving for the Persian Gulf," she commanded, "bright and early tomorrow morning, Colonel Waters."

Right then he would have lopped off his right arm if she had asked him so to do.

"Right ho," he had mumbled dazedly.

Chapter 19

Friday 12th June 1964
HMS Alliance, 23 miles East of Canet-en-Roussillon, Western Mediterranean

"TWO HUNDRED FEET UNDER THE KEEL, SIR!"

Lieutenant-Commander Francis Barrington opened his mouth to acknowledge the report but before a sound escaped his lips the control room deck beneath his feet made a passable attempt to step several inches sideways. A moment later the thunderous detonation of the single depth charge made the submarine's pressure hull ring like a badly cracked bell.

Closer than the first attempt!

"Wheel amidships!" He ordered coolly. "Make our heading zero-seven-zero!"

The commanding officer of Her Majesty's Submarine Alliance resisted the temptation to look up at the compartment's ceiling as the French frigate churned unhurriedly over the top of the boat.

He tried not to cringe as each sonar pulse burrowed into the ocean deeps; or to tense in readiness for the squealing, gravel-dragging echo of its contact with the steel shell of the submarine.

If the ship above them dumped another solo depth charge, or heaven forefend, a pattern of four, six or eight half-ton charges like she ought to have done right at the beginning of the hunt, Alliance was doomed.

Michael Philpott, the submarine's second-in-command stepped across to join his captain at the telescope stand.

"According to the boat's Jane's Fighting Ships," he announced, with the cheerful insouciance of a man discussing the latest football scores, "the pennant number seven-two-one indicates that chummy up above is the *Touareg,* as we thought, sir. She's one of the Buckley class destroyer escorts the Americans transferred to the French just after the forty-five war. Not all of the ships the Yanks transferred were fitted with Hedgehog launchers but they were all designed to carry up to two hundred depth charges."

Barrington nodded.

He was silently counting, very slowly.

One thousand and one.
One thousand and two.
One thousand and three.
One thousand and four.

He listened hard to the 3-bladed eight-and-a-half feet diameter cast manganese-bronze propellers driving the French warship away from Alliance at eleven knots.

One thousand and five.
One thousand and six.
One thousand and seven.

One thousand and eight.

It was almost more than he could do not to demand of the man on the hydrophones: "Charges in the water yet?" But he held his peace, and went on counting.

One thousand and nine.

One thousand and ten.

One thousand and eleven.

One thousand and twelve.

"Port ten!" He whispered urgently. "Come to zero-two-zero!" He patted Michael Philpott's shoulder and moved across to stand behind the man on the hydrophones. He bent down to quietly speak, very confidentially in the man's ear. "Tell me as soon as she turns. All I need to know whether she goes *right* or *left*."

Barrington went back to the plot table.

"The surface target has re-commenced a general sonar sweep, sir!"

He heard the pinging of the French frigate's sonar drifting into the distance; and went on redrawing and fine-tuning his plans.

"Make our depth one-five-zero please, Number One."

The submarine sank slowly into the deeps of the Gulf of Lions as she turned onto a northerly heading.

"Touareg?" He prompted his second-in-command.

"She was formerly the USS Bright, Skipper. She was built by the Western Pipe and Steel Company at the San Pedro Bay Shipyard. That's the modern port of Los Angeles, I think. Completed in 1944, and handed over to the French in November 1950."

Barrington grimaced.

"She's a long way from home now."

The Touareg's screws had very nearly receded beyond the range of human hearing.

Alliance steadied on her new course.

"The bottom shoals without warning in these parts, Skipper," Michael Philpott remarked.

"Yes. The people upstairs," Barrington rolled his eyes to the bulkhead, smiled ruefully, "know that too, Number One."

"The Touareg is turning, sir!" Hissed the hydrophone operator. "Turning LEFT. Repeat. TURNING LEFT."

Francis Barrington sighed.

"I don't think the chap on the bridge of *that* ship has played this particular game of cat and mouse before tonight," he remarked, just loud enough for *everybody* in the control room to hear it.

If the French captain had a Hedgehog launcher he would have used it on his first attack run.

The Hedgehog – or as it was more prosaically known, the 'Royal Navy Anti-Submarine Projector' – had been developed in the middle years of the 1939-45 war to overcome two apparently insuperable problems faced by all surface ships attacking submerged targets. The first of these problems was that sonar contact with a submerged target was lost as the attacking ship got to the crucial phase of its depth charge run; the obvious solution was to find a way of 'throwing' depth charges ahead of the attacking ship while it still held the target submarine in its sonar beam. The second problem was that dumping large bombs over the stern of a ship into the water 'around' where one *thought* a target was located was an inherently inefficient means of destroying the said target; since it relied upon the hydrostatic shockwaves of relatively distant – albeit large – underwater explosions to damage targets, rather than employing the much more efficacious method of directly 'hitting' the target.

Hedgehog solved both problems.

Firstly, it could be discharged at a submerged target while that target was still locked in the beam of the ship's forward looking active sonar; and secondly, a single hit by a round fired from it was almost always sufficient to breach the pressure hull of a submerged submarine.

In essence, the hedgehog was no more or less than a large multiple 'spigot mortar' capable of discharging some or all of its twenty-four sixty-four pound contact-fused rounds a distance of up to three hundred yards ahead of the vessel upon which it was mounted. Each seven-inch calibre round had a warhead of thirty-five pounds of Torpex. Experience in the Second World War was that whereas conventional depth charge attacks resulted in one kill in every sixty attacks; attacks by Hedgehog-equipped escorts had achieved a kill rate of better than one in six U-boats.

The Touareg ought to have used its Hedgehog and then run over Alliance's sinking corpse with a full pattern of at least eight big half-ton depth charges set to detonate half-way to the bottom. Instead, the captain of the frigate had minced around for over an hour before he started speculatively dropping single charges into the water; very much as if he thought he was on a training exercise or alternatively, he did not actually believe a single word his sonar men were telling him.

The French must have got a radar fix on Alliance's snorkel and come to investigate. If they did not know what they were looking at or did not credit that an enemy submarine could be operating so close inshore, perhaps his counterpart on the bridge of Touareg had already convinced himself he was chasing shadows?

"All stop!" Barrington commanded. The tone of his voice was suddenly agate hard. "Try to hold her at this depth please without turning the screws, Number One. Pass the word, all quiet; as quiet as the grave please."

Alliance was already running 'silent'; it did no harm to warn the crew that their captain had switched from evasion to hunter-killer mode.

The Touareg was searching in the deeper water to the south.

Barrington considered his options.

His orders were to remain on station undetected for as long as possible monitoring French and Spanish naval activity either side of the border. Now that the enemy knew – or at least strongly suspected – that Alliance was in the area his mission had altered. His rules of engagement permitted him to defend himself, or to take offensive action against enemy warships 'as necessary'.

The Touareg had dropped a couple of depth charges on him; now she was attempting to re-acquire her lost target. The next time Alliance was detected by the frigate's sonar there might not be an accommodating thermocline between her and the Touareg, conveniently deflecting the sonar beam and persuading his counterpart that he was chasing phantoms.

"Range to target?"

"Four thousand yards, sir!"

"Calculate a firing solution for the Mark Twenty in the aft starboard tube, Number One."

The Mark XX twenty-one inch torpedo was a passive sonar homing torpedo with a two hundred pound warhead and a range of over ten thousand yards. Once upon a time Francis Barrington would have regarded loosing off a 'fire and forget' missile at one's foes and stealthily creeping away to have been an underhand sort of way to wage war.

Damnably un-English!

But that was then and this was now.

The French had come within a whisker of sinking the County class destroyer HMS Hampshire in an unprovoked sneak attack. Here in the Mediterranean any French warship was fair game until such time as Flag Officer Submarines at Malta told Alliance's captain differently.

If he could lurk unseen beneath a transient thermocline that had no right to be where it was, and cold-heartedly sink his hunter at the flick of a button, so be it. Much though he considered himself to be a passably decent, moral man, Francis Barrington was not about to lose sleep over doing his duty.

Chapter 20

Saturday 13th June
Camp David, Catoctin Mountains, Maryland

In appearance Robert Francis 'Bobby' Kennedy had aged ten years in the last six months. In August the President of the United States of America was going to have to fight for his political life in New Jersey in a hotly *contested* Democratic Party Convention; and right now it was anybody's guess whether Hubert Humphrey or Eugene McCarthy, would beat his brother Jack to the nomination. That was bad enough but what was ten times worse was that even if Jack got nominated, the latest Gallup Poll showed him trailing behind independent Southern Democrat George Wallace in the South – which he had to carry to have any chance of re-election – and practically everywhere else he was locked in a losing race with *whichever* of the likely Republicans – Nelson Rockefeller, Barry Goldwater, Henry Cabot Lodge or perhaps, even Richard Nixon who had yet to declare for the race - might eventually win the Great Old Party's nomination. In the circumstances the choice of Atlantic City's Boardwalk Hall to host the Convention in August was wholly appropriate because the outcome was nothing short of a winner takes all crap shoot!

Unlike his younger – by over two decades – fellow Administration member, fifty-nine year old Secretary of State J. William Fulbright looked relatively fit and healthily tanned from his recent perambulations around the Mediterranean and the Middle East. He was a man who gave every indication that he was relishing the crisis management of his country's much weakened foreign policy hand. While others close to the President, National Security Advisor McGeorge 'Mac' Bundy and CIA Director John McCone, continued to press for a more 'pro-active stance' in the Middle East and South East Asia, and a 'more conciliatory approach' to former NATO, Australasian and southern African 'friends', he had insisted on a policy based on 'the facts on the ground' that implicitly recognised that there were *no circumstances* in which the United States would risk another global war. The homeland had suffered enough already. Whereas, the dramatically revised 'Soviet picture' which was slowly emerging from the first snippets of British *Jericho* material, the renewed discussions with Ambassador Dobrynin and one-time Soviet United Nations Representative Zorin, had alarmed – panicked actually – several of the *President's* other *men*, Fulbright had taken the altered geopolitical realities in his stride. The very fact that the Red Army was capable of putting two thousand tanks and a quarter of a million men in the field in Iran and Iraq spoke eloquently to the reality of the World situation; the first tentative, initial indications gleaned from the trickle of intercepts from the Jericho 'windfall' had simply confirmed what they already suspected.

Moreover, the fact that the British were in effect, demanding payment 'on the barrel' for every small consignment of raw *Jericho* material, and were still haggling about the price to be paid for the encryption keys to the first batches of the encoded transcripts thus far supplied to the National Security Agency, had eroded what little was left of his patience with the 'old country'.

Fulbright was not a man who liked to agree with the CIA – on anything in general or particular – but he was beginning to come around to Langley's point of view about Margaret Thatcher's increasingly bellicose administration in Oxford, England.

The day was coming when something would have to be done about 'that woman'!

Bobby Kennedy drained his cup of coffee and like a condemned man rose stiffly to his feet, shot his cuffs and straightened his shoulders, ready to walk to the gallows.

Fulbright collected his papers and filed them unhurriedly into a slim attaché case which he put under his arm as he got to his feet. If Bobby Kennedy had had to walk the hard yards he had in his two decades in the Senate he would not have been half as spooked as he was this morning.

Okay, Turner Catledge of *The New York Times* and Ben Bradlee of *Newsweek* had the story that, quote 'senior Administration figures have been in discussions with representatives of the Soviet Government'.

So what!

In Fulbright's opinion the Administration *ought* to have been 'in discussions' with Dobrynin and Zorin the day after the October War; and that the President had vetoed any attempt to re-open Dean Rusk's abortive post-war dialogue until recently was in retrospect, a bad mistake. The only thing that had really surprised Fulbright was that some idiot in the CIA had not already blabbed to the media about *Jericho*.

The two Soviet diplomats had had to be moved from Claude Betancourt's hideaway in Connecticut because newsmen had begun sniffing around the small town of Wethersfield, and gotten far too close for comfort to Oak Hill. Fulbright thought that was a pity, Camp David was way too public for his liking. Secure, but public; even before the President started using it as a transit camp for the families of British diplomats bombed out of Philadelphia, there had been far too many low level staffers and Administration members' wives and children roaming the place.

It did not help that the President kept allowing what he considered to be questions of 'right and wrong' to get in the way of taking care of business for the nation. Personally, like Jack Kennedy, Fulbright would have much preferred an internationalist agenda, for the US to be the World's peacekeeper and a good friend in need to its oldest European ally. Unfortunately, they did not live in that kind of World anymore. The option of being the global 'good guys' was pie in the sky. Yes, even now a second massive nuclear attack would obliterate the Soviet Union for all time; but no, that was not about to happen, leastways not under *this* President. Therefore, an accommodation had to be made with the Russians so that the resources necessary to rebuild the Union might be made available.

Given that the armed rebellion in Chicago had now erupted – like the putrescence from a ruptured cancer – across northern Illinois and Wisconsin, potentially threatening to spread across great swaths of the Midwest any remaining appetite for 'foreign adventures' had withered on the vine. If the disaster – there was no other word to describe what was going on in Wisconsin – was not contained fast the whole Midwest west of Lake Michigan might become a battlefield.

Worse, while that was going on, in the Deep South there were riots in the streets of the big cities most days and in the background there was the secessionist agenda of the West Coast Confederation. Until the last week or so this had been the problem that trumped all others on the President's agenda; not least because Governor Pat Brown of California, the most populous state in the Union was standing, virtually unopposed in the forthcoming Democratic Primary in his state meaning that at the upcoming Atlantic City Democratic Convention he was likely to bring one in four of all votes – and delegates – to the Boardwalk Hall.

Pat Brown was going to come to Boardwalk Hall with a list of demands the President could not refuse. Pat Brown – once upon a time a Kennedy loyalist – had become the king maker, or if he wanted, the king slayer. While Lyndon Johnson had been allowed to play the role of the Administration's elder statesman, secure in the knowledge that he would be on the JFK Presidential ticket in November things had seemed *under control*; but a week ago LBJ had retreated to his ranch in Stonewall, Texas.

The trouble was that as many as three, possibly four or five other states had been waiting to see what happened with the West Coast Confederation; specifically, what lengths the Administration would go to buy off California, Oregon and Washington State, before they too joined the states' rights campaign in earnest. Right now attention had shifted from the West Coast to the Midwest but nobody in the Administration had worked out if, or how, it helped or hindered the preservation of the Union, or Jack Kennedy's chances at Boardwalk Hall.

One way or another the Secretary of State knew he had to make a deal with the Russians; preferably before rather than after the Administration completely lost control of events. Watching LBJ and Bobby's people sniping at each other, there was no shortage of commentators who already thought that had happened. It was common knowledge that the President had reneged on the Administration-saving compact he had made with the wily Texan in the dark days of December. Bobby's friends had begun again to undermine LBJ behind the scenes and the news – as yet unannounced officially – that the Apollo Moon Program, publicly acknowledged to be Johnson's personal project was to be in effect 'mothballed', had been the last straw. In any event the break between

Jack Kennedy and his Vice President had become inevitable after what LBJ viewed as the 'disastrous outcome' of the Cape Cod Summit.

Nobody really knew if LBJ's retreat to his ranch in Texas was permanent. Most insiders suspected that the litmus test would be if his man, Marvin Watson, resigned as White House Chief of Staff. Thereafter, the Administration would face the nightmare prospect of its most senior – oddly, least sullied in the eyes of the American people if polls were to be believed – member pissing into the tent from the *outside* in the run up to the Atlantic City Convention.

Fulbright would have despaired if it had made any difference.

To cap it all Curtis LeMay had bluntly informed the President that the situation in Illinois and Wisconsin was 'out of control', and that 'the insurgency' now threatened the entire Midwest.

The American people did not know that yet.

After the Battle of Washington the Administration had been united, and that spring, buoyed by the President's renewed vigour and appetite for the fight his re-election had seemed against all the odds...*possible*. And then the hammer blows had begun to rain down.

In truth the Administration had been torpedoed below the waterline as early as that February day when Doctor Martin Luther King had been shot. King had lived but scores of his supporters had died in the panic at Bedford-Pine Park in Atlanta, trampled in the resulting panic. There had been the nuclear strike on the USS Enterprise in the Mediterranean; a strike that went unanswered; and in April the double humiliation of the Battle of Malta and the surprise Soviet invasion of Iran and Iraq. In hindsight, the most disastrous mistake had been to fail to eradicate the canker of rebellion in Chicago before it was too late.

Sacking Major General Colin Powell Dempsey, - the man who had 'dealt' with similar insurgencies in his own native state, Washington, who later had been instrumental in restoring peace to the countryside around DC, and been entrusted by the Chiefs of Staff to 'bring Chicago back under the rule of law' - in April at the behest of Illinois and other Midwest Kennedy loyalists had split the Administration.

It had been a point of no return; ever since then the Administration had been drifting and JFK's poll ratings had plummeted.

Curtis LeMay had also told the President that it was time to deal with what was in front of him, not argue about the way *he thought* things ought to be. The train for that debate had already left the station. The country was falling apart and it was high time somebody did something about it.

That was what today's conference with the Soviets was about.

The President's priorities were: one, to somehow – at any cost – to win the Democratic nomination; two, to restore the rule of law to the Midwest; three, to do whatever was necessary to keep the three West Coast states in the Union; and four, to avoid at all costs a new global war.

If an essential pre-condition for achieving any, or all of the above included coming to an accommodation with the Soviet Union - an enemy ninety-nine percent of the American public had been given to believe, by *their* President, had been vanquished for all time only eighteen months ago – then that was a price that was going to have to be paid.

On the undercard of the Administration's ongoing, ever-deepening woes was the small matter of somehow preventing Doctor Martin Luther King's *March on Philadelphia* turning into Governor George Wallace of Alabama's stepping stone to the Presidency in November. If Jack Kennedy could have backed out of his commitment to Doctor King to stand beside him on the steps of City Hall – the temporary home of the House of Representatives – he would have done it in a flash but there were some promises a man simply could not walk away from.

The last six months had been a Hell of a rollercoaster ride!

Before joining the Administration Fulbright had taken it as read that the sons of a monster like Joe Kennedy – heck, the man had had one daughter lobotomised to stop her embarrassing the family, and ostracised another for marrying outside of the Catholic faith – must have been born with mile-wide ruthless streaks. In retrospect if he had realised how conflicted Jack Kennedy was about October 1962, and how desperate Bobby was to be a least seen doing the right thing; he might not have accepted the offer to take the late Dean Rusk's place at the State Department. A man was perfectly entitled to have his own, profoundly held beliefs and to live according to his own ethical and moral code; but if he was to conduct his country's affairs abroad he had to leave all that behind him. Astonishingly, given all that had happened neither of the Kennedy brothers understood that...*yet.*

Fulbright and Bobby Kennedy emerged into the bright sunshine and strolled the short distance to the heavily bugged 'Soviet Chalet', two Marines falling into step with them as their feet crunched on the freshly gravelled pathway.

"I feel bad about this, Bill," the Attorney General admitted.

Fulbright ignored the admission.

"Jaw jaw is better than war war, Bobby," he retorted quietly.

The younger man was not convinced.

"This whole thing feels wrong to me, Bill. The Brits are actually fighting the Russian in Iraq. Right now. They aren't just going to pull out if we ask them. Heck, Bill," the President's younger brother hissed, "the Chairman of the Joint Chiefs says sending the Kitty Hawk into the Persian Gulf is asking for trouble! It's not like Curtis LeMay is the kind of guy who gets spooked by his own shadow! Don't you think he's got a point? I don't care how strong the Soviets may or may not be, there's no way they want to pick a stand-up fight with us. We ought to be playing hardball. And we *ought* to be talking to the Brits about this."

Fulbright groaned out aloud.

"We tried that, Bobby," he retorted. "Remember? Jack told

Premier Thatcher the way it was and she came out with all that crap about 'drawing a line in the sand'. Remember? She as good as called the President a coward in front of the rest of the Administration."

"Yeah," the President's younger brother conceded. "But then *she* came over to Hyannis Port and played nice. *She* didn't make any demands that embarrassed Jack. Heck, *she* even offered us a way to 'big up' the balance sheets of some of the Wall Street banks who expect the Treasury to bail them out, Bill. *And* she promised to help us out when the Warren Commission sits..."

Fulbright sometimes despaired of know it all college boys like the Attorney General.

"What this country needs isn't 'allies' who expect us to always be there to back them up. What this country needs is peace. If the President gives this country peace the people will forgive him, *us* anything, Bobby."

The President's brother did not reply.

"Peace is worth fighting for," Fulbright continued grimly. "If we have to we'll put ourselves between the Soviets and the British in the Gulf. It won't be pretty but if that's what we have to do to make our peace with the Russians, so be it!"

Chapter 21

Sunday 14th June 1964
Khorramshahr Railway Station, Iran

Rear Admiral Nick Davey was not usually the sort of old sea dog who normally felt like a fish out of water on land. Today his discomfort arose out of the stifling heat and a morning spent studying the latest charts of the Shatt al-Arab, its adjoining waterways and the maps of the surrounding desert and marsh lands.

There were very few Iranian civilians left in Khorramshahr. Those who had not moved out of the town, fleeing across the Arvand River into Iraq or north away from the recent fighting tended to keep a low profile. Their home town was now an armed camp periodically shelled – at extreme long-range in a somewhat random and desultory fashion – by troops still loyal to the Provisional Government in Isfahan; and subjected to hit and run night raids by fighter bombers of the Red Air Force. However, although neither the shelling nor the bombing was a serious inconvenience to the allied forces entrenched in and around Khorramshahr; the same could not be said of the latest clandestine hydrographic surveys of the Shatt-al-Arab. The results of the latter threatened to scupper Operation Cold Harbour, the naval component of Operation Lightfoot.

Lieutenant General Michael Carver, Commander-in-Chief of All Commonwealth Forces in the Middle East, and Major General Mirza Hasan Mostofi al-Mamaleki, officer commanding all Imperial Iranian Forces within the KAMDZ (Khorramshahr-Abadan Mutual Defence Zone), had listened to Nick Davey's briefing with the polite interest of men who did not really fully comprehend what they were being told.

Or at least, that was what he had thought until the two soldiers had brought him out to the railway station, more a *halt* in the margins of the urban area of the town where buildings transitioned into the arid, rocky wasteland of the desert.

Michael Carver pointed into the north east where the great curve of the Arvand River, the part of the Shatt al-Arab that swept down from the confluence of the Tigris and Euphrates Rivers north of Basra, past the eastern side of that city, and onwards to the south down the western flank of the Khorramshahr-Abadan position.

"Hopefully, the RAF can be persuaded to leave the one surviving pontoon bridge standing over the Arvand River connecting Basra to Iranian territory untouched. Fortunately, the Red Air Force doesn't seem to be able to hit anything much smaller than a city neighbourhood," he prefaced. "Basically, the RAF has been asked to leave the Basra suburbs nearest to the Arvand alone because the last thing we want is for the Red Army to arrive in the city and discover that the bridge is down and that most of the biggest barges have been sunk at their moorings. The object of the exercise is to get Marshal Babadzhanian to commit significant forces on the eastern side of the

Shatt-al-Arab and to do our level best to destroy those forces in detail."

"In and around Khorramshahr," al-Mamaleki grinned wolfishly as he stroked his magnificent bushy moustache.

"Hereabouts we are constructing defence works," Michael Carver went on, "including hundreds of revetments and hull down positions for our armour designed to channel any invading force down towards the town, and between it and the river or out into the open ground between Khorramshahr in the north where Hasan's armour will be waiting for them."

Hasan al-Mamaleki was jabbing at the big map where the Karun River south of Khorramshahr where it curved around the northern end of Abadan Island.

"When the Russians get here we will *bleed* them north of Khorramshahr and in the town before they get to the Karun. Then we will *bleed* them again as they try to throw bridges across the river. And when they get across the river we will be waiting for them in prepared fortifications three miles south." The Iranian officer smiled ruefully. "And if everything can be persuaded to go according to plan at the very moment the Red Army makes contact with our defence lines around the airfield on Abadan, *my boys* will come charging out of the desert to the north east of Khorramshahr and fall upon the enemy's flank!"

It sounded marvellous but even an admiral could see the obvious flaws in the master plan. Why would the enemy mount a major assault on the Khorramshahr–Abadan front when all he had to do was surround it, and bomb and starve the defenders into submission? Thereafter, in the face of ever growing local Red Air Force air superiority Nick Davey's ABNZ Persian Gulf Squadron would inevitably be driven from the seas of the northern Gulf, making the resupply of the Abadan garrison impossible in days rather than weeks. Thereafter, it would only be a matter of time before the garrison fell.

Nevertheless, he was a great believer in always making plans just in case the enemy did something unbelievably stupid. Such exercises were immensely good for maintaining morale. Prior to flying up to Abadan, itself over thirty miles from the Persian Gulf, Nick Davey and his staff had reviewed Operation Cold Harbour, the naval element of Operation Lightfoot.

"The main channel," he informed the two generals, "south of here is about ten metres deep depending on the seasonal flow of the Arvand River. It will be shallower in a month or so. The problem is that the main channel is not uniformly 'deep' or 'wide', gentlemen, especially once you get this far north." He jerked his thumb into the west. "Over there is Om-al-Rasas, a bloody great big sand bank through which three separate channels presently flow. The channel on the Khorramshahr side is the broadest of the three and the only one remotely navigable for my bigger ships. Stephen Turnbull of HMAS Anzac, whom I've spoken of before, reports grounding several times attempting to proceed north of here. The river is deceptive. If you stand on the bank hereabouts and look across to the other side it looks wide and inviting, the trouble is that apart from the deep channel, which moves about a bit without obvious rhyme or reason and sometimes divides into several narrow 'less' deep channels, the water is fairly shallow and transient mud banks are always forming and dissolving. This is a marvellous place for mucking about in a small boat, but it's not so clever if one's looking to bring one's gun line up river to support you fellows!"

Michael Carver already knew this.

Today's meeting was to apprise his ground commander, al-Mamaleki, of the *issues* which might derail the 'little surprise' they were concocting for Marshal of the Soviet Union Hamazasp Khachaturi Babadzhanian. As yet everything was surmise, a plethora of ifs and buts conditional upon the enemy's willingness to obligingly put his head in the noose.

Carver hated any plan which assumed the enemy would be prepared to take risks that he personally, would not consider even if a gun was being held at his head. But then he was a student of military thinking, a scholar of martial history and therefore, he understood that sometimes, just sometimes, apparently the best generals make really, really bad mistakes.

If any kind of trap was to be sprung it would have to be sprung after, not before, the Red Army had invested not just Basra but the entire Faw Peninsula south of the city. The Allies were too weak on the ground to confront the whole fighting strength of Babadzhanian's army group; that kind of a fight would only end one way. Moreover, there was no natural defensive barrier like the Karun River – over a hundred yards wide north of Abadan Island – in the west below Basra; so if the hugely stronger invading Red Army was to be drawn into battle it had to be on or around the line of the Karun around Khorramshahr where the terrain would naturally give the defence the advantage. Only in this way could the greatly outnumbered 'allied' forces hope to badly maul and possibly, locally, defeat a part of Army Group South. What happened after that was anybody's guess.

If the Abadan garrison and Hasan al-Mamaleki's tanks could inflict a significant reverse on the enemy; then it might be possible to mount some kind of flanking, or spoiling attack in the Umm Qasr sector; 'might' being the operative clause.

Notwithstanding, preparatory schemes needed to be thrashed out to cover the relatively small number of remotely likely eventualities.

The scenario under consideration today was one in which several of Nick Davey's ships fought their way through the narrow waterways into the basin of Umm Qasr, the southernmost port of Iraq; enabling Major General Tom Daly's small Anzac-led armoured force currently gathering in Kuwait to *pin* the Soviet forces likely to be in position south of Basra in place. Simultaneously the Commonwealth garrison of Abadan Island and Hasan al-Mamaleki's armour would draw the Red Army into battle *east* of the Arvand River in a killing ground of the Allies' choosing. Critical to this calculus was Davey's *main* 'gun line';

several destroyers and the cruisers Tiger and Royalist which *he* would have to fight the best part of fifty miles up the Arvand River from the mouth of the Shatt-al-Arab. 'Fight' being the operative word because on top of the virtually intractable problems of navigation in the waterway – probably at night – the whole length of the left bank of the river as his ships steamed slowly north would by then inevitably be in enemy hands, and presumably, emplaced with all manner and calibre of guns and rocketry.

The first time Michael Carver had spoken of the Navy's part in Operation Lightfoot, Nick Davey's reaction had been cheerfully resigned.

'My word, this sounds like Aboukir Bay all over again.'

Carver had not immediately been on the same wave length as the Navy man.

"Battle of the Nile, old man," Davey had explained. "Nelson took his battle line into the shallowest water *between* the French Fleet and the shore! Pretty much the sort of thing Peter Christopher pulled off on a smaller scale at the Battle of Lampedusa a few months back."

The soldier was a little disconcerted by how readily and enthusiastically the sailor had taken onboard his land-lubberly tactical concept for the coming campaign.

'So, you don't think the whole idea is insane?'

Davey had sobered.

'I'll lose a lot of ships and men. Perhaps, all my ships and most of my men,' he had declared, phlegmatically. 'But you don't have enough artillery in the whole theatre to fight a battle half this size; I do; therefore, the Navy *has* to steam into Um Qasr, *and* forty or fifty miles up the Shatt-al-Arab.'

'Oh, I thought you'd tell me I was an idiot,' Michael Carver had confessed ruefully.

Nick Davey had chuckled.

'What was it John Cunningham said when he was C-in-C Mediterranean Fleet at the time we were losing ships hand over fist evacuating Crete in 1941?' He had contemplated a moment. 'Yes, I remember; something along the lines of it taking the Navy '*three years to build a ship, but three hundred years to build a tradition*'. If memory serves me correctly he concluded '*the Navy will continue with the evacuation of Crete!*'

Chapter 22

Monday 15th June 1964
'The Angry Widow', 170 miles South West of Akrotiri, Cyprus

From the minute Guy French had walked through the gates of RAF Cranwell as a nervous, wide-eyed *boy* a little less than eight years ago he had spent most of the time preparing for war by continuously honing his flying skills. On that day in 1956 he had hoped to fly fighters, a Hawker Hunter or one of the other fast, agile silvery magnificently loud and outrageously nimble machines he had seen cavorting around the skies at Farnborough, at countless other air shows and at the various air bases at which his father had been posted during his childhood. However, fate had decreed that he was not destined to fly single-seaters and that he was to be a bomber man.

He had been promoted to flight lieutenant a year before the October War; flown an Avro Vulcan to the Baltic that night and to his and the rest of his crew's - not to mention everybody at RAF Brize Norton where he had made an emergency landing as dawn broke that awful morning – astonishment he had survived. Six of the nine No 83 Squadron Vulcans which had sortied from Scampton that night were never heard of again; all three surviving Vulcans had had their electronics suite burned out by EMPs – the Electronic Magnetic Pulses radiated by big bombs – and had been grounded for weeks and in some cases months, after the night of the war.

Rather than stooge around Scampton like a lost soul he had volunteered to fly transport aircraft, ending up in the left seat of a Comet 4 before being bumped up another rank and given command of a flight of three of the beautiful machines. Then a few days after the Brize Norton and Cheltenham atrocities in April, he was offered – completely out of the blue - a chance to retrain on Handley Page Victors. Having got used to the idea that he was going to be stuck in Transport Command forever and a day, he had leapt at the chance to fly out to Akrotiri to join No 100 Squadron. The rest was history; and now nine hours into a training exercise like no other he had ever flown, he was beginning to get used to the idea that the war was about to get very serious.

The Angry Widow, the Handley Page Victor B.2, to which he was assigned as second pilot, had taken off from RAF Akrotiri on Cyprus at 13:05 hours. With full fuel tanks and a fourteen ton mixed cargo of general purpose, blast, cluster and incendiary bombs crammed into her cavernous bomb bay, the bomber had climbed to forty-seven thousand feet and flown a jinking course to the west terminating fifty miles short of the Maltese Archipelago, flown south to within forty miles of the Libyan coast at Tripoli, then east to a point seventy miles north of Alexandria to rendezvous with a No 214 Squadron Vickers Valiant tanker at thirty-two thousand feet over the Eastern Mediterranean as it began to get dark.

The first pilot, an older Squadron Leader with nearly seven years seniority over Guy French, and his co-pilot were tasked to fly one hour on, one off throughout the scheduled fourteen hours and ten minutes of the exercise; and it happened that the first airborne 'pit stop' fell in one of Guy's 'slots',

It took three attempts to mate *The Angry Widow*'s airborne refuelling boom with the Valiant's trailing fuel drogue and it was fully dark by the time the Victor's outer wing tanks had been 'topped off'.

Breaking away Guy French had eased the big bomber all the way up to fifty thousand feet prior to levelling off.

"Bombs gone!" The navigator-radar officer cried from his position, facing backwards, in the rear of the crew compartment over Nicosia. However, the aircraft did not leap forward unburdened of its bombs for this was the first of three planned 'spoof' bomb runs.

Turning west and south the bomber repeated its earlier erratic track towards Malta, this time overflying the island of Gozo at twenty-two thousand feet, turning in a wide clockwise circle to commence its second 'spoof' bomb run, bleeding off height as it ran down the eastern coastline of the main island, lining up with the Grand Harbour's northern breakwater.

This time the simulation was not of a mixed high explosive and fire bomb 'package' spreading death and destruction across a broad swath of a heavily populated urban landscape but for a precision attack employing two six ton general purpose Tallboy bombs. For this part of the exercise, and for the second planned run – this latter simulating the dropping of a ten ton general purpose Grand Slam weapon – the accuracy of the 'drop' would be assessed by comparing radar and electronic records from *The Angry Widow*, with specially calibrated ground-based radar and tracking systems pre-positioned in and around the Grand Harbour.

The Angry Widow was the second of four 100 Squadron Akrotiri-based Victors scheduled to fly this 'war simulation exercise' so there was a healthy element of competition in finding out which aircraft eventually came out on top of the 'bombing tree'.

Climbing away into the night *The Angry Widow* headed for a second in-flight refuelling rendezvous with a Valiant tanker far out at sea.

Ahead of this exercise the Akrotiri-based Victors had been withdrawn from operations over Iraq and 100 Squadron personal restricted to the station until further notice.

It could *only* mean that the war was about to get *deadly* serious.

Chapter 23

Tuesday 16th June 1964
Kennedy Family Compound, Hyannis Port, Massachusetts

John Fitzgerald Kennedy, the thirty-fifth President of the United States of America stared distractedly out of the windows across the cloudy seascape of Nantucket Sound.

"Take a seat, Mac," he murmured. "You look all in."

McGeorge Bundy had been pacing the floor attempting to reconcile his conscience with the advice he had just given his President. The others in the room were deathly silent. They had listened to their President's long telephone conversation with Lyndon Johnson, nobody saying a word as the Vice-President's voice echoed, clicking and hissing around the big room on the ground floor of what, in happier times, had been called the 'Summer White House'. LBJ's tone had been frankly dismissive; that of a man whose wise, well-intentioned counsel had been ignored once too often.

The men in the room had been drinking black coffee and smoking - several of them chain smoking - all afternoon.

The President sighed.

"Ask Ted Sorenson to join us please," he said. "The way things are looking sooner or later we're going to have to present the American people with a *new* narrative. We'll need Ted for that."

Nebraskan born thirty-six year old Theodor Chalkin 'Ted' Sorensen had become the then Senator John Fitzgerald Kennedy's chief legislative aide as long ago as 1953. He was the President's special counsel, advisor and de facto go to chief speech writer. Riding the runaway political rollercoaster of JFK's caravan in the decade before the October War had been an exhilarating, frightening, marvellously disconcerting and fulfilling experience for the son of the Danish American former Attorney General of Nebraska who had graduated top of his law school class before heading east to seek his destiny.

Ted Sorensen had been the man who wrote the eight minute speech Jack Kennedy had delivered to the Union on the morning of Sunday 28th October 1962. That had been the speech that everybody believed had *stopped the bleeding.*

Before the war Ted Sorensen was one of the Administration's quiet men, discreet and forever at the edge of the frame in any picture in which he inadvertently appeared. He was one of the few irreplaceable gears in the engine room of the White House machine. Jack Kennedy had once referred to Sorensen as his 'intellectual blood bank'. Sorensen was the man who had crafted Kennedy's inauguration speech, the man behind the immortal phrase '*ask not what your country can do for you; ask what you can do for your country*', which had so caught the imagination of not just America but of the whole Western World. No man had done more to create the Presidential aura around JFK than the unassuming, modest lawyer who now entered the room blinking behind his horn-rimmed glasses.

Sickness had side-lined him throughout most of 1963; sickness both physical and of the spirit from which he knew he would never fully recover. However, like McGeorge Bundy he had eventually come back because his President had needed him.

Jack Kennedy waved his friend to a nearby vacant wicker chair. The President sat in his rocking chair, ashen but apparently relaxed despite the weariness etched in his no longer young face.

Over the last week Sorensen had been pondering how best to counter the lies and half-truths about the President's family and personal health circulating in the national press. He knew the President's sister Rose Marie had been in a home in Wisconsin for many years; the poor woman had suffered mental illness all her life. The 'Dr Feelgood' accusations about the quack shots German-born Max Jacobsen had given the Chief Executive around the time of the Bay of Pigs fiasco and the debacle of the Vienna Summit with Khrushchev in 1961, were harder to tie down and impossible to parry other than by point blank denials.

The problem was that everybody in DC had known about the President's 'alley cat' relations with half-a-dozen women, mistresses, conquests and 'friends', many of whom had had less than wholly upright *connections*. He was supposed to have slept with Marilyn Monroe for goodness sake! Some of the stories were preposterous, especially that one about his 'inaugural fling', they had all very nearly frozen to death on the steps of the Capital Building that day! The problem was that whereas, before the October War no newspaper man in Christendom would have dreamed of reporting that the President had seduced a Mafia kingpin's mistress, or 'banged' a debutante on his way to his inauguration in January 1961, the old taboos and *understandings* were starting to fall by the wayside. Presently, the whispering campaign was like a leak in a dam, just about controllable by plugging each small breach as it occurred. Inevitably, at some stage the dam would burst. Explaining away rumours and tall stories was one thing; this hastily convened 'war council' at Hyannis Port was another and everybody around Ted Sorenson seemed to be in denial. Whatever else happened in the next few months these rumours were going to destroy his friend if he did not get out there and fight back. Blanket denials were no good, it was too late for that; and now it seemed that there was something much, much worse in the wind.

Sorensen had known he would be summoned once the Vice-President had spoken. Bobby Kennedy and Bill Fulbright had come back from Camp David with angry resignation in their eyes. Robert McNamara had flown into Cape Cod like a corporate closer, and Marvin Watson, LBJ's man and since the spring the White House Chief of Staff had become increasingly unobtrusive, almost anonymous. Things were going badly in the primaries, in the country, *everywhere*. Then that morning Claude Betancourt had driven into Hyannis Port and Ted Sorensen had known that *this* conclave was 'the big one', literally, 'make or break' for the President's re-election campaign.

Sorenson wondered if his friend planned to throw in the towel.

The President seemed lost in his thoughts.

"Things are going to Hell," Bobby Kennedy said unhappily as Sorenson sat down, nodding acquaintance to the other men in the room. "Things are going to have to change. In fact, pretty much the whole shebang is going to have to change. Not today, or tomorrow, but sometime before the Convention."

The Attorney General's older brother stirred.

"We wouldn't do this if there was a better way, Ted," he explained, apologising before the younger man had any real notion what there was to be sorry for. "There's a storm coming," he added vaguely. "A perfect storm. There's what's going on in Iraq and the Persian Gulf. There's the Egypt thing, nobody knows how that will turn out in the end, or how Nasser will play things once he's stopped purging his Army and Air Force. There's the economy at home, stalled again; we actually need things like the," he paused, quirked a wan half smile at his stern-faced Secretary of State, "Fulbright Plan to mend Wall Street's balance sheets but we're going to have to print an insanely large amount of money to do it. And *if we do* it, we can't talk to the American people about it." Again he hesitated, shaking his head and gasping a sad guffaw. "Even though whatever happens we have to do it; unless we want to get ourselves into another stand-off with the British which might be unavoidable, anyway..."

Ted Sorensen tried very hard not to frown in confusion.

"The thing is," Bobby Kennedy interjected. "It isn't going to be enough to do things behind the scenes. We actually have to be seen to be doing things. Big things; things that are hard but that speak to the American people and that will need to be carefully timed and finessed..."

"Before the Convention," the President re-iterated, "maybe, starting in the next couple of weeks, or early next month." Jack Kennedy stopped rocking in his chair and fixed Ted Sorensen in his green-eyed gaze. "We've been talking to the Russians, Ted."

"The Russians?" Sorensen asked in bewilderment.

"Yes."

Bobby Kennedy coughed and his brother raised a hand, indicating for him to explain.

"Secretary Fulbright and I went to Camp David to meet with former Ambassador Dobrynin and UN Representative Zorin. We discussed what an open-ended US-Soviet non-aggression pact would look like." He balked at what he was about to say for a moment. "And what concrete *measures* would need to be put in place *on both sides* to make such a pact work in practice. Given recent history we both agreed that mere words will not suffice."

The Secretary of State leaned forward.

"We," Fulbright growled, "made certain demands of the Russians, and they made counter demands. As we speak Representative Zorin is in the air flying to Sverdlovsk to confer with the collective leadership of the USSR. He took with him the President's Special Emissary, Ambassador Thompson, and draft proposals designed to be the basis of future urgent negotiations."

Ted Sorensen was feeling a little like Alice must have felt when she fell through the looking glass.

"What are we offering them and what do we get in return, Mr Secretary?"

The men in the room were looking to him to sell this to the American people; to put the right words in the President's mouth, to make poison sound and taste like fine wine. Before he could do that he had to know what the bottom line was and to understand how bad things got if the deal did not get done.

"The Red Army halts at the northern borders of the Emirate of Kuwait and Saudi Arabia. Thereafter, an international peacekeeping force will be deployed in those countries and in southern Iran, creating a permanent 'buffer zone' to guarantee that there will be no further Soviet territorial incursion in the region. One year from the date of the end of major hostilities in the Persian Gulf the Soviets will bring to the table a proposal for comprehensive global nuclear disarmament. In the meantime a conference will be convened on neutral territory to discuss redrawing the spheres of influence in Europe agreed at Yalta in 1945. This will be a precursor forum for the discussion of long-term reconstruction planning for Western Europe and the 'viable' areas of the Soviet Union. At this time the matter of war reparations will be indefinitely shelved."

That sounded like good news. Not for the British, obviously but clearly that consideration was incidental.

Sorensen waited patiently.

"Additionally," Fulbright continued, "the Russians will 'blow' all their intelligence networks in the North American continent and send KGB officers to the US to work with the FBI in the rooting out of surviving Red Dawn cells."

It sounded to Ted Sorensen that this was going to involve a ruinously expensive bill of purchase. Intuitively, even before he had heard what it was going to cost he asked himself if it could possibly be worth it.

"In return we must make certain 'gestures' to Soviet sensibilities about the Cuban Missiles War..."

Sorensen's ears picked up the disingenuous note in the Secretary of State's voice.

"What sort of *gestures*?" He inquired with a vile taste in his mouth.

"In due course General LeMay will be stood down from his current post..."

The President intervened.

"We haven't settled anywhere near all the details yet, Ted. This is all still broad brush strokes. Re-jigging the makeup of the Joint Chiefs Committee is window dressing. Before any of that comes into play both sides need to commit to confidence building measures. For the Soviet side the first such 'measure' will be declaring a unilateral halt at the Kuwaiti and Saudi Arabian borders in Iraq, and a unilateral cessation of hostilities in Iran. On our part we will reciprocate by guaranteeing that the war in the Persian Gulf does not go nuclear."

Sorensen did not believe he had just heard his friend say that.

"Er, how can we make that sort of guarantee, sir?" This he asked before he thought better of it. He knew exactly how the President could make a guarantee like that *stick*. Everybody in the room knew how. The bile rose in his throat.

Jack Kennedy looked him in the eye.

"The Chief of Naval Operations is flying out to Bombay to consult with Read Admiral Bringle, the Commanding Officer of Carrier Division Seven. The CNO has personally assured me that the Navy will do its duty."

Chapter 24

At the time of the no confidence vote the governmental machine, the administrative infrastructure underpinning everything the Unity Administration of the United Kingdom did, had been in the process of establishing itself on a 'longer-term' basis in Oxford. Things had originally been set up on an ad hoc, emergency basis in the spring but now what had initially been foreseen as an unfortunate, albeit unavoidable three to sixth month disruption of the University and the City would be extended to at least a year, or perhaps two. Consequently, the major departments of state were being hastily re-configured as semi-permanent establishments pending the completion of a new 'Government Administrative Complex' on the London Road between the city centre and Headington.

While most major offices of state were expanding or re-settling their current host Colleges, the Cabinet Office had been removed – practically overnight to its new home in the Old Quad of Hertford College. Although the college traced its lineage back to the thirteenth century, the oldest building in the 'Old' Quad was of relatively recent – 'recent' in Oxford terms - construction, having been completed as 'recently' as the 1570s.

The Bodleian Library was directly opposite the main gate to Hertford College across Catte Street; and the famous Bridge of Sighs, one of the city's most famous architectural landmarks spanned New College Lane within its boundaries. William Tyndale, John Donne, Jonathan Swift and Evelyn Waugh were all Hertford men; but the Cabinet Office, the Private Office and the official residence of the Prime Minister had transferred to Hertford not because of its antiquity, or the credentials of its past alumni but because the Old Quadrangle, with its vines and still perfectly manicured lawn, offered sufficient 'working' space in a location which the Royal Marine detachment responsible for Margaret Thatcher's safety deemed, appropriately 'defensible'.

One of the first things the Prime Minister had learned when she became 'first among equals' was that it was essential to place *distance* between oneself and the hurly burly, minutiae of government business. That had not been easy at either King's College or Corpus Christi College where her rooms and Private Office had been sited cheek by jowl with departments and ministers competing for her attention and favour, and sometimes intent on dragging her into strictly 'departmental' matters which she expected her ministers to resolve.

Once the chaos of the removal to Hertford College had eventually subsided, the dust had had a chance to settle and everybody had got their feet under their new tables; the Prime Minister was confident that the benefits of reverting to a system analogous to No 10 Downing Street being the Prime Minister's secure base within the Whitehall milieu in pre-October War days, the relocation exercise would bear fruit. Unfortunately, presently the Old Quad was Bedlam!

It was for this reason that she had invited Airey Neave and Dick White to brief her on the latest disastrously bad news in her private rooms, a relative oasis of calm. She naturally assumed that when her Secretary of State for National Security and his chief spymaster asked for an urgent audience that they were bringing bad news, and she had braced herself for this eventuality.

Nobody ever brought her any good news these days.

The Prime Minister frowned as one of her AWP's – a robust, crisply uniformed Royal Marine - followed the two visitors into her rooms carrying a bulky reel-to-reel tape recorder. There was nowhere to put the device other than on the floor adjacent to the nearest available electrical wall socket. The Marine snapped to attention, careful *not* to crash his booted feet on her somewhat moth eaten carpet, turned and marched out.

"What's happened now?" The Prime Minister inquired briskly, and then mellowed. "I'm dreadfully disorganised, what with the move. I can't even offer you gentlemen a cup of tea at the moment, I do apologise."

Airey Neave glanced mischievously to his tall, elegant companion.

Sir Dick White, the Director General of the Security Services half-smiled and turned to Margaret Thatcher.

"We thought you would like to hear the latest intelligence from the de-briefing of Nicolae Ceausescu, Prime Minister."

"Oh, I thought we'd locked *that* horrible little man away in Scotland for the duration, Dick?" The woman queried, waving her visitors to take seats in the pool of evening sunshine dustily filtering into her 'meeting room'. There was a long table in the shadows, but beneath the window there were several comfortable chairs close to a cold hearth.

"That's what we hoped he'd think, too," Airey Neave chortled.

"We knew he wouldn't tell us everything he knew," Dick White went on. "In retrospect I think the decision not to employ 'coercive' measures against him was wise."

Trouble touched the Prime Minister's eyes for a moment; one of the IRA men responsible for the Brize Norton atrocity in April had died whilst under interrogation. He and his two associates had 'broken', told their torturers *everything* they knew; thankfully absolving senior Irish Government ministers and officials of all responsibility and thus making it possible to actively consider some relaxation of the UAUK's harsh sanctions against the Irish Republic. Nevertheless, that man's blood was on her hands and one day his name would no doubt be added to the growing pantheon of Irish Republican Army martyrs.

Margaret Thatcher had been a little shocked that the subject of 'coercion' had even been raised in the case of a half-dead, one-legged shipwreck survivor but then they lived in very strange times.

"We had Nicolae and his lady friend, Eleni, installed with the other 'incurables' up at Inverailort. I went up there and spun him a line about how much the Americans would love to have a chat with him and he swallowed it hook line and sinker," the Spymaster reported. "Anyway, we brought Nicolae and Eleni down to a safe house in Herefordshire and produced a couple of *CIA* men. Nicolae was under the impression he was straight off to the US but *my* tame *CIA* men put him right on a few things, just to soften him up. They sold him the line that they thought he had been leading us up the garden path and that frankly, they did not think he was a big enough fish to justify the 'gas to fly him back to Langley'."

Margaret Thatcher checked to confirm that she understood what her spymaster was telling her.

"*Your CIA men, Dick?*"

"Yes, Prime Minister. A couple of Americans on *our* payroll we recruited in Berlin a few years ago after they ran into a little trouble with their own people over some rather embarrassing smuggling allegations. They were well and truly 'blown' with their own people so it was a case of working for us or having to face the music back home. Anyway, we're still putting together a full report of the two sessions they had with Nicolae but we thought you'd like to hear one or two of the juiciest 'edits'. To give you a flavour of some of the *gems* Comrade Ceausescu served up in the belief that they would get him and his lady friend on the next flight to America."

The tall man rose and went to the tape machine, clicked a switch.

'*Nicolae,*' a man with a gravelly Bronx accent growled through the static background hiss. '*We're not here to pussy foot around. My boss in Langley wants to know if he's being sold a line by the Brits. It wouldn't be the first time. I've seen the transcripts the Brits have handed over but all that's about Red Dawn in the Eastern Mediterranean, or what was about to happen in Iran two months ago. You didn't tell the Brits about Tehran? That would have been a clincher. But if you didn't know about Tehran, what the fuck did you know about? The way I see it the Brits have lost interest in you. If you want us to help you, well, you've got to tell us something we don't already know.*'

There was a crackling, whispering silence that went on and on and on for what seemed like minutes but must only have been only ten to fifteen seconds.

'*Bucharest, or to be more accurate,*' Nicolae Ceausescu said slowly, as if he was feeling for the right words, '*Atopeni Air Base, was used by the Russians to clandestinely fly supplies and personnel to Western Europe. In the beginning there were flights to Germany and Austria, but not so many by the end. Most of the flights were to southern France and to Corsica. There was a continual traffic in men and mainly light weapons in both directions right up until the last few days in February. You see, many of the western leaders of Krasnaya Zarya had been in exile in the Soviet Union before the Cuban Missiles War,*' the man paused, gasped what might have been a laugh, '*in prison, obviously, or in mental hospitals where most of them still deserve to be. The war changed everything. The mad dogs were unleashed.'*

'The mad dogs?' This was a different, Ivy League Bostonian accent, cutting into the interrogation.

'*I only know what that KGB stooge Andropov told us. Before then we'd only suspected what was going on; once Andropov started singing everything suddenly made sense....'*

There was a new hissing, clicking interlude.

Dick White spoke quickly to fill the void.

"Nicolae reeled off a long list badly pronounced aliases, dates, places and so forth which will take a long time to decipher. My men brushed all that aside at the time so as to not let the little scoundrel take over the interview."

'*...The Collective Leadership, the Troika back in Russia lost control of Krasnaya Zarya so it did what Russians always do when they lose control of a thing, they turn on it like wolves and tear it limb from limb. Red Dawn, as you call it, had become a bigger threat to the Soviet Union than the West; capable, some feared of turning what remained of the Motherland's nuclear arsenal against itself. Even now the Soviets only have tenuous footholds in Greece, Yugoslavia, Bulgaria and Anatolia, they actually control little or nothing, Krasnaya Zarya controls the mountains, the hinterland of Asia Minor, and the forests of Transylvania. But that doesn't matter, the Red Army controls the banks of the Bosphorus, Red Navy submarines control the Aegean and the Black Sea; Krasnaya Zarya stands between the West and any realistic prospect of reintegrating anything between Italy and Syria back into its sphere of influence. Central Europe is a depopulated wasteland; Krasnaya Zarya guards the ground to the south and when the Red Army stands on the shores of the Persian Gulf the Russians will be safe as if behind a great wall. And they will have their hands on seventy percent of the World's oil...'*

'*Most of that is schoolboy speculation and surmise, Nicolae,'* the educated voice interjected urbanely. "*What do you know that we don't know?'*

There was a pause of about five seconds.

'*In the south of France the Front Internationale, the faction that Krasnaya Zarya infiltrated and took over after the Cuban Missiles War is nominally under the control of a man called Jacques Duclos but the real power, behind the throne as the British say, may be a Krasnaya Zarya apparatchik called Maxim Machenaud. He was trained by the man you know as Arkady Pavlovich Rykov, one of whose aliases I borrowed to escape from my enemies after I was forced to flee from Bucharest. Duclos was Stalin's man in the French Communist Party, and after Stalin, he became Khrushchev's puppet.'*

It was apparent that the interrogator had had no interest in Jacques Duclos; presumably because it was a name he was already familiar with. He moved past the subject of the French 'leader'.

'*Maxim Machenaud?'*

'*The man is a fanatic. His father fought with the Marquis, the*

French Resistance. He was a communist, one of the many communist freedom fighters that hypocrite Churchill sold out to the Nazis to curry favour with de Gaulle's Free French in 1944. His fifteen year old sister was raped and murdered by Nazi collaborators a fortnight after D-Day, his older brother was executed in Paris by the Gestapo two days before the city was liberated, and his mother died in Ravensbrück concentration camp in January 1945, probably of starvation and typhoid.'

'Okay, so the guy's got a beef against the Brits?' The Bronx-accented phoney CIA man asked impatiently. 'A lot of people have got a beef against the Brits! So what?'

'Around the beginning of the year the Soviets suspended shipments of arms to the Front Internationale. Partly, this was because of an acute shortage of long-range transport aircraft, but also I think it was because Machenaud was making increasingly onerous demands. He wanted nuclear warheads, for example. Not bombs or missiles, just warheads; presumably to load onto fishing boats to sail into English ports. Anyway, around the time Bucharest was destroyed I learned that the KGB was talking to the Front Internationale about 'diversionary operations' in the Western Mediterranean. The larger part of the French Navy in the Mediterranean was wiped out, more or less, by the strikes on Marseilles and Toulon and although the surviving fleet receives a trickle of oil from North Africa and from a refinery in Genoa, the ships that remain have been forced to stay in port most of the time due to a shortage of fuel. The deal was that the Red Air Force would fly gold bullion into Italy to buy oil, and the French Navy, or rather the ships based in Corsica would attack the British. The quid pro quo was that the KGB would undertake to start flying in weapons and Spetsnaz detachments to help the Front Internationale push back the 'armed bands' threatening the eastern and northern borders of the area under its control. Machenaud controls practically all the undamaged territory of France south of the line Nantes-Tours-Dijon-Besancon but the eastern border with Germany and Switzerland is almost completely porous. The eastern border of the Front Internationale's territory is more or less the north to south line of Besancon-Grenoble-Nice. The local chieftains in and around Toulon and Marseilles already act independently of Machenaud and his followers in Clermont-Ferrand in the Auvergne, and to all intents these two 'factions' of Krasnaya Zarya might by now be physically separated by elements coming into southern France from the east...'

'What elements?'

'I don't know. Andropov said the bandits were survivors of American and British armed forces and their civilian camp followers.'

'And these armed groups are powerful enough to push back the Front Internationale?'

'In some places, yes; or at least that was what my people were telling me in the weeks before Bucharest was bombed...'

Chapter 25

Tuesday 16th June 1964
Headquarters of Army Group South, Baghdad, Iraq

Marshal of the Soviet Union Hamazasp Khachaturi Babadzhanian had spent much of the previous twenty-four hours helpless in his sick bed, wracked with agonizing spasms that set his guts on fire every few minutes. Never a man prone to putting on weight he had lost nearly ten kilos during the campaign, his ribs were starting to stick out and he felt weak all the time. This was his second debilitating bout of dysentery; everybody in Baghdad had the runs from the bad water, and was worn down by fevers and bites, boils and ulcers caused by the clouds of insects, and the dirt and the physical wear and tear of continually being on the move along crumbling roads and over rough ground. During the day the temperatures in the open were forty to fifty degrees Celsius, and if the skies cleared at night the temperatures plummeted, and men awakened – if they could sleep at all – feeling as if their bones were filled with ice.

He hated this country.

He hated an enemy who would not stand and fight.

The Iraqi Army had evaporated into the deserts that flanked the broad marshy flood plains of the Euphrates in the west and the Tigris in the east. Whole units had abandoned their vehicles on the side of the road, thrown their uniforms on the ground, picked up their rifles and disappeared into the endless marshlands, or gone home, melting into the anonymous, sullen-faced populations of the towns and cities Babadzhanian's mechanized divisions had driven through on the way south.

He carried on studying the big map table, reading and re-reading the symbols that denoted units and their rates of movement, current status and fighting strength, appraising and re-appraising the balance and the actual striking power of each formation of his two armies.

The spearhead of 10th Guards Tank Division had halted in Diwaniyah, two hundred kilometres south of Baghdad last night. Its men were exhausted and it had out run its supporting mechanised infantry. Major General Vladimir Andreyevich Puchkov had been beside himself with impotent rage to discover the local Iraqi militia, prior to running away, had opened the outlet valves on the town's small central oil storage bunkers and mined the approaches to the site.

An armoured personnel carrier – an eight-wheel BTR-60 - had run over a mine and the resulting explosion had ignited the whole depot and a large part of the town.

With elements of five Brigades of 3rd Caucasian Tank Army stretched out along the roads between Baghdad and Diwaniyah in absolutely no kind of battle order, calling a short 'stop' to the headlong advance made eminently good military sense; but still it chafed abominably. That was the 'tanker' in Babadzhanian's soul. You drove forward until you could go no further and then you fought on, because anything that was not 'movement' was unacceptable. The trouble was he had no choice but to accept a lot of unacceptable things these days.

Every transport aircraft that flew into the hastily repaired and reopened air bases around Baghdad discharged more 'replacements' and 'reinforcements' to fill the gaps in the ranks. Thus far in *Operation Nakazyvat* Army Group South had suffered some two thousand three hundred dead – over half in bombing raids – and another seven thousand injured or seriously wounded. That was nothing when compared with the Red Army's butcher's bill in any of the big battles of the Great Patriotic War against the Nazis. The trouble was that there were, on most days, around fifteen to twenty thousand men listed as 'sick or unfit for duty', desertions were listed in hundreds, and at least a thousand men had just gone *missing*. Not missing in action, just missing. They had gone for a walk, to have a piss or a crap, and they had never come back. That was how the locals played guerrilla warfare; no pitched battles, hardly any real ambushes, not even a lot of mines by the roadside or booby-traps set in abandoned vehicles or houses; they just waited for their moment and they snatched the unwary. Days later mutilated bodies with no dog tags, clothes, or anything to identify them would turn up. It was hardly surprising his boys were starting to shoot anybody who looked at them the wrong way!

Babadzhanian knew the attrition would only get worse the longer the campaign went on. Until his tanks were parked on the shores of the Persian Gulf, *and* he had neutralised the British garrison at Abadan he could not spare the troops necessary to police *any* of the ground his Armies had conquered. He was so short of men; the whole Red Army was so short of trained infantrymen that ninety percent of the 'replacements' he was being sent were men drafted straight from penal battalions. Some of these 'prisoner soldiers' had had a week or so of basic training, but hardly any of them knew which end of their rifles the fucking bullets came out of!

Nevertheless, his T-62s had cut south towards Basra like a red hot axe through butter. The drive to the south had been virtually unopposed, mocking the caution with which he had mandated that both his Armies progress within the confines of the flood plains of the Euphrates and the Tigris, so as to be capable of supporting each other in extremis, as they gathered themselves for the assault on Basra.

It had only been in the last forty-eight hours that he had recognised that Iraqi resistance was so feeble that 3rd Caucasus Tank Army *alone* was perfectly capable of taking Basra 'on the run', before rushing down into the Faw Peninsula to complete the conquest of western Iraq. Planning for both his tank armies to converge on Basra had been a reasonable, *conservative* schema right up until the moment events on the ground had convinced him that the Iraqis were every bit as beaten, demoralised and comprehensively routed as they seemed to be.

Given the reality of the battlefield he now considered it would be unforgivably profligate, both in terms of time and resources, to 'waste' both his Armies on Basra and consequently he had decided to drastically alter his battle plan.

The revised 'grand scheme' for the conquest of Iraq and south western Iran, swallowing up, rather than simply 'investing' the prize of Abadan Island had crystallized in Babadzhanian's mind between the fever dreams. The enemy was too weak to mount any kind of major counter attack above Basra that might justify both his tank armies operating 'shoulder to shoulder', able to instantly support the other in a crisis. The Iraqi Army – that part of it which had not already laid down its arms – was in headlong flight from his advancing T-62s. As for the Iranians in and around Abadan, they seemed to be too busy fighting some kind of pointless civil war to worry about Army Group South's relentless approach.

This was the moment, *the* moment of decision.

Thus, he had determined to throw caution to the winds; to strike with every available man, tank and aircraft directly at the critical strategic objectives laid down in the preparatory briefing paper he had submitted to the Collective Leadership a year ago which had ultimately resulted in Operation Nakazyvat.

Puchkov would continue in command of the spearhead of 3rd Caucasian Tank Army charged with driving all the way to the south of the Faw Peninsula past Basra; thereupon to seize the port of Umm Qasr and to threaten the northern border of the oil-rich Emirate of Kuwait.

Meanwhile, Kurochnik's tanks at the head of 2nd Siberian Mechanised Army would abandon the original line of advance down the right hand, western bank of the Tigris River when it reached Amarah; and instead swing left and 'charge' straight down the left hand, eastern bank of the river towards Khorramshahr and Abadan.

On the face of it Babadzhanian's two armies would be operating too far apart – not to mention separated by the Tigris, one of the great rivers of the world - to be in a position to offer mutual battlefield, or logistical support if either ran into trouble.

It was the sort of scenario which would have had war gamers scratching their heads in bewilderment. What happened if either the western drive on Basra and the Faw Peninsula or the eastern advance down the far bank of the Tigris ran into significant opposition?

It was a fair question; but not one that Babadzhanian judged relevant. It was the time to execute all out Blitzkrieg tactics. There were *no* significant enemy forces positioned anywhere along the altered lines of advance of his advancing armies. The British had a garrison at Abadan and spies reported a small build-up of tanks south of the Kuwaiti border; the British also had ships in the Persian Gulf, but not enough aircraft to seriously challenge the local air superiority achieved by the Red Air Force as far south as Hillah and Kut. With every advance of his T-62s new forward operating bases were opened for the MiG-21s and the dozens of S-75 surface-to-air missile batteries rushed south from the Motherland – where they had previously been standing idle, useless ever since the end of the Cuban Missiles War - which had already driven the RAF out of the sky over central Iraq. And what use were ships on the sea? It did not matter how many ships the British had because not one of them was worth as much as a single T-62 in a land battle!

Nevertheless, he confidently expected several of the more obsessively cautious members of the General Staff of the Red Army back in Chelyabinsk to wet their pants when they discovered what he had done!

Babadzhanian sighed as he ruminated upon the giant composite map of southern Iraq.

He would act now and tell the fools back home later.

First, it was necessary to effect a minor but significant reallocation of fighting power between his two armies.

"3rd Caucasian Tank Army will surrender 2nd Guards Tank Division to 2nd Siberian Mechanized Army. To rebalance matters 8th Guards Mechanised Brigade will be re-assigned to 3rd Caucasian Tank Army as soon as it completes refitting in the Baghdad area."

2nd Guards Tank Division was laagered south of Baghdad. Several of its units having been detached to assist the suppression of the Kurdish northern cities; the Division was at approximately sixty percent strength with one hundred and forty operational T-62s.

8th Guards Mechanized Brigade had been badly mauled in air raids and was still equipped with older T-54 and T-55 main battle tanks.

Second, it was necessary to articulate the revised priorities in such a way that his key commanders, specifically his two trusted 'hard chargers', Puchkov and Kurochnik would henceforward operate with an unambiguous understanding of what he expected of them.

"With immediate effect 3rd Caucasian Tank Army's objectives are redefined to be: one, to proceed south with all speed to invest and capture Basra via Samawah; two, to invest the Faw Peninsula and seize the port of Umm Qasr at the earliest date. Secondary objectives: one, to support operations on the eastern bank of the Arvand River opposite Basra and against Abadan Island as required; two, to fortify the western bank of the Shatt al-Arab at its southernmost point, and to fortify the port of Umm Qasr."

Pens scratched. The mood around the Army Group Commander was calmly grave.

"With immediate effect 2nd Siberian Mechanized Army's objectives are redefined as following: one, to disregard all previous orders in respect of a line of advance south from Kut to Basra via Nasiriyah, and all references in former orders relating to operating in such a manner to always be in a position to offer mutual support to 3rd Caucasian Tank Army's advance; two, the Army is to proceed with all speed to Amarah, there to advance south down the line of the eastern bank of the Tigris River to Al Qurnah; three, at Al Qurnah the Army will re-group to advance on and take by force majeure the town of

Khorramshahr preparatory to assaulting Abadan Island. The jumping off line for this operation will be on the eastern bank of the Arvand River five miles south of Basra. Further to the above, it is my intention that 2nd Siberian Mechanised Army be in position to begin the assault on Abadan no later than 00:01 hours on 1st of July."

Babadzhanian felt the wide-open eyes of his staff boring into his back.

Nobody in the Red Army ripped up orders which had had to be sanctioned and authorised by the Politburo; because if things turned out badly losing the battle was likely to be only the beginning of one's troubles.

Everybody around him was holding his breath.

He fixed the Red Air Force liaison officer in his sights.

"Red Air Force," Babadzhanian sniffed, hoping he would finish dictating his orders before he fainted and had to be carried back to his sick cot in the next room. "The Red Air Force's priority is to give all necessary support to both lines of advance until 2nd Siberian Mechanised Army is in position to commence offensive operations against the Khorramshahr-Abadan sector. The Red Air Force and the Officer Commanding 2nd Siberian will summit a fully worked up joint land-air attack plan for this operation not later than forty-eight hours prior to the planned H-Hour."

Babadzhanian looked around.

"Any questions?"

Chapter 26

Friday 19th June 1964
Leningradsky Prospekt Hotel, Chelyabinsk, Soviet Union

Fifty-nine year old Llewellyn E. 'Tommy' Thompson, Jr. was that most unlikely of Americans; a man who had, if not fallen in love with, then always missed Russia when he was elsewhere.

Born in Las Animas, Colorado the son of a rancher, he had studied economics at his native state's University in Boulder and entered the US Diplomatic Service via a Foreign Service Tutoring Group while working in the Georgetown office of Price-Waterhouse in Washington DC. His first overseas posting was to distant Ceylon in 1929, where he was a Vice Consol. In 1933 he was sent to Geneva, becoming Consul in 1937 and later served as US representative at the International Labour Office. After coming back to America in 1940 his next appointment was as a Second Secretary to the Embassy in Moscow. Becoming a fluent Russian speaker he had remained in Russia until 1944. His service had included the period in 1941when German tanks approached so close to Moscow that all diplomatic missions had been evacuated to Kuybyshev, not returning to the capital until the dark tide of Nazi aggression had receded far to the west. His reward for his stint in Russia was a two year spell in London between 1944 and 1946, and an extended period in Washington DC where he had met and married his wife, the artist Jane Goelet in 1948.

President Kennedy's Special Emissary looked out of his second floor – somewhat starkly furnished and decorated - apartment in the virtually deserted hotel on the avenue for which the building was named. He did not see the bleak sameness of the urban architecture or the drab clothes of the men and women on the street below; he saw the trees in full leaf, the blue grey twisting chord of the Miass River in the near distance and *felt* the weight of history on his shoulders.

It was good to be back; good to discover that there were still unbombed places in this extraordinary country which his compatriots at home so often completely misunderstood. He missed his wife's presence, her patience and wit would have gone down well with his hosts once they had got to know her; but this first trip was too dangerous, a voyage of discovery best sailed single-handed, or in his case, with a small coterie of State Department volunteers. It was not that he mistrusted anything that Valerian Alexandrovich Zorin had told him, simply the innate prudence of a man who had already been around the 'diplomatic block' several times.

He and Zorin had met frequently over the years.

Thompson had been present at practically every major US-Soviet diplomatic encounter since the Second World War starting with the Potsdam Conference on July 1945. He had served in Austria as Occupation Commissioner and then as Ambassador in Rome, where he had brokered a settlement between Italy and Yugoslavia over Trieste, and had been a key player in the treaty negotiations which concluded with Austrian independence in 1955. Notwithstanding that he had been an ambassadorial appointee under Democrat President Harry S. Truman; Eisenhower had asked him to return to Moscow in 1957, where he was instrumental in persuading Nikita Khrushchev to visit America in 1959. In fact during his spell in Moscow he and his wife had become very friendly with the Khrushchevs, frequently staying at the Soviet leader's home.

President Kennedy had sought Thompson's advice over the Berlin crisis of 1961, and again in October 1962 after his tour of duty in Moscow had ended. Thompson often he wondered how things might have turned out if he had still been in Moscow, in a position to exploit his friendship with Khrushchev at the height of the Cuban Missiles disaster. However, he had been in Washington, not Moscow...

Thompson tried very hard not to think those kinds of thoughts.

Everybody carried their own personal parcel of guilt for what had happened on the day of the October War and in that respect he was no different to any of the other peripheral players in that tragedy.

Thompson viewed the cavalcade of big, blocky black limousines approaching the hotel from the east. Apparently, at night the whole leadership cadre of the USSR went underground in the huge pre-war bunkers in the countryside around Sverdlovsk, some one hundred and thirty miles to the north, or into the so-called 'Kursk Bunker' complex located east of Chelyabinsk. At first, he had assumed his hosts were afraid of Curtis LeMay's missiles and bombers; but he had discovered this nocturnal exodus from the cities was a more recent thing, prompted by the British bombing campaign in Iraq where the RAF had repeatedly demonstrated the capability to target troop concentrations, road junctions and bridges with very large bombs.

Given that this was a part of Russian over which the Russians had engaged and successfully shot down ultra-high flying U-2 spy planes, this paranoia seemed a little overblown. However, even to a Russophile like Thompson, there were many facets to the Russian character which would inevitably remain hidden forever.

The US Special Emissary gathered his wits and swallowed his misgivings. His companion was watching him closely, reading his thoughts.

Valerian Alexandrovich Zorin, the man who had been chairing the Security Council on that fateful day Adlai Stevenson, his US counterpart had confronted the USSR before the court of World opinion about the Soviet medium range ballistic missiles on the island of Cuba touched Thompson's arm.

"Millions of our people died in the war," he remarked, almost idly. "And yet we always worry about our scruples."

"The British were our allies," the American retorted gently, wearily.

"And our friends too in the Great Patriotic War." Zorin shrugged, feeling old and worn. "But now history is against them. That is the way of things. When we throw them out of Iran they will take somebody else's oil. As will your country when circumstances, and history, demand it. Better we settle our differences before, rather than after the *next* war."

Thompson shivered inwardly.

After the next war, if there was a next war - God help us – there might be not be anybody left to talk to when the smoke cleared.

The US Special Emissary to the Soviet Union turned away from the window and surveyed the room. He had anticipated being whisked off to a dacha in the country, not thinking that the Troika would pay a call on him in his hotel suite. It made a kind of sense in one way; his small delegation and a battalion of KGB security men currently occupied the top two floors – the second and third – of the Leningradsky Prospekt Hotel, and the only other guests seemed to be military or party officials, so security was hardly any kind of issue. However, in another way it was *odd*, very un-Soviet. In the old days his hosts would have made a big fuss about holding a meeting like today's in a sumptuous, or overblown setting, some great hall or theatre, or in the heart of a sprawling, hugely intimidating Red Army base. Somehow, an ugly 1950s hotel with fading *Intourist* message boards, and damp patches on the corridor walls hardly seemed in keeping with the occasion. As always the trouble was figuring out exactly what kind of message the Soviets were trying to send him.

This was a thing that became a little less opaque when he discovered the identity of the two men the Collective Leadership had sent to conduct 'exploratory' talks ahead of the 'plenary session' scheduled for the next morning.

Sixty-four year old Vasili Vasilyevich Kuznetsov was one of four First Deputy Foreign Ministers of the Union of Soviet Socialist Republics. He worked for Alexei Kosygin, the member of the Troika whose responsibilities included the administration of the first post-Cuban Missiles War Five-year Plan and Foreign Policy. Kuznetsov 'managed' the Western European Department of the Soviet Foreign Ministry.

Born in Sofilovka in the Kostroma Governate of Tsarist Russia north east of Nizhny Novgorod, Kuznetsov had joined the Party in 1927. By profession an engineer he had been permitted to travel to the United States between 1931 and 1933 to study at Carnegie Mellon University. His two years studying and living in Pittsburgh, Pennsylvania might have made a less careful, less assiduously 'reliable' man than Kuznetsov horribly vulnerable in the years of Stalin's purges and Laverentiy Beria's witch hunts but in hindsight, he had survived relatively easily. Like many men in the middle echelons of the Party apparatus he had remained anonymous, safe, going about his work unmolested by the famine in the Ukraine, the butchery of the Red Army's officer corps, and the constant NKVD trawls for fresh gulag fodder. Perhaps, he had just been lucky; he preferred to think he had simply been too 'useful' to be culled in those far away times. Besides, he had always honestly believed that people exaggerated how bad things were under Stalin. Those were hard times and any leader worth his salt would have been a hard task master.

His good fortune probably had a lot to do with the fact he had not achieved a 'visible' position in the Soviet Government, or the Party until he was in his late thirties in 1940. By that age a man understood when to keep his mouth shut, who to talk to, and which subjects were safe to discuss. He had risen through the ranks unspectacularly, eventually being entrusted with the chairmanship of the *Soviet of Nationalities* succeeding Nikolay Mikhailovich Shvernik and had been appointed First Deputy Minister of Foreign Affairs in 1955, where he had worked anonymously in the long shadow of Andrei Andreyevich Gromyko.

Now and then he reflected that had Gromyko survived the Cuban Missiles War the Motherland might not have marched back down the road to a new, never-ending war with such enthusiasm. But that was his heart talking; his head said that the war faction – even after it had broken the back of Krasnaya Zarya inside the Soviet Union – would have won out whatever Gromyko had done.

Kuznetsov and Thompson had enjoyed coolly cordial relations before the October War. The Foreign Ministry man was accompanied by Major General Sergey Fyodorovich Akhromeyev. In the same way that Kuznetsov was representing Alexei Kosygin, Akhromeyev was Marshal of the Soviet Union Chuikov's man.

Thompson knew nothing of Akhromeyev; which was probably exactly why the Minister of Defence had sent him to this 'exploratory' meeting.

The opening pleasantries were soon concluded and the men settled around a large teak table in a bare-walled former bedroom. Nobody had touched up the paintwork where the cots had rubbed against the wall and the air was vaguely musty, a desultory setting for an opening exchange hedged around with dangerous pitfalls.

"Your British allies have threatened the Motherland with nuclear war," Kuznetsov said without preamble, his voice level and his tone collegiate. "They are clearly set upon the destruction of my country."

Thompson listened.

After a moment of contemplation he decided not to respond.

Kuznetsov understood and respected his counterpart's silence.

"I am instructed by the Supreme Soviet," he continued "that the general conditions specified by the American side are, subject to detailed negotiation, a satisfactory basis for proceeding with these discussions. In the spirit of mutual co-operation and the interests of global peace I am therefore authorised to communicate to you draft terms for an armistice of not less than five years between the Union of Soviet Socialist Republics and the United States."

Chapter 27

Friday 19th June 1964
Corpus Christi College, Oxford

Field Marshall Sir Richard Hull the Chief of the Defence Staff was the last to arrive at the early evening conference. The afternoon had turned showery with periodic dark clouds scudding across the Oxfordshire countryside threatening sudden thunderclaps and short, vicious downpours. One such was looming over the city as the weary old soldier trudged up the stairs to the appointed meeting place with the Secretary of Defence.

"It never rains but it pours," William 'Willie' Whitelaw the jowly, hang dog-faced Member of Parliament for Penrith and the Border observed cheerfully as he shook Hull's hand. Although Whitelaw was only forty-five – his forty-sixth birthday was at the end of the month – he had the look of a much older man. It was not just the bad diet, the privations of the last two winters, or the stresses of the terrible decisions which had to be taken day after day that wore a man down. It was living with the grief of having lost so many family members and friends, the knowledge that nobody yet understood how permanently poisoned the World had become, and the sense of despair that sometimes afflicted any parent when they contemplated what the future held for their children and grandchildren that slowly, insidiously, inevitably corroded the soul. Not everybody was afflicted with the general *mal de mere*, many of the young simply wanted to pick up the traces and get on with living; it seemed to be the older people, the generation who had lived through the Second World War who were the worst hit, aging faster, and weary before their time.

The Chief of the Defence Staff was relieved to find that there was to be only one other participant at the meeting. Sometimes, things were best kept to the smallest possible circle until somebody had made a decision what to do next, and in his judgement this was precisely one such time.

"Good to see you looking so well, Peter," the soldier said, nodding to the bespectacled, grey-haired, distinguished man standing at the Defence Secretary's side. Peter Alexander Rupert Carington, 6th Baron Carington, had the look of a cancer patient. The skin hung off his once trim frame, his pallor was waxen; he might have been sixty-five, not forty-five years old like his friend Willie Whitelaw. Carrington had been First Lord of the Admiralty at the time of the October War, escaped the bombs but not the vagaries of the subsequent fall out clouds which had claimed the lives of his wife and two eldest children. In the recent post-confidence vote reshuffling of the pack of junior government ministers conducted to lock the Labour Party into the UAUK, Carrington had been one of a handful of Tory 'minor grandees' brought in from the cold. Officially, he was 'Navy Minister'; although everybody knew he was actually Willie Whitelaw's deputy.

Eton and Sandhurst educated Carrington had been commissioned into the Grenadier Guards in the 1945 war, winning a Military Cross for valour. He had stayed in the Army until 1949, thereafter entering politics, serving in Winston Churchill and Anthony Eden's administrations as Parliamentary Secretary to the Ministry of Defence and in the latter 1950s as High Commissioner to Australia. Returning from Australia Harold MacMillan had brought him straight into the Cabinet as First Lord of the Admiralty. Like Whitelaw, had he emerged from the cataclysm of October 1962 unscathed he might as easily have found himself contending with Edward Heath, Ian Macleod and Peter Thorneycroft, Margaret Thatcher's current Chancellor of the Exchequer, for the leadership of the immediate post-war United Kingdom Interim Emergency Administration.

A flash of lightning momentarily illuminated the humid, airless first floor annexe in which the three men stood. A water jug and several glasses had been placed on a table in the corner of the room, otherwise the only other furniture in the ancient, wood-beamed former Don's study were four battered Queen Ann style chairs.

Willie Whitelaw gestured at the chairs.

Whitelaw and Carrington were in morning suits, perspiring in the lingering sultry humidity of the day. Sir Richard Hull was similarly sweltering in his uniform. Distant rumbles of thunder rattled the leaded panes of the windows, another flash of lightning flickered in the eyes of the men confronting the latest disaster to befall British arms.

"The First Sea Lord is down at Plymouth at present," the Chief of the Defence Staff reiterated, "conferring with Flag Officer Submarines and Rear Admiral Collingwood."

"Presumably Admiral Collingwood has been brought in to advise if and when HMS Dreadnought might be available for operations in the South Atlantic?" Lord Carington inquired rhetorically.

"Yes, Minister," Sir Richard Hull acknowledged. Earlier that day HMS Oberon; listed as missing forty-eight hours ago had been re-classified as 'lost in action'. The submarine's last known position approximately accorded with Argentine Navy boasts that it had depth charged and destroyed a British submarine south east of the Falklands Archipelago four days ago. "As you will be aware HMS Grampus is being withdrawn from operations in the Western Mediterranean with a view to redeployment to the South Atlantic, and Finwhale and Sealion are in mid-passage to relieve boats which have been on station since the commencement of hostilities. Theoretically, HMS Dreadnought could be in the war zone within sixteen to twenty days if she sailed now."

"What does Admiral Collingwood have to say about that, Sir Richard?"

"He reports that although Dreadnought can be made ready for sea in a matter of days that she will not be 'operational' for several months. Damage and machinery faults incurred in the boat's two war patrols have thus far been 'patched' not 'repaired'."

Rear-Admiral Simon Collingwood was the man who had taken

command of HMS Dreadnought – then still fitting out in a graving dock at Barrow-in-Furness – on the night of the October War and commanded her on her first two patrols. In response to the Prime Minister's demand to build a nuclear undersea fleet, the then First Sea Lord the late Sir David Luce had promoted him two ranks and installed him in Barrow as the Navy's 'nuclear boat supremo'; a task which by all accounts, Collingwood had thrown himself into with the same one-eyed professional determination with which he had commanded Dreadnought in action in the North Atlantic and the Mediterranean.

The Defence Secretary coughed.

"Basra?" He asked pointedly. "Is it true that all the bridges are down including the pontoon crossing of the Arvand River?"

"The Iraqi forces in the city appear to have blown them up," the Chief of the Defence Staff explained, oddly sanguine about the news. "It might mean that they plan to make a stand at Basra."

"What does General Carver make of it?"

Sir Richard Hull hesitated. It was far from a straightforward matter to know what was in Michael Carver's mind at the best of times.

"He views the development with equanimity, sir."

"What does that mean?"

The soldier grimaced. Once one got into the business of second guessing the man who was actually 'on the spot' that was a very bad road to travel.

Lord Carington pressed him.

"It was my understanding the *Jericho* intercepts indicated that the Red Army planned to throw its whole weight south down the floodplains of the Euphrates and the Tigris towards Basra before crossing the Tigris at Al Qurnah and at Basra – by pontoon bridge if necessary – prior to mounting a strike south of Basra into the Faw Peninsula and east to envelope Abadan? Without any way to get across the Arvand River at Basra the Red Army might elect to consolidate before it mounts further operations. In that event it would be too well-entrenched, possibly within weeks, for us to ever dislodge or challenge it and Abadan would become a liability?"

"*Jericho* is almost three weeks out of date," Sir Richard Hull reminded his political masters. "Other than fragmentary evidence from traffic analysis and the helpful propensity of the Soviets to broadcast their presence in various locations as if nobody was listening, we are in the dark as to their actual progress towards Basra. We have surmised their most likely lines of advance; but we know very little and can know very little more, until such time as the Red Army draws closer to Basra." He mopped his brow with a handkerchief. "Operations in the South Atlantic are the purview of Flag Officer Submarines in Plymouth. Likewise, operations in the Persian Gulf are in the capable hands of the C-in-C Middle East."

The Defence Secretary reluctantly accepted this; and even more reluctantly moved on to the real reason for this unscheduled conclave.

The announcement of the relaxation of sanctions against the Irish Government in Dublin had been quickly followed by an inflammatory, quasi triumphal speech by Sean Lemass, the Taoiseach – Prime Minister – of the Republic and had led to a weekend of rioting in Londonderry and Belfast, and a new rash of sectarian killings and attacks on property across the six counties of Northern Ireland. Buoyed by virulently partisan statements from its supporters in America, the Irish Government was giving every impression that it had won some kind of great moral victory. While it was unclear whether Lemass, a veteran of the 1916 Rising, had intended to set Ulster on fire from end to end his blatant pandering to his own Fianna Fáil party faithful on the steps of the Irish Parliament building, might well have just lit the blue touch paper igniting a second Irish Civil War.

"Ulster," Willie Whitelaw groaned. "You will be aware that one of the options on the table is the suspension of the Northern Ireland Government at Stormont and the institution of direct rule from Oxford," he prefaced glumly. There were already twenty-four thousand British troops stationed in the six counties, troops which would have been invaluable to Michael Carver in the Persian Gulf. "Another option is a complete withdrawal of our forces, their dependents and members of the civil administration and their families, whose lives would obviously be in danger if they remained behind in the aftermath of such a withdrawal."

The Chief of the Defence Staff blanched at either 'option'.

To his mind a civil war restricted to the six counties of the north was one thing; acting in such a way as to make that civil war general throughout all thirty-two counties of the island of Ireland was unthinkable.

"Um..." He looked *his* Ministers in the eye. "A total pull out as opposed to a planned withdrawal carried out over a period of years with the consent of all the major parties, would tend to exacerbate, rather than relieve out current military over-stretch," he said diplomatically. "In the case of the imposition of direct rule you must realise that nothing short of martial law will suffice at the outset. There are no more troops that can be safely sent to Ulster. The barrel is empty, gentlemen."

Sir Richard Hull prided himself that he was 'above politics' and that his loyalty was to the Crown in the person of Her Majesty the Queen. That the politicians in England and Ireland had let the situation in Northern Ireland reach this pass after all that they had been through since the October War beggared belief.

The country was now fighting what amounted to a World War, *alone* thanks to the 'politics' of its transatlantic 'friends'. Throughout the twentieth century successive British governments had pandered to the sectarian whims of the so-called 'loyalist' and 'unionist' majority in Ulster; it was inevitable that one day there would be a reckoning. Unless something was done to regain order on the streets of Northern Ireland the sectarian unrest and violence could easily spread to Glasgow. What was to stop other cities on the mainland, their populations beset with hunger, austerity without end, living in squalor in the detritus of a war which had killed millions, forced to watch helplessly as disease took away the elderly and the young while their 'leaders', few of whom had any real legitimacy in this post-cataclysm brave new world prattled and politicked as if the sufferings of the nation were as nothing, rising in revolt?

In many ways the Chief of the Defence Staff was amazed it had not happened already!

The soldier shook his head.

"Sir," he replied, "You have asked the Army, the Royal Navy and the Royal Air Force to fight wars on oceans and continents thousands of miles apart. Every day service men are dying in foreign wars while in this city," he waved dismissively with his right arm, "their leaders are behaving as if they have no understanding whatsoever of their privations, or of those of their families at home. You talk to me about 'options' to keep the lid on Ulster. Frankly, we are beyond that, sir."

Whitelaw and Carrington exchanged thoughtful looks in the way politicians will when they have the courage to admit to themselves that actually, they have very little control over *events*.

"Other than elements of the 1st and 5th Royal Tanks based in Wiltshire, in combination amounting to a brigade strength armoured battle group," the Chief of the Defence Staff explained, "the British Army has no strategic reserve. Moreover, even this 'reserve', would be unsustainable in the field for want of spare parts, ammunition and the skilled men required to support it. It was for this reason that I advised early in the Middle Eastern crisis against attempting to deploy it in the Gulf. Otherwise, the Army is fully engaged on police-keeping duties the length and breadth of the United Kingdom, and in managing ongoing salvage and recovery operations in the bombed areas. There are no more troops to be sent to Northern Ireland or to 'manage' the fallout from any kind of precipitate withdrawal from that province. Let us speak plainly," the soldier counselled gravely, "if there is a political resolution to the current strife in Ulster it is self-evidently *not* within the wit or the gift of the current administration in Stormont Castle. We have lost control of civil order in Northern Ireland, how long will it be before we lose control of the situation in Glasgow, or in the countryside around the Mersey Estuary, or around London as refugees return to the less damaged suburbs, and bands of brigands group together to attempt to 'mine' the vaults of the City of London? Damn it! The Navy has had to take over policing the country around the submarine base at Barrow!"

William Whitelaw understood exactly what Sir Richard Hull was telling him. If anybody had ever been in any doubt, the time for half-measures had long gone.

Chapter 28

Saturday 20th June 1964
HMS Tiger, Tarout Bay, Persian Gulf

Even with all the scuttles wide open and several fans blowing it was still uncomfortably sultry in Rear Admiral Nicholas Davey's day cabin. Even the two Saudi ministers seemed a little hot and bothered, although not so much on account of the afternoon heat but because they felt like supplicants.

Lieutenant General Michael Carver was carrying the dust of Abadan Island on his shoes and figuratively, on his shoulders as he and Major General Thomas Daly joined the Flag Officer, ABNZ Persian Gulf Squadron, and his guests in the relatively spacious cabin in the stern of the cruiser. Carver affected nodding bows to the two Saudis before hands were cursorily shaken.

"Forgive my keeping you waiting," he smiled, tight-lipped. 'My flight was delayed by a little local *difficulty*."

The Red Army was flooding past Basra into the Faw Peninsula and was in the process of investing the western bank of the Shatt al-Arab. Carver's aircraft had had to take a detour east over Iranian territory in order to remain outside the likely engagement envelopes of the surface-to-air missile systems the Soviets would undoubtedly be striving, as he spoke, to emplace opposite Abadan.

"Is it true that the Soviets are already on the outskirts of Umm Qasr?" Asked thirty-six year old Sultan bin Abdulaziz, the Saudi Minister of Defence and Aviation.

"We believe so, sir," Carver confirmed, his tone significantly more sanguine than his premonitions. There was disturbing evidence that a combination of the complete breakdown of organised Iraqi resistance and the drastic – positively Draconian - steps to reorganise the Red Army's logistical train, had supercharged the recent acceleration of the Soviet advance. South of Basra the enemy's spearheads would be parked on the northern shore of the Persian Gulf possibly within hours; in the east the pathfinder elements of the 2nd Siberian Mechanised Army were exploring his picket lines north of Khorramshahr along the Iraqi-Iranian border. The Soviets had discovered a second wind after being briefly bogged down in central Iraq; now the Red Army was sweeping all before it supported by a Red Air Force which had achieved virtual aerial supremacy over much of the conquered lands. "Presently, the enemy is probing our lines north of Abadan."

Michael Carver had no intention of discussing the situation east of the Shatt al-Arab with his Saudi 'allies' in any kind of detail. Regardless of whether they had come onboard HMS Tiger to ask for help, or to pledge their own support to the cause; the secrets of Operation Lightfoot were going to remain just that, *secret*.

He nodded to the tall, balding Australian commander of the small

'Anzac Brigade' currently guarding the northern Kuwaiti border.

Daly was stern-faced. He and Michael Carver had met several times in England when he was posted to the Staff College at Camberley after the Second World War and their recent conversations had been nothing if not 'frank' concerning the prospects for the coming ground campaign.

"My boys have established strong defensive positions south of the Iraq-Kuwait border," he explained. "Command is now unified under a combined Australian-British Staff and Kuwaiti officials are doing what they can to mobilise local defence militias to release my troops from lines of communications duties. It is my assessment that the Soviet forces across the border are in urgent need of rest and replenishment and possess only limited offensive capabilities at this time. That said, it is apparent that enemy forces already in the Faw Peninsula and the desert north of the Saudi Arabian and Kuwaiti borders are already numerically superior to those available to the Anzac Brigade we are attempting to build up at the present time."

The two Saudi ministers listened in quietly respectful silence.

Thirty-three year old Ahmed Zaki Yamani, Minister of Petroleum and Mineral Resources, probably the most 'westernised' member of the Saudi government was in every respect the coolest man in the room. While Prince Abdulaziz fomented and glowered like a man about to explode, Yamani simply stroked his goatee beard and pondered the possibilities.

Yamani was of that generation of privileged young Saudis whom necessity had decreed should be educated abroad to learn what they might about the ways of the World. The son of a Qadi – a respected judge and scholar of Islamic law – who was currently the Grand Mufti of Indonesia and Malaysia, Yamani was among the first of his contemporaries to rise to prominence in the Kingdom. Having earned a law degree at King Fouad I University in Cairo, the government had sent him to the Comparative Law Institute at New York University, where in 1955 he had earned a master's degree in Comparative Jurisprudence. He had married Laila, an Iraqi woman in Brooklyn, thereafter moving on to Harvard Law School to collect a second master's degree. Returning to the Kingdom he had become an advisor to the government during the 'troubled' period when Kind Saud and Prince Faisal were vying for power; adroitly avoiding burning his boats with either of the competing factions. His reward had been his appointment as Minister for Petroleum and Mineral Resources, the Kingdom's key economic post.

Nick Davey, for once in his life in a grimly sober mood had suggested his guests take chairs and called for 'refreshments'; coffee rather than the normal pink gins with which he customarily entertained 'visitors'.

Yamani glanced at his Saudi companion, momentarily arching an eyebrow.

It was the only prompt the Minister of Defence required.

"The Crown Prince had decreed that all the *former* American war stores depots within the boundaries of the Kingdom will be opened with immediate effect, for the use of the Kingdom's national armed forces and the use of the Australian, British and New Zealand Commonwealth Expeditionary Force."

"That is most gratifying, Your Highness," Michael Carver remarked mechanically. *Better late than never.* Although, not that much better. To the best of his knowledge there was no available inventory of what was actually stored in the 'war stores depots' and in any event, most of the ammunition was the wrong calibre for *his* guns, and practically all the heavy equipment was mothballed and partially disabled. He waited, knowing that Abdulaziz knew this already.

"Movement orders have been issued to the 1st and 4th Royal Saudi Divisions. The 1st will entrain at Riyadh for transfer to Dammam as soon as possible. The 4th, which as you know is based at Jeddah, will embark at that port for transit by sea to Dammam. The Crown Prince has instructed me to personally liaise with you, General Carver, as to the future disposition and employment of these formations."

The Englishman allowed himself a half-smile.

The Saudi 1st Division based north of the capital was equipped with American M-60 and M-48 tanks. It was 'active' whereas the 4th Division in the south was a 'reserve' formation equipped with a mishmash of up-gunned World War II era Shermans and American Army cast off M-48s. More pertinently, the 1st Division could be transferred relatively swiftly, say in a couple of weeks, from Riyadh to Dammam and thence at worst, to a blocking position south of the Kuwaiti border, or at best, onto ground west of Kuwait where it might threaten the right flank of 3rd Caucasian Tank Army as it continued to pour into Basra Province.

Michael Carver was determined to strike while the iron glowed red in his hand.

"Nick," he inquired, turning to his host. "Would you have a map of the ground west of the Kuwaiti border to hand by any chance?"

Within a minute the five men were standing over a relief map of the western Persian Gulf.

"Let me be plain with you," he warned the two Saudis. "I do not have in mind some kind of grand blocking or defensive battle with the Red Army. That said, I do intend to engage it and to destroy a substantial part of it in southern Iraq. However, before I can do that I need two things from the Kingdom."

He made eye contact with both Prince Abdulaziz and Yamani.

"The RAF will need every free fall general purpose bomb it can get its hands on from the Riyadh war stores depot. Aircraft can land next to it, load up and fly missions directly against targets in Iraq assuming the necessary logistical and maintenance arrangements can be put in place in the next few days and the principle available runway is lengthened by some five hundred yards. Jeddah is too far away for this purpose."

He looked up again, seeking nods of agreement before dropping his eyes to the map spread across the table between the four men. He jabbed a forefinger at the desert fifty miles west of the Kuwaiti border.

"If by hook or by crook *we* can assemble fifty, ideally a hundred Centurions, M-60s and M-48s here," he said, "with sufficient mechanized infantry in support, and fuel enough for two to three days hard fighting," now he smiled a saturnine, predatory smile, "Tom," he half-smiled to the Australian, "might just give the Soviets a run for their money!"

Chapter 29

Saturday 20th June 1964
Kennedy Family Compound, Hyannis Port, Massachusetts

Before the October War Ted Sorensen was one of the few irreplaceable gears in the engine room of the White House machine. Jack Kennedy had once referred to Sorensen as his 'intellectual blood bank'. It was Sorenson who had crafted Kennedy's inauguration speech, the man behind the immortal phrase 'ask not what your country can do for you; ask what you can do for your country', which had caught the imagination of not just America but of the whole Western World. Back in those days the words had come easily; these days nothing came easily, and nothing would ever be simple again.

"We're not just talking about walking away from the Fulbright Plan, are we?" He asked, looking up from the notepad on his knee. He and Bobby Kennedy were sitting on the porch of the old Kennedy family house enjoying the sunshine in the cool breeze blowing off Nantucket Sound. "That's why we're keeping Ben Bradlee and the other news guys away from the President, isn't it?"

His questions were entirely rhetorical. However, he had needed to ask them; if only to salve his conscience.

"You could say that," his friend agreed.

The President had called the Chiefs of Staff to Camp David that weekend. It was one thing for Curtis LeMay to say he had the other Chiefs 'onside', another entirely for the Commander-in-Chief to look his most senior military advisors in the eye and ask them the question.

Nobody actually thought 'the situation' in the Persian Gulf would end up with the United States being dragged into a shooting war; but LeMay was right to demand that if his people were being asked to go into harm's way they needed to be armed with a lot more than just 'stern words and good intentions'.

After the US Sixth Fleet in the Mediterranean Carrier Division Seven was the most formidable naval battle group on the planet. Its ships were crammed full of every technological marvel the American taxpayer could afford, and its flagship, the USS Kitty Hawk boasted an air group comprised of more than eighty of the most advanced fighting aircraft ever to take to the skies.

Sorenson took off his glasses and distractedly cleaned them.

"Back before the war," he observed, "we'd have made soundings about this stuff. We'd have tried to figure out who we could talk to. We'd have gone out of our way to talk to people like Ben Bradlee. Now we're flying blind, Bobby."

The Head of the Philadelphia Bureau of *Newsweek*, Ben Bradlee had been a Kennedy family friend, an insider, for many years but ever since the Battle of Washington Ben had not been buying anything the Administration had to sell. The Attorney General got to his feet, paced briefly, turned to his companion.

"Here's the thing, Ted," he prefaced. Jack had asked him to take a couple of days 'out' with Sorenson to work through how to deal with the media if and when something *really* bad happened in the Middle East. "CIA says the Red Army has bet everything on the Iran-Iraq thing. Every card on the table, last throw of the dice, the whole shebang. The Chiefs don't buy it. LeMay's got this crazy idea in his head that the whole thing in the Gulf is just some kind of large scale 'diversion'. He's afraid they're going to hit us someplace else; Japan, maybe, or Norway, or Sweden. He may have a point, the Russians screwed us over so badly we never saw any of *this* coming."

"Does it actually matter if the Soviets have another army someplace else?"

"I don't know. But it matters if their fleet of new nuclear submarines in the Pacific survived the bombing in October sixty-two!"

Sorenson thought this was beginning to sound a little paranoid.

"I thought we had the Polaris boats and twenty or thirty other nuclear subs, Bobby?" He asked the question, moved on immediately. "Besides, look at the problems we've got in Illinois, Wisconsin and the Pacific North West. Things must be ten times worse in Russia?"

His friend chewed this over for some seconds.

"Jack will do anything to avoid another nuclear exchange with the Russians," he said eventually. "*Anything*, Ted. He'd open the grain stores and hand the Brits a blank cheque if they'd draw in their horns. There's this thing in the Gulf. The problem down in the South Atlantic. The Mediterranean is a problem, too. The *situation* in Egypt is really bad news. The Brits are out of control. Heck, *that* Thatcher woman threatened to nuke Chelyabinsk and Sverdlovsk!"

Sorenson's brow furrowed.

"That was only if *they* used nukes against us again, Bobby," he reminded his friend. "In retrospect wasn't that what the Soviets got away with back in February hiding behind their Red Dawn proxies?"

"That's another thing. The deal we're looking for with the Soviets undercuts Red Dawn over here."

"But not in Europe or anywhere else?"

Bobby Kennedy pretended he had not heard this.

"If Premier Thatcher was more reasonable," he explained. "Or if somebody else was in charge over there in Oxford, maybe things would be different. But we've got to the point where we can't *deal* with *that* woman!"

Ted Sorenson sighed. "Margaret Thatcher isn't Fidel Castro, Bobby." His friend flinched as his he had been struck. "Heck," Sorenson went on, "if we can talk to the Soviets we ought to be able to talk to our friends!"

Bobby Kennedy's jaw worked but no words formed on his lips.

The other man took off his glassed, squinted thoughtfully at the Attorney General.

"Don't you think?" He asked, gloomily.

Chapter 30

Saturday 20th June 1964
Merton College, Oxford

Frank Waters had been putting off this moment for several days; ever since he had learned his fate and had the balance of what he like to call his mind, rather more than somewhat perturbed at the Neave's dinner table just over a week ago. In a life of thrills, spills, and misadventures marked by numerous deeds of gallantry and no little calumny, the last few weeks had been well, downright... *strange*. Not to mention extraordinarily invigorating.

He had confidently expected to be taken out and shot right up to the night his KGB guards marched him onto that Tu-114 transport and he had found himself manacled in a seat twenty feet away from Kosygin, Shelepin and that wishy-washy scientist chappie Sakharov. In retrospect the *most* peculiar thing about *that* nine-hour flight had been his *interviews* with first Shelepin, the KGB top dog, and later, with Sakharov.

Shelepin whom Frank Waters strongly suspected was the sort of creature who *liked* hurting and killing people – he had seen a lot of men of *his* type over the years – had coldly quizzed him about Brize Norton, and various politicians whom he had never met or honestly and truly, would not recognise if they were standing in front of him. And then Sakharov had sat down next to him and with the dowdy, stern-faced interpreter 'Natasha' impatiently translating with the ill-grace of one who would much rather have been somewhere else, they had had a fascinating little chat.

Sakharov had eyed Frank Waters's restraints apologetically.

'Comrade Natasha Nikolayevna must remain so that Comrade Shelepin and our intelligence services may be apprised of our conversation, Colonel,' he had explained. 'If you are agreeable we will converse in Russian.'

This had set his mind off on a tangent.

Natasha? Why had the woman adopted the westernized form of her first name? Nikolayevna, *daughter of Nikolayev* suggested her given name was Natalya. Had she been a spy somewhere? Or worked in an embassy in the West before the war?

'Kak vy khotite, tovarishch,' he had agreed.

As you wish, comrade.

Sakharov had tried to sell him the line that carrying on the war was 'stupid'. After the 'madness' of the Cuban Missiles War it was the interests of every man, woman and child on the planet that there should be a peace conference. He believed, apparently in all sincerity, that nuclear weapons should be renounced forever. The old soldier had thought that all sounded rather like pie in the sky. He would have discounted the Soviet scientist as a crank but for the sadness in his eyes and the uncomplicated *genuineness* which positively leeched from every pore in his body.

Natalya Nikolayevna had not batted an eyelid when the scientist explained that he was the man 'responsible for building the hydrogen bombs which had destroyed London and other British cities'. Or when he had expressed the hope that one day 'men of science of all nations will unite in the cause of peace'.

Returning to England the Army had fed the returning hero a succession of hearty square meals before he realised that everybody else seemed to be on half-rations. Although the medicos wanted to build him up after his experiences in the East he had felt horribly guilty about getting special treatment. It went against the grain; one for all and all for one, there was a bloody war on and everybody was supposed to be in it together. Notwithstanding, he had carried on 'tucking in' and within a few days he had felt stronger, fitter and begun, slowly to put a little flesh back on his bones. It was only now that he realised he had been in a bad way a fortnight ago, literally a bag of bones, a bit of a scarecrow in fact.

He had undergone half-a-dozen de-briefings, each re-examining many of the things he thought he had covered in previous sessions. The first couple of 'debriefs' left him exhausted but as his strength returned he had become his old, combative self and rather enjoyed the cut and thrust of the process. People tended to underestimate how much starvation, illness and being periodically beaten up tends to impair the working efficiency of the old grey matter; but a few restorative square meals, convivial company and a shot or two of antibiotics had worked wonders.

Frank Waters had only just recovered from his first encounter with *The Angry Widow* by the time he found himself standing in front of her a second time. Some clot had decided he had earned an MC – a Military Cross – for his troubles in Iran. He already had a VC, so what was the point of that? In any event, he had made himself as presentable as possible – as one does for these things – and turned up on parade at King's College for the awarding of the said superfluous medal, stepped forward and found himself again gazing into those steely, topaz eyes.

The woman had seemed to be surrounded by some kind of glowing aura... She had pinned the Military Cross on his breast, and stepped back half-a-pace, eyed the ribbons covering his heart with obvious approbation.

'You are running out of room, Colonel Waters," she had observed brightly.

God in Heaven he had very nearly swooned!

'You must visit me for tea before you rush off abroad again,' *she* had commanded and he had been putty in her hands.

He had been terrified that he would in some way contrive to comprehensively blot his copybook at 'tea' that afternoon. He might easily have done so had not Lady Patricia Harding-Grayson – apparently the Prime Ministerial chaperone and confidante – and the Thatcher twins been present. Their mother had been very keen for them to meet 'another very brave English hero'.

Honestly and truly Francis Harold St John Waters, VC, MC and assorted other gongs he had forgotten the names of, had *never* met a woman like Margaret Thatcher. He did not know how to begin to describe, let alone how to come to terms with his infatuation with the woman; and it utterly bewildered the cynical, shameless womaniser that he had long ago become.

Given that in a day or so he was flying out to the Persian Gulf, where things looked 'dicey', to say the least, he had determined to make an attempt to do the right thing. One way and another it was high time he started doing 'the right thing'.

Mrs S.H. Waters, Meadow Cottage, Ughill Moors, South Yorkshire.

He looked at the address for several seconds before appending the date to the heading of the letter. His hand-writing had grown less ornate, scratchier with the years, the 'artistic temperament' his masters at Charterhouse School had so decried in the 1930s, had been slowly knocked out of his calligraphy!

Dear Shirley...

This was a thing best kept short and sweet with a minimum of sentimentality. This he repeated silently, like a protective mantra.

> *You will have learned by now that I returned to England a couple of weeks ago in somewhat unlikely circumstances. I apologise for not having communicated with you sooner. You will, I hope, understand that it has taken me a few days to get my bearings again. Thank you for your kind letter filling me in on your new domestic circumstances and your wish for a divorce.*

Oddly, he was sorry he had not written 'sooner'. Not like me at all! He shook his head and focused on the matter in hand.

> *Things have been unhappy between us for many years. This has been my fault. There is nothing to be gained by dwelling on the past. Suffice to say that I wish you and young Harry all possible happiness with Eric. Eric and I have never really got on but unlike me he is a good sound fellow and I genuinely wish you both well.*

No, no, no. No matter how much you want to tear the letter to bits and throw it in the bin you have to stick to your guns! Do the decent thing, man!

For once in your life, do the decent thing!

> *You will be interested to know that I have taken legal*

advice vis-a-vis our marital 'situation'. The upshot is that under an adjunct to the emergency laws currently governing civil society many of the previous injunctions and 'complications' concerning the dissolution of marriages, and so forth, are not what they were prior to October 1962. Essentially, we may be divorced if I submit a written application to the Registrar of Births, Deaths and Marriages here in Oxford confessing my many and despicable marital infidelities. On your side this will require a separate notarized document by your own hand. In the event that this is your wish, the divorce may be granted upon a satisfactory financial agreement being agreed between the two of us in respect of your maintenance and the costs of bringing up and educating young Harry.

He took a very deep breath.

I acknowledge that I have been remiss in providing for you and Harry in recent years. In recompense I have instructed my solicitors in Oxford, Messrs Leese and Oliver, to place in trust the unspent back pay which I have accumulated in the last years I have been abroad on foreign service. The aforementioned trust is for the purpose of paying for Harry's future education.

He had got his second wind now. Things were so much easier when a chap made up his mind what really mattered to him!

I should inform you that – for reasons I will not trouble you with at this time – I shall soon be retired from the Service. The powers that be have been so kind as to ensure that I will depart on a 'full pension'. While this stipend is hardly a King's Ransom these days, I have written to the Paymaster General's Office here in Oxford directing that one-half of my pension should be paid in favour of you henceforth without let or hindrance, or limits of time in final settlement of any claims outstanding in respect of our divorce.

He sighed.

Please convey to Eric and young Harry my good wishes.

And signed off.

Yours obediently, sincerely...

He was a free man again.
Free to make a damned fool of himself again!

Chapter 31

Saturday 20th June 1964
Prime Minister's Rooms, Hertford College, Oxford

Walter Brenckmann senior nodded acquaintance to William Whitelaw and Field Marshall Sir Richard Hull in the lobby outside the Prime Minister's Private Room. The Secretary of State for Defence and the Chief of the Defence Staff were grim-faced, departing the scene as the United States Ambassador to the Court of Woodstock walked in.

Hands were shaken perfunctorily, pleasantries briefly exchanged in a tight-lipped, strained way and then the US Ambassador was face to face with Sir Henry Tomlinson, the Cabinet Secretary and Margaret Thatcher's greying, most civil of Civil Service gatekeepers.

"Ambassador, thank you for coming over at such short notice."

"I am always at the Prime Minister's service, Sir Henry."

"How is your lovely wife, Walter," Sir Henry Tomlinson inquired now that the tiresome formalities were concluded.

"She has a speaking engagement at a Women's Institute 'gala' this evening in Abingdon. This afternoon she was planning to visit a nursing home at Whitney."

Joanne Brenckmann had determined to carry on spreading as much 'goodwill' as was humanly possible however 'badly the President behaves', for so long as the 'Brenckmann family was involved in the diplomacy business'. Both husband and wife believed it was their joint role to present the 'human face' of their country to their British 'friends'. They would worry about defending themselves before the House Un-American Activities Committee *after* rather than before, they were summoned home if and when John Fitzgerald Kennedy lost the election in November.

"The Prime Minister is just having a chat with the Secretary of State designate for Northern Ireland. That shouldn't take too long."

"Oh," Walter Brenckmann had not known what to make of the rumours he had heard in the last few hours. Part of the problem was that the State Department told him nothing about anything – on account of the fat they already thought he had gone 'native' – and lately his primary ambassadorial role had been as an apologist for things he did not know had happened until his hosts told him about them. It was a bizarre and dispiriting way to conduct 'diplomacy' and daily he reconsidered his 'position'. "This is a little sudden..."

"I suspect that's the way the new Northern Ireland Secretary feels about it. Lord Dilhorne's a real brick, stepping up to the plate," the Cabinet Secretary explained. "He was Lord Chancellor at the time of the recent war. Prior to his elevation to the peerage he was a member of Mr MacMillan's Cabinet serving in the capacity of Attorney General for England and Wales. In those days he was just plain Sir Reginald Manningham-Buller. He's just the man for the Ulster brief. I think he must have felt somewhat out of it lately."

"The home rule of Northern Ireland has been suspended?" Walter Brenckmann asked artlessly in his surprise.

"Yes. Had to be done, I'm afraid. And a thing that has to be done is best done quickly, what?"

"Absolutely."

The US Ambassador was introduced to the ashen-faced bespectacled, old-looking man who emerged from the Prime Minister's room a few minutes later. The poor fellow looked as if he was trudging towards the gallows.

"I'd offer you a cup of coffee but the latest *substitute* for coffee is so unpleasant that you'd think I was trying to poison you, Walter," Margaret Thatcher declared taking the Ambassador's hand and guiding him to a comfortable chair. "It will have to be tea, I'm afraid."

There had been moments during the last twenty-four hours when Walter Brenckmann had expected to see tanks on the streets of Oxford and politicians being led off to prison in handcuffs. His CIA people, jeremiads to a man, despite not being any the wiser to what was going on had supposedly got wind of rumours that the Army's patience with the UAUK was wearing thin. His intelligence 'experts' had been rubbing their hands together in near glee forecasting dire 'repercussions'.

"You must be wondering what on earth has been going on?" Margaret Thatcher put to her friend.

"Well, yes," the man shrugged, quirking a half-smile. "And no, Margaret."

"The Chief of the Defence Staff exercised his right to speak to me yesterday," the Prime Minister told him. "We had a very frank and open discussion and by word and deed I was able to assure him that *my* Government would always *listen* most closely to the professional advice he was kind enough to give it. Understandably," she continued, "certain of my colleagues feel undermined by recent events. However, one does not change one's team on the eve of the 'big match'."

Walter Brenckmann nodded, held his peace.

"Tom Harding-Grayson reminded me not so long ago of something that Winston Churchill said of America," the woman went on cheerfully.

"Oh?"

"Please don't be offended," the Margaret Thatcher cautioned, her eyes becoming hard, 'but dear Winston once observed that 'you can always count on the Americans to do the right thing," a steely smile, "but only 'after they've tried everything else'."

Walter Brenckmann did not know whether to be amused or insulted.

"I would not dream of saying it to any other American in Oxford," Margaret Thatcher said, very soberly, "but I think we are running out of time. Here in England, in the South Atlantic; certainly, in the Middle East, Walter. Please do not imagine for a minute that I do not understand, and sympathise with President Kennedy's domestic political woes. I have no idea how I would cope with nightmares like what is going on in Chicago at the moment, or if parts of England or Wales or Scotland seemed to be slipping into the hands of secessionists. If and when I am ejected from government I will probably be allowed to disappear into obscurity, I can be fairly confident that my successor will be unlikely to want to exact physical or judicial revenge upon me or my kith and kin. Whereas, if Jack Kennedy loses in November his enemies will, one way or another do their level best to destroy him."

She waited while a tea service was placed on a table between them.

"President Kennedy and I agreed a personal pact at Hyannis Port earlier this month. If I remain in office I will honour my side of the bargain. Now it is the time for him to reciprocate."

The US Ambassador frowned, totally confused now.

"I'm sorry...I was led to believe that the Summit was a complete failure?"

"That was part of the pact, Walter." They were alone in the room and suddenly it was uncannily, eerily quiet. "We broke the Soviet codes in April," the woman explained in a bare whisper. "GCHQ is currently sharing *some* small part of that intelligence with a joint NSA and the CIA task force set up to handle *Jericho*. Had we not had *Jericho* we would have abandoned the northern shores of the Persian Gulf within weeks of the Soviet invasion of Iran. Now, of course, it is too late."

Walter Brenckmann opened his mouth but no words came.

"Furthermore, I promised President Kennedy that no British civil servant or military officer would testify before the Warren Commission until after the November Election. Insofar as the Scorpion Affair rumbles on, I will give permission for Congressmen and Senators to interview British officers under oath in the United Kingdom at a time of the House's choosing. The action I have taken to remove the blockade of Irish ports – at great cost in terms of the general situation in Ireland - is a token of my commitment to my side of the deal. I invited the President to broker peace in the South Atlantic and I agreed, by default, not to pursue American conglomerates for their predatory acquisitiveness in the aftermath of the October War."

"What about the Fulbright Plan?" The Ambassador asked softly.

"That was my idea. Or rather, it was the Chancellor's, Peter Thorneycroft's idea, if one is being honest. For all its problems it has two recommendations. It might forestall the United Kingdom's bankruptcy for another year, and it *will* boost the balance sheets of the Wall Street banks who sign up for it. Presumably, this will buy off much of Wall Street's previously very public disdain for the Kennedy Administration."

The thing which constantly wrong-footed Walter Brenckmann about Margaret Thatcher was that she was a dazzling contradiction; brutally pragmatic and borderline mendacious one minute while capable of being almost childishly idealistic and 'damn the torpedoes' the next. Nothing that had happened in the last six months had dented her belief in the rightness of things. For all he knew she bitterly regretted and resented the compromises she had had to make in her Premiership; but she remained utterly resolute, implacable in her quest to get where she and her country needed to be in the future. Where an older, wiser, more seasoned political operator might already have allowed necessity and expedience to modify her convictions, she still possessed a sustaining vision that seemed very nearly impervious to hard knocks. She had had hard knocks a plenty lately. Frankly, he did not know how she kept on battering away, or had remained the angry, driven woman he had first met in Cheltenham in December.

"Please," Margaret Thatcher suggested, "when next you speak to Secretary of State Fulbright, or the President, I would be most grateful if you would remind the Administration that the time to do the 'right thing', is *now*."

Chapter 32

Thursday 25th June 1964
USS Kitty Hawk, 129 miles East of Muscat, Arabian Sea

It was one of those balmy nights at sea when God smiled on all mariners. After the sharp monsoon storms Carrier Division Seven had passed through after leaving Bombay seven days ago the short, steep seas had smoothed to a mirror-like, billiard table calm. In the heavens the Moon glistened off the surface of the ocean, not like a baleful overseer but as a distant nocturnal Sun perfectly lighting the way for the big grey warships.

Lieutenant-Commander Walter Brenckmann junior had come off watch at midnight, returning to his cabin to write up the journal he kept with the particulars of the last twenty-four hours, and started writing a letter home to his mother before, still restless, he had come topside to observe deck operations. Every day he was learning, becoming a better officer and he hoped, a better man. He had become too much a 'nuclear boat man', too imbued with a submariner's take on the Navy, the World, on everything in fact and that would almost certainly have become a problem in years to come.

To be out here in the Arabian Sea on the Kitty Hawk, a giant floating 'war city' with nearly six thousand other men, he could not but be awed by what his country was capable of when it set its mind to it. The big carriers were all about a thing strategists called 'global force projection'; object lessons in power politics which made it strange that after departing Bombay, Carrier Division Seven had headed straight back to within easy striking distance of the Persian Gulf.

At this moment one of the carrier's twin-turboprop Northrop Grumman E-2 Hawkeye airborne early warning, reconnaissance and electronic warfare aircraft, was loitering over southern Iran at the edge of the Abadan Defended Airspace Zone, its sophisticated electro-magnetic 'ears' trawling the airways for 'intel' deep into Iraq. To enable each Hawkeye to stay on station for extended periods one of the Kitty Hawk's three Douglas EKA-3 Skywarriors – specially modified bombers converted into airborne re-fuelling tankers – periodically sortied to 'top up' the duty Hawkeye's tanks. The British had sent up fighters to check out the first Hawkeye on station thirty-six hours ago; since then they had let the spy planes go about their business unmolested.

Even on a ship the size of the Kitty Hawk, over a thousand feet long with a flight deck so huge that it would have swallowed several whole football fields there were few places that a man could safely 'goof off' to watch the world going by. On a carrier a man was either on duty or he kept out of the way. Danger lurked everywhere topside as twenty-ton supersonic jets came and went, afterburners flamed, steam catapults discharged and hundreds of men moved across the vast steel stage like crouching, waving, shouting players in some insanely choreographed lethal ballet. The whole eighty thousand tons of the Kitty Hawk resounded with the thump of aircraft hitting the deck, throttles wide open in case their hooks missed a 'wire' ready to 'bolt' back into the air. The roaring scream of afterburners shook the behemoth to her keel when a pair of McDonnell Douglas F-4 Phantoms rocketed off the bow catapults. Off the ship's starboard quarter there was the constant thrumming of a Sikorsky SH-3 Sea King; airborne in a search and rescue role whenever Kitty Hawk was launching or recovering her birds.

Walter had pulled on a jacket over his normal fatigues and headed for the stern of the carrier where, half way beneath the massive overhang of the flight deck and the water churning under the taffrail twenty feet below, surrounded by massive mooring posts and chains, he joined perhaps a dozen other men of all ranks and trades. Some men smoked, some talked in low tones with friends, but most men came to the stern for no better reason than to stare into the darkness or the roiling water astern and to think their own thoughts.

In the light of the full Moon a North American A-5 Vigilante strike bomber was clearly visible at least two to three miles out as it lined up for its final approach. The Vigilante was a huge aircraft to be operating off a carrier, seventy-six feet long and weighing in at over twenty tons if was landing back onboard with its full ordnance load. The A-5s had been exercising night and day since Kitty Hawk cleared Bombay, which was unusual because the Vigilante's main role was to deploy the nuclear bombs – some thirty or so – which were locked down in the ship's Atomic Munitions Magazine.

The 'good will' visit to Bombay had been a colourful if rather lack lustre affair. The Kitty Hawk and two escorts had docked, the Marine Corps band had paraded on the quayside, the Fleet Commander had gone ashore to make a round of courtesy calls, one or two local dignitaries had come onboard the flagship but Indian troops had kept visitors out of the docks, and Indian Navy patrol boats had chased away inquisitive sightseers in the main anchorage. Shore leave had been strictly limited and then, as a tropical storm blew over Bombay the visit had been over, the dampest of damp squibs as driving rain swept across the city in the Kitty Hawk's wake.

Walter stared at the full Moon.

Another full Moon; another month at sea completed.

Walter had hoped that there would be a new batch of mail from home awaiting the fleet at Bombay. At sea on a deterrent cruise in a Polaris boat a man knew that there would be no mail from home, he got used to the idea and after a while it did not bother him. Life in the surface navy was different; a man expected news from home, anticipated regular contact and when there was no mail it irked him in unsettling, uneasy ways.

This was yet another thing that Walter Brenckmann's submariner alto ego had grown accustomed to lately; although as lessons went it was nowhere near as troubling as having one's horizons, quite literally expanded in ways he could not have predicted. His life in the undersea navy had been a cloistered affair, his view of the World limited by the proximity of the nearest bulkhead, his tactical appreciation wholly focused on the efficient running of his department, the boat and surviving the numerous perils of the deep.

Ever since he had stepped onto the Kitty Hawk he had been confronted by new realities; viscerally aware that he was involved in a bigger, infinitely more complicated drama.

The raging of the A-5 Vigilante's engines raced ahead of the swooping bomber, gleaming like a silver eel in the loom of the all-seeing Moon.

It was as if Kitty Hawk had gone to war stations the minute she cleared the breakwater of the port of Bombay. There had been no announcement of a new mission; simply the posting of a revised, intensive program of air operations involving every element of the carrier's eighty-one strong mixed air wing of supersonic fighters, nuclear bombers, attack aircraft, tankers, spy aircraft and helicopters.

Carrier Division Seven's stated mission remained unchanged; to protect US tankers, to maintain the freedom of navigation in the Persian Gulf, to evacuate and or to assist US citizens, American diplomatic outposts and commercial interests in the Arabian Peninsula. The President had promised the American people that not one GI's boot would be placed 'East of Suez', and that the US Navy was in the Arabian Sea on a 'peacekeeping mission'.

Walter flinched involuntarily as the A-5 Vigilante fell onto the aft deck of the carrier like some screaming prehistoric raptor. Its jets raged, subsided as the restraining wires - 'traps' - arrested the bomber's forward momentum with the controlled violence of a high speed car wreck.

Upon high the Moon saw it all.

About a thousand yards off Kitty Hawk's port quarter the old modernized Cleveland class cruiser Providence (CLG-6) held station, her odd futuristic silhouette painted with yellowy edges in the lunar glow.

While the Providence retained one of her Second World War triple six-inch turrets forward, augmented with a twin five-inch dual purpose turret mount in place of her original main battery 'B' turret, her after superstructure had been replaced with towering radar towers and the unmistakable pillars of a twin-rail Mark 9 RIM-2 Terrier surface-to-air missile launcher. The US Navy had had so many ships at the end of the 1945 war that it had run out of men to man them, and finished the war owning such a plethora of redundant spare hulls rusting in mothballs that whenever possible Congress had forced the Navy to convert 'what it had' – rather than build fresh hulls - as the new guided weapons technologies came on stream. A rash of hybrid, odd-looking ships like the Providence had been the result; big gun ships stripped of most of their guns, compromised to mount new 'space age' systems as yet untested in battle.

Walter watched the silhouette of the cruiser lengthen.

Phosphorescent water bubbled under her sharp stem, and then the silhouette began to shorten as she heeled into a turn away from the flagship.

Moments later the klaxons began to sound on the Kitty Hawk.

And men were running to their battle stations.

As Walter Brenckmann ran – as if his life depended upon it because for all he knew it did – he could not stop himself thinking again about the possibility that one or more of the dozens of Soviet nuclear submarines under construction at the time of the October War had actually survived the holocaust.

Even in the bowels of the great aircraft carrier everybody felt, rather than heard, the reverberation of the big underwater explosion.

The men who had been running, now *sprinted* towards their duty stations.

Chapter 33

Thursday 25th June 1964
Abadan Island, Iran

Colonel Francis St John Waters, VC – he had been promoted to sweeten the pill of being summarily consigned to the Reserve List – had not yet wholly got used to the idea that he had been handed into the pastoral care of the British Broadcasting Corporation. It was odd not having a licence to kill any more; and he had entertained any number of reservations about the reception he could expect to receive on this his first assignment, when he renewed acquaintance with the daunting person of the Commander-in-Chief of all Commonwealth Forces in the Middle East.

The new Acting Director General of the British Broadcasting Corporation, upon learning of his prior *acquaintance* with the C-in-C, in league with Nick Ridley, the Secretary of State for Information, had decreed that the former SAS man's cobbled together 'news team' would go to the 'north of the Gulf', while Barry Lankester's 'civilian-led' team would cover 'the south'.

The Acting DG, thirty-six year old David Attenborough had struck Frank Waters as a good enough sort, likeable if not clubbable and clearly not overly impressed with curmudgeonly old military types like him; but a decent enough sort for all that. He was some kind of zoologist by profession by all accounts who would probably have been much happier making films about wildlife than rebuilding the BBC. To give him credit he had been crystal clear what he expected from his two 'Persian Gulf' teams.

'Find out what is going on, talk to the people who matter and send reports home by the swiftest possible means at regular, ideally daily, intervals.' To which he had added a second, entirely sensible caveat; 'don't worry about editing your material in the field, there are plenty of people back in England who can do that.'

It was no secret that Lieutenant-General Michael Carver and Frank Waters had crossed swords not once, but twice back in those long ago days when Rommel was making monkeys of a succession of British 'desert generals' in the sands of Cyrenaica. That had been over twenty years ago but the British Army could be positively elephantine when it wanted; it might not be overly keen to apply the hard won lessons of old wars but it forgot nothing.

There was a chill in the desert air as a fluky breeze gusted off the Shatt al-Arab beneath the rising silvery Moon. In the clear, starry desert night the temperature was tumbling, the cold pinching men's faces burned by the merciless Sun only hours before.

Parked in dead ground beneath camouflage netting, Frank Waters discovered that the C-in-C had installed himself in a command truck that would not have been out of place in the Western Desert in 1942.

Michael Carver met him under the netting outside the lorry,

stepping out of the impenetrable shadows.

Hands were shaken.

Frank Waters sprang open the attached case he had brought with him from his film unit's temporary tented base at RAF Abadan. He held out a bottle of Laphroig Malt Whiskey.

"A peace offering, General," he smiled toothily.

Carver accepted the bottle, hefted it briefly.

He shook his head.

"Lately, I've been thinking about those days when XXX Corps seemed to be the only thing between the Afrika Korps and Cairo more often than I ought," he confessed ruefully.

Frank Waters had first encountered Michael Carver when he was GSO1, the senior staff officer of the 7th Armoured Division – the 'Desert Rats' – in 1942. Apart from the fact that both men in their own ways thought that the top brass in charge of 8th Army at the time was simply not up to the job, there had been absolutely no meeting of minds.   Waters was the junior man, a scruffy good for nothing irregular on the payroll of the Long-Range Desert Group, the forerunner of the SAS. In those days before Bernard Montgommery showed up in the desert, Carver had bigger problems than the needs of Waters's fighting column; like for instance, constantly having to dissuade his superiors from continually driving the Division's tanks straight down the muzzles of the Afrika Korps' dug in 88-millimetre tank-killing guns.

Michael Carver had never been one to tolerate fools gladly or otherwise, and to give the man credit he rarely differentiated between fools of high or low rank. Allegedly, on at least one occasion later in the war Montgommery had had to step in to save him after he had told the wrong senior officer *exactly* what he thought about him. Carver had won the Military Cross at Tobruk in 1941, adding two Distinguished Service Orders before the end of the war; all three decorations were for valour in the face of the enemy, as were practically all his – very numerous - mentions in despatches. Aged twenty-nine in 1944 he had been the youngest brigadier in the Army.

"Babadzhanian isn't Rommel, sir," Frank Waters suggested.

"Neither am I." Michael Carver grimaced. His gaze, seemingly cool, warmed and briefly there was something akin to mischief in his eyes. "Come inside and we'll break open your peace offering."

Carver indicated for his visitor to perch on a low stool, he sat on a Spartan canvass cot. The two men raised their glasses.

"Old friends," they agreed.

In the distance the sound of thunder whispered.

"The Soviets are in the northern suburbs of Basra," Michael Carver said, as if this was of only passing interest. A few days ago he had gratuitously, positively shamelessly exaggerated the southern progress of the Red Army hoping to jerk his erstwhile Saudi allies into action; the latest intelligence reports indicated his pessimism had now been vindicated. "They lobbed artillery into the city last night about this time. Not for very long, I think they're short of ammunition. We suspect advance elements of the Red Army have already bypassed Basra to the west and are extending south into the Faw Peninsula. Flying columns could be in Umm Qasr in forty-eight hours. Hereabouts, it will probably be a few days yet before they are in any position to shell Abadan." He sipped his drink, seemingly the most sanguine man in the Middle East. "All in all things are developing nicely."

Frank Waters frowned.

"We're not beaten yet, then?"

"Not yet," the other man, the older by five years, agreed. "The RAF lost a couple of aircraft taking out the bridges over the Euphrates at Al Qurnah two days ago. I sometimes think the Royal Air Force is afraid it is missing out on all the fun. It seems somebody in Cyprus was under the misapprehension that the enemy needed those crossing to reinforce the push towards Basra. Anyway, I'm sure the Soviets will have concluded that we are still 'in the dark' about their true intentions, which is all to the good."

"*Their* true intentions, sir?"

Michael Carver stood up and beckoned Frank Waters to join him at the big map on the left hand side of the truck.

"If you want to seize Abadan Island you have three options. One, secure the opposite, western bank of the Shatt al-Arab and mount an amphibious assault. Bad idea, the Arvand River is well over half-a-mile wide and the first waves of the assaulting force takes eighty to one hundred percent casualties. Two, using Basra as a base of operations one bridges the Arvand River at places of one's own choice with pontoons, transferring forces to the eastern shore under cover of local air and artillery support. This is what the Iraqis did a month or two ago but they failed to achieve concentration and were routed in detail as soon as my Centurions came upon their flank. Three, you take the major river barriers out of the equation. Crossing the Tigris at Al Qurnah north of the confluence of the Tigris with the Euphrates does *not* meet this criterion." He jabbed his right forefinger at the small town of Amarah on the Tigris River over a hundred miles north of Basra. "However, if you transfer your forces onto the eastern bank of the Tigris at Amarah – effectively the last place you can rely on bridging the river between Baghdad and the Persian Gulf – you can advance down that bank all the way to Khorramshahr without encountering another significant water obstacle. Moreover, you have a hundred miles of ground to advance over in which to get yourself organised to mount a proper assault on the Iranian forces holding Khorramshahr, and thereby preventing an advance to the northern bank of the Karun River. Thereupon, the enemy is confronted by just that single river barrier to bridge before enveloping the low hanging fruit of Abadan Island by *force majeure*. By which time," he concluded, "Red Army formations will already be in control of the western bank of the Shatt al-Arab."

Frank Waters was so shocked by Michael Carver's candour that he was a little lost for words.

"A whole Soviets tank army is coming down the eastern bank of the Tigris?" He blurted.

The other man nodded.

"Yes."

Frank Waters might not be any kind of grand strategist but he had a street fighter's nous for practical battle tactics; and the news he had just heard sent a shiver down his spine. An irresistible wave of armour was washing down the eastern bank of the Tigris River towards him and it could be here not in weeks but days.

"My word," he chuckled thoughtfully, "the beggars really have got us by the, er, nose," he offered lamely.

"Quite," Michael Carver concurred. "In fact my Staff takes the general view that the blighters have got hold of us by a much more sensitive part of our anatomy, Waters," he observed pithily. "Moreover, I should imagine that's precisely the way Comrade Babadzhanian thinks, too."

"But you don't, General?"

Michael Carver shook his head.

"Not entirely. No."

He pointed to the line of the Karun River where it curved around the northern end of Abadan Island.

"If I was Babadzhanian I'd stop there," he said. "In my own sweet time I'd ford the Karun twenty or thirty miles east of Abadan and again, in my own sweet time I'd besiege the whole island. Shell and starve us out, basically. That's the obvious thing to do. Trying to get armour and ground troops onto Abadan Island is asking for trouble." He sighed. "Let's go for a walk."

The Moon was so bright a man had to shade his eyes to see beyond the shadows. The forward headquarters was close to the southern bank of the Karun River; and the slow moving mud-laden waters glittered in the moonlight.

"We outnumbered Rommel and the Italians two or three to one at El Alamein," Michael Carver reminded his visitor. "But we knew that in advance, just like we understood the lay of the land in front of us. We're outnumbered here. That's a given, there's nothing we can do about it," he explained, matter of factly, as if he was discussing dispositions at a regimental parade.

"How many tanks do you think are coming down the eastern bank of the Tigris in our direction, sir?"

"I've no idea; several hundred, certainly. Perhaps, half of whatever Comrade Babadzhanian's got left after his little odyssey through the Mountains of Iran a thousand miles to the Persian Gulf. Practically the whole mobile weight of 2nd Siberian Mechanized Army."

"I heard that we have some Iranian units on our side?" Frank Waters inquired cautiously.

"Yes," the C-in-C acknowledged tersely.

"The Russians would be idiots to try and cross *that* river," Frank Waters observed, staring across the hundred yard wide channel. "The channel must be ten or fifteen feet deep hereabouts?"

"Easily," the C-in-C agreed. "Going back to El Alamein," he went on, "if Erwin Rommel had had a water obstacle like this in front of his lines he could have held out forever."

"So that's the plan, sir?"

Michael Carver shrugged.

"We shall see. The trouble one always has with setting any kind of trap," he thought out aloud, "is persuading one's quarry to put some significant part of his anatomy into it. In an ideal world I'd like to do Babadzhanian's armour serious harm on the northern bank of the Karun River, and then have the blighter attempt a full scale amphibious operation to put a brigade or two of T-62s on *my side* of the water. Right now most of my plans revolve around isolating and destroying his spearheads around Khorramshahr; if the Russians carry on coming after that," he chuckled mirthlessly, "well, that would be too much to hope for. Either way, if Marshal Babadzhanian thinks he's just going to roll right over the top of us he's got a very, very nasty shock coming to him!"

Chapter 34

Thursday 25th June 1964
Victor B.2 'The Angry Widow', 20 Miles East of Krasny Kut, Saratov Oblast, Soviet Union

After topping off her fuel tanks from a No 207 Squadron Valiant at thirty-three thousand feet over the Caspian Sea, *The Angry Widow* had turned towards the Ural Mountains. In the days before the 'off' there had been endless speculation about what might remain of the pre-October War Soviet air defence system; secretly nobody had thought any aircraft could possibly penetrate this far into Soviet territory – no matter how devastated it was – without getting shot down. But then nobody had really anticipated that the air defence environment this far inside the Soviet Union would be so electronically 'dead'. There were lights on the ground, here and there, but no big settlements, no hubs of any kind of industry and radar activity was so sparse as to make it child's play to navigate between the few widely separated lukewarm 'hotspots'.

Thus far the crew of *The Angry Widow* had come across nothing to contradict the intelligence assessment of the mission briefing officer: 'The western and previously most populous areas of the Soviet Union west of the Ural Mountains are not dead zones, in fact we believe many millions of people still survive to inhabit all bar the most hard hit places. Sections of many large cities survive damaged but habitable and in the countryside significant communities were untouched by the direct effects of the bombing.'

However, from what *The Angry Widow's* instruments reported the threads that bound modern societies together – electricity, telecommunications and industrial organisation – had been comprehensively cut to shreds in the lands over which it had flown. If large numbers of people still lived beneath the Victor's flight path as it weaved and jinked across the great hinterland, they were not living as they had before the cataclysm. If the evidence of the electronic warfare panel was to be taken at face value, great swathes of the Soviet Union had literally been bombed back into the Stone Age.

Squadron Leader Guy French remembered the night of the October War, dodging the plumes of nuclear strikes across a landscape where huge firestorms raged, whole forests were burning and EMPs – Electro-Magnetic Pulses - had eventually trashed every piece of 'hardened' radio, radar, guidance and bomb aiming kit on his Avro Vulcan.

Reports of the recent raids on targets in southern Iraq had talked about massively 'beefed up' Soviet missile defences and the southward 'creep' of a formidable co-ordinated Red Air Force air defence command and control system. A Vulcan flying out of Dammam-Dhahran and two Cyprus-based Canberras had gone missing on operations over Basra and Al-Qurnah in the last week and other missions had been forced to abort short of their targets in the face of increased enemy fighter activity. Baghdad had been 'off limits' for last ten days; a thirty mile zone around the city having been saturated with surface-to-air missile batteries.

Ahead of today's operation the Intelligence boys at Akrotiri were speculating that the Soviets might have risked weakening the air defences of 'the homeland' to 'stiffen' the air cover over their ground forces in Iraq. Guy French was sceptical about that; he would wait and see what awaited *The Angry Widow* and the other three 100 Squadron Victors east of the Urals. The Moon was rising in the eastern sky, painting the bomber's way to its target, still two hundred miles distant.

Each of the four Victors carried different bomb loads. *City of Lincoln*, the Squadron CO's kite carried a ten-ton Grand Slam and four thousand-pounders in her belly, *The Angry Widow* a pair of six-ton Tallboys, *Eight East* thirty-six one thousand pound general purpose bombs, and *Remember London* an eighteen-ton mixed cargo of two thousand pound 'blast' munitions and magnesium and phosphorus based incendiaries.

The *City of Lincoln* and *The Angry Widow* had come out on top in the 'Grand Harbour Bombing Contest', and thus earned the right to cart the biggest bombs to Chelyabinsk, or more correctly, to a suspected bunker complex located some distance to that city's north-east. The 'also rans' in the 'contest' were tasked to bomb the centre of the built up area of the city from fifty thousand feet at the same time the two 'winners' descended to nineteen thousand feet to strike at the suspected 'command and control centre' six miles east of the Miass River.

In his concluding remarks the Squadron Commander had cheerfully told the crews of the four Victors – to a man veterans of the night of the October War - that this was a 'press on at any cost job' and the decision to mount the operation on a full Moon night had been calculated to 'send the enemy a message'.

The message in question was presumably that only mad dogs and Englishmen flew over hostile territory by the light of the silvery Moon...

The chaps had taken this in good heart; it was not as if any of them wanted to live forever. The men of the V-Bomber Force had been a fatalist crowd before the war; now, well there was a general acceptance that they had all been living on borrowed time ever since that night.

Guy French ought to have been more interested in exactly why the bunker complex outside Chelyabinsk was so important that it justified the likely loss of four irreplaceable Victors, and the risking of three supporting Valiant tankers and two Vulcans flying electronic counter measures missions deep into former Soviet airspace. But the *why* was so much less important than the immediate *how*, that the former was completely subsumed by the latter. Flying the mission was *everything*, the reasons *why* incidental. That was the way it had been on the night of the October War, and that was the way it must have been for his father when he was flying Lancasters over Germany in Hitler's War.

Theirs was not to make reply. Theirs was not to reason why. Theirs was but to do and die. Into the valley of Death flew the twenty men of No 100 Squadron...

It was all he could do to suppress a mischievous chuckle beneath his chaffing oxygen mask. Death was too good a fate for a man who could so shamelessly misquote Alfred, Lord Tennyson's Homeric ode to the egregiously gallant folly of a former age. Flying at the speed of a rifle bullet *The Angry Widow* rocketed east above the Ural Mountains.

The navigator's voice sliced through his co-pilot's thoughts.

"Initial Point in sixty seconds on my mark...NOW!"

The mission profile called for a rapid high speed descent at the commencement of the bomb run over ninety miles short of the target. In moments flaps would be extended, air brakes activated, throttles dragged back and the huge bomber would literally drop like a stone into the darkness. Anybody watching on a ground-based radar screen would suspect that his contact was out of control, crashing.

"THIRTY SECONDS!"

"Pay attention everybody," the Aircraft Commander drawled. "Hold onto your straps."

"TWENTY SECONDS!"

"Instrument check, co-pilot," the man in the left hand seat inquired solicitously.

"A-OK. All readings are nominal, sir."

"Jolly good!"

"TEN SECONDS!"

The roller coaster ride was about to begin.

"FIVE! FOUR! THREE! TWO! ONE!"

"Showtime," the pilot grunted as the flaps and air brakes extended into the near supersonic airstream ripping over and under the Victor's wings and along its space age fuselage, and as the four great Rolls-Royce Conway turbojets buried in her wing roots rapidly spooled down to half-power.

It was like being simultaneously punched in the stomach and dropped off a cliff. Both pilots lurched forward hard against their straps; and experienced the uncanny sensation of their intestinal tracts attempting to exit their bodies via the top of their heads.

It was a miracle *The Angry Widow* did not shed her wings in protest; which, all things considered was the reason that in the normal course of things one simply did not do this sort of thing to a 'beast' like *The Angry Widow*.

Unless, of course, there was a job to be done.

Guy French wanted to yell his exhilaration to the glowing yellow orb of the rising full Moon.

In that moment of monumentally heightened, almost erotic awareness when everything was suddenly so *immediate* the Moon seemed so close that if he reached out he could touch it...

Chapter 35

Friday 26th June 1964
HMS Alliance, Lazaretto Creek, Malta

Lieutenant-Commander Francis Barrington snapped to attention as the Commander-in-Chief of all British and Commonwealth Forces in the Mediterranean Theatre of Operations stepped onto the deck of the submarine. High above his head a skull and crossbones adorned black Jolly Roger flag flew from the jury-rigged rope and tackle attached to the boat's raised attack periscope. Down on the pressure casing the crew was dressed on parade, sweating in the late morning heat.

Air Marshall Sir Daniel French acknowledged Barrington's salute and smiled a quick, wolfishly predatory smile.

"*Another* damned fine job, Commander Barrington," he declared loudly, so that everybody heard it. "*Another* damned fine job done by a damned fine boat, captain!"

"Thank you, sir."

Alliance's return to Malta had been a royally celebrated affair.

Last night Alliance had been visited by Vice Admiral Grenville, C-in-C Mediterranean Fleet and earlier that morning the newly designated Acting Prime Minister of the Maltese Archipelago, Dom Mintoff and several other senior members of his 'all party' civil administration had come aboard.

The avenger of the 'Hampshire atrocity' had been greeted out at sea by the Battle class destroyer HMS Oudenarde and over-flown by RAF Hawker Hunter fighters as she passed east of the Grand Harbour breakwaters and steamed into Marsamxett. The ramparts of Valetta had been crowded, likewise the ruins on Manoel Island with cheering and waving civilians and service personnel.

Malta itself still seemed wrecked from end to end.

Valletta's skyline was smashed and smoke blackened; in Lazaretto Creek the old depot ship Maidstone still sat on the bottom, traces of bunker oil escaping through the surface booms fouling the crystal clear waters. Work was still going on to clear a wreck from the main channel and a new mole was being built to shelter Msida Creek from the east winds that blew down Marsamxett carrying the dust from countless streets half-blocked with rubble and debris.

The orders for Alliance's next deployment had been awaiting her return.

ALLIANCE WILL MAKE GOOD DEFECTS STOP REFUEL STOP
RE-ARM AND VICTUAL FOR A THIRTY DAY WAR PATROL
AND RETURN TO HOME WATERS NOT LATER THAN TEN
DAYS AFTER ARRIVING LAZARETTO CREEK, MALTA STOP
ALLIANCE TO DRAW CHARTS FOR ONE WESTERN TWO
APPROACHES BRISTOL CHANNEL AND THREE IRISH SEA

AND MAKE PASSAGE AT BEST SUBMERGED SPEED TO HM
NAVAL BASE BARROW-IN-FURNESS STOP THERE TO
REPORT TO FLAG OFFICER 10TH SUBMARINE SQUADRON
STOP ALLIANCE TO ADVISE ARRIVAL DATE BY SECURE
COMMUNICATIONS AFTER COMPLETING PASSAGE OF
STRAITS OF GIBRALTAR STOP PROMOTIONS AS FOLLOWS
STOP BARRINGTON FH TO COMDR STOP PHILPOTT MJ TO
LT. COMDR EFFECTIVE RETURN TO HOME WATERS
MESSAGE ENDS

Nobody knew very much about the 10th Submarine Squadron
other than it was the personal fiefdom of Rear Admiral Simon Horatio
Collingwood, the man who had commanded HMS Dreadnought on her
first two war patrols, the Royal Navy's anointed 'nuclear boat
supremo'.

Francis Barrington had no idea what use an old – albeit
substantially modified – World War II designed 'A' Class boat like
Alliance would be up in Barrow, allegedly, the place where the Navy's
undersea fleet of the future was to be built.

He would worry about that when he got home. In the meantime
the damaged port shaft which had cut short Alliance's patrol in the
Gulf of Lion, courtesy of a randomly dumped French depth charge,
needed to be repaired and that was going to be a dry dock job. Later
that day he had an interview scheduled with Commodore Renfrew, the
Admiralty Dockyard Superintendent but he entertained no
expectations of jumping the queue. One of the big US Navy missile
destroyers based at Malta had just taken up residence in Dock No 2,
and HMS Victorious, resembling a half-burned hulk rather than a fleet
carrier was moored in Kalkara Creek waiting to get into Dock No 1.
Every ship in the Mediterranean Fleet was either broken or worn out
and the influx of dockyard workers from the Clyde and the Tyne, had
found it hard going stepping into the shoes of the Maltese workers
killed and injured in the Battle of Malta.

Barrington had assumed that Air Marshall French would simply
want to shake a few hands and depart; in fact he asked for 'a tour' of
the submarine and insisted on shaking *every* man's hand. Such was
the C-in-C's propensity to stop and chat that he was on Alliance well
over an hour before his anxious aides contrived to drag him ashore to
his next appointment.

Alliance's place in the blockade of the French Mediterranean coast
had been filled by HMS Anchorite, an unmodernised sister boat which
– until the last couple of months - had had at least two superior
claims to fame than Francis Barrington's command.

Firstly, in 1960 Anchorite had been the first Royal Navy
submarine to visit Tonga since the Second War, and secondly,
Anchorite was the only boat in the Fleet which had had a rock named
after it; specifically, a previously uncharted 'rock' in the Hauraki Gulf
off Auckland which it had discovered by employing the well-known
hydrographic mapping technique known throughout the Service as

'inadvertently colliding with it'.

Returning to Malta on one shaft Alliance had been routed well away from the Corsican waters in which she had exacted revenge for the sneak attack on HMS Hampshire.

Vice Admiral Grenville had cheerfully informed him that after Alliance had 'done her execution' the RAF had 'flattened most of Ajaccio and the surrounding countryside', apparently, 'just to make a point'. Since then the boats of the 2nd Submarine Squadron – five Amphion class boats reinforced with a pair of new, advanced and very stealthy 'O' class 'Oberons', the Oracle and the Otter – had 'pretty much bottled up what's left of the French Mediterranean Fleet in Toulon and Marseilles and put the lid on any ongoing coastal traffic'. It seemed everybody was a little jealous that Alliance had 'stolen all the glory' before the enemy had run for cover.

Francis Barrington had profusely apologised for being greedy and Grenville, a ruddy-faced, four square man who probably would have been on his element on the quarterdeck of one of Nelson's ships of the line at Trafalgar had guffawed enthusiastically.

The Commander of HMS Alliance watched his latest visitor's barge chug towards the near shore along the western rim of Lazaretto Creek. The roads had been re-opened through the ruined houses in Msida and Gzira, wisps of grey smoke rose here and there in the urban sprawl from the cooking stoves lit by families returning to their bombed homes.

"It's all very well being honoured and feted by the great and the good, sir," Lieutenant Michael Philpott observed ruefully, "but it makes a nonsense of watch rotas and work schedules!"

Barrington chuckled. "Be thankful for small mercies, Number One," he counselled sagely. "The last time we did something heroic the same people who are queuing to come onboard and pat us all on the back had us put in quarantine for a fortnight!"

"Very true, Skipper," the younger man concurred. Sobering a little he added: "It will be good to get home before the end of the summer after the last couple of winters."

Standing on the deck of the submarine in tropical whites with the sun beating down so fiercely that exposed metal was hot enough to sear unprotected flesh, or to flash fry an egg in seconds it was a little incongruous to be thinking of English winters. They had assumed Alliance would be stationed at Malta for the foreseeable future, and in a World which could come to fiery end in a moment that had seemed like forever. Now they were looking forward to going home and it mattered not one jot that they had no real idea what awaited them in England.

Barrington looked to his wrist watch. It would be noon in a few minutes.

"Normal harbour stations from twelve hundred hours, Number One. Send as many men ashore as we can spare. Our people deserve an opportunity to let off a little steam."

Chapter 36

Saturday 27th June 1964
Kursk Bunker, Chelyabinsk, Soviet Union

One of the two six-ton bombs which had landed within the security perimeter of the bunker complex, had demolished a gymnasium where over a two hundred slave workers and political offenders assigned to Penal Battalion 507, had been sleeping. The whole building had collapsed and a fire fed by a ruptured gas main had eventually consumed the entire structure. Had anybody survived the blast of the huge bomb they might have been rescued from the wreckage before the fire took hold; had that is, anybody cared or had the fire fighters not been fully occupied elsewhere.

A second six-ton – a so-called Tallboy - bomb had struck the edge of the four-metre thick reinforced cupola protecting the central, 'command bunker' from which the Red Air Force directed the air defence of the 'Sverdlovsk-Chelyabinsk Defended Region'. The bomb had carved some fifteen feet into the earth passing through the metre-thick roof of the broad circular communication walkway between the air defence centre and the 'political bunker', where senior Party and Red Army and Air Force leaders and their families sheltered in a still deeper warren of tunnels and rooms some twenty metres underground when there was an air raid alert.

In comparison with the modern deep bunkers around Moscow which, ironically, very few senior Party figures had been able to reach before the first American missiles arrived on the night of the Cuban Missiles War, the Kursk complex was relatively shallow and built to survive an attack with Hiroshima-size bombs exploding not on top of, but 'air bursting' near it. Some thought had been given to the 'survivability' of the facility if attacked with large conventional precision munitions but, not much. This was hardly inexplicable since the notion of Yankee or British bombers flying this deep into the Soviet Union carrying six and ten ton 'earthquake' bombs would, prior to October 1962 have seemed risible, if not laughable.

The detonation of this second huge bomb in the downward sloping circular passageway had undermined one of the structural members supporting the southern edge of the 'bomb proof' four thousand ton cupola above the air defence centre, and completely collapsed the tunnel over a length of approximately forty metres. At the same time the concrete 'lid' had dropped nearly a metre splintering internal walls. Deep underground massive concrete slabs had exploded like giant hand grenades, all the lights had gone out and water from nearby subterranean reservoirs, and the tanks of diesel kept topped up to power internal generators if Chelyabinsk was destroyed by a nuclear strike, had started to flood into, and inundate, the lower levels of the complex from countless crushed and ruptured pipes.

All of this had happened in the thirty-seven seconds before a ten-ton Grand Slam bomb screamed down from four miles high like a supersonic crossbow bolt. It had struck the grassy ground ten feet above the three-metre thick reinforced concrete roof of the Red Army's Central Communications Room in the linked Kursk No 2 bunker. Although this initial obstruction significantly retarded the progress of the bomb the great projectile nevertheless plunged another five metres, passing through a second two-metre concrete ceiling before its fuse, set to explode its four ton Torpex explosive warhead – with a blast yield equivalent to over six-and-a-half tons of TNT - 0.25 seconds after impact had blown up in middle of the single most critical command and control centre in the entire Soviet Union.

First Deputy Secretary and Deputy Chairman of the Communist Party of the Union of Soviet Socialist Republics, Alexei Nikolayevich Kosygin and his wife were buried somewhere in the flooded 'political bunker'.

Minister of Defence and Commander of the Red Army, that seemingly indestructible old Bolshevik Marshal of the Soviet Union Vasily Ivanovich Chuikov's body lay somewhere in the wreckage of the Kursk No 2 bunker.

When the British Grand Slam bomb had exploded it had lifted the whole northern section of the complex several feet in the air, forming a thirty metre wide crater into which the pulverised remains of the 'nuclear bunker' had fallen seconds later.

At a stroke the RAF had snuffed out the lives of the wiliest political operator in the Politburo, and the Motherland's most famous living soldier. It seemed almost incidental that over five hundred other people had died, or were still missing in the attack on the Kursk Bunker complex.

Forty-five year old Alexander Nikolayevich Shelepin stood beside the Chairman of the Communist Party, Leonid Ilyich Brezhnev as a rain squall unleashed its passing anger on the desperate salvage operations in the hole above where the Red Army's Central Communications Room had once been.

The stench of death was in the air.

"My people think only one man," Shelepin breathed angrily, "successfully ejected from the bomber we shot down. It was one of the pilots. The local Party official in charge of the search squad put a bullet in his head."

Brezhnev's eyes narrowed and his bear like countenance furrowed.

"Yes, yes," the First Secretary of the KGB sighed impatiently. "I have already had the idiot sent to a labour battalion in the east. We could have put a bullet in the fascist's head any time. If my boys had got hold of him first we might have discovered how the bastards did *this*."

"Sergey Georgiyevich should be arriving in Chelyabinsk this afternoon," Brezhnev remarked, staring distractedly into the chaos of the crater. He had over-ridden his own personal objections to promulgate Admiral of the Fleet Sergey Georgiyevich Gorshkov, since

1956 the Deputy Defence Minister, as Chuikov's replacement because there was no other viable candidate for the post other than Hamazasp Khachaturi Babadzhanian and right now the Commander of Army Group South had other, pressing business in Iraq on his mind.

Besides, Brezhnev accepted that while Shelepin could stomach Gorshkov's elevation to the Collective Leadership, the notion of inviting Hamazasp Khachaturi Babadzhanian onto the top table was anathema. Forty-eight hours ago that would not have mattered; but that was before two of the three man 'Troika' which had emerged out of the ashes of the Cuban Missiles War, and a dozen other senior Party, Red Army and Red Air Force members of the high command had been murdered by the British.

"*This*," Shelepin spat, much in the fashion of a Cobra spraying venom into its prey's eyes, "would never have happened if Chuikov hadn't sent all those fucking anti-aircraft missiles to Iraq!"

Brezhnev had considered the transfer of fifteen of the twenty-one S-75 batteries allocated to the defence of the Sverdlovsk – Chelyabinsk region a calculated gamble. Something had had to be done to stop, or at the very least, deter the British from constantly bombing bridges, roads and towns along Babadzhanian's line of march south of Baghdad; and transferring the bulk of the S-75s had seemed a good idea at the time. It had, in fact, succeeded in its aim driving the RAF from the skies of central Iraq.

However, Shelepin was right; the massed batteries of S-75s which had been in place around both Sverdlovsk and Chelyabinsk until a few weeks ago would have made short work of the four RAF V-Bombers which had wreaked so much havoc in the nearby city and the Kursk bunker complex. As it was three of the four bombers had got away having been able to make their bomb runs untroubled by the handful of light guns protecting the city.

The Red Air Force claimed to have shot down a second bomber north of the Crimea. The downed aircraft had supposedly crashed in a 'dead zone' known to be heavily contaminated by radiation from an American bomber which had crashed during the Cuban Missiles War, and although search teams had been sent to investigate the reported 'downing', as yet no reports had been received in Chelyabinsk.

This was hardly surprising since all secure communications now had to be filtered through the Defence Ministry complex in Sverdlovsk, where arrangements were in hand to relocate the reconstituted 'Troika' and its large – temporarily disrupted - administration.

"Well," Brezhnev concluded, knowing that in time the blame game would erode the former Chuikov's reputation and be ruthlessly employed by Shelepin to undermine the 'Hero of Iraq', Babadzhanian. There was nothing he could do about it so he was not about to waste time worrying about it. "It doesn't really matter, does it? The British gave us a kick in the guts. Now we have to get on with things. We will take our revenge on them in the Persian Gulf. The KGB can have its inquest into how *this*," he waved at the rubble, "was allowed to happen later."

Inevitably, the raid had taken the shine off the Red Army's triumphant march south to the Persian Gulf.

Overnight the news had been received that advanced units of Major General Vladimir Andreyevich Puchkov's 10th Guards Tank Division had taken the Iraqi port of Umm Qasr and closed up to the Kuwaiti border. Other than a few isolated pockets of resistance in the Kurdish north, the whole of Iraq was in Soviet hands. Soon, Abadan would be over run and then it would only be a matter of time before south eastern Iran capitulated.

On the eastern, Iranian bank of the Arvand River, powerful spearheads of the 2nd Siberian Mechanised Army, commanded by the relentless former paratrooper Konstantin Yakovlevich Kurochnik had rolled over a weak Iranian armoured regiment opposite Basra and were preparing to advance south on Khorramshahr. The only thing that had not gone to plan was the failure of the Red Air Force to achieve and to maintain any degree of local air superiority over the eastern half of Basra Province; but in the scale of things, this was only a minor fly in the ointment. The Red Army now held the Faw Peninsula opposite Abadan Island and in the next few days, heavy artillery and dozens of Katyusha rocket launchers would be brought forward. Then, squeezed between the massed guns of 3rd Caucasian Tank Army in the west and by the irresistible tide of advancing 2nd Siberian Mechanized Army's armour, the end would come quickly.

Albeit over a month behind schedule, Babadzhanian's 'grand strategy' was finally playing out *exactly* as he had predicted.

"I want Yuri Vladimirovich in Baghdad as soon as possible," Shelepin asserted, having decided not to challenge Brezhnev's authority at this early stage in the life of the new Troika.

Like a wily old boxer too wise to be distracted by his opponent's fancy footwork and untroubled by his educated jabbing and feinting, Brezhnev had anticipated this demand and already weighed its merits. There were other candidates as qualified, and possibly, more suitable to assume the role of Commissar General in the conquered territories than Yuri Vladimirovich Andropov. However, at a time like this placing the 'best man' in post was not actually the primary consideration.

Whether he liked it or not Brezhnev had accepted Shelepin as Alexei Kosygin's de facto replacement in the 'Troika', and Sergey Georgiyevich Gorshkov, as Chuikov's. In the 'new' collective leadership Brezhnev would command the Party, Shelepin would remain the First Secretary of the KGB and responsibility for internal security, and Gorshkov, for the defence of the Motherland. Inevitably, Gorshkov would be the junior member of the ruling triumvirate because unlike his predecessor he could not and never would, speak for the Red Army. This suited Brezhnev and Shelepin perfectly; while they needed Gorshkov to counterbalance Babadzhanian, the man they expected to return home from his triumphs in Iran and Iraq like Julius Caesar after the Gallic Wars angling to be Tsar one day, they had no intention of 'sharing' real political power with a mere 'Admiral'.

"Yes, send Andropov to Baghdad," Brezhnev agreed. "It will give him ideas above his station but I'm sure you'll keep an eye on him."

Shelepin snorted what might have been laughter.

"Assuming," Brezhnev went on, his voice as unyielding as the Siberian permafrost, "*your* people and *my* people don't start another Civil War in the meantime."

The master of the KGB looked to his companion dead eyed.

"There is no profit in that for either of us, Comrade Leonid Ilyich. If there is to be peace we must present a united face to our enemies. Do you not agree?"

"And afterwards?"

Shelepin shrugged.

"Afterwards is another country, my friend."

Chapter 37

Saturday 27th June 1964
USS Kitty Hawk, Straits of Hormuz, Persian Gulf

In contrast to her approach the first time she had encountered Carrier Division Seven HMAS Anzac cruised towards the flagship out of the haze at a sedate fifteen knots. About a mile behind her the silhouette of the New Zealand frigate, Otago, recently arrived from Australasian waters slowly turned south.

Anzac's bridge signal lamp began to wink.

Lieutenant-Commander Walter Brenckmann junior mouthed the letters of the message silently, formed the words on his lips as he gaze zeroed in on the destroyer.

MV CONNAUGHT MINED IN WATERS OFF KARAK ISLAND STOP LOCAL IRANIAN FORCES BELIEVED HOSTILE STOP SAFE CHANNEL ON SOUTH SIDE OF THE STRAITS MESSAGE ENDS.

There was a short interregnum while the destroyer awaited acknowledgement from the carrier.

RESPECTFULLY SUGGEST YOU CLEAR KISHM ISLAND BY TEN PLUS MILES TO THE SOUTH MESSAGE ENDS.

The Straits of Hormuz were only twenty-nine miles wide at the narrowest point, and beyond it as shipping entered the Persian Gulf Kishm Island guarded the Iranian coast for many miles.

There was another gap in the signalling as the Anzac drew nearer.

PROVIDENCE SHALL NOT BE FORGOTTEN.

Shortly afterwards Anzac reduced speed to about eight knots and as she passed through Carrier Division Seven she dipped her flags, all of them, including a huge battle flag streaming from her main mast yard, to half-mast. The destroyer had manned the rail of her foredeck, and on the flying bridge her officers had doffed their caps to the Kitty Hawk.

Clear of the big ships of the flagship's escort the Battle class destroyer increased speed and turned to catch up with Kitty Hawk.

MAY I SPEAK DIRECTLY TO CINCCD7 STOP SCRAMBLER CODE ONE-ONE-THREE MESSAGE ENDS.

It seemed that the sinking of the USS Providence had changed the world hereabouts between the time of Carrier Division Seven's first meeting with the captain of the Anzac and now.

From the moment the torpedo had exploded beneath the keel of the modernized World War II cruiser, Carrier Division Seven had been on a war footing. Wherever the flagship sailed there were sonar buoys in the water and a pair of Grumman S-2 Tracker twin turboprop anti-submarine aircraft in the air co-ordinating the movements of the Kitty Hawk's screening destroyers and frigates. The SSN USS Permit had been left behind in the deeper waters of the Arabian Sea to guard the entrance to the Persian Gulf, and every man on every ship was looking for an opportunity to exact payback on the cowards who had killed over a hundred of their comrades onboard the Providence.

Having been previously ordered to maintain a 'peace time level of anti-submarine warfare readiness' nobody was blaming Walter Brenckmann for what had happened; but that did not make him feel any better. In the days since the sinking a dark, brooding anger had clouded his waking mind and he knew it was not going to blow away any time soon.

Notwithstanding there had been no announcement, nor any dissemination of new mission orders, nobody onboard the Kitty Hawk honestly believed any of that 'peace keeping baloney' any more. The news that Admiral Bringle intended to 'take Carrier Division Seven into the Persian Gulf to exercise the US Navy's right of free and unfettered passage in international waters' had not come as any surprise to anybody.

Now as the great carrier passed through the Straits of Hormuz there had been another change.

No neutral had any place in the Persian Gulf.

The Red Army had parked its tanks on the northern shore; Abadan was likely to fall within days and everybody understood that the British and their allies were not going to just let it happen.

Within days the waters into which Carrier Division Seven was passing would run with blood, and Walter Brenckmann honesty did not know how he and his comrades onboard the Kitty Hawk could possibly stand back from the coming fight.

Chapter 38

Monday 29th June 1964
Sultan Abdulaziz Air Base, Riyadh

Construction work was still going on to extend and widen the taxiways and row upon row of general purpose, blast and anti-personnel munitions were stacked - apparently randomly arrayed - on pallets and in the sand beneath the merciless Arabian sun as Squadron Leader Guy French clambered from the sweaty, nevertheless relatively cool pressurized crew 'bubble' of Victor B.2 *The Angry Widow* onto the burning tarmac. The heat shimmered off the desert creating a haze which blurred the lines of the control tower in the middle distance.

The briefing officer back at RAF Akrotiri on Cyprus had remarked that the runway on which *The Angry Widow* had just landed 'did not exist a fortnight ago' and looking around Guy French could believe it. He moved into the shadow of the port wing, unzipping and unlatching his flying suit down to the waist and peeling the sweltering, clinging fabric down until it was bunched around his hips as the other crew members had already done. Still the perspiration poured off him.

The Chelyabinsk operation already felt like a lifetime ago.

No 100 Squadron would have basked in the satisfaction of a job well done; had it known it had actually *done the job well* and but for the loss of the CO's kite *City of Lincoln*. The boys who had carpet bombed the middle of Chelyabinsk could justifiably claim to have hit the nail on the head, not so *The Angry Widow's* crew. For all Guy French knew the Victor's two Tallboys had gone down in open countryside. However, even though one of the ECW – electronic countermeasures warfare – Canberras based at Akrotiri had also failed to return, the top brass seemed pleased enough. The only fly in the ointment on Cyprus was that the raid had more or less emptied the bomb dumps of medium capacity general purpose bombs and high capacity blast munitions; which was why *The Angry Widow* was sitting on the broiling concrete apron of an air base in Saudi Arabia, literally in the middle of a veritable sea of precisely the sort of devices that were in critically short supply at its home base.

There were bombs of every denomination, 250-pounders, 500, 1000, and 2000-pounders, smoothly rounded general purpose jobs, blunt-ended cylindrical thin-skinned explosive-packed monsters, devices stencilled 'AP', some with cameras in their noses, others with tail widgets containing pre-wired components of their terminal guidance systems. Some bombs had over-sized tail flukes, and others stubby, business-like stabilisers.

It seemed that the US Air Force had left this veritable cornucopia of devastation in Arabia because it was cheaper than carting it all the way home but the RAF was not about to get 'proud' about the scraps it was about to scoop up off the Yankee table.

There had been talk in the Mess about 'trundling down to Riyadh, bombing up and heading straight off to Basra'; that sort of talk had been quashed early on. No, *The Angry Widow* was to take onboard thirty-eight thousand pounders – twenty-four high capacity blast bombs and fourteen of the medium capacity general purpose variety which could be set to explode anywhere between 0.25 seconds after impact to forty-eight hours later – and stroll back up to Akrotiri.

Operating from Riyadh sounded all right the first time a fellow said it, and in the future circumstances might mandate it but presently, it was all a little bit too ad hoc for the brass in Cyprus.

In the near distance the first long, low train of bombs dragged behind a small, khaki camouflaged tractor. From the other side of the air base two fuel bowsers slowly trundled, in loose formation, across the great expanse of shimmering concrete towards where *The Angry Widow* sizzled, sighed and creaked as her engines cooled from the trip down to Arabia, and her flight surfaces warmed in the blazing afternoon sunshine.

The Angry Widow's navigator/bomb aimer wiped the sweat off his brow and grunted disgustedly.

"I don't suppose there's anywhere around here where a chap can get a cup of tea, I suppose?"

Chapter 39

Commander Stephen Turnbull marched up the seaward companionway and stepped into what had, prior to the aircraft carrier's conversion to a heavy repair ship – basically, a floating dockyard – been the hangar deck.

HMS Triumph had been moored just far away from the Royal Fleet Auxiliary Ammunition Ship Retainer when that she blew up to avoid crippling damage. Although a number of shells and several tons of wreckage had fallen on her old flight deck, bridge, on the quayside and in the water all around her, mercifully none of the munitions had actually detonated. Although two men onboard had been killed by falling debris, less than a dozen members of her crew had suffered serious injuries and within hours of the disaster, Triumph would have been able to cast off and go to sea under her own steam.

The nearest of the two blackened, twisted parts of the Retainer lay half-sunken less than two hundred yards away, a section of her bow canted up at an outrageous angle. The operation to salvage unexploded munitions had begun within forty-eight hours and Triumph had become the clearing house for all 'fixed' rounds – that is rounds which incorporated their own 'fixed' propellant charge – and shells, recovered from the harbour and the surrounding land which had been made or declared safe by Royal Navy clearance teams or the Royal Engineer bomb disposal experts.

"What's it look like, Malcolm?" Anzac's captain inquired cheerfully of his gunnery officer. Thirty year old Malcolm Speedwell was clad in grubby dungarees, sensible attire given that from the moment the destroyer had come alongside Triumph three hours ago after her high speed run back from the Straits of Hormuz he had been clambering over the ordnance stacked on the hangar deck floor.

Speedwell was a lean man with a distance runner's physique. A reservist he had been teaching in a Melbourne school until six months ago before joining Anzac ahead of her re-commissioning trials.

The younger man pushed back his cap.

"I wouldn't like to load any of this," he struggled for the word, "*stuff* into *my* guns until we've got all the rust and muck off them, sir," he confessed, gesturing at pallets loaded with extraordinarily filthy, oxide streaked 4.5-inch fixed semi-armour piercing and high explosive reloads. A large number of the rounds bore chalk marks, mostly 'ticks' but here and there one displayed a 'cross'.

"I'm surprised there are so many left," Turnbull chuckled. The Tobruk and a couple of Royal Navy ships had come in to Tarout Bay to top up their main battery magazines in the last week or so; he had been a little afraid the shelf would be bare by the time Anzac arrived.

"Tobruk must have taken the best *stuff*," the other man

complained, but his heart not really in it.

"We'll take all the HE we can get out hands on, Malcolm," the older man declared. "Unload some of our SAP reloads if you have to. I don't think we're likely to get stuck into a ship to ship knockabout in these waters."

"No, sir."

Turnbull noted the smaller cache of rusty 6-inch fixed rounds for HMS Tiger's main battery. The cruiser's advanced quick firing automatic guns could theoretically shoot twenty rounds a minute, but not *those* rounds. The slightest imperfection in the confirmation of a reload would result in a jam, and a potentially catastrophic turret breakdown which might take minutes or even hours to put right. In the heat of battle that might be fatal.

Anzac's two twin 4.5-inch turrets were old-fashioned, crew handled mounts. Assuming the salvaged reloads did not foul up the magazine hoists too badly the gun crews could be relied upon to sort out any problem manually.

HMNZS Royalist, the ABNZ Squadron's other cruiser had brought all her own main battery reloads from New Zealand. Well, every single 5.25-inch HE reload and anti-aircraft proximity fuse her crew had discovered rifling through the naval ordnance depots in Auckland and Wellington in the days before she sailed for the Gulf.

"A transport came up from Aden while we were at sea, sir," Speedwell remembered belatedly, angry with himself for not reporting it earlier. "There's a pile of crates set aside for Anzac. Forty-millimetre ammo, sir. Some of the rounds had been in store down there in Aden for years. But it all looks in good condition. There are clips for the single barrels and loose rounds for the belt feeds on the twin mounts; probably more than enough to fill our ready lockers twice over."

"That's some good news at last!"

"Yes, sir."

Turnbull left his gunnery officer to get on with his work and went in search of Triumph's captain to pay his respects. For all that he had a well-earned reputation for being a decidedly 'awkward customer', Anzac's captain did not need reminding that the last man in the Persian Gulf he wanted to upset, in any way, shape or form, was the man who 'owned' practically every spare part for thousands of miles in every direction.

He headed up to the disused flight deck, now crammed with lifting derricks and workshops serviced by lumpy tractors amidst a horribly un-naval tangle of pipes and power cables. He had just entered the island bridge on the starboard side of the ship when he heard the ululating wail of air raid sirens.

The banshee wailing began far away and swept closer like a wave piling up on a beach before breaking.

Onboard Triumph the ship's klaxons sounded.

Turnbull found former carrier's captain on the port bridge wing, binoculars slung casually around his neck and a Sten gun in his meaty hands.

"I heard you were sniffing around the four point five inch stash," the other man chortled. "Never fear, we made sure we held enough back for chaps like you who know how to use it!"

"Very good of you, sir," Turnbull smiled. He looked curiously at the Sten gun.

"Yes, yes! I know we're all supposed to be cowering behind the nearest slab of armour plating," Triumph's captain admitted ruefully. "And I know you can't hit a barn door at a hundred paces with this bloody thing but blast it," he exclaimed, turning irascible as he hefted the Sten gun, "if one of the bastards comes close enough I bloody well intend to let him have it!"

Chapter 40

Wednesday 1st July 1964
RAF Abadan, Iran

"We could have all have been killed!"

The man who had voiced this somewhat hysterical complaint was the fellow the BBC had given the title of 'producer/director', and theoretically the man who had been placed in charge of Frank Waters little band of intrepid 'broadcasters'. The chap's name was 'Brian' – Brian Harris - and he was about Waters's own age, although clearly of a much more nervous disposition. When they were introduced 'Brian' had mentioned he was 'with Monty' in the desert; presumably hiding under the old rascal's caravan most of the time if today's performance was anything to go by!

"Well," the former SAS man grinned, "there is a war going on, old man."

The other members of 'the crew' – cameraman Michael, sound engineer Ken and boyish general factotum Robin - were of that twenty to thirty year old generation who had grown up in the Second War, done their National Service in peace time – if they were very unlucky in Korea or Malaysia – and settled into nice safe, cushy jobs at the BBC in the years before the fiasco of October 1962. At some level they had accepted that they were in a 'war zone'; in another they clearly did not think the 'war' part of the 'war zone' had anything to do with them.

"A bloody Russian tank almost rolled over us!" Brian protested angrily, his voice breaking with angst.

"Well," Frank Waters shrugged, trying to be diplomatic. One had to make the effort with these civilian types. "It *might* have if it hadn't been blown to bits by the anti-tank boys we were with at the time."

"That's the last fucking time we let you drive the fucking truck!" This from the white lipped 'sound man' Ken.

The old soldier was beginning to get a little vexed by the attitude of his companions. Constructive criticism and a bit of live and let live joie de vivre was one thing; but it was not as if he had allowed himself to be press ganged into the BBC to be at these blighters' beck and call. In fact, had not the Prime Minister more or less personally begged him to do the decent thing and help out the Ministry of Information in this time of national crisis, he would have dug his heels in and stayed put in England.

Or perhaps not...

Actually he did not know what he would have done. He was putty in *that* woman's hands and he had not had the heart, or the least inclination to refuse her anything; what with one thing and another how could a man refuse anything to a woman who had him drooling from *both* sides of this mouth?

In picturing her face he was momentarily so transported to another, dream world that he completely forgot he was sitting in a dusty, fly-blown tent with four jumped up little Bolsheviks who were under the impression he worked *for them.*

"Frank," Brian demanded, "are you listening to us?"

"Er," Margaret Thatcher's perfect countenance cruelly dissolved from his mind's eye and he came back down to earth with a jolt. "Why, were you saying something?"

"We can't go on this way, Frank!"

That was usually a woman's line? Wasn't it?

Brian Harris seemed to get a grip of his emotions.

"You three buzz off, *the Colonel* and I need to have a chat."

The other Bolsheviks sloped off into the evening, muttering mutinously.

Frank Waters sighed. Things had come to a head when he had wanted to stand up and talk to the camera as the first T-62 had hooved into view in the distance. The bloody thing had still been miles – well, a few hundred yards away – at the time and he was only trying to be helpful.

"You might be a gold-plated bloody hero, Frank," Brian Harris explained, badly wanting to scream in his *presenter's* face. "But the rest of us are mere mortals and we plan on being *living* mere mortals when this thing is over and done with. You might have a death wish but *we* don't!"

Frank Waters scowled.

I don't have a death wish!

I wouldn't have lasted this long if I had a bally death wish!

"That's uncalled for," he objected sulkily. Besides, getting killed would rather mess up his plans to – hopefully, yearningly – renew acquaintance with the astonishing woman whose smile, like Helen of Troy's had so many others in olden times, launched him on this latest odyssey.

"Is it?" Brian retorted angrily. "We're here to tell the people back home what is going on. How the fuck are we supposed to do that if the first time we 'go into action' you get us all killed?"

That was a little unfair.

It was not as if he had actually *waved* at the nearest T-62...

"And don't even think about telling me we got a really good shot of 'the action' today. It is our job to get the best possible 'shots' of the action every day, not just the day we all get blown to bits! War correspondent! You're just a bloody mad man!"

In the distance there were two explosions; Red Army artillerymen zeroing in the ground, most likely while the 2nd Siberian Mechanised Army massed opposite Basra for the final assault. During the day the Soviets had mounted two separate armoured probes exploring the strength of the Iranian forward defensive positions north of Khorramshahr.

Major General al-Mamaleki's boys had held their nerve; that had been a pleasant surprise and one that boded well for the coming days. Michael Carver had introduced him to the Iranian tanker yesterday evening and had been a little put aback to discover that the two men already knew each other.

'I thought you were dead, Frank!'

The two old acquaintances had sized each other up for a moment. Of the two Mirza Hasan al-Mamaleki was wearing much the better, the same handsome, marvellously moustachioed, superbly kitted out soldierly man he had always been.

'Me too, old man,' he had chortled.

When Carver had told him that al-Mamaleki was his 'deputy on this front with full powers to act in my name and on my behalf', Frank Waters might, briefly, have been susceptible to being floored by a blow from a very small feather. Later he had wondered how the Australian officers he had chatted with in the Mess at the airfield felt about *things*, or if they even knew about it. High command was a notoriously murky thing, and all things considered he had decided it was best not to open up that particular can of worms.

"And about that gun you insist on carrying around with you everywhere?" Brian Harris was saying peevishly. "That's just not done. You work for the BBC now, we are neutral..."

"Steady on, old man," Frank Waters snapped. Some things were sacrosanct; personally, he had never been 'neutral' about anything in his whole life and he jolly well was not going to turn over new leaf now! The bloody man would be asking him not to carry the stiletto he kept strapped to the inside of his right calf next! "Dash it! It's only a small gun!"

The Walther PPK practically disappeared into his hand!

"BBC employees do not carry firearms!"

"This one bally well does!" And there it was; his old life and his new one in direct opposition.

Brian Harris groaned, made a visible effort to calm down.

"I was terrified this afternoon," he confessed. "We all were. You were enjoying yourself."

"Yes." Frank Waters confessed.

Brian took a long, ragged breath.

"Okay, let's start again. You haven't a clue what I'm upset about, have you?"

Frank Waters shrugged, much in the fashion of a naughty schoolboy.

"You fellows did seem a tad rattled when we were out there in the desert," the old soldier conceded. He was not an unreasonable man, just a born awkward case. "Look," he continued, "I'd much rather we were all chums in this but it simply won't work unless we're all on the same wavelength. I came out here to report from the battlefield, not from some communications trench miles away from the front line."

A silence settled between the two men, albeit a silence broken by the faraway crump of sporadic explosions and the frequent deafening roaring of jet aircraft taking off nearby.

"Perhaps," Brian suggested eventually, "we should try a different approach tomorrow?"

"I'm all ears."

"How about if you and I make a private pact that in front of the others you are the boss?"

That sounded good to the former SAS man.

Far too good to be true, nevertheless he went on listening.

"And in return," Brian went on, "you promise to look after the rest of us and to do your level best to make sure none of us gets killed or injured?"

Frank Waters thought about it for some moments before sticking out his right hand. Solemnly, the two men shook on the compact.

Chapter 41

The dysentery which had plagued Marshal of the Soviet Union Hamazasp Khachaturi Babadzhanian had laid him low again for most of the last twenty-four hours. His uniform now hung off his wasted frame like his oversized cadet kit had on the day he had, as a skinny nineteen year old, entered the Alexander Miasnikyan Unified Military School in Yerevan, Armenia at the beginning of his military career. His physical weakness was all-pervading, there was nothing he could do to stop his hands trembling and if he attempted to stand for more than a few minutes he became nauseas.

Neither Vladimir Andreyevich Puchkov nor Konstantin Yakovlevich Kurochnik betrayed any sign of having noticed the Army Group Commander's debilitation.

"Relax, relax," Babadzhanian muttered.

His two most trusted field commanders stood easy, waiting patiently, silently.

"I'll keep this short and sweet," Babadzhanian declared hoarsely, his throat feeling like it was coated with sand, his lungs burning with every breath he took. "Operations on the western side of the Shatt al-Arab have moved from an offensive to a consolidation phase. The movement of forces south of Basra into defensive emplacements and the build-up of armour and materiel ahead of a resumption of the drive south into Kuwait is beginning..."

It took him several moments to recover his breath.

"You are wasted in the Faw Peninsula sector," he said to Puchkov. "Your division will remain where it is. It can refit and integrate replacements around Umm Qasr but I have other work for you."

The hard-charging commander of the 10th Guards Tank Division flashed a predatory smile.

"I want you in charge of the 19th Guards Tank Corps," Babadzhanian told him. "Kurochnik will bring you up to speed."

Puchkov's smile faded.

In approximately thirty hours 19th Guards Tank Corps, bulked up with two thirds of 2nd Siberian Mechanised Army's armour was due to hurl itself at the – supposedly flimsy – Iranian Army lines north of Khorramshahr, ahead of taking on the – probably - more robust British defences at Abadan beyond the formidable water barrier of the Karun River.

"Your predecessor," Babadzhanian explained, "wanted to delay until all 2nd Siberians' armour caught up with Kurochnik's boys. We don't have time to hang around. Whatever we do we must not allow *our enemies* any opportunity to regroup until *all* the objectives of Operation Nakazyvat have been secured."

Konstantin Yakovlevich Kurochnik tried very hard not to frown.

There were all sorts of outlandish rumours going around as to what was going on back home. There had been some kind of major upheaval in Chelyabinsk; half the Politburo had been replaced, Marshal of the Soviet Union Vasily Ivanovich Chuikov was gone, his place taken by Admiral of the Fleet Gorshkov. There was even loose talk that there had been some kind of disaster, possibly an explosion at the Kursk bunker. The only thing he knew for certain was that Yuri Vladimirovich Andropov, First Deputy Secretary of the KGB had been, or was about to be installed as the Commissar General of the new Soviet Republic of Iraq.

Kurochnik was under no illusion that when Babadzhanian spoke of 'enemies' he was looking over his shoulder, rather than to his front at the weak Iranian and British forces which 2nd Siberian Mechanised Army was about to crush beneath the tracks of its massed T-62s.

However, this was not to say that Kurochnik was over-confident or in any way complacent about the coming battle. His experiences in the early stages of the campaign back in Iranian Azerbaijan had reminded him, not that he had needed reminding, that Operation Nakazyvat had been mounted and conducted on the basis of 'intelligence' that did a disservice to the description 'shit useless'.

If the Iraqi Army had put up any kind of fight or if the British Royal Air Force had continued wrecking roads, knocking down bridges, and turning towns along the southern lines of advance into rubble, Operation Nakazyvat would probably have stalled just south of Baghdad. Granted, no plan survived first contact with the enemy but the invasion of Iran and Iraq had been prosecuted on a wing and a prayer. It was an absolute miracle that things had turned out so well.

This was the problem, of course.

That day when he had been standing on the roof of the City Governor's house in Urmia after his paratroopers had taken the city with negligible casualties, he had been asking himself exactly the same questions he was asking himself now. South of Baghdad the Red Army had motored towards the Persian Gulf as if it was conducting summer manoeuvres in the Ukraine.

So why do I have a nagging suspicion that I am about to put my hand into a meat grinder?

Until he had walked into the room and seen for himself that Comrade Marshall Hamazasp Khachaturi was as ill as worried staffers – all loyal men who had been with him, in some cases since Budapest in 1956 – had claimed, Kurochnik had been planning to voice his mounting concerns about the veracity of the 'big intelligence picture'.

He had also meant to raise his worries about whether a 'bridging plan' that involved two battalions of combat engineers towing a hundred and fifty pontoons down the Arvand River from Basra – assuming bombing did not destroy the pontoons in the meantime – could be guaranteed to throw two bridges capable of carrying T-62s and T-54s across the Karun River when the time came. Over-running Khorramshahr was one thing, bridging the Karun River and sustaining operations south of it was another altogether. He was an airborne commander; heavy duty combat engineering and the prospect of handling large armoured formations in the heat of what was likely to be the most serious fight of the whole campaign was alien to him.

However, looking at Marshal Babadzhanian he felt guilty for even considering worrying the great man with his own pathetic worries.

"The bastards won't know what's hit them, sir!" Puchkov promised grimly.

Kurochnik's last doubt died.

"We'll roll straight over the bastards!" He agreed grimly.

Babadzhanian rallied briefly, forcing a deathly, ashen grimace.

Chapter 42

Thursday 2nd July 1964
Prime Minister's Rooms, Hertford College, Oxford

Sir Thomas Harding-Grayson had watched the storm clouds gathering, and braced himself for the flood that would almost certainly sweep the Unity Administration of the United Kingdom to perdition. In hindsight he was very much afraid that his plotting and scheming around the fringes of the unfolding disaster might, when one day it came to light as it surely would, damn him to a particularly dark place in the purgatory into which future generations of historians would surely assign most of Margaret Thatcher's ministers.

Oddly, his conscience was clear.

It had been necessary to hamstring Egypt; otherwise Nasser would have sought to take advantage of the inevitable catastrophe unfolding in the Persian Gulf; that in turn would have led to a never-ending war with Israel and probability, rather than possibility that other Arab countries, fomented by and to the long term profit of the victorious Soviet Union would be sucked in. At least he had succeeded in limiting, for now, the damage always providing the United States came to its senses in time to deter, or to physically obstruct Soviet ambitions to conquer the Arabian Peninsula.

Confronted by so many ifs and buts, by so many unquantifiable clauses and caveats, possibilities and disasters, one could only do so much. He ought to have recommended that British and Commonwealth forces be withdrawn before this final, inevitably bloody denouement; but Margaret Thatcher would never have stood for that.

She had drawn her line in the sand and that, was that!

Had she taken any other stance the resolve of the Chiefs of Staff might have crumbled and the UAUK would have fallen anyway. Geopolitical grand strategy had ever been thus; the ineluctable product of impossible choices and a raft of decisions made under impossible circumstances.

History was after all, in most ages the autobiography of a madman. That was the only lesson of history.

"Margaret," the Foreign Secretary said, trying not to plead. "Much as we all hope that things turn out for the best in the Gulf we must prepare for other," he shrugged apologetically, 'eventualities.'

Tom Harding-Grayson had got into a lot of trouble playing Devil's Advocate before the October War, and he expected to be in even deeper water soon. Nevertheless, he stuck to his guns.

"We have done our best. We have stood by our 'friends' in the Middle East. We have tried to do what we can. The crisis has immeasurably strengthened our ties with Australia and New Zealand and the rest of the 'white' Commonwealth but now we are looking down the barrel, as it were. I hope and pray that things do not turn out as badly as they might; but how long will our strengthened ties to our Commonwealth allies survive if there is a massacre..."

The Prime Minister gave her friend a sympathetic, quizzical look as she raised her tea cup to her lips. With the moment of decision drawing very close she had discovered a new serenity. Knowing that there was little to do except wait for the latest news, good, bad or disastrous and that there was absolutely nothing more that could be done to influence the outcome of the forthcoming trial by fire was perversely...*comforting*.

It fell to Willie Whitelaw, the gaunt-faced Defence Minister - who looked at his wit's end - to remind the Foreign Secretary that the die was cast.

"Whatever happens," he sighed, "there will always be *politics* on the other side, Tom." There spoke the old soldier who had fought from Normandy to North West Germany with the 6th Guards Tank Brigade in 1944 and 1945, who had seen too many friends and comrades killed before his eyes in those days to have any illusions about the coming battle.

The Prime Minister put down her cup and saucer.

The trio were sitting around a table in the pool of late afternoon sunshine streaming in through the old, leaded windows which overlooked the ivy-festooned Old Quad. At this time of the evening Cabinet and Private Office staffers mingled on the lawn of the Old Quad, chatting, enjoying cigarettes, standing or sitting in small, confidential groups taking advantage of the Prime Minister's recent edict relaxing the Draconian 'security regime' within the walls of Hertford College. The College was surrounded by a veritable ring of steel and her AWP – her faithful Royal Marines informally styled themselves *Angry Widow's Praetorians* - patrolled the corridors. The ad hoc 'body guarding arrangements' of the early part of Margaret Thatcher's premiership were a memory and she had mandated a more pragmatic approach, at least within this sanctuary. Down on the lawn lovers would be flirting, old friends complaining about their minister's foibles, exchanging gossip, behaving like normal people ought to behave in a 'normal' World.

"I wish," she remarked, lost for a moment in her thoughts, "that I still *believed*. If I still *believed* I would pray for our safe deliverance."

Tom Harding-Grayson was suddenly aware that his friend's mesmeric steely blue gaze had settled on his face.

"I feel sometimes as if the situation with the Americans is my fault, Tom."

"No, no, no," Willie Whitelaw objected instantly.

The woman raised a hand.

"I ask myself what Winston Churchill would have done in my place," she explained. "Franklin Roosevelt was an isolationist President of a Depression-wracked isolationist nation. He was the original 'America First' man of the twentieth century; whereas, Jack Kennedy was, and probably still is in his heart, an internationalist, a man who has travelled the globe, a decorated war hero who studied at Oxford, who spent many of his formative years here in England when his father was Ambassador to London. Unlike FDR, Jack Kennedy actually *likes* us. And yet he and I have been unable to build any kind of 'special relationship', let alone a war-winning coalition of the kind Roosevelt and Churchill built in the 1940s."

The Foreign Secretary roused himself.

"Winston Churchill was half-American, Margaret. He was in his sixties by the time he became Prime Minister. The man had had a lifetime in politics and government, he was a bestselling international author, perhaps the most famous and well-known Englishman in Christendom by the time he and Roosevelt started talking Realpolitik in 1940. You must not be hard on yourself. You began from a standing start; Winston Churchill had had a forty-year run up, forty long years at the top table before he faced his great test."

In response Margaret Thatcher quirked an unhappy smile: "He was a great man. The greatest man of our century," she retorted sadly.

There was a knock at the door.

A woman in a faded twin set entered and delivered a folded note to the Prime Minister.

Margaret Thatcher read silently.

"The Argentine Forces of occupation on East Falkland have just released photographs of the execution of ten civilian hostages in front of Government House in Port Stanley," she said dully.

When she looked up there was tempered steel in her eyes.

Chapter 43

Thursday 2nd July 1964
HMAS Anzac, 35 miles east of Bandar Bushehr, Persian Gulf

The Battle class destroyer was closed up at Air Defence Station One as astern the ships of the gun line slowly disappeared into the gathering dusk. The battle plan for Operation Cold Harbour had been torn up around noon upon the receipt of the latest intelligence from Abadan and England.

Something had happened and HMS Centaur's Westland Wessex helicopters had fetched the captains of every ship in the Umm Qasr and Shatt al-Arab gun lines to a hastily called conference. The old carrier and her escorts, HMNZ Otago, and the anti-submarine frigates Palliser and Hardy had been loitering forty miles astern of the 'gunboats', from where her Sea Vixens and Scimitar interceptors could screen their advance north.

Rear Admiral Davey had greeted his captains in the carrier's wardroom with no little bonhomie but wasted no time getting down to business.

'Within the next twenty-four hours the enemy *will* assault the *Allied* defences north of Khorramshahr.'

Commander Stephen Turnbull had asked himself how Davey could possibly know *that* for certain; while not for a minute doubting that he was utterly *certain* of it. Ever since Anzac had arrived in the Gulf he had been struck by the confidence of not just Nick Davey, but by the C-in-C, General Carver, and the commander of Australian Ground Forces, Tom Daly, in the 'intelligence picture'; today the Fleet Commander had not been just 'confident', he had been *convinced*.

'This and other *factors* mean that the focus of Operation Cold Harbour will be to provide the closest possible fire support for Allied land and air forces in the Abadan Sector.' He had grinned broadly. 'The RAF has undertaken to *deal* with the Russians in and around Umm Qasr, while we busy ourselves with the work that needs to be accomplished in the Shatt al-Arab.'

The gun line was to be led by Anzac.

'To my mind,' Nick Davey had explained to his band of brothers, 'when in years to come good men talk of our deeds the name *Anzac* should be the first on their lips. Tonight we fight as men of the Commonwealth dedicated to the rightness of our cause. *Anzac* will blaze the trail!'

At that moment there had, very briefly, been a suggestion of a tear in Stephen Turnbull's eye.

'Second in line will be Diamond,' Davey had continued, nodding acknowledgement to the captain of the newly arrived Daring class fleet destroyer. 'The flagship will follow close astern of Diamond; and after Tiger, the Tobruk, with Royalist bringing up the rear.' These latter two ships had been slated to bombard Umm Qasr until the change of plan.

'The minesweepers Tariton and Stubbington will hang back two miles behind Royalist. In the event any of the ships in the gun line are sunk or have to be abandoned, Tariton and Stubbington will *sweep up* survivors who are *washed* down river.'

Davey had given the youthful lieutenants commanding the two small Ton class minesweepers a meaningful look and added: 'I don't want either of you fellows getting ideas above your station and attempting to engage the enemy with your pop guns!'

Both men had been crestfallen to receive this injunction.

'Gentlemen,' Nick Davey had announced soberly, 'Anzac will lead us across the bar of the Shatt al-Arab at twenty-two hundred hours tonight. Captains may independently engage any target of opportunity on the Iraq side of the Arvand River in the event the gun line is fired upon. Please be mindful that the main battle will be nearer Basra than the Gulf shore; so keep your powder dry for as long as possible.'

There were *housekeeping* and *operational* contingencies to spell out.

'Once battle is joined if a ship ahead is disabled or unable to manoeuvre the following ship should pass it to port. That is, between the enemy and the stricken ship. In some quarters this is called the Aboukir manoeuvre in honour of Admiral Lord Nelson at the Battle of the Nile,' Nick Davey had quipped jovially. 'I think in later years we will as likely refer to it as the Christopher manoeuvre; in honour of my old friend's scallywag son Peter!'

The band of brothers laughed together as if they were one man.

'No ship may stop to give aid to another during the battle,' the Squadron Commander ordered, somewhat quietening the mirth. 'Once abreast of Abadan captains will slave main battery fire control to the artillery directors on Abadan Island, or manually comply with all requests for fire support from ashore irrespective of the tactical situation on the Arvand River. The priority is to stop the Red Army in its tracks and give it the bloodiest possible nose; ships in the gun line may support each other at need but *not* at the expense of delaying or ignoring the main mission.'

Davey made no attempt to sweeten the pill.

'Captains are ordered to ground their ships and to continue the fight in the event they judge their commands are in danger of foundering.' He hesitated, as if worried he would choke on his next words. 'If things go badly it may be necessary to scuttle every ship in the gun line in the main channel to deny its use to the enemy.' He had moved on swiftly. 'Line of command. If I am incapacitated Squadron Command passes to Tiger.' He had glanced at the cruiser's captain, forty-six-year-old Hardress Llewellyn 'Harpy' Lloyd, a well-liked man had won a Distinguished Service Cross commanding MTB 34 in a fight with German E-Boats in the North Sea in August 1942. 'After Tiger, Anzac," Davey had nodded to Turnbull, 'then Royalist, then Diamond, then Tobruk.' He allowed himself a rueful chuckle as he fixed his gaze on the two boyish minesweeper captains.

'If either of you find yourselves in command I suggest you make best speed out to sea and get yourselves underneath Centaur's air umbrella sharpish, boys!'

The older men in the wardroom had chortled grimly.

Replaying the briefing in his head after his return to Anzac, Stephen Turnbull had been under no misapprehension that Operation Cold Harbour was anything other than a one way ticket to a very particular kind of Hell.

Chapter 44

Thursday 2nd July 1964
HMS Tiger, 35 miles east of Bandar Bushehr, Persian Gulf

Rear Admiral Nicholas Davey stared down into the gloom and watched, distractedly as 'A' turret swung slowly from port to starboard and back again. The cruiser had taken heavy seas over her bow in the South Atlantic during her passage to the Persian Gulf and the turret had suffered minor breakdowns and mechanical 'misalignments' ever since. Ideally, Tiger would have gone into dockyard hands for a few days to have the problems properly investigated. The turret crew was currently testing the latest 'fix'.

Davey and his Flag Captain, 'Harpy' Lloyd had remained onboard HMS Centaur that afternoon after the other commanders had been ferried back to their ships, joining the carrier's captain on deck to greet Rear Admiral William Bringle as he jumped down from the US Navy Sikorsky SH-3 Sea King.

Salutes were exchanged, hands shaken.

The Commanding Officer of Carrier Division Seven turned to the officer at his shoulder, who was carrying an attaché case in his left hand.

'This is Lieutenant-Commander Walter Brenckmann,' Bringle had said brusquely. 'He was a member of the reception party that time you came onboard Kitty Hawk, Admiral Davey.'

Nick Davey recognised the younger man. Flying in the face of protocol he stuck out his fleshy right hand in welcome.

'Yes, I recall you, Mr Brenckmann.'

"Mr Brenckmann is acting as my flag lieutenant at this time."

Davey let this go unremarked.

The welcoming committee and the two American officers went below and settled in chairs in the carrier's captain's day cabin.

'To what do we owe the pleasure of your unexpected visit, Admiral Bringle?' Davey had enquired solicitously. It was the US Navy had requested the 'urgent conference', not him.

Bringle had hesitated.

'I have received new orders to protect US industrial, mineral and shipping interests in the Persian Gulf and the authorisation to use lethal force if required. While I am expressly instructed to act independently of all other friendly or neutral forces in the region in my mission, I wish to avoid any inadvertent or accidental clashes between the ships and aircraft of our respective commands.'

'Very commendable, sir," Davey had declared, intrigued and a little bit bewildered by his counterpart's apparent change of tune; the last time they had spoken Bringle had wanted to keel haul him!

'To that end it is essential that ABNZ forces and Carrier Division Seven observe separation rules and,' the American had paused to measure his words, 'and adopt standard operating procedures including shared communication frequencies sufficient to avoid unfortunate *incidents.*'

Several hours later Nick Davey was still trying to unpick Bringle's meanings; reading and re-reading between the lines of their brief, somewhat strangled conversation. Normally, he was the last man to waste time deconstructing such 'courtesy visits' and 'conferences' but there had been something dissonant in Bringle's eyes and all the time his elders and betters were talking; his 'flag lieutenant', Brenckmann, had clearly had no idea what he was doing witnessing the meeting.

'It is important that our ships do not get *mixed up* with each other,' Bringle had said. The American had been circuitous, ambiguous, and reluctant to say anything definitive about *anything*. It was as if he had flown across to the Centaur for the sake of 'flying across'. *To be seen to have flown across to the Centaur.* But nothing had actually been said, agreed or negotiated which could not have been communicated and signed off in a two minute chat over the scrambled TBS system. And then there was the presence of a *witness*. Davey was glad he had called in Harpy Lloyd, to 'even up the odds'.

Tiger's Captain had thought the whole episode was odd too.

At the end, just as Bringle and his flag lieutenant were rising from their chairs to leave, Nick Davey had asked his counterpart a direct question.

'What's all this about, Bringle?'

Bringle had looked him in the eye, thought better of it and flicked his focus over Davey's right shoulder.

'I'm just making sure we are playing from the same old NATO playbook, Admiral Davey. Carrier Division Seven's mission is to keep the peace. *And that is what it will do...*'

The Commander of the ABNZ Persian Gulf Squadron became aware of a presence at his right shoulder.

"Will you join me for a stroll, sir?" Inquired Captain Lloyd, the cruiser's commanding officer.

The two men left the bridge and went to the lee rail, amidships. They stared into the night awhile.

"This is a rum business," Harpy Lloyd observed quietly.

"Yes," Davey agreed with a sigh. "I keep thinking about the way the Yanks let us down at Malta. That," he added, "and how my old friend Julian Christopher must have felt when he realised he'd been stabbed in the back."

Tiger's Captain ruminated unhurriedly.

The seconds passed slowly.

"At Malta we were looking to the US Navy to stop somebody creeping up on us while our back was turned, figuratively speaking," Harpy Lloyd offered. "Here, well, we're not actually counting on their help. We know we're on our own. The Americans have been honest enough about that."

"Um..."

"I don't like Admiral Bringle keeping station with Centaur either," the cruiser's commanding officer admitted. "I know sea room is in short supply in these waters, but twenty miles is nothing, less than two minutes flying time for most of the aircraft on the Kitty Hawk. Centaur's radar suite is so old if somebody on one of those new-fangled Hawkeye planes hits the wrong switch she'll be completely in the dark. And we're going to need every one of Centaur's Sea Vixens and Scimitars to keep the Red Air Force off us in the next day or two."

However, that was not what was gnawing at Nick Davey's soul.

"Why on earth would you want to operate the biggest and the most powerful aircraft carrier in the World right on top of one of the oldest and smallest, Harpy?"

"To make some kind of point?"

"No, surely there are better ways of doing that?"

The cruiser's Captain turned and looked aft down the length of his ship in the darkness.

"Perhaps, they just feel a little left out of things, sir," he suggested dryly.

Nick Davey chortled.

"Perhaps," he countered, "I'm thinking too hard about all this. You're right. We know the Yanks aren't going to ride to our rescue like the Seventh Cavalry! I'm sure they'll keep out of our way when the real fighting starts."

Chapter 45

Squadron Leader Guy French had been more than a little surprised, and mightily impressed by the apparent 'completeness' of the 'targeting information' and the 'comprehensive picture of the general air defence environment' in and around the southern Iraqi port of Umm Qasr.

'Umm Qasr stands on the part-canalised Khawr az-Zubayr section of the Khawr Abd Allah estuary leading to the Persian Gulf. The port itself, which is planned to be Iraq's deep-water gateway to the World is as yet uncompleted, work having only started in 1961, after the Iraqi government made the strategic decision to disregard the objections of the local shipping moguls in Basra and to go ahead with the port project. Before the October War the Iraqis were building a major road down the western side of the Faw Peninsula, effectively bypassing Basra to connect the planned port with the rest of the country. That road, albeit not yet completed, was of inestimable value to elements of the 10th Guards Tank Division and miscellaneous brigades of the 3rd Byelorussian Mechanized Division, the 7th Guards Tank Division and the 15th and 22nd Mechanized Infantry Divisions, all of which are occupying hurriedly thrown up defensive positions in and around Umm Qasr. The majority of these formations are currently refitting, presumably to enable them to resume the advance south into the Arabian Peninsula in due course. Meanwhile the 14th Ukrainian Combat Engineer Regiment is in the process of deploying in the port area to activate the existing limited deep water port facilities and to supervise the building of an emergency air base in the desert fifteen miles north of the Kuwaiti border. It is likely that several thousand slave workers, organised in so-called penal battalions followed the forward units of the 3rd Caucasian Tank Army into the Faw Peninsula in the last week.'

Umm Qasr had just been a small fishing village as recently as 1958, separated from Kuwait by a narrow inlet. The Allies had built temporary docks and unloading wharfs during the Second World War, ironically, to send war supplies north by road to the Soviet Union. Alexander the Great was supposed to have set foot in Mesopotamia for the first time at Umm Qasr in 325 BC; until the twentieth century its only real claim to fame.

The Iraqi Navy had established a base at the port in the late fifties and by 1961 a consortium of West German, Swedish and Lebanese companies had been granted the concession to develop the port and to connect Umm Qasr to the north with a new railways line.

No. 100 Squadron's Victors had been sitting idle since their 'jaunt' down to Riyadh to load up with unwanted American bombs. They had flown back to Akrotiri with unfused, relatively 'safe' cargoes; although landing with twenty tons of ordnance in one's bomb bay was always an 'interesting' evolution. Squadron armourers had ensured that all five Akrotiri Victors were 'ready to go' within eighteen hours of their return to Cyprus, and the V-Bombers' crews had been at QRA – Quick Reaction Alert – status ever since, living in tents and shed-like 'chalets' close to the runway, enjoying the sunshine, catching up on their reading, playing cards, smoking and drinking endless mugs of tea and coffee, aching for the word to 'GO!'.

The Angry Widow, Guy French's kite was a Mark B.2 with upgraded engines, avionics and electronics which could be 'fired up' by the pressing of a single button. The ninety ton bomber could be rolling within as little as two minutes of the balloon going up.

The Chelyabinsk operation had turned out to be Guy French's last trip in the second, right-hand seat of *The Angry Widow*. The Squadron CO had not returned from the operation and *his* pilot had stepped into his shoes, handing the baton, so to speak, to Guy.

Although it was not as if it was a new experience, he had been his aircraft's captain on the night of the October War and countless times since flying Comet jetliners for Transport Command; to be the man in the left-hand seat of a V-Bomber, in charge again was a little strange. Coming to Cyprus had been a huge adventure, now it was suddenly as deadly serious as it should have been to him long before the Chelyabinsk operation.

Each aircraft had its own target and every aircraft was carrying a mixed bomb load of medium capacity 'eggs' including several with fuses set to detonate minutes and hours after impact, high capacity blast bombs and at least half-a-dozen anti-personnel mines each designed to distribute scores of smaller 'bomblets', cluster bombs to saturate the target area with lethal shrapnel.

No. 100 Squadron's Victors were scheduled to bomb within a five minute window shortly after fighter bombers, RAF Hawker Hunters and a handful of Royal Fleet Air Arm De Havilland Sea Vixens based on Saudi Arabian territory within fifteen minutes flying time of Umm Qasr 'suppressed' the 'local air defences'. Two Dhahran-based Avro Vulcan V-Bombers, initially acting in an electronic warfare role, would subsequently drop cargoes of cluster bombs and delayed action one-thousand pound general purpose bombs into the carnage caused by the Victors. In the event that there were any Red Air Force interceptors 'stooging' around over the Faw Peninsula two Gloster Meteor night fighters would loiter in the vicinity prior to and immediately after the bombing strikes.

The Angry Widow was tasked to obliterate a 'divisional holding area' located in the desert roughly equidistant between Umm Qasr and Safwan, a border village some fourteen miles east north east of the port. This 'holding area' within two to three miles of the Kuwaiti border was thought to be where elements of the 10th Guards Tank Division had halted to throw up defensive sand berms behind which to laager, rest, refit and assimilate replacement equipment and men.

Tonight the route to the target crossed into Israeli and then

Jordanian air space for the first time. After the operation instead of turning for home and retracing their steps 100 Squadron's Victors were tasked to fly down to Riyadh, to refuel and take on another full bomb load before returning to Akrotiri via a 'transit' corridor authorised by the Egyptians over Sinai. Egypt, unlike the Israelis and the Jordanians had accommodated RAF over flights from the outset of the Soviet invasion of Iraqi territory; but in the wake of the coup – fighting had raged in the streets of Cairo for nearly a week – had become something of a sleeping partner in the war.

The Angry Widow waited at the runway threshold, a *beast* purring with latent power straining to rumble forward.

In the distance the CO's aircraft, *Waltzing Matilda* – the CO's mother was Australian – climbed into the eastern sky, her navigation lights winking distantly.

"Number Two," the controller's voice broke into Guy French's thoughts. "Report aircraft status please."

"All flight systems OK, control."

"You are clear to take off, Number Two. Repeat. You are clear to take off."

The throttles advanced, the *beast* trembled, leaning into her locked brakes.

"Brakes off!"

The Angry Widow smoothly, irresistibly surged forward into the night.

Chapter 46

Thursday 2nd July 1964
Field Headquarters of 4th Royal Tank Regiment, Abadan, Iran

Lieutenant General Michael Carver had read, and re-read Read Admiral Nicholas Davey's terse 'IMMEDIATE AND MOST SECRET' communication several times, initially not really knowing what to make of it. In fact, the first couple of times he had perused the flimsy message slip he had wondered if there had been some kind of blunder in the decryption process.

USS KITY HAWK TASK FORCE IS SHADOWING HMS
CENTAUR...

It had crossed Carver's mind that after the torpedoing of the USS Providence, Carrier Division Seven might be ordered to make some kind of knee jerk, retaliatory gesture; although what form that 'gesture' might take and against whom it might be directed had been less clear.

USN NOW ASSUMES PROVIDENCE ATTACKED BY RED NAVY
SSN...

The Kitty Hawk's aircraft had attacked and sunk a likely candidate with airborne launched homing torpedoes and the USS Permit, attached to the American fleet had supposedly 'driven off a second suspected hostile submarine'.

CARRIER DIVISION SEVEN IS OPERATING ON A WAR FOOTING
AND WILL AGGRESSIVELY ASSERT USN RIGHT TO SELF-
DEFENCE IN INTERNATIONAL WATERS BY ACTIVELY
ENGAGING ANY AIRCRAFT OR SHIP OR SUBMARINE WHICH
ENTERS ITS ENGAGEMENT ZONE OR THREATENS UNITED
STATES SERVICE PERSONNEL, CIVILIANS OR COMMERCIAL
AND INDUSTRIAL INTERESTS...

'Don't the Yanks own a slice of the refinery complex on Abadan Island, sir?" Carver's GSO1 queried, as energised and as surprised as his Chief by Davey's signal. "And if Admiral Bringle has actually gone out of his way to confer with Admiral Davey, does that mean the whole weight of Carrier Division Seven stands behind us?"

I AM UNHAPPY THAT CARRIER DIVISION SEVEN IS
SHADOWING CENTAUR BATTLE GROUP AND HAS ASSERTED
ITS OWNERSHIP OF MUCH OF THE AIR SPACE OF THE
NORTH WESTERN GULF...

"I don't know," the Commander-in-Chief of all British and Commonwealth Forces in the Middle East confessed. For a man like Nick Davey to admit that he was 'unhappy' about something was an unambiguous admission that he had no idea whatsoever what the Americans were playing at.

Given that at this very moment allied forces in the Middle East were irrevocably committed to a desperate last gasp, winner takes all battle plan be-devilled with countless critically dependent parts – the failure of any one of which might plunge the whole enterprise into confusion – the Americans could not have chosen a worse juncture to throw yet another imponderable into the mix.

"But," Carver added, "whatever it means, our, er, erstwhile allies obviously don't plan on sitting on their hands in the next few hours."

And why had Nick Davey made a point of saying that the Americans 'assume' the USS Providence was sunk by a Soviet submarine. Don't they 'know'?

Further discussion was rudely interrupted.

Both Carver and his GSO1 instinctively threw themselves to the dirt floor of the shallow desert bunker. All the old hands went to the ground like boxer's caught by a haymaking left hook, only the younger men, including several who had been in the Army many years and served in several colonial bush fire wars, failed to instantly hit the deck; presently, they all followed their C-in-C's lead momentarily.

A man got used to the rumble of distant artillery dropping shells onto somebody else's head. All the old Eighth Army sweats, and the men who had fought in Sicily, Italy, France and Germany in Hitler's war instantly recognised the subtle change in the 'background' noise.

Carver had yelled: "GET DOWN!" As he was hitting the ground, his battle-tuned ear noting the faraway whistle of the approaching barrage.

The first salvo fell long.

Mainly, he guessed in open ground near the bank of the River Arvand.

The next ten-round salvo fell closer to the headquarters; the ground flinched and heaved in pain, dust filled the air. Debris from the third salvo crashed onto the roof of the bunker.

Everybody was automatically pulling on their gas masks.

The Soviets had never signed up to the 'rules of war' that Great Britain, its European allies and the United States had taken for granted. The enemy had never recognised the need to treat prisoners decently, or differentiated between combatants and non-combatants, or accepted any distinction between chemical, biological and other weapons of war. Thus far in the Iran-Iraq invasion the Red Army and the Red Air Force had not employed chemical or biological weapons – at least not against British or Commonwealth troops - but that was no guarantee they would not start using them now.

There was no counter battery fire.

Everything depended on trapping large elements of 3rd Caucasian Tank Army in the Faw Peninsula, and sucking the main fighting strength of 2nd Siberian Mechanised Army into the prepared killing ground around Khorramshahr north of the Karun River. The Iranian and Commonwealth forces dug in waiting for the main assault had been virtually 'playing dead' for the last week, letting the enemy come on, and on. A couple of small scale sacrificial armoured 'demonstrations' near the Iran-Iraq border south of the Basra industrial area apart, Carver had done everything possible to convince the invaders that the road south to Abadan was barely defended and that the task force on Abadan Island was hunkering down, resigned to its fate and awaiting the end.

All aircraft had been evacuated from RAF Abadan in the last few days, and his tanks, guns and missiles were heavily camouflaged in ballast pits and revetments. Out in the desert to the east of Khorramshahr his Iranian ally, Hasan al-Mamaleki's armour was practically buried in the sands below the foothills of the Zagros Mountains. Meanwhile, pickets armed with recoilless anti-tank rifles sniped at the edges of the oncoming leviathan's flanks at long range, and hastily laid deliberately poorly concealed minefields to inconvenience the advancing T62s, otherwise the Red Army was moving steadily forward as if it was already planning its victory parade.

If the Soviets had had the patience to move – or the foresight to prioritise the movement of – 3rd Caucasian Tank Army's artillery south of Basra into the Faw Peninsula to command the Shatt al-Arab and to fire directly into the Abadan defences from across the Arvand River from the western bank, each and every aspect of Michael Carver's 'master plan' would have come to nought. As it was only light guns had been emplaced across the river thus far and 2nd Siberian Mechanised Army's heavy guns were being brought forward in stages on roads clogged by the narrowness of the front on which it was advancing.

There was a fourth, and a fifth salvo, each creeping back towards the Karun River; and then the shocked silence which followed every barrage hung in the dust and smoke fouled air. Above ground there was the sound of running feet, and engines firing up.

Michael Carver stiffly picked himself up off the floor.

There had been no gas alarm sounded so he pulled off his mask

He sniffed, looked around.

Either the Red Army was short of big guns or of ammunition, or of both. Whichever condition applied it probably meant that the massed armour of the army bearing down on Khorramshahr was also, most likely, short of fuel. The Soviets were not anticipating a long fight, or if they were, they were in no state to sustain it.

"Send to Admiral Davey," he prefaced. "IMMEDIATE AND MOST SECRET." He paused, composing his thoughts. "ALL PLANNED OPERATIONS ARE GO STOP REPEAT GO STOP GOOD LUCK AND DAMN THE TORPEDOES MESSAGE ENDS."

Chapter 47

Thursday 2nd July 1964
Foreign Ministry Annexe, Kuybyshev Prospekt, Sverdlovsk

Sixty-four year old Vasili Vasilyevich Kuznetsov, until forty-eight hours ago one of four First Deputy Foreign Ministers of the Union of Soviet Socialist Republics would have hesitated before *demanding* a face to face meeting with the two senior members of the newly reconstituted *Troika*.

Under the former 'collective leadership' arrangements his boss, Alexei Kosygin had overseen the post Cuban Missiles War Five-year Emergency War Plan and Foreign Policy – the latter something of an oxymoron in the present situation since the foreign policy of the Motherland had been until a few days ago to wage war in every practical way against the murderers of October 1962 – while Kuznetsov had 'managed' the Western European Department. In this role he had worked closely with First Secretary of the KGB Shelepin and his deputy, Yuri Andropov. In that capacity he had been instrumental in the initial post-war facilitation of Red Dawn 'actions' in the Mediterranean, France, and the United Kingdom; and in recent months, the dismantling of several those networks abroad and the purging of its senior officers at home. Throughout, he had proved himself to be pathologically loyal to the Party, ideologically 'sound' and demonstrably diligent in the discharge of his duties. Given his age, deep into his sixties, he was also relatively physically robust and able. However, since he had been inherited his old friend Alexei Kosygin's 'Foreign Ministry', he was beginning to wish that, like other surviving senior members of the pre-war Party elite who had never previously aspired to the highest offices, he too had been put out to pasture in a modest country dacha.

Kuznetsov would have been perfectly happy to see out his declining years as the governor of a collective farm, or the director of road repairs for some remote province far from the dangerous tensions of the capital. He was starting to feel as if an invisible deadly plague had blown through Sverdlovsk and everybody – except him – had contracted some kind of death wish.

Even if the Americans kept to their side of the bargain Alexei Kosygin and he had brokered with US Special Emissary Thompson in Chelyabinsk, a prospect which was so unlikely as to be utterly implausible in any sane universe; what was there to stop the British sending their V-Bombers back to the Motherland to finish General LeMay's unfinished business?

What profound lesson, for example, had the great men of the Politburo or the 'brilliant' men around Brezhnev, Shelepin and Gorshkov concluded from the post-Cuban Missiles *experience* that had convinced them that the British would meekly bow to 'the inevitable', and pack up their guns and go home in the Persian Gulf?

Had the brutal lessons of the Mediterranean campaign taught them nothing?

By seizing back Cyprus the British had not only outflanked Red Dawn in Turkey but re-installed their air force and their navy in the Eastern Mediterranean. The British had got close enough to Nasser in Egypt – the same Nasser a British Prime Minister had likened to Adolf Hitler and attempted to depose by force less than a decade ago – to completely destabilise the one significant military power in the Middle East for years to come. Had his superiors learned nothing from the Battle of Malta? Yes that had been a strategic diversion, not a coup de main; so what? Practically every naval asset and nine out of every ten irreplaceable soldiers, sailors and airmen thrown into that desperate 'master stroke' had been lost, including over two thousand elite airborne and Spetsnaz troopers and nearly a third of the airlift capability of the whole Red Air Force! As for the Red Navy; all that now survived 'west of Suez' were a few old submarines hiding in the Black Sea!

Even as he had been haggling over the 'essentials' of an Armistice with the Americans, that self-important imbecile Gorshkov had come within a whisker of scuppering the whole 'peace process'!

What had the man been thinking torpedoing a US warship in the Arabian Sea in the middle of the most sensitive diplomatic negotiations in the history of the Soviet Union?

What was going to happen back in Philadelphia when it became publicly known that all the President's men had, at the time of the sinking, *elected* not to worry about the tiny matter of sunken cruiser and the loss of over a hundred men of her crew?

Sometimes he honestly wondered if his superiors had the remotest idea what they were doing!

Did his masters have no concept of what was really going on?

The Kennedy Administration's had come to a historic determination that the guiding principle of American policy would be the avoidance of another global war. The axiomatic corollary to this was President Kennedy *needed* to sell the story that *he* had averted a new global catastrophe and safeguarded cheap Arabian oil for US industry and consumers. If blood had to be spilled then it was supposed to be British blood; and when that happened *he* had to be able to make the case that sooner or later, somebody had had to put a stop to the British government's seemingly insatiable post-imperial warmongering before *they* blew up the whole World!

Meanwhile, while the collective leadership had been engaged in the most sensitive and dangerous talks with the Americans since the Cuban Missiles War, the Red Navy had been pursuing its own 'torpedo-based foreign policy'!

It beggared credulity!

Perhaps Hitler had been right; the big lies were the best...

Both Leonid Ilyich Brezhnev and Alexander Nikolayevich Shelepin were looking at Kuznetsov with the thoughtful suspicion of men who had never imagined the day would come, when a faithful old Party apparatchik like him would stick his head above the parapet. Kuznetsov had never seen that day coming either; but then his interpretation of the telegrams and the reports pouring into the Foreign Office building on Lenin Avenue, was obviously at a complete divergence from everybody else's.

Brezhnev and Shelepin understood that most of the people around them were predominantly preoccupied with what the recent deaths of Kosygin and Chuikov signified for them personally. In this climate of uncertainty, mistrust and naked fear they intuitively mistrusted practically everything anybody said to them unless it specifically conformed to what they had already decided coincided with their own, personal best interests. This was therefore, the worst possible time to be asking inconvenient questions.

This was especially so because each 'leader' had had his own entourage of faithful retainers and ambitious younger 'Party climbers' to nourish and promote, none of whom were senior enough to have shared their masters' fate in the wrecked Kursk Bunker complex. Those men – and women – were presently preoccupied vying for advantage in the chaotic aftermath of the disaster, and formed a volatile caucus of discontent and a fertile medium upon which the regime's enemies might easy foment a future coup. The easiest way for one of the young 'pretenders' currently seeking rapid advancement into the role, job or position of a dead or seriously injured government or Party official was to show his or her ability to make problems 'go away'.

Or to denounce anybody who was obviously better qualified...

It was in this atmosphere that Kuznetsov was doing his best to ensure that the biggest, most intractable problem facing the Motherland did not 'go away'. In fact, right now he was brandishing it in the faces of the only two men in the Soviet Union who could condemn him to a penal battalion with a casual flick of the finger.

Vasili Vasilyevich Kuznetsov felt it to be his duty to become 'a problem' to the ruling Troika; because somebody had to speak out against the madness before it was too late.

Kuznetsov had always been Kosygin's man, anonymous with an unblemished record; one of those loyalists who had never questioned anything, who had blindly – right or wrong – faithfully followed every instruction from on high. The only other thing in his favour was that because he had always been Kosygin's man, he was never going to be a viable figurehead around whom the suddenly dispossessed 'cliques' might collect.

"Comrades," Kuznetsov prefaced apologetically. "Thank you for making time for this meeting." The second level, bare-walled room in the fallout shelter was coolly clammy. The building above it was being repopulated by Ministry 'refugees' from Chelyabinsk and had been empty until twenty-four hours ago, surplus to requirements. Chairs had been found from somewhere and the three men sat around a table nursing glasses of Vodka. Brezhnev was already on his second glass; Shelepin had sipped distrustfully at his drink, while Kuznetsov was wistfully eying the rest of the bottle.

He sighed.

"I have only recently become aware of the full details of our somewhat," he grimaced uncomfortably, "abbreviated recent contacts with the British and other events outside my former sphere of responsibility. You have done me the honour of appointing me to my current post," he hesitated, feeling the thin ice cracking under his feet, "and it is my duty to advise you to the best of my humble abilities, Comrades."

Shelepin and Brezhnev had agreed to this unscheduled 'conference' at this place because their staffs could not agree another suitable location at short notice. The decision to transfer the Politburo and the surviving administrative machinery of the Troika to Sverdlovsk the day after the attack on the Kursk Bunker, had risked paralysing key ministries for several days but Brezhnev and Shelepin, Andropov and others, including Admiral Gorshkov had deemed it necessary lest the attack on the Kursk Bunker was the prelude to an internal Party putsch. They were all men who had first come to prominence under Stalin, and Nikita Khrushchev had been no less conspiracy adverse than the 'man of steel'. The maxim was that it was better to see plots and coups where there were none; than to risk missing the real thing.

Everybody agreed that the British V-Bombers which flown through the Red Air Force's defences undetected and unopposed until moments before the bombs began to drop - with terrifying precision into the beating heart of the regime – could not have struck with such pin point precision without the help of traitorous elements in the highest levels of the government. There could be no other explanation for the disaster than that counter revolutionary elements in Chelyabinsk had been working in league with the enemy. There must were traitors in their midst and Shelepin's men were already conducting the first interrogations in the basements of KGB detention centres across the city.

At the very moment the Motherland needed to be most focussed on the business in hand in the Persian Gulf, the leadership and the whole Sverdlovsk-Chelyabinsk command zone was a chaos of house arrests, suspicions and denouncements.

"It is my understanding that Comrade Gorshkov is travelling to Iraq at this time?" Kuznetsov inquired rhetorically.

The other men nodded.

"I have no military insights," the Foreign Minister confessed, "on the situation on the ground or at sea, or in the air in the Middle East but forgive me," he swallowed dry-mouthed, "I feel that in recent days military considerations seem to have rather overtaken 'political' considerations."

Shelepin shook his head.

"Say what you mean to say Vasili Vasilyevich!" He demanded, his brow furrowing with impatience.

"Forgive me," the older man gulped. The First Director of the KGB had been the man to whom Nikita Khrushchev had entrusted the 'tidying up' of the entire security apparatus of the USSR in the late fifties; the man to whom the High Command had turned to make the embarrassing evidence about what had really happened in the Katyn Forest in 1940 'disappear'.

"It was my working assumption throughout my talks with Special Emissary Thompson that similar bilateral exchanges were going on in secret with the British. That in fact the two Imperialist aggressors were being, in effect played off against each other to our advantage."

The other men were looking at him with blank-eyed hostility.

"Comrades," he pleaded, knowing that like a mouse which had eventually found the courage to roar in the face of not one, but two hungry lions, he might be sealing his own fate, "this is madness."

"Madness?" Shelepin purred threateningly.

"Comrades, I am a good Party man. I am a patriot. I am an old man, my family is gone and I do not care what happens to me personally. I believe we have confused regaining control of the Krasnaya Zarya abomination with avenging ourselves on the West; and now we have confused achieving a quick victory in the Persian Gulf with the long term interests of the Motherland. A miniscule, tiny fraction of the resources we have frittered away in Iraq would have been much better invested in France to secure the Krasnaya Zarya regime in the south; a regime now possibly critically undermined by the destruction of its surviving fleet and the blockade of the Gulf of Lions by British submarines. Likewise, if we had allowed Krasnaya Zarya to run its course, the whole of the Balkans and northern Italy would now be in our hands; admittedly, under the stewardship of zealots but nevertheless fanatics nominally under *our* flag. As it is our territorial gains in the Eastern Mediterranean in the Aegean and Turkey remain outflanked and threatened by British naval power, and our hold over those now mostly wasted areas is tenuous at best. The tank divisions we have 'used up' seizing hundreds of square kilometres of useless desert and marshland south of Baghdad ought to have been employed to secure our hold on the Anatolian littoral, Comrades. Southern France ought to have been a bridgehead from which to intimidate Franco's Spain which would, inevitably have forced the British to devote resources they don't have to guarantee the security of the Channel coast of Northern France. Instead, we are fighting the British in the Persian Gulf for oilfields that we don't need. We already have the oil of the Caucasus and of Iraqi Kurdistan. Why are we bankrupting our military capabilities south of Baghdad? It is madness, Comrades!"

Leonid Brezhnev drained his glass and poured another measure of Vodka.

"We will build new tanks. We will train new soldiers," he grunted. "I know you are a good Party man, Vasili Vasilyevich. You may even be right in your analysis. Before the Cuban Missiles War we were surrounded by enemies but we were powerful, we could afford to play the long game, to 'spread ourselves thinly', as they say, in many places and still be strong in many, many other places. Testing the British in the Western Mediterranean was a gamble. It was Chuikov's idea. It was a mistake but we had no way to reinforce our French 'friends'. Sometimes, one must throw one's 'friends', particularly the fanatical ones, to the wolves. Besides, Krasnaya Zarya has served its purpose."

Brezhnev drained his latest glass and rose heavily to his feet.

"I do not think the British will bomb us 'back to the stone age'," he declared morosely. "There is no profit in that for them. This they know. Hopefully, they will bomb the Americans!"

Shelepin put down his half-empty glass and stood up.

"That's too much to hope for," he scoffed sourly.

He eyed Kuznetsov like a cat eying a vanquished competitor, with contemptuous dismissal.

"In days to come we shall remember who was true to the Party."

Kuznetsov had so much more he had to say yet when he opened his mouth but no words came forth.

Chapter 48

23:08 Hours
Thursday 2nd July 1964
Dulaim Province, Iraq

The two 617 Squadron Avro Vulcans had taken off from Dhahran-Dammam Air Base after dusk, climbed to thirty-four thousand feet over Sinai and 'loitered', awaiting orders. Ninety minutes after take-off they took turns topping off their tanks from a 214 Squadron Vickers Valiant. Both Vulcans – nicknamed by their crews *Just Jane* and *Rattle and Shake* were adorned with appropriately lascivious fuselage art – carried a single Yellow Sun free fall bomb fitted with a Red Snow W28 one megaton thermonuclear warhead.

The Red Snow devices had been supplied to the RAF pre-October War for fitting to the Blue Steel stand-off missile then under development in the United Kingdom. The warheads carried by the two 617 Squadron Vulcans were unmodified US Mk 28 hydrogen bombs engineered to marry up with the standard Yellow Sun chassis.

There had been brief debate about whether it was appropriate to employ 'American' weapons on this particularly 'British' mission; however since the only other option was to employ either the four hundred kiloton (tested) version of the Green Grass all-British bomb, or the (untested) one megaton version of the warhead which nobody knew for sure would actually *initiate*, matters of national pride and sovereign propriety had been set aside. In any event a four hundred kiloton warhead was *not* going to do the job; and a one megaton bomb that might or might not explode when one pulled the trigger was a 'nonstarter'. The decision had gone all the way back up the chain of command to Oxford, where the Chief of the Defence Staff had explained the situation to the Prime Minister and that lady had plumped for *Red Snow*.

The crew of Vulcan *Just Jane* had purloined the aircraft name and its *art*, a nubile young lady sitting astride a plummeting bomb, from the nose of a Lancaster bomber on which the pilot's uncle had flown thirty missions to Germany in 1944. When a man flew with 617 Squadron the legacy of the Dambusters; Guy Gibson, Leonard Cheshire and a host of other Bomber Command legends flew on one's shoulders like guardian angels.

Après moi le Deluge!
After me, the flood!

Dulaim Province stretched from Baghdad to the Syrian border in the northwest, and from the Jordanian border in the west to the Saudi border to the south west. Named for the tribes which had historically laid claim to much of the uninhabited, virtually uninhabitable Syrian Desert of Iraq it was fifty thousand square miles of – mostly – unpopulated wilderness. The further west one flew from Baghdad the fewer the settlements, beyond Al-Fallujah and Ramadi there was mile upon mile of...*nothing.*

In an ideal world the RAF would have much preferred to have dropped the Yellow Suns carried by *Just Jane* and *Rattle and Shake* somewhere out in the wilds where no human foot had stepped for decades. Unfortunately, 'not killing anybody' had never been an option; so the thing had become to kill as few people as possible. Whereas dropping the bombs far enough away from Baghdad, Ramadi and Fallujah to avoid killing tens of thousands of innocent civilians just about worked, according to the slide rule calculations of the physicists and ops types back at base; dropping the damnable things on *nothing* did not work. In the end two 'compromise' drop points had been established and in the last week both *Just Jane* and *Rattle and Shake* had flown three separate simulated missions against 'beacon delineated' target zones far out in the western deserts of the Arabian Peninsula, periodically harassed by 'friendly fighters' and 'locked up' by equally 'friendly' air defence radars.

The best intelligence was that to reach the assigned 'drop points' both Vulcans would have to fly at least fifty miles inside the engagement envelopes of the multiple S-75 surface-to-air missile batteries defending Baghdad.

The men flying *Just Jane* and *Rattle and Shake* that night knew they were not coming back; each man had written a last will and testament, and left a letter to their next of kin. Unusually in the post-October War RAF, of the ten men flying the mission, all but one actually had a next-of-kin to write to; four had surviving wives and children, another two sweethearts back in England, or parents or siblings still alive despite the predations of the twenty months since the October War.

No man complained about his lot.

The Red Army was about to consign the last hoorah of the British Empire to the dustbin of history and there was nothing to be done but to well... keep on fighting until one could not.

Just Jane and *Rattle and Shake* received the order 'EIGHTY EAST' at 22:08 hours.

Both aircraft acknowledged within seconds.

Just Jane and *Rattle and Shake* climbed to fifty-three thousand feet with their throttles wide open and headed north. Tonight fuel economy was not an operational factor. There would be a 214 Squadron Valiant tanker lurking just over the Saudi Arabian border on the way back but nobody believed either Vulcan would be topping off their tanks 'on the way back'.

Just Jane signalled she had crossed through the IP – the initial point of her bomb run – at 22:56 hours.

MOHNE.

Rattle and Shake signalled within ninety seconds.

EDER.

At their IPs each Vulcan nosed down into a shallow drive to attack at Mach 1.1, over seven hundred miles per hour. Their sonic booms preceded their coming by fifty miles, rumbling across the ground ten miles below.

At 23:09 *Just Jane* signalled in plain language.

GONER.

At 23:11 *Rattle and Shake* signalled, also in the plain.

GONER.

No further transmissions were received from either Vulcan...

Chapter 49

23:09 Hours
Thursday 2nd July 1964
USS Kitty Hawk, 38 miles south west of Kharg Island, Persian Gulf

Lieutenant-Commander Walter Brenckmann was on the bridge when the *incident* occurred. The plot indicated Hawkeye Zero-Three had been flying a standard reconnaissance pattern over southern Iran nearly two hundred nautical miles distant from the flagship. Then, without warning the airborne command and control, early warning spy plane had begun to orbit over the eastern foothills of the Zagros Mountains.

Flight operations had flashed an alert to the bridge. It was not a panic alert; more a 'be aware of a possible problem' sort of alarm. Shortly afterwards the CAG – Commander, Air Group - requested permission to vector two McDonnell F-4 Phantoms over Iranian airspace to support Hawkeye Zero-Three.

Then things had rapidly spiralled out of control.

"I have Hawkeye Zero-Three on the Command Circuit!"

"Put it on the bridge PA!" Walter had ordered, assuming the distant Hawkeye was broadcasting on the command circuit because it had an emergency. In that event everybody on the bridge needed to know immediately *exactly* what was going on.

Kitty Hawk was closed up at Air Defence Condition Two but *not* in an 'engagement posture', this being the case aircrew safety remained the number one priority of the OOD.

"This is Hawkeye Zero-Three requesting permission to talk to Captain Epes. Over."

Walter Brenckmann blinked into space.

'What?" He muttered under his breath. Gathering his wits he demanded a handset.

"This is the OOD. State your emergency, Hawkeye Zero-Three? Over!"

Walter had looked to the bridge plot.

Both F-4s had already gone supersonic in Iranian air space.

"Hawkeye Zero-Three. State your emergency. Over!"

The ether hissed, Walter turned, looking to the warrant officer manning the communications consul.

"The channel is good, sir!"

The speakers crackled.

"Hawkeye Zero-Three requests immediate verification of mission protocol Foxtrot Bravo. Repeat. Hawkeye Zero-Three requests verbal verification of mission protocol Foxtrot Alpha. Over!"

It was at that juncture that Captain Horace Epes strode onto the bridge.

"Captain on the bridge!"

"Take that off the speaker!" He ordered angrily as he strode across to Walter Brenckmann and held out his hand for the TBS microphone. With his free hand he held the headset the communication yeoman held out to his ear. "This is Captain Epes. Mission protocol Foxtrot-Bravo is LIVE. Repeat LIVE."

Walter was a little unnerved to realise that the commanding officer of the biggest warship in the World was trembling with what could only be rage. He was forcing out every word he said between clenched teeth.

"Acknowledge, Hawkeye Zero-Three."

Everything on the bridge had momentarily come to a halt.

Captain Epes had control of the 'Hawkeye Zero-Three' situation. Walter was the OOD and he needed to be looking where the ship was going; likewise, he needed everybody around him to keep their eyes on the ball.

"Hawkeye Zero-Three is aborting its mission!" Captain Epes reported. "Call the two F-4s back to Mother."

The older man came to join Walter Brenckmann behind the helmsman's back. Epes waited for his orders to be acknowledged and logged. He was leaning slightly towards the OOD when a new, baffled report came over the bridge speakers.

"Hawkeye Zero-Three and CAP Zero-Five and Zero-Six have gone off air!"

Actually, the whole northern segment of the air plot had gone down.

"EMP!" A man called. "One confirmed EMP bearing three-three-zero degrees magnetic."

"Second EMP!"

Captain Epes had forgotten whatever it was he was going to say to his young OOD.

"Does CAP have an eyeball on the nukes over Iraq?"

The aircraft flying combat air patrols forty thousand feet above Carrier Division Seven would have a line of sight hundreds of miles north.

"Affirmative. Very distant, sir."

Suddenly Walter Brenckmann was suddenly thinking about the bizarre exchange he had witnessed between Admiral Bringle and his British counterpart on HMS Centaur that afternoon. He was experiencing the uncanny sensation that he had come in half-way through a movie; and it was as if the projectionist had mixed up the order in which the reels ought to be shown. He recognised the faces of the characters but everything was happening in the wrong order and he had no idea whatsoever of the chronology or the context of the underlying narrative arc.

"Centaur is launching birds!"

"I have the bridge, Mr Brenckmann," the commanding officer of the USS Kitty Hawk declared.

"You have the bridge, sir," the younger man acknowledged. "Permission to report to my duty station in CIC, sir?"

"Affirmative. Carry on."

In his role as Carrier Division Seven's Acting Anti-Submarine Warfare Officer, Walter's responsibilities mainly concerned the operation and deployment of the Kitty Hawk's ASW Squadron of Grumman S-2 Tracker twin turboprop aircraft and sonar 'dipping' helicopters. The carrier's attendant ASW screen of four guided missile destroyers armed with a variety of ASROC – Anti-Submarine Rocket Launchers – and the latest version of the World War II Hedgehog spigot mortar system – were under the command of a hard-arsed four-ringer who as a Lieutenant (junior grade) had briefly served on the Buckley class destroyer escort USS Reuben James DE-153), with Walter's father in the winter of 1944-45 in the North Atlantic.

The Kitty Hawk's CIC was darkly crowded as Walter went to his desk. The Operations Officer of ASW Squadron 72, a mustang in his forties who had started his Navy career as an observer/gunner on Avenger torpedo bombers in 1945, nodded acknowledgement of his presence.

"We have a situation developing, sir," he reported.

Walter studied the big Battle Board in the middle of the CIC, then referred back to the smaller ASW 'threat plot'.

Six miles on the Kitty Hawk's starboard bow the Coontz class guided missile destroyers Dewey (DLG14) and William V. Pratt (DLG13) had turned onto a northerly heading and stepped on the gas as if something very big and very scary was chasing them. Two miles off the carrier's starboard beam the cruiser Albany (CG10) was manoeuvring to close the range with the flagship.

The Battle Board lights indicated that all three ships were spooling up their missile systems; the destroyers' Terrier launchers were at 'ready', the cruiser's Talos and Tartar systems were coming on line.

"What?" Walter mouthed.

The Kitty Hawk's Tannoy blared warning bells.

"Now hear this! Now hear this! Air action is imminent! Air action is imminent!"

The Battle Board now showed the carrier's own twin Terrier surface-to-air launchers at 'ready status'. Mounted either side of the stern in revetments in the aft flight deck Walter Brenckmann had always tacitly assumed it was too dangerous to 'load the rails' of either launcher while landing operations were in progress.

The Battle Board showed eighteen of the Kitty Hawk's aircraft in the air and two in a landing pattern. Other aircraft were queued to take off.

Eighteen aircraft up!

Why?

Six McDonnell Douglas F-4 Phantoms, four A-4 Skyhawks, four A-6 Intruders, two Hawkeyes and two tankers. The board changed. One helicopter had landed; another Sikorsky SH-3 Sea King was taking off.

The klaxons were blaring.

"ACTION STATIONS! ACTION STATIONS!"

"The Dewey is flushing her birds!"

What?

What the fuck was the Dewey shooting at?

Moments later the William V. Pratt fired a second salvo of two Terriers.

The bulkhead doors were swinging shut.

There were NO alerts or threats showing on the Battle Board.

That was the thing that stuck in Walter Brenckmann's memory whenever he thought about that night.

THE BOARD WAS CLEAR...

The only other contacts on the Battle Board were those of the Centaur battle group; Centaur and her three escorts, with the British oiler Wave Master escorted by a small minesweeper several miles astern. Other than Kitty Hawk's aircraft the only other contacts on the Battle Board were two pairs of sub-sonic Royal Navy De Havilland Sea Vixens and obsolete Supermarine Scimitar fighters proceeding *away* from Carrier Division Seven.

And then he realised what was going on.

The Dewey and the William V. Pratt were shooting at the British aircraft...

Suddenly, there was a horrible sick, sinking feeling in Walter Brenckmann's guts.

Chapter 50

23:09 Hours
Thursday 2nd July 1964
Al-Rasheed Air Base, South West Baghdad

Fifty-four year old Minister of Defence, Admiral of the Fleet Sergey Georgiyevich Gorshkov was in a foul mood by the time his personal Tupolev Tu-114 finally landed. He had hoped to fly down to Basra in the morning and have a private face to face, clear the air and reset the rules of engagement sort of stand up shouting match with Hamazasp Khachaturi Babadzhanian. Babadzhanian had never had much time for Gorshkov; and the feeling was mutual. However, that was old history and right now it was vital that the two men presented a united front and that their personal feelings – mainly loathing and disdain in equal proportions – did not interfere with the successful conclusion of Phase One, the conquest of Iraq and the seizure of Abadan, of Operation Nakazyvat.

Gorshkov had been briefed on the latest developments before he left Sverdlovsk. Although he had intuitively mistrusted the bullish confidence of the Red Army and the Red Air Force staff officers who had been at pains to convey the inevitability of the triumph of Soviet arms over the weak, pathetic, post-Imperial rump of the British Empire, actually he was pleasantly surprised how well things seemed to be going.

However, the memory of what two small Royal Navy ships had done to the *entire surviving Red Navy Black Sea surface fleet off Malta* at the beginning of April was still lividly, excoriatingly, horribly fresh in his mind.

Gorshkov had been onboard the Project 57A guided missile destroyer Gnevny, one of the old battle cruiser Yavuz's and the big Sverdlov class cruiser Admiral Kutuzov's four close escorts during the whole of the Battle of Malta. He had watched those two small British ships driving towards the big guns of his capital ships through a firestorm of shot and shell; one had dropped out the fight burning fiercely, the other had just kept on coming until everybody on the bridge of the Gnevny had honestly believed it would ram the Yavuz. On and on she came; by the time she swung around to fire her torpedoes she was so close to the big ships that neither could depress their main battery guns sufficiently to engage her.

The captain of the Gnevny had launched two P-15 Termit anti-ship missiles at the British destroyer but the other ship had been *too* close; the missiles had harmlessly roared out to sea before their clumsy analogue guidance systems could acquire their target. If that day had taught Gorshkov anything it was that a man underestimated the British at one's peril; if he had not disembarked onto a submarine ninety minutes after the battle he would have been killed when the Gnevny was sunk by strike aircraft flying off the USS Independence.

The Americans had come late to the fight but it had been those two small British ships which had already won the battle by the time the 'US Cavalry' belatedly 'turned up'.

And now those idiots in Sverdlovsk were telling him 'the Battle for Iraq is winding down!' According to them the enemy was 'beaten', and that 2nd Siberian Mechanised Army's four hundred tanks were about to 'roll over the top of the British and their *Arab* friends at Abadan'. Apparently, it would all be over in the next twenty-four hours! The RAF's raid on Chelyabinsk had been no more than one 'last spasm of defiance', spies on Cyprus left behind from the Krasnaya Zarya occupation reported that the British had 'run out of bombs', and that 'bomber losses had been so heavy in the campaign over Iraq that there were never more than a handful of aircraft stationed at Akrotiri and Nicosia'. As for the collection of old and as for the obsolete ships the enemy had collected in the Persian Gulf well, 'our people in Dammam blew up most of their ammunition!'

Sergey Georgiyevich Gorshkov was not a man who took a staff officer's word for anything without substantive and compelling corroborative evidence. The painful lessons of the Battle of Malta; and everything the High Command had learned about the British way of war in the last couple of years ought to have been burned in the psyches of *every* soldier in the Motherland by now.

The British *did not* know when they were beaten.

If the British were to be defeated on the battlefield it was not enough to deny them Abadan, or to sink their ships, or to destroy their army and air force in detail. The British would always keep coming back for more in just the same way the Americans would one day attempt again to bestride the globe.

It still beggared belief that the idiots in Chelyabinsk had neglected to brief him on the progress of the negotiations with the Americans until a day ago! But then in the Soviet Union before, and certainly after, the Cuban Missiles War a man got used to having his credulity regularly tested to breaking point. A month ago the numskulls had given him the task of ensuring that the Kitty Hawk never got anywhere near the Persian Gulf; that she should be disabled, or preferably, sunk. The priority had been to make it impossible for Carrier Division Seven to intervene on the British side in the defence of Abadan and the northern borders of the American client states of Kuwait and Saudi Arabia. Unfortunately, the talks with the Americans had been so secret nobody had told him they were even going on until after one of his boats had sunk that Yankee cruiser!

Things could of course, have been worse. If everything had gone to plan the two Red Navy Pacific Fleet Project 659 class nuclear submarines K-45 and K-122, would have sunk or crippled the USS Kitty Hawk, and then the *Troika* might have truly understood what *his* Red Navy was still capable of!

K-122 had gone silent shortly after the attack on the USS Providence and K-45 had been driven off by a US Navy nuclear submarine whose presence had not previously been suspected. K-45's commander had requested permission to follow the Americans into the Persian Gulf; Gorshkov had forbidden it. If the Yankees failed to keep their side of the Faustian pact they had made with the Troika, Carrier Division Seven would have to come out into the open ocean again, and by then another boat, the K-151 *might* be fit for operations. In the meantime he had ordered K-45 to make her best speed south to rendezvous with a supply ship.

The collective leadership had locked Gorshkov out of things since the Battle of Malta; carrying the war to the US Navy in the Arabian Sea was his ticket back onto the top table. His enemies had been circling like vultures over a wounded animal when the RAF had serendipitously eliminated Kosygin and Chuikov; the former had never trusted Gorshkov, the latter had always viewed him as a threat, a rival.

Brezhnev was different. He had been Nikita Khrushchev's man, as had Gorshkov. Back in July 1955 when Gorshkov had been First Deputy Commander-in-Chief of the Red Navy, Khrushchev had brutally purged his chief, Admiral Nikolai Kuznetsov. Admiral Kuznetsov, who was no relation to the newly appointed Foreign Minister, had been a 'big gun navy' man and Khrushchev wanted a fleet of small missile armed vessels and as many submarines as could be built *as soon as possible*. Kuznetsov had wanted to spend decades building up a battleship and aircraft carrier navy like the British and the Americans, and this had sealed his fate. When the old battleship Novorossiysk, a ship taken from the Italians in 1945, had blown up at anchor at Sevastopol – most likely having activated an undetected magnetic mine laid by the Germans a dozen years before – Khrushchev had used this act of 'gross negligence' to discredit Kuznetsov and to install Gorshkov, the Red Navy's most implacable missiles and submarine advocate in his place.

In 1955 the Red Navy had been no more than a coastal defence force equipped with obsolete equipment; but in the years before the Cuban Missiles War Gorshkov had laid the foundations for a massive twenty-year expansion. Under his plans the Red Fleet would eventually possess over three hundred submarines, a third of them nuclear powered by the early 1970s, modern destroyers, cruisers, and a national, and hopefully, an international infrastructure of bases and ports to give the Red Navy a truly 'global reach' to match that of the US Navy which dwarfed the shrinking maritime power of the old British Empire.

October 1962 had changed all that.

The Northern Fleet had ceased to exist in the war; as had the Baltic Fleet. The Black Sea Fleet had been luckier, but not much and its surviving strength had now been largely expended in the battles with the British and the Americans in the Mediterranean. Only in the Pacific had a small part of the new fleet that Gorshkov dreamed of building survived intact. Five Project 659 nuclear powered submarines had been under construction in hardened pens, or at sea, running trials or on patrol on the day of the war. Other ships had been completing on the slips of the Leninskiy Komsomol Shipyard, at Komsomolsk-na-Amur in the Far East of the USSR. Amur had been targeted by at least one ICBM and several bomber strikes; two B-52s had been shot down within twenty miles of the yards where the K-151 had been under construction. Fortunately, the nearest big bomb had gone off over twenty kilometres north of the yards, and the city around it had been only lightly damaged. While out in the Sea of Okhotsk and the Sea of Japan the US Seven Fleet had ruthlessly hunted down submarines and ships of the Pacific Fleet, Amur had been ignored, presumably already marked down as 'destroyed' on US Navy target lists.

Since the Cuban Missiles War two new, improved Project 659 boats had been laid down although the construction of both vessels had progressed slowly due to lack of prioritisation. K-1 and K-2 were respectively only twenty-four and thirty-one percent complete at this time, but reactor fabrication was on schedule and both boats might be in the water as early as this time next year. Elsewhere at Amur anti-submarine patrol boats, small guided missile frigates and destroyers were approaching completion.

The rebirth of the Red Navy had begun...

The big airliner was turning off the main runway when the lights in the cabin flickered.

Once, twice and then went out.

The thunderous roar of the four great fifteen thousand horse power Kuznetsov NK-12MV power plants seemed to pause, then pick up again at a much lower output. The whole aircraft lurched, juddered as if the brakes had suddenly been applied and released before its momentum carried it forward again.

Gorshkov leaned forward in his seat and looked out of the window at the lights of the suburbs of Bagdad straggling sporadically across the north eastern horizon in the night.

The whole cabin suddenly lit up, so brightly that it was as if an anti-aircraft searchlight had been pointed down the length of the fuselage.

The light had originated somewhere to the west.

Had it been to the east the Soviet Minister of Defence would have been blind; his retinas burned out by the thermonuclear airburst.

Chapter 51

"GONER!" The navigator/radio operator reported tersely.

Squadron Leader Guy French knew that even at this altitude the distant flash of thermonuclear explosions would probably not be visible but he turned his head to glance sidelong anyway. There were some human responses no man could avoid.

The 617 Squadron boys had their job to do; he had his.

Their job was half done; his was just beginning.

"Come up by ten knots, skipper," he heard in his helmet from the navigator/bomb aimer. "Two-zero miles to run. Repeat two-zero miles to run on my mark. MARK!"

The bomb bay doors were opening.

Guy French felt the increased drag tugging back on the controls through the multiple powered servos and gears that physically separated his hands from the huge bomber's control surfaces.

"Negligible air defence activity," reported the EWO – the Electronic Warfare Officer – dispassionately.

The Red Army had advanced at such breakneck speed that in the end it had literally fallen over in an exhausted, disjointed jumbled heap in and around the port of Umm Qasr and spread itself randomly across the western side of the Faw Peninsula; more in the fashion of an exhausted horde, a rabble than a conquering army. The spearhead tanks had out run their supply lines, their communications, and the range of the Red Air Force. In recent days the RAF had surrendered the skies south of Basra, fallen back as if it was ceding the field to an obviously superior enemy, despite knowing that the invaders had no meaningful air defence command and control capability anywhere south of, or indeed, over that city.

Lately, Guy French he wished he still had a picture of Greta, his dead fiancée. Greta and he would have been married a year by now but for the October War.

She had died that night of the war and all his personal possessions had gone missing in the confusion of the days and weeks afterwards. The Squadron had thought he was dead for nearly a week and by the time he had been reunited with his old billet it was as if he had never existed in the first place.

Sometimes he struggled to conjure Greta's face in his mind's eye; it was as if his memories were inexorably eroding the farther he travelled, and the more distant he became from the man that he had been before the cataclysm. He had come so far already that what he had mistakenly believed was a lust for revenge, was really simply a quest for *justice*. If the dead were forgotten, or if the living left them too far behind then what had the whole dreadful business been about in the first place?

The Angry Widow was travelling at nearly a mile a second, a giant barb-shaped rifle bullet racing towards the pre-selected AP – aiming point - where she would automatically release her bomb load in a five-second minutely choreographed 'dispersal pattern' designed to do the most damage, kill the most people and to make it as hard as possible to clear up the mess afterwards.

The rain of ruin began to fall from the Victor's bomb bay.

Hundreds of incendiaries, phosphorus and magnesium sprinkled with Napalm bomblets, cluster bombs with hundreds of deadly, killing and maiming sub-bombs ejected just above the ground or scattered across the target area creating a booby-trapped, lethal environment covered in small deadly anti-personnel mines to inhibit the rescuers and salvagers.

A dozen high capacity thin-skinned blast bombs levelling everything within a hundred feet of their impact points; and a clutch of general purpose bombs burrowing deep into the ground before exploding within a microsecond of landing, or delay-fused to explode only when the medics were attempting to treat the injured and to recover the bodies of the dead.

The bombs went on falling...

Guy French's father had regaled him with tales of how a Lancaster would bound upwards when her bombs dropped; the Victor hardly trembled under his hands as her deadly cargo began its descent, evenly, smoothly unloading, the contents of her cavernous bomb bay spilling earthward in a precisely calculated automated sequence which balanced the creation of the optimum possible bedlam on the ground, with a release sequence that neatly and evenly distributed the peak stresses imposed on the V-Bomber's airframe.

"NO HANG-UPS!"

Guy's father had once told him about the day he brought a two thousand pound bomb with a live delayed action fuse back from Essen. Nobody had known how much longer there was to run on the timer. He had landed away from base and the bomb disposal boys had carted the bomb off to a nearby quarry where it had exploded five minutes after they drove away from it.

That was when he saw – or perhaps, imagined that he saw – the momentary very distant lightning flash of the first of the 617 Squadron Yellow Suns shining above Dulaim Province over four hundred miles away to the north-north-east.

The Angry Widow's radio operator called out: "GONER."

Both of 617 Squadron's Vulcans had dropped their eggs.

Chapter 52

Marshall of the Soviet Union Hamazasp Khachaturi Babadzhanian had collapsed in a heap in the officers' latrine. By the time several worried, panicking members of his staff found him he was unconscious in a spreading pool of bloody faeces and vomit.

In practically any other army Babadzhanian's deputy would have immediately been informed of his superior's incapacitation and assumed temporary command of Army Group South. In practically any other army the nearest available medical practitioner would have been called without delay to attend to the stricken man. But then in practically any other army everybody would have known who exactly - in the Army Group Commander's absence or incapacity - was now in charge. However, in the Red Army nothing was ever simple, and the general rule of thumb was that 'if in doubt, pass a decision up the line'. Or, in cases where this was particularly *problematic*, 'try to find somebody else to make the decision that *you* ought to have taken'.

The situation was further complicated by the fact that earlier in the day Babadzhanian had sent his nominated deputy – largely side-lined ever since the two men had angrily disagreed about the balance of forces committed to the respective western and eastern thrusts of the drive south from Baghdad - forty-seven year old Lieutenant General Semyon Konstantinovich Kurkotkin had been sent north to Baghdad to 'keep that bastard Andropov out of our hair until we've sorted out Abadan!' Relations between the two men had deteriorated further when Kurkotkin had had the temerity to remind his superior officer that the chain of command ought to be preserved intact until Abadan was 'sorted out'. Needless to say the two men had parted on extremely bad terms.

Although Babadzhanian sometimes allowed key field officers to get close, and occasionally to be taken into his confidence, he was an old-style officer; a subordinate obeyed his orders or there was trouble. It did not help that Kurkotkin, a Muscovite, was known to be a favourite of several senior members of the surviving 'Moscow clique' within the Red Army high command, a younger, post-Great Patriotic War group which until a few days ago had been kept firmly under the gnarled thumb of Babadzhanian's recently murdered mentor, Marshal of the Soviet Union Vasily Ivanovich Chuikov.

Strictly speaking, this meant that in Kurkotkin's absence the next man in line to stand in for Babadzhanian was forty-two year old Lieutenant General Viktor Georgiyevich Kulikov, a nakedly ambitious man who had made no secret of how much he resented having had 'a jumped up fucking paratrooper like Kurochnik' given command of 2nd Siberian Mechanised Army's armoured push to the south. Kulikov had personally communicated his unhappiness to the Defence Ministry the day before the bombing of the Kursk Bunker. In retaliation Babadzhanian had broadcast his mistrust of Kulikov by promoting his own man, Vladimir Andreyevich Puchkov, the hard-charging commander of the 10th Guards Tank Division to command the corps which was, at this very minute, moving up to the start line to begin the assault on Khorramshahr.

Out of a misplaced sense of loyalty to their master, Babadzhanian's staff officers never really seriously considered informing the commander of 2nd Siberian Mechanised Army of the Army Group Commander's collapse. After all, Marshal Babadzhanian would probably be back on his feet in the morning, or in a few hours, or days at the worst; and nobody needed the *disturbance* of a new man marching in and interfering with the smooth functioning of the Army Group Headquarters. *Everybody* was confident that that was what Marshal Babadzhanian would think too; and anybody who did not think that way was not about to risk the wrath of the great man by inviting Kulikov into *his* headquarters without direct orders from...*somebody* in authority.

The other dilemma was that Babadzhanian's staff knew that they could not just call in *any* doctor; because that was a sure fire recipe for spreading any number of alarmist rumours. Compounding this problem was the fact that the headquarters' surgeon was currently visiting a field hospital in the south of the city, and doctors in general were incredibly scare commodities in this part of the World. Thus, initially the only medical help on call was a pair of frightened medical orderlies, two youngsters no better trained than stretcher bearers, possessing only the most rudimentary knowledge of first aid. Therefore, while trusted runners were despatched in search of 'reliable' doctors, it happened that the senior ranking officer in the Red Army lay on a soiled cot in a back room of his headquarters babbling feverishly, shitting and pissing himself in between convulsions utterly oblivious to everything going on around him.

And then, at approximately 23:15 hours with 2nd Siberian Mechanised Army only minutes away from launching the biggest set piece armoured assault since the Great Patriotic War ended in 1945; the headquarters of Army Group South lost radio communication with Baghdad, Umm Qasr and the forces about to pour south across the Iraq-Iran border on the eastern bank of the Arvand River above Khorramshahr.

At the critical moment as the great offensive approached 2nd Siberian Mechanised Army lost the ability to co-ordinate its attack with the Red Air Force and its own artillery; and most of its key field commanders were suddenly robbed of the wherewithal to actually command the units rolling south. What had been up until then a closely marshalled, expertly choreographed juggernaut rumbling irresistibly across the border had become, in a split second, like Goliath blinded by a slingshot, a giant blundering sightlessly towards its fate.

Chapter 53

23:15 Hours
Thursday 2nd July 1964
Basra Industrial City, 3 kilometres north of the Iranian border

The Western oil and shipping conglomerates which had achieved footholds in southern Iraq before the Second World War, the forces of occupation during and after that war and at various times since, the French, British and US combines that had sought to establish and maintain a presence in Basra Province, had colonised the eastern bank of the Arvand River opposite the city. From small beginnings these *interests* and *concessions* had spread along the left bank of the great river, and begun to extend inland until they had created the ugly, disorganised industrial sprawl which now sat squarely across the path of the advancing Red Army north of the Iraq-Iran border.

The Iraqi Army had abandoned the eastern bank after its abortive sortie into Iranian territory north of Khorramshahr in April; subsequently, sporadic shelling had driven out the last civilians and in the weeks since there had been widespread looting and the random burning of workshops and trading stores.

On the right hand wing of the armoured leviathan coiled to hurl itself at the Iranian forward positions across the border the skeletal ruins would inevitably hinder progress. The street plan of the old 'industrial' area would also tend to channel armour, mobile artillery and motorised infantry columns down predictable 'tramlines'. However, on the left the armoured spearheads and their supporting guns and shock troops could surge down towards Khorramshahr over relatively open, good ground.

2nd Siberian Mechanised Army held all the cards but only a fool would risk gifting a weaker foe the opportunity to attack an exposed flank. In mandating that the advance go ahead on the widest possible front Major General Konstantin Yakovlevich Kurochnik's new Corps Commander, Vladimir Andreyevich Puchkov had demonstrated, for all his predatory gung ho tanker's appetite for haste, that he was not about to completely throw caution to the winds.

The two men stood in the semi-darkness beneath an awning stretched between two BTR-60 eight-wheel armoured personnel carriers. Fifty metres away the Arvand River poured down towards the distant Persian Gulf. Other vehicles, including BTR-40 armoured transporters and several thin-skinned trucks were parked in the surrounding ruins. Such was the advanced mobile headquarters of the 19th Guards Tank Corps.

The former paratrooper had explained that Lieutenant General Kulikov, the man in charge of the army on the eastern bank of the Arvand River, had issued direct orders demanding that the two wings of the 'assault force' should advance in an 'unbroken line'.

Puchkov grinned wolfishly.

"Fucking old woman!" He grunted dismissively.

Having just been appointed to command the greatest deployment in battle of Soviet armour since the Great Patriotic War he had no intention of 'pussy footing around!' He was a veteran of Kursk, the most epic clash of armour in history, and Marshal Babadzhanian had not sent him across the river to 'play chess' with the enemy. The men of Army Group South were tired, hungry, there was sickness – dysentery, possibly typhus and cholera in the ranks – and its equipment was worn out. The once invincible invasion force was a pale shadow of the all-conquering armies which had massed in the Caucasus in the months before Operation Nakazyvat; the three hundred and seventy tanks moving up to the start line were all that they had left – every single tank that was still capable of motoring for another twenty-four, or at a pinch thirty-six hours – and if *he*, Vladimir Andreyevich Puchkov did not get the job done quickly 'the job' was probably was not going to get done at all!

Puchkov knew he did not need to tell Kurochnik any of this. Kulikov, the Army Commander, was a well-connected Party loyalist to whom command of 2nd Siberian Mechanised Army was a stepping stone to the Chief of Staff's post and a seat on the Politburo sometime in the next five years. Nobody doubted Kulikov was also a very competent soldier, albeit of the cautious, methodical kind; but Babadzhanian would not have sent his most trusted mad dog tank commander across the river if Kulikov was actually the hard charger he claimed to be!

What needed to be done tonight and in the next day or two was a job for an old school tanker, not one of the leading members of the 'new wave'. Left to his own devices Kulikov would feint this way and that, box clever until he saw an opening to go in for the kill; when what was needed was somebody, like Puchkov, to wade straight into the fight and deliver a quick, brutal, crushing knockout blow.

Puchkov looked at his watch.

Not long to go now.

Time was his enemy.

His artillery would run out of ammunition inside three hours if it failed to observe proper discipline. Kurochnik's tanks had full shell racks but that was all; there were no reloads south of Baghdad. Likewise, once his tanks ran out of fuel that was that. It was a prospect which might have daunted a lesser man.

What remained of Puchkov's own exhausted and depleted 10th Guards Tank Division was currently laagered threatening the Kuwaiti border east of the port of Umm Qasr. He had had precisely nineteen serviceable T-62s – of the one hundred and sixty he had entered Iran with three months ago - by the time what was left of the Iraqi Army had fled in panic into Kuwait. Most of the tanks he had started the campaign with lay broken, cannibalised and abandoned along fifteen hundred kilometres of impossible mountain and desert roads between the Caucasus and the Persian Gulf.

Notwithstanding the imperious presence of the veteran tank

commander Konstantin Yakovlevich Kurochnik *was* worried.

Not because he had any actual evidence that the final offensive of the Iraq War was going to be particularly bloody, or in any way problematic but because ever since Army Group South had crashed into northern Iran he had been asking himself if, and when, the enemy would finally make a stand.

After Abadan there was nowhere left to make that 'stand'.

Red Army and KGB Intelligence reported that all that stood between his lines and Abadan was the remnants of several Imperial Iranian tank brigades, about fifty or sixty tanks – British supplied Centurions and American M-48s, neither of which he considered a match for his T-62s in a stand up fight – in and around Khorramshahr. The Iranians had been engaged in and significantly weakened in vicious battles first with the Iraqis, and then with their own people in the east while Army Group South had still been subduing the north. The British were known to have strengthened their garrison on Abadan Island but they had only about thirty tanks at most, a few aircraft and a couple of batteries of surface-to-air missiles; if the British had not been cowering all this time behind the water barrier of the Karun River his armour would have run straight over them without noticing them!

But still Kurochnik fretted.

It was not the pressure of having high command suddenly thrust upon him. He had been yearning for this day since he was a cadet; no, nor was it the odd sensation of separation he felt from the front, of no longer being in the rifle line with his boys. He had always known that this was inevitable someday. No, what was really troubling him was a thing he had never expected at this elevated level of combat command; specifically, how easily a man could be euphorically swept along by a tide of events over which he had absolutely no control. Previously, he had exercised command on the basis of what he could see with his own eyes. He had dealt with whatever was in front of him and afterwards, worried about the next step when he got used to the idea he was still alive. In the last few weeks he had had undreamed of responsibility, the power to influence the lives and fates of tens of thousands of men, to in some small way *make* history; in retrospect he now realised that he had actually been in control of very little.

As a battalion and regimental commander he had been in actual command of everything; now he was like the conductor of an orchestra, frantically waving his arms but totally in the hands of his musicians, trusting to other virtuosos.

Bizarrely, he found himself wondering what it must be like sitting on a barrel drifting down the Arvand River, gripped by the tide, his destiny to be carried inexorably down the Shatt al-Arab to the blue waters of the Persian Gulf...

"What is it?" Puchkov demanded, drawing Kurochnik aside and lowering his voice.

The former paratrooper was shorter than the towering scarred tanker.

"The last couple of days I've been thinking about that time in Urmia," he confided. "Once I knew your boys were coming up the road I knew everything would turn out okay in the end."

Puchkov scowled.

"This is a big thing," he retorted. "You haven't been here before. I have been here before. Any man who says he doesn't think he's about to put his hand into a meat grinder before a big attack is a liar, Comrade Konstantin Yakovlevich."

The two men made eye contact, two hard, battle-tempered men neither of whom could afford the luxury of doubt.

While they had been talking both men had been peripherally aware of the constant low-level jabbering of voices, many distorted by interference and the constant tapping patter of Morse code transmissions seeping out of the nearby communications trucks.

It was several seconds before both Puchkov and Kurochnik became aware of the unnatural...*silence.*

A man cursed angrily from within the nearest radio lorry.

"Everything's fucking dead..."

"What's dead?" Kurochnik demanded irritably.

The stillness, the sudden quietness seemed horribly threatening.

"All the fucking radios, sir!"

"What about the fucking radios?"

"Everything just died..."

Chapter 54

The destroyer had felt its way up river like a blind man in a flood. Observing complete electrical 'silence' with every piece of modern communications and radar equipment physically switched off, Anzac had groped into the black waters at the entrance to the Shatt al-Arab with her captain praying that the bar had not shifted since his last reconnaissance four weeks ago. Creeping forward showing only a shaded stern lamp, Commander Stephen Turnbull had expected the Battle class destroyer to run aground at any moment.

He had queried the order forbidding the use of sonar to 'ping' the way ahead but been tersely informed by the flagship that 'all ships in the gun line will observe a complete electronic blackout'.

Stephen Turnbull stalked his bridge like a caged big cat.

The sky was strangely overcast, the stars only occasionally twinkling through gaps in the clouds. On the water the darkness was stygian. It was virtually impossible to visually distinguish the banks from the stream. Every twenty minutes Anzac idled in the stream, put an old-fashioned lead over the side and plumbed the depth of the channel beneath her keel. More than once she had almost touched bottom. Behind her HMS Diamond, the big Daring class fleet destroyer sometimes ran so close that lookouts on Anzac's stern and Diamond's bow had no option but to frantically signal each other with hooded torches to avoid a collision. Behind Diamond the flagship, Tiger was invisible, the cruiser's silhouette lost in the impenetrable gloom. Nobody on Anzac had any way of knowing if HMAS Tobruk or the old New Zealand cruiser Royalist were still in company.

Unable to use his sonar to keep in the middle of the deep channel, Anzac had crawled north. As midnight drew near the leading ship of the Persian Gulf gun line was less than half way to Abadan.

Turnbull was a wise enough old hand to know that Admiral Davey would not have hobbled Anzac with the electronic 'blackout' unless he had good reason; but it vexed him not to know what that reason was!

If crawling up the Shatt al-Arab blindfold had been the plan all along; why the Devil had the squadron not trained for the eventuality?

Shades of the disaster in the Java Sea all those years ago...

In the face of a greatly superior enemy fleet the beleaguered ABDA – American, British, Dutch and Australian – force had been beset by confused and contradictory orders, and was eventually harried to its doom. It had taken Stephen Turnbull most of the last two decades to forgive the men responsible for that shambles...

Suddenly, he blinked into the night.

Was that a shooting star?

Or lightning?

Having caught exactly the same brief flash of light at the edges of their peripheral vision, the bridge lookouts had trained their glasses a point west of due north.

Glasses searched the blackness as seconds dragged into a minute, and then two...

There was another spike of light.

Not *in* the sky but somewhere below the horizon which fleetingly *lit* the heavens and subsided to black.

"Was that big nuke?" One man asked hesitantly.

In a moment Stephen Turnbull understood the electronic 'blackout'.

Big bombs detonated so high in the atmosphere that their fireball barely kissed the ground miles below sometimes – given the right atmospheric conditions - radiated a massive electro-magnetic pulse of energy, an EMP which was capable of overloading and short-circuiting electronic equipment scores, perhaps hundreds of miles away. Nearer to the explosion transformers would fail, power lines burn out under massive short-lived voltage overloads, and transistors, capacitors and fuses would self-destruct or trip out. Sometimes circuitry would spontaneous catch fire if the EMP was big enough and close enough.

Arc Light...

"The flagship is signalling, sir!"

Two miles down the river and a little further to the right hand side of the main channel a big lamp was winking high on the Tiger's bridge.

"SWITCH EVERYTHING BACK ON STOP!"

The yeoman repeating the message sounded... *baffled.*

"PROCEED WITH ALL SPEED TO AL SEEBA AND ANCHOR ON THE IRAN SIDE OF CHANNEL STOP!"

Past Al Seeba on the Iraq bank of the Arvand River the waterway proscribed a huge westward semi-circle. Anchored in the main channel opposite Al Seeba the gun line would be in an ideal position to provide ground controlled indirect fire support to the Allied forces on Abadan Island and around Khorramshahr.

"GUN LINE WILL ANCHOR IN LINE ASTERN IN SAILING ORDER TO PRESENT STARBOARD BROADSIDES TO THE ENEMY MESSAGE ENDS!"

Stephen Turnbull chuckled to himself in the darkness.

"Sonar!" He called. "Start active pinging. Warn the engine room to be ready to make revs for up to ten knots!"

Things would start to get really hot very soon now.

Chapter 55

The Defence Minister of the Soviet Union had been unceremoniously rushed to the nearest air raid shelter while the crew of his Tupolev Tu-114 made urgent preparations to get the aircraft back into the air. Things only began to calm down – a little – when there were no subsequent nuclear strikes. A few minutes before midnight Admiral of the Fleet Sergey Georgiyevich Gorshkov ordered his bodyguards to take him to the Air Defence Control Centre located on the perimeter of the air base.

"What happened?" He demanded, storming into the strangely darkened basement room beneath the old control tower. Some of the electric lights were on but all the radar screens were dead. The familiar background chatter of radio talk was absent.

The Red Air Force commander of the Al-Rasheed Air Base stamped to attention before the newcomer.

Two suspected enemy aircraft had been picked up at extreme range by forward mobile radar stations located in the Syrian Desert some one hundred and fifty kilometres west of Baghdad. Thereafter, both contacts had been tracked as they flew arrow straight courses towards central Iraq.

Neither aircraft had at any time deviated from its course.

Neither aircraft had attempted to jam ground or airborne radio and radar frequencies.

"They just kept on coming," the base commander reported. "Even when they were 'locked up' by several S-75 batteries they just kept coming. No evasive manoeuvres, no counter measures. They ignored the missiles coming towards them..."

The first big bomb had gone off several kilometres above Buhayrat ath-Tharthar, a man-made two thousand square kilometre lake designed to collect and contain the spring flood waters of the Tigris, located some one hundred kilometres north west of Baghdad. The bomb had exploded roughly equidistant – some thirty-five to forty kilometres from the two nearest concentrations of population, in Samarra and Ramadi.

The second bomb had gone off above an area known as the Karbala Gap more than a hundred kilometres south east of the capital, some forty-five kilometres northwest of the nearest major town, Karbala.

Gorshkov suddenly understood what had happened and why.

The British had mounted two suicide raids to drop big thermonuclear bombs in two locations where they could be assured that there would be few, if any civilian casualties.

The RAF could have easily bombed Baghdad and Basra.

Targeting the two cities would have generated equally disruptive electro-magnetic pulses and killed thousands, possibly tens of thousands of Soviet combatants; but the British had been too squeamish to do that.

It was a lesson that Sergey Georgiyevich Gorshkov would file away in his pocket for later. In the meantime he did not need to consult a tactical or strategic genius to know that the bombing of central Iraq was anything other than the calculated prelude to some kind of massive counter attack.

Except, that made no sense at all; the British and their allies were beaten, holed up in their precious enclave on Abadan Island while their Iranian 'friends' squabbled amongst themselves in the deserts around Khorramshahr. True, the British had their famous V-Bombers; they had a small aircraft carrier somewhere in the Persian Gulf with a couple of dozen sub-sonic Sea Vixen and Scimitar interceptors onboard. As for their 'surface fleet', a collection of old destroyers and a couple of World War II type cruisers well, what use was that to anybody...

His predecessor, Chuikov had authorised the sabotage 'actions' against the British fleet at Dammam, and if the opportunity arose for one of Gorshkov's 'toys' – as he called the new, supposedly 'unproven' nuclear Project 659 submarines – to have a 'pot shot' at any 'British ship' encountered. Otherwise, the ABNZ squadron had been ignored by the High Command and to his knowledge, had never figured at all in Babadzhanian's thinking.

A telephone was ringing.

Land lines would be relatively immune to EMP, with few vulnerable relays and electronic exchanges. In Iraq everything would still be mechanical, the civilian telephone network switchboards manually operated.

Another telephone rang.

The first reports were finally coming in.

Gorshkov was suddenly thinking about the Battle of Malta.

The British had been caught by surprise, the US Navy, represented by a powerful squadron of modern guided missile destroyers which the Red Navy's battle fleet had anticipated having to confront in Maltese waters with no little trepidation, having unexpectedly sailed away and left the Maltese Archipelago undefended. And yet at no time had the British considered laying down their arms and surrendering; in fact, at the lowest ebb of the battle when his big ships were pouring shells onto the RAF's airfields, the Royal Navy's dockyards and two battalions of elite Spetsnaz supported parachute troopers were assaulting the British headquarters at Mdina, the resistance had become unyielding, reckless, and utterly irrational.

The way that old British destroyer had come roaring out of the shadow of the main island, ploughing through forests of shell splashes to get to grips with his ships had been a nightmare...

"Comrade Defence Minister," a tremulous voice murmured,

breaking into Gorshkov's darkling premonitions.

"The enemy has bombed," the man gulped nervily, "or rather, is still bombing the port of Umm Qasr and the advance units of 3rd Caucasian Tank Army laagered around it."

There was a dreadful, sick, sinking feeling in Gorshkov's stomach.

It was like watching that lone British destroyer charging at his big ships off Malta all over again. On and on it had come like a rabid dog worrying at the legs of a pack of enraged Brown bears, undeterred by the knowledge that a single blow from the swinging claws of any of the circling beast would surely rip off its head.

Something made him check the time.

It was now one minute to midnight.

Chapter 56

"What are we doing here?" Brian Harris had learned the folly of *volunteering* as a very young man in Burma twenty years ago. *Volunteering* had got him into the Chindits, operating behind the Japanese lines with Orde Wingate's gang of heroes, or madmen, depending upon one's point of view. Living off the jungle, fighting the Japanese at their own game had seemed quite a good idea until he was actually 'in the jungle' and the RAF, which was supposed to regularly drop supplies to the Chindits, kept dropping *their* supplies onto Japanese positions. Once he had extracted himself from the Chindits he had found himself on the front line of the bloodiest battle of the whole Burma campaign at Kohima. What with one thing and another he had decided he had had quite enough to do with the military by the time he got back to England in the spring of 1946.

Frank Waters had asked the others if they were 'up for a little jaunt across the Karun River', and for reasons beyond Brian Harris's ken – he had assumed the mad former SAS-man would have much preferred to wander around the battlefield alone - the idiots had signed up for the escapade.

'Look, it's got to be better than waiting for the next shell to land on our heads sitting around here beside the airfield,' the old soldier had proposed, grinning that infuriating, toothy grin of his. Actually, he had had a point. Every few minutes the Red Army lobbed a salvo of half-a-dozen rounds into the positions of the 2nd Rifle Battalion of the New Zealanders' Canterbury Regiment. The 'Canterburies', whose forward company was dug in along the river bank guarding the southern bulge of the so-called Minushahr Peninsula around which the Arvand River proscribed a two-mile wide meandering half-circle on its way south, were keeping their heads down. The shelling seemed a little aimless to a veteran like Brian Harris; several of the others felt differently, as if each round was personally aimed at them. In any event they had 'borrowed' a Land Rover, Frank Waters had talked them across the pontoon bridge on the Karun River and they had seen how far 'north' they got.

'Cards on the table time, chaps,' Frank Waters had declared. 'I might be new at this *presenting* lark but I do know my stuff when it comes to finding places where there are likely to be *stories*.'

Brian Harris was still not sure how Frank Waters had talked the sentries into allowing them to drive across the Karun River pontoon bridge onto Iranian soil, and then to motor unmolested into the southern outskirts of the damaged town. By then the other members of the crew had realised the error of their ways and were panicking.

The former SAS man had driven them back to within a few

hundred yards of where they had witnessed the long-range duel between Soviet tanks and Iranian anti-tank gunners the previous day.

"Steady on, chaps," Frank Waters rebuffed the complaints. "I've been given to believe that the general idea is to catch the Russians in the open to the north of the town. We're perfectly safe here. Safe as houses, in fact."

Given that most of the surrounding 'houses' looked, even in the dark, like burned out shells this was hardly reassuring. Initially, Frank Waters had been disappointed that so little appeared to be 'going on'.

The Red Army kept on lobbing shells over the top of Khorramshahr, other clusters of shells thumped down into the desert to the north and the east but not much was actually happening until a little before midnight there was the sound of equipment clanking, and boots tramping in the street.

"Who the Devil are you?" Growled a subaltern with the badge of the Royal Tank Corps on his battledress as a torch was shone from face to face.

"BBC, old man," Frank Waters retorted insouciantly, standing and extending his hand in welcome. He introduced himself with casual bonhomie and the young officer straightened. "I'm Frank Waters of the British Broadcasting Corporation."

"Colonel Waters, sir," the much younger tanker apologised. Momentarily, he paused to allow his brain a chance to assess the situation. "You really can't stay here, sir. If things go according to plan this will be pretty much the worse place to be for miles around!"

The activity the BBC men could hear in the nearby streets was the bringing forward and emplacing of L2 BAT – Battalion Anti-Tank – 120-millimetre recoilless anti-tank rifles adjacent to pre-positioned hidden ammunition caches. Elsewhere in and around Khorramshahr a battery of eight twenty-five pounder guns was similarly being brought forward. Further forward several still several Centurion tanks lurked, screened from the north by the ruins, hull down, invisible.

"I think the idea is to funnel the Soviet armour down towards us," the Royal Tank Regiment officer explained. "Obviously Iranian artillery will be firing on the enemy flank from the east while this is going on. If the enemy over runs or bypasses the town, then we are to attempt to pull back across the Karun – hopefully before the bridges are blown up – and fill in any gaps in the line."

Brian Harris rolled his eyes in the gloom. He had been labouring under the misapprehension that Waters had given him his word to 'keep the chaps safe' the previous day.

"Frank," he suggested, "we ought to get out of here while we can."

"Get out of here? Not on your life, matey!"

"I'm really not sure you should be this far forward, sir," the subaltern added helpfully.

"General Carver said I could go wherever I want," Frank Waters told him sharply. His tone was magisterial, threatening that if there was any more of this nonsense about skulking about miles behind the front he would personally take the matter to his good friend, the Commander-in-Chief. "And that is exactly what I propose to do. The people at home have a right to know the story of the Battle of Abadan and I bloody well intend to be the one telling it to them!"

Chapter 57

00:53 Hours
Friday 3rd July, 1964
Abadan, Iran

Lieutenant-General Michael Carver had moved up to the forward headquarters of the 4th Infantry Brigade. 'Brigade' was something of a misnomer; the formation was essentially a two thousand-strong all-arms 'battle group' tasked with guarding the northern flank of Abadan Island. Although it had the muddy breadth of the slow-flowing Karun River between it and Khorramshahr, if the Red Army broke through in force the coming battle, the brigade's role was not so much to attempt to stop the enemy in his tracks but to withdraw in good order, slowing down and mauling the Soviet juggernaut as it drove towards the more substantial 'redoubts' protecting the island's one, now evacuated air base.

The last operational aircraft had flown out of RAF Abadan before the Soviet gunners found their range. The seven serviceable Hawker Hunter fighters and both the surviving Canberra bombers would join the aircraft based in Kuwait and Saudi Arabia. Aircraft from HMS Centaur ought to have been loitering over Abadan; but these had not materialised as yet. No matter, he knew the Navy would not let him down.

Michael Carver would not have been human if he had not had doubts, horrible doubts, about how the ruses and stratagems so carefully, agonisingly calculated in the last few days and weeks would actually play out in practice. The trouble was that however he analysed the 'facts on the ground' the enemy had three or four times as many tanks, at least three times as many guns, and seven or eight times as many combat 'effectives'.

On paper Hasan al-Mamaleki's Third Imperial Armoured Division had well over two hundred and fifty main battle tanks, including forty Mark II Centurions with L7 105-millimetre L/52 rifles but of these tanks only one hundred-and-thirty were actually 'ready to roll', and in the last fortnight as many as forty of his Mark I Centurions and M-48 Pattons had had to be deployed in the eastern desert, and since become locked in a low intensity attritional campaign with units of the Iranian Army still loyal to the post-Shah Provisional Government faction in Isfahan. Intelligence gained from interrogating deserters indicated that the Provisional Government, headed by a distant relative of the Shah – who was apparently backed by the CIA - who had been living 'like a playboy' in the United States until the destruction of Tehran, had recently ordered 'punitive action to be taken against the traitor al-Mamaleki'. Having counted on a force of two hundred tanks to counter the oncoming flood of Soviet armour, al-Mamaleki currently had around ninety to hand.

Carver had sent a troop of 4th Royal Tank Regiment Centurions, six of his precious Mark IIs over the Karun River to Khorramshahr to release ten of his Iranian friend's M-48s to re-join al-Mamaleki's main force to the east, and concentrated his most potent anti-tank units, equipped with lethal L2 BAT 120-millimetre recoilless anti-tank rifles in the ruins of the town and dug in around the derelict station directly in the path of the most likely enemy route of advance.

British and Commonwealth forces would be the anvil – at Khorramshahr – against which Hasan al-Mamaleki's mighty armoured hammer would later smash the invaders.

But not quite yet, not tonight; only when the moment was right...

At dusk Carver had ordered forward all eight of his sixty-three ton FV 214 Conqueror heavy tanks to take up hull down positions watching over the 'Karun Line' on the southern Abadan shore. Initially designed as the 1945 war was ending in response to the hugely superior German panzers that British tanks had faced during that war, and to the Stalin IS-3 monsters of the victorious Red Army, the Conqueror mounted a giant 120-millimetre rifled cannon capable of 'killing' anything that came, literally, within miles of it. Safe in prepared revetments with fields of fire that dominated the northern bank of the Karun River, the Conquerors might not stop the whole of 2nd Siberian Mechanised Army in its tracks but they would wreak fearful carnage before they were overwhelmed, or driven back.

Carver had held the remainder of his tanks – eighteen Centurion Mark IIs – back in two mobile groups of nine, each supported by armoured cars, and improvised 'grenadier' companies, men drawn from 3rd Battalion, the Parachute Regiment, mounted in armoured personnel carriers and, for want of other transport, Land Rovers, Jeeps and every kind of thin-skinned vehicle that could be found, in reserve. If and when the 'Airfield Line' was broken these two sub battle groups of the 4th Royal Tank Brigade would plug the breech. Or that at least, was the plan. Minefields had been laid all around Khorramshahr, and here and there on Abadan Island where the enemy would be forced 'off road' by zeroed-in seventeen and twenty-five pounder batteries 'hidden' within the deactivated refinery sprawl to the east of the abandoned air base.

Carver stood on a firing step in one of the trenches radiating out from the access road up to the one still-intact pontoon bridge connecting Khorramshahr to Abadan Island, raised his binoculars to his eyes and peered into the gloom.

He had once dreamed of a second Cannae in the marshes above Basra; what he had got was a desperate defensive battle in which he had no choice other than to hurl every asset at his command into the fire in a single spasm of violence. And when he had expended his 'last throw of the dice' – his exact words to Field Marshall Sir Richard Hull, the Chief of the Defence Staff – if the enemy still remained on the field of battle, *everything* would be lost.

He had dreamed of a tactically elegant, crushing manoeuvre.

What he had eventually ended up with was a scheme with so many inter-related critically dependent elements that *anything* could go wrong at any time and bring the whole castle crashing down around his ears. Such was the razor-sharp knife edge that he was walking that if, for a single moment, the enemy realised what he was attempting to do his 'last throw of the dice' would be for nothing.

He had not seen the distant lightning in the northern sky but his communications staff had informed him that 'test equipment' had been 'partially disabled' by EMPs at around the anticipated hour.

The fires of Umm Qasr were clearly visible in the west.

They flickered and pulsed on the rim of the horizon, reflected off the clouds and pillars of rising smoke in the night.

The RAF had pummelled Umm Qasr and the surrounding 'laager areas' on schedule, although as yet he had no idea what losses the bomber force had suffered.

There had been no news from Rear Admiral Nick Davey's ABNZ gun line; but neither had there been flashes of gunfire from the supposedly Red Army-occupied western bank of the Shatt al-Arab. In fact the darkened Faw Peninsula gave every appearance of being deserted, neutral.

Nick Davey's ships *would* be on station south of the bend of the Arvand River opposite the village of Al Seeba on the Abadan side of the main channel when the time came. Davey had given him his word and that was good enough for Michael Carver.

As for the question of whether or not the United States Navy would, when push came to shove, come to the party well...

He would wait and see.

In the meantime he did not intend to hold his breath.

The entire northern horizon beyond Khorramshahr suddenly blazed with fire.

00:58 hours.

Hundreds of Katyusha rockets were climbing skywards, and the muzzle flashes of countless of guns rippled like diamonds shining momentarily in the fierce light flooding out of an open furnace door.

"INCOMING! INCOMING! INCOMING!"

Michael Carver watched the searing trails of the Katyushas proscribing a great arch of fire across the canvass of the desert night, arching towards their distant targets like a storm of modern fiery arrows.

Not that much had really changed since English longbow men had been the masters of the European battlefield. Gunpowder, cordite, various flavours of high explosive had enhanced the range and killing power of weapons; but in the end it all amounted to the same thing. Blood and shit and pain beyond measure, such was the test of the profession of arms.

The great trial of his life had commenced.

He watched a moment longer, then, with a sigh, stepped down below the parapet.

Chapter 58

The President of the United States of America's voice was angry, worried and a little afraid. All this Margaret Thatcher heard in his first words.

"Thank you for taking my call, Prime Minister."

The transatlantic line was periodically very nearly blocked with bursts of static, the rest of the time it was just 'clicky', prone to the customary vexing attenuations of tone and volume.

While Tom Harding-Grayson, the Foreign Secretary and his wife Patricia had come over to Hertford College to offer their moral support, William Whitelaw, the Secretary of State for Defence and Sir Richard Hull, the Chief of the Defence Staff were present for strictly 'operational reasons'. Two days ago the Prime Minister and her Deputy, James Callaghan, had agreed that the latter – and a 'backup operations team' led by the Chief of the Air Staff, Sir Christopher Hartley - would base himself in the Chilmark Emergency Command and Control bunker in Wiltshire, just 'in case the worst happens'. Airey Neave and Alison Munroe, whose departments were responsible for the Intelligence Services, and Supply, Transportation and Energy respectively, had already joined Callaghan in the bunker. On the night of the October War there had been nobody in authority in a 'safe place'; consequently, when the 'worst' *had* happened it had taken several weeks – disastrous weeks in terms of civil disorder and the alleviation of the distress of the sick and injured – to restore a semblance of 'national order'. Whatever happened tonight that was *never* going to be allowed to *happen* again.

Tom Harding-Grayson held a second handset to his head and Willie Whitelaw was leaning close enough to hear most of what was said at the Philadelphia end of the line.

"I am always happy to *take* the President's call," Margaret Thatcher replied coolly. Since taking the decision to authorise *Arc Light* strikes forty-eight hours ago – albeit a licence hedged around with caveats that had driven the Chiefs of Staff to distraction – she had felt physically sick most of the time. Her *mal de mere* had had nothing to do with the fact that once the strikes took place it was inevitable that Jack Kennedy and she would have to have *this* conversation; it was wholly to do with having let the thermonuclear genie out of the bottle *again*.

The Chiefs of Staff had come to her and in soberly chilling terms made their case. What it amounted to was simple. If they were to play David to the Soviet Union's Goliath; Goliath must first be blinded so that he might be brought crashing to the ground and God-willing, be hacked at until he surrendered or expired from his wounds.

'If we fail to inhibit the enemy's ability to co-ordinate his greatly superior forces against us at the critical moment,' Sir Richard Hull had concluded, "we will suffer a defeat so total that our ability in future to exert influence on the global stage will be at an end.'

"My people," Jack Kennedy prefaced, "are telling me that the electro-magnetic pulses of two medium sized nuclear devices have been detected over Iraq in the last ninety minutes?"

"They are correct in that assumption. RAF V-Bombers conducted strikes some sixty miles to the west of Baghdad over sparsely populated areas," Margaret Thatcher retorted. "What of it, Mister President?"

The Secretary of Defence flinched.

Tom Harding-Grayson's expression remained inscrutable.

"What of it..."

The Prime Minister cut through the hissing background static.

"I trust and pray that you are not going to ask me why I did not give you forewarning of the activation of *Arc Light* protocols, Jack?"

Jack Kennedy had been about to ask her exactly that.

"Margaret, we moved the Kitty Hawk into the Persian Gulf specifically to deter the Soviets reaching for the nuclear trigger," he responded. He honestly did not believe *he* was having *this* conversation with the woman who had talked him out of retaliating against the Red Dawn strikes back in February. "Now if the Soviets 'go nuclear' we'll all be dragged into this thing."

The woman tried not to groan out aloud. "Mister President," she said between clenched teeth. "The reason RAF V-Bombers attacked Chelyabinsk eight days ago with 'conventional' bombs was to ensure that the Soviet High Command could have no doubt, no doubt whatsoever, that *we* are fully prepared to complete the work General LeMay's boys left unfinished in October 1962. If the Soviets retaliate with nuclear weapons we will do likewise."

"Margaret, you can't..."

"Further," Margaret Thatcher added, a hectoring note rising stridently in her voice, "if the worst comes to the worst I will not hesitate to bomb the Red Army all the way back to Baghdad!"

Understandably, this prompted a shocked silence.

"Are you still there, Jack," the woman asked peremptorily after a gap of about ten seconds.

"Er, yes..." The President regained his composure, his voice hardened. "I will be no part of that," he declared. "In fact I must tell you now that I have already broadcast a message to the Soviet leadership disassociating myself from British actions. Via the good offices of former Ambassador Dobrynin, whom you may know elected to remain in the United States after the Cuban Missiles War, we have been in communication with the *Troika*, the collective leadership of the Soviet Union in recent days energetically endeavouring to defuse tensions arising from the sinking of the USS Providence in the Arabian Sea..."

Even Tom Harding-Grayson's eyes widened at this revelation.

Next to him the Secretary of State for Defence made a choking noise. Across the room the Foreign Secretary's wife's face had turned ashen.

Margaret Thatcher lowered the telephone handset from her face and covered the mouthpiece with her left hand.

It was too awful to contemplate. It was the Suez crisis of 1956 all over again except exponentially worse; back in 1956 President Eisenhower had *only* threatened to sell the pound sterling and to withdraw existing credit lines. Now an American President was holding a gun at a British Prime Minister's head.

It ought to have been a moment of...*defeat.*

Strangely, it was a moment of blinding clarity that suddenly brought things into pin-sharp focus.

The United States had been talking to the Soviets behind the back of its former 'special' ally.

Carrier Division Seven had been sent into the Persian Gulf to stab British and Commonwealth forces in the back.

There was a heavy knocking at the door and a Royal Marine rushed in brandishing a flimsy message sheet which he breathlessly presented to the Prime Minister.

SECRET AND IMMEDIATE STOP ATTENTION FIRST SEA
LORD AND ALL COMMANDS STOP FLAG OFFICER
COMMANDING ABNZ PERSIAN GULF SQUADRON TO
ADMIRALTY STOP AIRCRAFT AND SHIPS OF CENTAUR
BATTLE GROUP ATTACKED WITHOUT WARNING BY US
FORCES IN THE GULF SOUTH OF KHARG ISLAND STOP
EXPECT IMMINENT AIR ATTACK ON ABNZ GUN LINE STOP
THE GUN LINE WILL STAND ITS GROUND STOP ENGLAND
EXPECTS STOP DAVEY MESSAGE ENDS.

In that moment Margaret Thatcher was beyond fear, her anger was like ice in her veins, exploring every pore in her body. Her thoughts slowed, turned coldly, once, twice and then again around the altered reality of the World.

She offered the message sheet to the Chief of the Defence Staff.

"This is," he fulminated disgustedly, "this is, disgraceful, I don't..."

"Believe it, Sir Richard," the Angry Widow said softly. She raised the telephone to her ear.

"Margaret, I..."

She ignored Jack Kennedy's preamble to what she assumed would be some kind of profoundly insulting, patronising plea to her for him to be heard out.

"President Kennedy," the woman retorted frigidly. "I took you for many things. Some of those things were uncharitable, others it now seems, unjustly creditworthy. As we speak the United States Navy is murdering British and Commonwealth sailors, airmen and in all likelihood soldiers in the Persian Gulf. Once again you have attacked *my people* without warning, their blood and the blood of all those who will die in the next few days, weeks and perhaps, years will be on your hands for all time."

Field Marshall Sir Richard Hull had passed Rear Admiral Davey's message to his political master. Willie Whitelaw was staring at it in blank disbelief, aghast...

He looked to Margaret Thatcher with desperate eyes.

The lady was glacially calm.

"Mr President," she enunciated clearly, her tone so implacable that it made the hairs on the back of the necks of all the men in the room stand up in sympathy. "Once again it seems as if the United States has stabbed *Great Britain* in the back..."

"Margaret, I..."

"As we speak American airmen and sailors are murdering British and Commonwealth personnel in the Persian Gulf."

There was a hissing silence on the line for several seconds.

"Margaret, I'm receiving news as we speak..."

"Mr President, I will not let this stand!" Margaret Thatcher had spoken softly but to those who had heard her words it felt as if she had screamed them in their face. "Do you hear me?"

The Prime Minister was trembling with an incandescent rage that threatened to see the phone in her hand hurled across the room. Her teeth were gritted so hard she had to pause to consciously relax her facial muscles before she could continue. The words which came out of her mouth were those of a stranger, a woman whose acquaintance she had never previously made. Those around her could be in no doubt that in that moment she was channelling the terrible righteous anger of the whole nation.

"Do you hear me, Mr President?"

"Yes, I hear you, Prime Minister..."

"This will not stand," the woman said, her voice trembling with deadly intent. "Be assured that I will use every gun, every bomb, every bullet, every weapon that I have at my disposal..."

She broke off to snatch a ragged, spitting breath.

"Every weapon that I have. I swear I will avenge this betrayal one day. Do your worst. I will fight you with my own eye teeth if I have to!"

The man at the other end of the transatlantic line was literally lost for words. Around Margaret Thatcher the room was dreadfully quiet.

"My own eye teeth," the Angry Widow ground out between clenched teeth. "May you rot in Hell!"

Jack Kennedy said something that she did not catch as she clunked the receiver back in its hooks with such force that the two cups of tea on the table next to her stepped an inch to one side slopping most of their contents into their saucers.

Margaret Thatcher looked around the circle of shocked faces.

Presently, she focused on General Sir Richard Hull.

"I will," she said very slowly, "not let this stand," she informed the Chief of the Defence Staff. "*All* options are on the table," she added, "including *Arc Light*."

Chapter 59

The cruiser reverberated with the rushing clank of chains as her anchors ran out at her bow and stern while her screws held her steady against the current. The ship's motion changed as her shafts stopped turning and the anchors bit into the bottomless silts of the main channel.

In the north the sky was torn with Katyushas and the flash of exploding ordnance flickered like a distant electrical storm through the clouds of dust and smoke.

HMS Tiger's two main battery turrets had trained to starboard. Likewise the two twin three-inch mounts which could be brought to bear on that beam. For now the guns remained silent; awaiting their call. Astern of the flagship the destroyer Tobruk and the old Second World War anti-aircraft cruiser Royalist were riding on their anchors, broadside on to eastern bank of the river, their bows pointing approximately due west.

Rear Admiral Nicholas Davey had read the emergency signal twice, digested its contents swiftly, and returned to the cruiser's bridge.

He had handed the decrypt to his Flag Captain.

Hardress Llewellyn 'Harpy' Lloyd looked up.

His tone was bleak. '*Et tu, Brute?*'

Davey was having trouble choking back the bile rising in his throat. He had held off signalling the other ships of the gun line and addressing the cruiser's crew until he *knew* – until he absolutely *knew* – what was going on. Of course he had *known* the moment he received the first message, broadcast in plain text, from HMS Centaur. Since then the reports of the Fleet Air Arm pilots of the carrier's handful of airborne Sea Vixens and Scimitars had confirmed and amplified the magnitude of the betrayal.

One by one those gallant voices in the sky flying above the *atrocity* had fallen silent as the Kitty Hawk's F-4 Phantoms, and the advanced surface-to-air missiles of the carrier's escorts methodically hacked the Centaur's aircraft out of the sky. Three Sea Vixens tasked to suppress a suspect Red Army 'concentration area', where several dozen armoured and other vehicles had been spotted by a high-flying Canberra photo-reconnaissance mission thirty-six hours ago; had turned back intent on targeting Carrier Division Seven. Amidst the jabbering of American airmen gloating about their 'kills' it was impossible to know if the Sea Vixens had got through.

Nick Davey thought it unlikely.

Centaur would have been a sitting duck; her aircraft helpless when the *enemy* turned on them without warning. The old carrier's escorts; the Otago, a Rothesay class general purpose frigate, and the two Blackwood class anti-submarine frigates Hardy and Palliser had nothing with which to fight off a sneak overwhelming air attack. Otago had a quadruple GWS 21 Sea Cat launcher but she probably would not have had time to spool up her birds before the *enemy* was on top of her. The New Zealand frigate's twin 4.5-inch main battery and single 40-millimetre gun was practically useless against fast jets, likewise the Hardy's and the Palliser's three Bofors cannons. Hardy and Palliser both mounted 21-inch torpedo tubes; but again, they were no use against fast jets!

Thus far the *enemy* had left the fleet oiler Wave Master, trailing some miles behind the Centaur Battle Group escorted by the Ton class minesweeper Bronington unmolested. However, from the signal sheet Davey had just handed to his flag captain this was a situation the US Navy was about to address.

Wave Master and Bronington were too far away to communicate via normal ship-to-ship VHF scrambled radio and in any event the *enemy* attack had been accompanied by heavy multi-frequency jamming. The Royal Fleet Auxiliary Wave Master was a Second World War build which had been laid up in Singapore awaiting disposal for scrapping at the time the October War. Her communications suit was not so much basic, as antediluvian. Hence the plain text Morse code signal she had dashed off before the US Navy's jamming silenced her for good.

CENTAUR AND OTAGO DESTROYED OR IN SINKING
CONDITION STOP HARDY AND PALLISER CONDITION
UNKNOWN STOP TWO HOSTILE SURFACE UNITS CLOSING
MY POSITION AT HIGH SPEED STOP BRONINGTON
DETACHED WITH ORDERS TO MOVE INSHORE STOP THE
BASTARDS ATTACKED WITHOUT WARNING STOP GOD
SAVE THE QUEEN MESSAGE ENDS

Davey looked to Tiger's captain.

"They'll have picked this up at Abadan and re-broadcast it to C-in-C Land Forces. Resend it to Fleet Headquarters in England anyway please."

"Yes, sir."

"In the meantime with your permission I will address the crew, Captain."

He was passed a handset.

"*This is Admiral Davey,*" his voice echoed around the ship. "*A short time ago we received news of an unprovoked attack on the Centaur and her escorting vessels by aircraft and ships of the United States Navy. The Centaur and the Otago have been sunk and there is no word of the Hardy or the Palliser. It is likely that the gun line will also come under attack in due course. However, our mission remains unchanged. We have come up river to fight the enemy at our front. If and when we are attacked by the cowards at our backs, we will deal with that as best we may.*" He paused, looked around at the grim determination on the faces of the men of the bridge watch. *"All that we can do now is stand to our stations, to do our duty and to fight like Hell!"*

This reverberated around the ship.

"That is all. God save the Queen!"

Nick Davey handed the microphone to the small man at his shoulder, not initially realising who it was.

Fleet Chief Petty Officer Spider McCann took the handset and surrendered it to the boyish bridge talker to stow in its cage on the nearby bulkhead.

"My apologies, Mister McCann. I didn't know you'd returned to the bridge."

"Things will get warm soon, sir," the other man observed, stoically calm as if what happened next was of no real concern of his.

Davey chuckled lowly. "This sort of thing must be getting a little 'old hat' for you, Mr McCann?"

The senior Chief Petty Officer in the Royal Navy pondered this respectfully.

"Aye, sir," he confessed. "I'd say that as we're anchored with about eight or nine feet of water under the keel *this* big cat isn't going to sink that far," he shrugged. "When we get clobbered, I mean. So that's on the plus side. The other times the Yanks tried to sink me, Talavera had several hundred feet of water under her keel, thousands most likely that time off Cape Finisterre. After the Battle of Malta she went down in about a hundred fathoms they say. I thought my time had come that night Captain Christopher took the Talavera inshore off Lampedusa. Then there was that time that Phantom got blown off the deck of the Enterprise in February and it looked as if it was going to land on Talavera's bridge," he quirked a rueful smile, "right up until a sea carried the ship to leeward and the plane just clipped us on the way down. So this is well," he sighed, "more of the same I suppose. Except it's different every time, just like when I had the honour to serve with you and Captain Christopher's father in the Med all those years ago. If you'll forgive my impertinence, sir."

"God, those were days," Nick Davey recollected fondly, before his mind turned over less fond memories. He had been on HMS Resolution – part of Force H along with the battlecruiser Hood and the battleship Valiant - that day in July 1940 when the battleship's 15-inch guns had fired on the French Fleet anchored in Mers-el-Kebir. That had been an act of treachery but had the French Fleet fallen into Adolf's Hitler's hands the Germans would probably have won the war...

So what was treachery?

What was treachery and what was simply the evil of war?

How on earth would historians view tonight's betrayal in a hundred years' time?

Chapter 60

01:26 Hours
Friday 3rd July 1964
Basra Industrial City, 3 kilometres north of the Iranian border

The virtual loss of all radio communications did not have any immediate effect on the launching of the attack. The Red Army method was to issue orders, demarcate objectives and timescales and to expect its commanders to 'get on with it'. Directives had been issued, the operation was supposed to proceed on 'tramlines', with senior commanders intervening only if necessary. The problem was that now the firing gun had been fired the absence of normal communications made it very nearly impossible to actually know what was going on at the front. Yes, unit commanders were expected to do what had to be done to achieve their own objectives; but no, broader tactics and the management of combined forces was the job of divisional and corps leaders and none of them had functioning radio communications with their troops.

Major General Konstantin Yakovlevich Kurochnik had no idea what was going on along the Iranian border north of Khorramshahr. He had sent motorcycle 'runners' forward to report but as yet none of them had returned; in the meantime a handful of spare radio sets had been discovered, and previously discarded sets were being hurriedly cannibalised for working parts. This might help him talk to other headquarters but the problem remained that he was not hearing anything from his assault units.

He had a timetable predicting where given units would be by a certain time; but no way of finding out if that timetable was already hopelessly behind or ahead of schedule.

Leaving a small radio relay party in the ruins of Basra Industrial City he was moving up onto the heels of the first assault wave. The communications 'problem' was not about to be solved quickly and he needed to know what was going on at Khorramshahr.

The initial short, sharp softening up barrage had petered out as individual artillery batteries exhausted their ammunition quotas. Once their stocks of ordnance fell to sixty percent the guns fell silent and prepared to advance south. Every assumption was that the T-62s of the 19th Guards Tank Corps would over run the defenders of the Khorramshahr Station line; swiftly brush aside the feeble Iranian armoured presence east of the town and take command the north bank of the Karun River well before dawn. At some stage a cursory surrender demand would be communicated to the British. If that offer was rejected artillery and combat engineering units would be brought up to bridge the river and to support the final assault on Abadan Island. The final offensive of the Iraq War would surely sweep all before it...

Such was the plan.

Vladimir Andreyevich Puchkov, the cavalier veteran tanker the Army Group Commander Marshal Babadzhanian had inserted into the command chain of 2nd Siberian Mechanised Army, mainly to stop its existing commander Lieutenant General Viktor Georgiyevich Kulikov stealing *his* thunder, was so irrepressibly bullish that he completely discounted the 'minor communications problems' the Army was experiencing.

"Look. All that's between us and the British on Abadan Island are a few rag heads driving kit that can't hurt us at any kind of range, and a slow-flowing river our engineers can bridge with their eyes closed! Maybe the British will give us a proper fight. Our boys deserve a little fun!"

"With the comms net down we could be walking into a trap," Kurochnik objected respectfully.

Puchkov viewed him with something akin to sympathy.

If you had spent you whole career being thrown out of aircraft with a gun and couple of magazines of ammunition and told to make the best of a bad deal; he quite naturally assumed any sane man would be a pessimist.

"You go forward," he grunted. "I'll sort out the fucking traffic jam up here!"

The 'traffic jam' was actually the Army Commander's responsibility but he was still sulking about his treatment at the hands of the Army Group Commander. Kulikov it seemed, had felt that right from the outset of Operation Nakazyvat Marshal Babadzhanian had treated him like a 'sergeant major', not an equal in the great crusade to restore the pride of the Red Army and to win for the Motherland a place in the sun. At this critical moment in the campaign Kulikov was therefore, still sitting in his headquarters over thirty kilometres away in Al-Hartha nursing his wounded pride.

With the radio net down for all the good he was doing in Al-Hartha the Army Commander might as well have been hiking in the mountains of the Moon.

Chapter 61

The main barrage had fallen to the north and the east of the town. Having studied the map by torchlight to refresh his mental picture of the lay of the land hereabouts, Frank Waters assumed that the Red Army had been hitting positions in and around the Railway Station, and more than somewhat preoccupied with the extensive trench lines and the amateurishly camouflaged anti-tank revetments fanning out from the eastern side of the town all the way down to Karun River.

Initially, he had wondered what was going on out there until belatedly he had realised *nothing* was going on; and that the real defensive works were farther east under so much camouflage netting that people were likely to inadvertently fall into them if they did not know they were there. The Russians did not have the monopoly on 'smoke and mirrors'.

The intensity of the opening barrage had slackened noticeably after about a quarter-of-an-hour, continued in a decidedly desultory fashion for another ten minutes and ended in something of a whimper.

"Those chaps are short of ammo," he told his companions. "They didn't have enough rounds to flatten everything so they only hit the things they thought were going to cause them the biggest headaches. It makes a chap wonder what exactly they are expecting to find down this way?"

The others had pressed themselves flat against the walls, attempting to make themselves invisible.

"This is insane. We ought to get out of here while we can."

Brian Harris, the producer knocked this on the head.

"No, that won't work I'm afraid. Frank has gotten us all into a fine old mess again. Haven't you Colonel?"

"Oh, don't be so wet!" The SAS man retorted cheerfully. "It's too dark to start filming anything I suppose?"

This was greeted with abrupt negatives.

"Let's start doing some words of wisdom for the radio then?"

Nobody argued with him. The bulky tape machine was unpacked and a large, unwieldy microphone of the shape and approximate proportions of proportions of a Neolithic stone axe was pressed into Frank Waters's hands in the darkness.

"Tell me when you are ready?"

Frank Waters was not the man to shirk a new challenge.

However, he hesitated now.

What do I say?

Tricky, very tricky...

Oh, I know!

First things first! The good people at home need me to mark their cards for them. Therefore, the first thing on the agenda was a *sit rep*.

"Yes, I'm ready!"

The soundman began counting down.

"Five. Four. Three. Two. One. Go!"

Frank Waters took a long breath.

"This is Frank Waters. We're sheltering in the ruins of a town called Khorramshahr in Iran. You've probably never heard of this place before. No matter, it is a few miles north of Abadan and the Red Army is under the mistaken impression that Khorramshahr is ripe for the picking."

He paused. Nothing like a dramatic pause to lend a fellow a smidgen of gravitas; a man learned a thing or two from twenty years briefing SAS cut-throats!

"If the enemy knew that Khorramshahr was packed full of chaps looking down the sights of the best anti-tank weaponry in service with any Army anywhere in the World, he'd be quaking in his boots. And that's ignoring all those Iranian tanks hidden out there in the desert. Scores of the beggars, hull down and buried under so much camouflage netting you'd have to pretty much step on the bally things before you know they are there..."

The bark of distant guns crashed out.

Jet engines roared high above the ruined town.

The unmistakable WHOOSH of a Bristol Bloodhound surface-to-air missile launching seemed much closer than it actually was. Within seconds another Bloodhound launched.

"Things are starting to happen now," Frank Waters declared cheerfully. "We have tanks shooting at each other to the north. A couple of Bloodhounds – they can hit targets twelve miles high – have just blasted off from somewhere on Abadan Island. If you listen very closely you can hear the approaching rumbling and rattling of a lot of tanks. Russian tanks! I'm reliably informed that the beggars brought all their most modern tanks, T-62s on this adventure. Mean looking beasts with a really big gun, but no match for Centurion Mark II in a straight fight. If the Russians get past us here in Khorramshahr the one hundred and twenty millimetre cannons of the Conquerors back on Abadan Island will chew these fellows to pieces at two miles. Here in Khorramshahr our boys will let the enemy come right up to us before we let them have it. The first Soviet tanks will follow the best road, the easiest contours in the land, and the least rubble-strewn streets; once our boys have knocked them out the next wave will have to come at our positions less directly, exposing their vulnerable side armour to our guns..."

Heavy machine guns rattled, instantly more guns were firing, chattering madly in the gloom. Multi-coloured tracer and incendiary rounds flashed and curved through the night, bullets ricocheted through the ruins like enraged, supercharged bees.

"Goodness, these fellows seem to have arrived down here at Khorramshahr in no time at all! We must have waved them through our lines. I've heard hardly any of our tank guns firing yet...."

A brilliant blue flare ignited high overhead.

And then a second red flare.

And every Centurion's cannon and every anti-tank gun and recoilless rifle in the World seemed to belch forth death in the next ear-shattering, apocalyptic split second.

Chapter 62

02:32 Hours
Friday 3rd July, 1964
Abadan, Iran

Lieutenant General Michael Carver had watched and listened from the relative safety of the observation trenches on the southern bank of the Karun River, as the Soviet spearhead had come to a fiery, very bloody juddering halt in front of Khorramshahr. The flames of burning T-62s and smashed armoured personnel carriers licked and flickered beyond the town, casting red-tinged shadows far into the desert. However, Carver knew that this was only first contact. The Red Army could afford to take casualties; this early in the battle he could not and it was this fact which banished any temptation to unleash Hasan al-Mamaleki's armour against the Soviets' partially exposed left flank in an immediate counter attack.

The trap was nowhere near fully 'baited'.

Nor would it be ready to be 'sprung' before the Russian bear had been bloodied, gored and tormented virtually to distraction; and that was going to be a foul business not likely to be completed quickly.

If he sprung the trap even minutes too early, or late his vastly outnumbered men and tanks would be consumed by the battle to no good purpose...

And that would be criminal...

The 'blooding' of 2nd Siberian Mechanised Army before the walls of Khorramshahr was but the first of a series of vicious gambits designed to *bleed*, madden and weaken the great ravening beast bearing down on his positions.

Presently, the Soviets would be struggling to reconstruct their communications net; news of this setback – for his enemy the destruction of twenty or thirty tanks was a *setback*, not a disaster – south of the Railway Station at Khorramshahr would take a little while to percolate back up the line. In the meantime, the rest of the Soviet juggernaut would be rolling forward. Nobody on the Russian side would actually know what had just happened to the 'first wave' until the second wave found its way blocked by the wrecks of burning tanks and APCs; at such times the fog of war became nigh impenetrable. Nevertheless, the second and third waves would inexorably roll south until they encountered what was left of the first. The advance might pause but it would not stop, that was not the Red Army way.

Theoretically, there was 'space' to exploit in the desert to the east of Khorramshahr but advancing on Abadan 'around the houses' extended the attackers' flank. Before the enemy swung around the 'urban obstacle' in its path he would extend his line many miles east, hoping to bring the 3rd Imperial Iranian Armoured Division to battle. From previous encounters with Iraqi and Iranian armour the Soviets would expect to brush Hasan al-Mamaleki's tanks aside; and therein lay the Soviets' next first surprise.

The enemy was not to know that Hasan al-Mamaleki had pulled his armour back over ten miles in places precisely to *avoid* contact with the Soviet spearheads. In fact his pickets – light tanks and a few sacrificial anti-tank units – were deployed so as to convince the Russians that there was absolutely no threat to their left flank.

Carver ordered his driver to take him back to his headquarters.

After the concentrated violence of the opening barrage which had fallen mainly on the frontier and desert positions where, until a week ago, Iranian tanks and infantry had been dug in, the shelling had become sporadic, an apparently random thing. However, although rounds were only falling on Abadan Island at a rate of only one or two a minute; already big fires were burning in the northern refinery complex.

"Admiral Davey's gun line has anchored in the main channel north of Al Seeba, sir," Carver was informed as he strode into the buried operations room. "Contrary to our expectations he has encountered no opposition as yet."

"We launched four Bloodhounds?" The Commander-in-Chief inquired, almost as an afterthought.

"Three against presumed hostiles approaching from the north, sir," another staff officer reported. "One possible kill. The fourth launch was against an unidentified contact over the entrance to the Shatt al-Arab. We think this was probably one of the Kitty Hawk's Hawkeyes. Regrettably, the target successfully evaded the missile."

Michael Carver went to the big composite wall map of the Abadan-Basra-Khorramshahr-Faw region, began to study it as he thought his thoughts.

"Admiral Davey is on the scrambler, sir."

A lesser man's heart would have sunk at this news.

Carver had absorbed the disastrous news from the Gulf about the Centaur Battle Group with a mixture of disgust and despair, forced himself to move on. *Forget about Naval air support.* What next?

"Hello, Nick," he drawled laconically into the handset he was handed.

"Things are going to get a bit *sticky*, Michael," the other man replied in similarly untroubled tones. "Further to my last signal Centaur has either been disabled or sunk and none of her birds are transmitting any longer."

Carver had been counting on Centaur's air group to provide some minimal level of cover over Abadan Island, without it he had only the Bloodhounds and they were useless against low flying fast jets. The nearest air support was based hundreds of miles away in Dammam. Emergency forward airstrips had been prepared in Kuwait but there was only a minimal maintenance, ordnance and re-fuelling infrastructure in place at those desert airfields; and in any event none of the Hawker Hunters or obsolete Seahawk Fleet Air Arm fighters – the latter hastily retrieved from mothballs and ferried out to the Middle East in recent weeks – had the operational endurance necessary to loiter more than a few minutes over Abadan flying from those bases in Kuwait. He was also painfully aware that none of the ships in Nick Davey's gun line moored north of Al Seeba was equipped with modern surface-to-air missile systems.

"Yes," Michael Carver mused out aloud. "I think *sticky* is probably about the size of it, Nick. Obviously, things are happening very quickly and the situation is somewhat...*fluid* at the moment. That said I am minded to carry on regardless with Operation Lightfoot and its surviving naval components."

Nick Davey hesitated.

"Yes, dammit!" He concurred after a gap of perhaps two to three seconds. All things considered both men recognised that they were already so far up the creek without a paddle that it was of only of passing consequence how many hungry crocodiles were circling 'the boat'. "If the bastards,' there could be no doubt whatsoever that he was referring to the United States Navy *not* the Red Army, "attack Abadan or my gun line there's precious little we can do about it. No point worrying about it."

It was Michael Carver's turn to pause for the briefest of interregnums, thinking a hundred thoughts at once against the darkling background of a tactical environment that could hardly be less propitious. Before the cowardly attack on the Centaur he had been confident that given the expenditure of sufficient Allied blood he could hold Abadan for several days, possibly weeks; albeit the whole island would be comprehensively wrecked in the process. With the assistance of Hasan al-Mamaleki's the 3rd Imperial Iranian Armoured Division he had hoped to not just blunt but to mutilate the Red Army's striking power in the Persian Gulf. What he had never considered was the possibility that at the very moment battle was joined north of Abadan he would be threatened, by an overwhelmingly powerful American naval and air force at his back.

"We shall proceed as planned," he determined urbanely. "My gunners will be calling on the inestimable services of your squadron shortly, Nick. There's nothing we can do about what's going on down in the Gulf..."

Actually, there was *something* he could do about it.

He just did not know if it was feasible or if the people back in Oxford would go along with it.

"Good luck, Nick," he signed off.

Chapter 63

02:40 Hours
Friday 3rd July, 1964
Al-Rasheed Air Base, South West Baghdad

True to form the newly installed Commissar General of Iraq had gone to ground within seconds of the first air burst west of the city. There were only two underground bomb shelters on the base and First Deputy Secretary of the KGB Yuri Vladimirovich Andropov and his entourage having commandeered the deepest one, had absolutely no intention of coming out again until it was 'safe'.

Defence Minister of the Soviet Union Admiral of the Fleet Sergey Georgiyevich Gorshkov was disgusted, but in no way surprised to discover that the base 'operations centre' was so full of men in green KGB uniforms and snivelling Party apparatchiks; that most of the Red Air Force officers and men manning the command centre responsible for *all* air operations in Central and Southern Iraq had been expelled from the complex to make room for the influx.

He turned to the head of his personal security detachment, a Siberian Lieutenant-Commander of the Red Navy Security Police who had been with him at the Battle of Malta and who had no love for the Muscovite coterie cowering in the corridors of the bunker.

"Get these fuckers out of here!"

Gorshkov had drawn the Makarov pistol he had carried ever since he got back to Chelyabinsk in April. He brandished it to force his way through the crowd.

"Shoot anybody who doesn't want to move!"

"You can't just barge in here and start ordering *my* people about!" Andropov complained angrily.

The newly appointed Commissar General had not risen to his feet on Gorshkov's entrance. The Minister of Defence slapped his gun down on the desk between him and the KGB man and leaning towards Andropov asked: "So what's the plan? Skulk away down here until the war is over? Or do you plan to get off your fat arse and start doing your fucking job, Comrade Commissar?"

Andropov's battered face coloured with anger in the pale illumination of the bunker's naked light bulbs. The commotion in the corridor outside the room was clearly unnerving him.

Gorshkov did not wait for a reply.

"I'm moving all your KGB fuckers out of here so the Red Air Force controllers can get on with their jobs. We're under attack and you and I are going to be seen *above ground* doing our duty!"

"The line of command must be preserved..."

Gorshkov picked up the Makarov.

"I'm the *line of command* while we're under attack. The *Commissar General* is supposed to be *managing* the civilian government of the Protectorate of Iraq. If you want to stay down here that's fine by me; I'll put a bullet between your eyes and find somebody with the guts to do the fucking job!"

The operations room was still crowded when the two men shouldered their way through to the command table.

"Anybody who does not have a job to do in this room get out now!" Gorshkov shouted. He stopped himself firing a shot into the roof; the bullet would have probably ricocheted around the concrete walls killing and wounding several men. At a time like this he could not afford to risk losing key men. "Anybody who isn't in the Red Air Force get out!"

Nobody moved.

Gorshkov sighed, pointed the Makarov at the nearest KGB man in a green uniform and pulled the trigger. The bark of the gun was painfully loud in the confined space.

"Who's next?"

Andropov was staring at him. He swallowed hard.

"All the radio equipment is short-circuited," he said lamely.

"The fucking land lines will be okay. Has anybody found out what's going on elsewhere yet?"

No, nobody had found out *anything*.

There were a lot of people at Al-Rasheed Air Base who deserved to be shot; that was a thing Gorshkov would attend to in the morning if they were all still alive when dawn broke.

Telephones were ringing insistently.

Two KGB troopers dragged their fallen comrade out into the corridor trailing a viscous slick of dark blood on the floor.

"I am Gorshkov!" The Minister of Defence shouted. "I am in command. I will shoot anybody who does not obey my orders." He knew exactly what the priorities were in the fog of confusion that must already be spreading across the whole of occupied Iraq. "Communicate by land line to all commands that the authority to deploy nuclear and chemical weapons is absolutely *denied* by my order under the powers vested in me by the Central Committee of the Party."

"We are under attack, Comrade!" Andropov hissed in his ear.

"No, we're not," the dark-eyed Admiral with the boot black moustache retorted angrily. "The air bursts were precisely targeted to cause the maximum disruption to our communications net and the minimum loss of life and damage on the ground. Baghdad would no longer exist and we'd already be vaporised if the British had meant to hit the city!"

Gorshkov seized Andropov's elbow and dragged him into a corner. He leaned close.

"We made a pact with the Yankees. They guaranteed that *they* would *deal* with the British if they *went nuclear*."

Andropov opened his mouth like a beached fish, sucking air and drowning all at once.

"That's why I'm here. To make sure nobody fucks up!" Gorshkov added. "The ground war will be over in a few hours and the Yanks will *deal* with the British navy and air force. That's the deal and no matter how fucked up it is that is *the deal*. This is the price we pay for a 'peace with honour' with the Americans. *That price will be paid.* Operation Nakazyvat *ends* on the northern shores of the Persian Gulf." He quirked a sour grin. "For five years, anyway," he added with the scowl of a man who is tasting ash in his mouth.

Gorshkov viewed Andropov thoughtfully for a moment.

If the Commissar General had not already had a bowel movement he had the appearance of man who was about to have one.

"Get your people on side," Gorshkov grunted disgustedly and turned away.

Fucking civilians!

Chapter 64

02:48 Hours
Friday 3rd July, 1964
USS Kitty Hawk, South of Kharg Island, Persian Gulf

Lieutenant-Commander Walter Brenckmann had felt the deck quiver rather than jolt or flinch beneath his feet. Down in the Kitty Hawk's darkened CIC the bulkhead lights flickered momentarily. The carrier had been turning to port, heeling one, two degrees and shortly after the 'bump' her wheel went over again and she settled on her new course. All seemed as before; and then the faraway grinding, thumping reverberation set the deck plates trembling and the flagship of Carrier Division Seven began to slow in the water.

The battle ought to have been a foregone conclusion; that in its aftermath the biggest warship in the world had briefly been reduced to walking pace was testimony to naked courage of the vanquished.

Nearly three hours had passed since the final shot was fired.

Since then Kitty Hawk had worked back up to twenty-seven knots and resumed normal air operations.

Walter glanced at the ship's chronometer repeater above his head. 02:49.

Crewmen had brought round jugs of strong black coffee a few minutes ago.

No threats were visible on the big Battle Board in the middle of the compartment, and everybody spoke in low, ultra-controlled tones. It was all very bloodless; or rather, *conscienceless* although Walter Brenckmann wondered if that was quite true. On reflection he decided that *unconscionable* probably better described what had happened in the last few hours.

The *enemy* – the British, the Australians and the New Zealanders – had, once they got over their shock and realised they were under attack, fought back like lions. He had watched it all in slow motion as the symbols and nomenclature displayed on the Battle Board had told the whole disgraceful story.

To start with he had honestly believed that there had been some terrible mistake.

Then he had realised that what was going on only looked piecemeal, knee-jerk, and unpremeditated because the crew of Hawkeye Zero-Three, sent to loiter over Southern Iran over an hour in advance of the battle had refused to be any part of the atrocity. What had supposed to have been a choreographed, meticulously executed slaughter had suddenly had to be improvised very nearly out of thin air by the shell-shocked duty operations team in the carrier's CIC.

'NOW HEAR THIS! NOW HEAR THIS!'

The speakers had boomed and Admiral Bringle's dead pan baritone had filled the air.

'IN ACCORDANCE WITH EXECUTIVE ORDER ZERO-ZEVEN-

EIGHT SLASH SIX-FOUR CARRIER DIVISION SEVEN IS AUTHORISED TO CLEAR ALL HOSTILE SHIPPING FROM THE PERSIAN GULF AND TO CONDUCT OPERATIONS TO SECURE AND MAINTAIN AIR SUPERIORITY OVER THE COASTAL REGION BETWEEN THE STRAITS OF HORMUZ AND DAMMAM-DHARHRAN.'

In the CIC men had been giving each other bewildered, quizzical looks by that juncture. The unreality had deepened the next moment.

'SHIPS AND AIRCRAFT OF THE AUSTRALIAN, BRITISH AND NEW ZEALAND EXPEDITIONERY FORCE DEPLOYED IN THE GULF HAVING FAILED TO DISENGAGE AND DESIST IN OFFENSIVE OPERATION IN IRAQ AND IRAN ARE FORTHWITH TO BE REGARDED AS HOSTILE. CARRIER DIVISION SEVEN WILL DISCHARGE ITS DUTY. THAT IS ALL!'

Walter had contemplated requesting permission to be relieved of his duties in the CIC; he would have in the event he had been asked to play any direct part in the night's foul business. Instead, he and his ASW watch had been passive, horrified witnesses; his threat table having remained empty throughout the 'action'.

The Coontz class guided missile destroyers William V. Pratt (DLG-13) and Dewey (DLG-14) had shot down two aircraft shortly after they launched from HMS Centaur, approximately seventeen nautical miles north of the Kitty Hawk. The cruiser Albany (CG-10) had flushed two Bendix Talos long-range naval 'beam riding' surface-to-air missiles less than a minute later.

Almost as an aside to the naval battle which unfolded south of Kharg Island, the two F4 Phantoms sent to intercept Hawkeye Zero-Three were engaged by air defence systems in the Abadan area, and forced to engage full reheat to escape out to sea.

Working up to flank speed the converted World War II era heavy cruiser Boston (CAG-1) – whose conversion had left her forward triple 8-inch turrets in place – had manoeuvred astern of the flagship to bring her broadside to bear on the frigate HMNZS Otago, at a range of approximately fifteen miles.

Otago had begun to fire on the approaching Coontz class destroyers – then still seven to eight miles away – with her twin 4.5 inch guns. HMS Centaur's other escorts, the ASW frigates Palliser and Hardy, the former some three miles closer to Kharg Island than the carrier at the beginning of the action, and the latter two miles astern, had immediately increased speed and steered to put themselves between Centaur and the ships of Carrier Division Seven. These two smaller ships, each displacing a little over a thousand tons with a maximum speed of around twenty-five or six knots, only carried a handful of anti-aircraft cannons between them and *nothing* else for protection against air attack.

HMNZS Otago was a more capable ship, albeit no match for any of the larger more modern US ships she was up against. She had a quadruple GWS Sea Cat surface-to-air missile launcher and – depending upon which intelligence report one accepted – either six or twelve torpedo tubes. Palliser and Hardy both had two twenty-one inch torpedo tubes.

'What are they doing?' Somebody asked in disbelief when it was patently obvious *what* the Centaur's outgunned and outmatched escorts were *doing*.

Walter Brenckmann had watched the tragedy play out on the Battle Board with a sick feeling in the pit of his stomach and the bitterest of bile rising in his throat.

This was HMS Talavera's and HMS Yarmouth's *death run* off Malta all over again, except this time the British and the New Zealanders' enemy was exponentially more powerful and with every aircraft the Kitty Hawk launched off her catapults the odds became more impossible.

There was dumb horror when Otago's Sea Cats scored a 'lucky hit' on one of the four A-4 Skyhawks falling on her like vultures on a carcass. The surviving pilots coolly reported near misses and a hit amidships with a thousand pound general purpose bomb.

Walter tried and failed to imagine the scene playing out fifteen miles away in the night. Across a watery battlefield lit with star shells, flares and the flash of guns Kitty Hawk's Phantoms, Skyhawks and Intruders were homing in on their targets guided by the invisible electronic fingers of their radars.

The air search and gunnery sensor returns from *all* the big ships of Carrier Division Seven were constantly being fed back into the Kitty Hawk's CIC, updating the Battle Board in real time. It was a space age battle being found with blood and iron; in the bowels of the great carrier it was hard to remember that the labels and tracks on the Battle Board told of and foretold the death of incredibly brave men.

The Otago was dead in the water; still shooting back at the Dewey and the William V. Pratt as the range closed

The Boston switched its fire from the Otago to Centaur.

The carrier held her course.

How courageous was that?

She kept on launching aircraft until either a hit from one or more of Boston's three hundred and thirty-five pound high explosive shells, or a bomb from one of the circling A-6 Intruders put a hole in her flight deck.

HMS Centaur had turned away to the north.

Two A-4 Skyhawks caught up with her; turning her into a floating torch within minutes.

The Dewey and the William V. Pratt stood off Otago's starboard bow and poured 5-inch rounds into her as the Boston relentlessly closed the range with the sinking aircraft carrier.

The Palliser and the Hardy were left to the Air Group.

To Walter Brenckmann the 'whole show' was an object lesson in exactly why the management of fluid modern battlefields ought not to be left in the hands of competent men with clockwork minds.

Rear Admiral Bringle never once came down to the CIC during the battle; leaving its conduct to his Flag Captain, Horace Epes and Kitty Hawk's Commander (Operations), a man who had spent most of the last twenty years ashore lecturing at Annapolis and in staff jobs in Washington DC. The man clearly thought he was refighting the Battle of Midway!

Achieving local air superiority trumped all other considerations. After that knocking out the enemy's carrier was the thing that really mattered. Thereafter, the Otago had to be 'dealt with' because it had the most capable radar and communications suite in the Centaur Battle Group. The ASW frigates were 'no real threat' so they could be 'sorted out later'.

In the course of the battle over half Kitty Hawk's airborne 'assets' were committed north of the 'engagement zone' enforcing 'air superiority' over large tracts of empty air space above Southern Iraq, Iran and the Persian Gulf around Kharg Island. Those assets ought to have been killing 'enemy' ships. It was only when first HMS Palliser and shortly afterwards, HMS Hardy approached within eight miles of the Kitty Hawk's guard ship, the gun-denuded missile cruiser Albany that the Operations Officer had...*panicked.*

Suddenly, the bombs wasted on the already burning and dead in the water Centaur and in trying to end Otago's absurdly unequal gunnery duel with the Dewey and the William V. Pratt, meant that bar two F-4 Phantoms flying top cover, everybody else's bomb racks were empty. The situation was further exacerbated by the fact that four of Carrier Division Seven's major surface units had not been required to, let alone ordered to either engage the enemy, or to put themselves in a position to so do.

Early in the 'action' Walter had queried this; suggesting that the Charles F. Adams class destroyers Towers (DDG-9) and Lawrence (DDG-4), or the Forrest Sherman class John Paul Jones (DD-931) or Du Pont (DD-941) ought to supplement the fleet's ASW screen in the absence of the Dewey and the William V. Pratt on Carrier Division Seven's northern flank'.

He had been tersely requested to mind his own business.

In the event the commanding officers of the Towers and the John Paul Jones had taken matters into their own hands. Both ships had come careening around the stern of the carrier to engage the two small Royal Navy frigates steadily forging ever closer to the Kitty Hawk.

War is chaos, chaos is war...

That was not the way it was supposed to be!

Carrie Division Seven had been on a peacetime goodwill cruise until a few days ago and as a result it had gone to war with a poorly drilled operations team, without a Plan 'A', or 'B' and by the time those two British frigates had got within torpedo range of the flagship if there had ever been a Plan 'C', nobody had shared it in advance with anybody else in Kitty Hawk's CIC.

If Kitty Hawk's crew had been driven hard for the last two months things would have been different; but you simply could not build a 'team' in the middle of a battle. It mattered not that Carrier Division Seven had crushing might on its side; too many of its senior officers were fighting from memory, trying to read the moves from a text book.

Walter had left his post and walked across to the Operations Officer.

'Those ships carry the British Mark Eight torpedo, sir,' he reported urgently, not believing that he was having to tell the other man *this*.

The other man had been so intent on studying a nearby consul that he started with alarm. Not to mention offence at the quiet anger in Walter Brenckmann's voice and hooded eyes.

'What?'

'They might already have launched torpedoes at us, sir.'

'Yes, yes...'

Walter wanted to grab the Commander (Operations) by the lapels and shake him; he probably would of had the other man not been a head taller and eighty or ninety pounds heavier. Instead, he had settled for pointing at the Battle Board.

'I recommend we deploy the Lawrence and the Du Pont to *arrest* the fleet oiler attached to the Centaur Battle Group, sir.'

'Arrest?'

'British Royal Fleet Auxiliary oilers do not mount any ordnance, sir.'

The tanker had been escorted by a smaller vessel, probably one of the four hundred ton coastal minesweepers the British had had stationed in the Gulf before the Soviet invasion of Iran and Iraq.

In the confusion – and the bungling onboard the Flagship - it had got away into shallow water pursued by salvoes of 5-inch shells from the chasing destroyers.

RFA Wave Master had been boarded by men from the Du Pont and was presently being escorted back to the rest of the fleet.

Both HMS Palliser and HMS Hardy had been sunk; Palliser by naval gunfire from three destroyers, Hardy by a single thousand pound bomb which had capsized her in less than sixty seconds.

The Kitty Hawk had belatedly begun to make a turn away from a 'possible' torpedo attack. That had baffled Walter; surely you always turned *towards* approaching missiles? A ship's bow was much less prone to catastrophic damage than its stern; it was basic seamanship...

The torpedo had detonated somewhere inconveniently adjacent to where the carrier's starboard outer propeller shaft exited the hull.

The shaft had not been fractured, nor the propeller lost.

What had happened was that the shaft had become deformed – probably only bent out of alignment by a degree or two – while it was turning at ninety percent of maximum revolutions.

Before the shaft could be stopped it had opened up three-feet wide rent in the aft hull around the shaft, wrecked every bearing in the two hundred feet long tunnel within the ship carrying it back to the machinery spaces; and torn the guts out of the after turbine in Engine Room Four. Kitty Hawk had taken on nearly fifteen hundred tons of water and her flank speed had been reduced from over thirty-three knots to around twenty-seven, by good fortune rather than design, sufficient, given a healthy wind over the bow to conduct normal flight operations. Counter-flooding and pumping bunker oil from one side of the ship to the other had already stabilised her minor starboard list, and nobody had been killed or seriously injured by the hit.

Two aircraft, the A-4 taken out by Otago's Sea Cats, and an A-6 Intruder – most likely shot down by one of Centaur's Sea Vixens – had been lost. A single hit from a 4.5inch round fired by the New Zealand frigate had killed seven men on the William V. Pratt and injured another five. Otherwise, the battle had been bloodless on the American side.

Walter Brenckmann felt the carrier heel into a new turn.

He watched the compass repeater steady onto a new bearing.

North-north-west; farther into the Gulf.

All the better to twist the knife *deeper* into one's friend's back.

Chapter 65

00:25 Hours (GMT – 3 hours behind Gulf time)
Friday 3rd July, 1964
The Prime Minister's Room, Hertford College, Oxford

"The *bastards!*" Margaret Thatcher spat. "The absolute *bastards!*"

The men in the room were staring at their feet.

"Quite," Prime Minister, Sir Henry Tomlinson the Cabinet Secretary agreed stoically. Everybody was on their feet and this was never a good thing when the moment called for the most level of heads and the calmest possible judgement to be exercised.

William Whitelaw, the Secretary of State for Defence looked daggers at Tom Harding-Grayson, who met his angry scrutiny with cool eyes.

"Dammit," Whitelaw complained, "we should never have gone down the road of playing fast and loose with the Americans. Undermining them with the Saudis! And as for all the trouble we've caused in Egypt..."

His voice trailed away when he realised everybody was looking at him as if he was an idiot. Everybody, that is, apart from Airey Neave, the minister in charge of the Intelligence Services, who was viewing him with murder in his eyes. Neave had turned up unannounced only a few minutes ago after deciding, without consulting anybody, that he was not going to 'skulk about in that blasted bunker at Chilmark while my friends are above ground in Oxford!'

Everybody tacitly assumed that the notion of being forever parted from his protégé, Margaret Thatcher's side by the vagaries of war, had been too much for the hero of Colditz.

"The Yanks undermined their own position in Arabia without any help from us, Willie," Airey Neave objected testily. "As for Nasser and the Egyptians, we could hardly leave biggest Army and the biggest Air Force in the whole bally Middle East free to stab us in the back at a moment of *Colonel Nasser's choosing!*"

"Well, a lot of good it's done us!" Observed Peter – Lord, the 6th baron in his lineage – Carington, Whitelaw's Minister of State and of the Navy, his closest political advisor. However, his tone was conciliatory, as if to say 'well, we did the best we could but all things considered it didn't turn out quite as well as it might'.

Margaret Thatcher had used this fraught interlude to compose her thoughts. She waved at the chairs, each threadbare and somewhat careworn in different ways – much like her companions – spread around the room.

"Everybody sit down please. If we are going to jump up and down every time we hear the next piece of appallingly bad news we shall get nowhere!"

The Prime Minister looked to Sir Henry Tomlinson, the greying eminence grise who ran the Home Civil Service, and therefore, commanded the sinews of the entire governmental infrastructure of the less than united, United Kingdom. The old man nodded to the Foreign Secretary who had just come back into the room.

"I took it upon myself to talk to Ambassador Brenckmann," Tom Harding-Grayson explained. For the first time that anybody could remember he looked and sounded utterly exhausted. "Poor Walter is beside himself," he groaned. "Nobody in Philadelphia is taking his calls and everybody at the embassy is a state of near catatonic shock, actually."

"It's not too late for us to put out some kind of statement of our peaceful intent," William Whitelaw suggested. "Something to, er, hold the line until tempers have cooled..."

The Chief of the Defence Staff, Field Marshall Sir Richard Hull shook his head as the other man spoke.

"With respect, sir," he groaned, "I have a nasty feeling that it is already *too late*." He looked at his watch, a habit he was trying to curb.

Not yet one o'clock in the morning Greenwich Mean Time – not that Greenwich existed any more, courtesy of the Yanks – which meant it would be dawn at Abadan in an hour or so.

"Look," he went on, "we always knew we were getting into murky waters deploying *Arc Light*..."

"The Americans would probably have stabbed us in the back regardless of *Arc Light*," Lord Carington remarked philosophically.

"Possibly," the old soldier agreed. "In any event this, or something like it, was one of the scenarios that we 'gamed' at my headquarters. Our 'gaming' produced a series of graduated responses; only one of which is actually remotely feasible in the likely short timescales available for us. I say 'one', actually there are two possible responses. The other response would be to do nothing. However, it is not my feeling that *this* government will wish to seriously contemplate *doing nothing*."

Margaret Thatcher tried not to frown too hard.

"Where else do we think American forces might turn on us?"

"American naval and air forces significantly outnumber our forces in numerical strength and technical capabilities in the Mediterranean, Prime Minister." The Chief of the Defence Staff held up a hand because he had not finished. "However, most of the big ships of the US Sixth Fleet are currently tied up in Malta and Gibraltar, Prime Minister. In those ports the US Navy still gives every appearance of docility..."

What Margaret Thatcher said next dumbfounded all her political colleagues. If she had produced a freshly caught flat fish – perhaps, a Dover Sole - from her handbag and gone around the room slapping each man in face with it, she could not possibly have prompted looks any more astonished.

"Intern those vessels," the lady decided. "Immediately."

"Margaret," Airey Neave said, starting to object before he thought better of it. He glanced to Sir Richard Hull. "Er, can we actually do that, CDS?"

The soldier nodded.

"There might be bloodshed. But yes, we can have," he smiled "a *shot* at it." He looked around the room. "It happens that after his previous experience relying on the US Navy the C-in-C Malta and Admiral Grenville, C-in-C Mediterranean Fleet had their staffs develop a set of contingency plans for exactly this kind of *situation*. Although, I'd hasten to add none of us actually saw *this* particular *thing* coming."

Margaret Thatcher's expression was icily severe.

But in her topaz blue eyes there was a glint of grim...mischief.

"You're telling me that you already have plans in hand to intern the US Navy vessels docked at Malta and Gibraltar, Sir Richard?"

"Yes, Prime Minister. I took the liberty of activating them as soon as I received the first cables from Admiral Davey, and General Carver's subsequent request for *Arc Light* strikes against the USS Kitty Hawk Battle Group in the Gulf."

"We will await the arrival the Chief of the Air Staff before considering that latter *request*," Margaret Thatcher decided tersely. "How soon can we *arrest* the ships of the Sixth Fleet?"

The Chief of the Defence Staff tried not to smile; it seemed as if he had read the mood and the resolve of his Prime Minister perfectly. While all the wise men around her might have vacillated in this hour of crisis she had – instinctively, intuitively – acted. Exactly as he had anticipated she would react, decisively and with unshakable resolve.

Since the soldier had already issued the orders to Air Marshall Sir Daniel French in Malta to act against the US Fleet at five o'clock local time in Malta, Margaret Thatcher's question was one that he could answer with great exactitude. Again, he checked his watch.

"In about two hours from now, Prime Minister."

"Very well. Do it!"

Chapter 66

03:30 Hours
Friday 3rd July, 1964
Khorramshahr, Iran

"This is Frank Waters talking to you from the front line in Khorramshahr," said the dusty former SAS man after he had finished coughing the dust and drifting cordite smoke out of his lungs. While he tried very hard not to hurry, or to speak with the urgency of a man who has a train to catch; every instinct in his body told him that if he and his BBC news crew did not get out of the ruins of Khorramshahr soon they would never get out.

After the Soviets had driven into the first trap the Red Army had done exactly what it always does in such situations. It tried to do the same thing again; with predictably even more bloody and fiery results which had left practically everything combustible in the wrecked town burning fiercely.

"This is truly heroic stuff!" Frank Waters exclaimed cheerfully. "I've just pulled the cotton wool,' actually it was strips of a field dressing, "from my ears and they are still ringing like bells with the sound and fury of our guns!"

The trouble was that it was only a matter of time before the Red Army went to Plan 'B'. Specifically, it would saturate the whole area with artillery fire, and then it would attack again with everything it had. If downtown Khorramshahr had been a bad place to be a couple of hours ago it was going to get massively more uncomfortable very soon now.

"This will be a very short report. The surviving anti-tank squads are starting to pack up. I don't know what the Centurions around us will do. I honestly don't know how they can possibly extricate themselves from the town. The whole place has been fearfully knocked about. I can't imagine how the Soviets are going to get T-62s through the streets. Streets! Well, there aren't any streets anymore!"

Frank Waters paused, partly to get his breath, partly to think about the brave men who had died and were about to die attempting to hold back the next tide of Soviet tanks. He ought to have worked out Michael Carver's game plan a lot earlier than he had; but then that was why he was a freebooting lone wolf, and Carver was the British Army's greatest living tactician.

Michael Carver meant to bleed the Red Army white and in so doing block and delay its approach to the northern bank of the Karun River. He would let the T-62s come onto his defences, on and on and when the leading regiments had been decimated several times over, challenge the beggars to get across the two or three hundred feet wide slow moving muddy God-given water barrier of the Karun River south of the town. Then when he had the 2nd Siberian Mechanised Army's spearheads fully engaged across the river on Abadan Island he would unleash Hasan al-Mamaleki's 3rd Imperial Iranian Armoured Division on the invaders' left flank.

The Red Army had charged Michael Carver's guns so fast that it had not had time to fully study and understand the battlefield, nor to appreciate the clinical pragmatism of its adversary's mind. Some time later today the entire – by then badly bloodied - first wave of the Soviet assault force would be backed up between the Karun River and the urban sprawl of the Basra Industrial Area the other side of the northern border with Iraq. If everything went according to Carver's plan the defenders of Abadan would be directly to the enemy's front in pre-prepared lines beyond the Karun River, Iranian armour would be poised on its left and the ABNZ floating gun line would threaten its right hand flank.

"Stop recording!" The old soldier commanded.

"Frank, what are we doing?" Brian Harris asked.

"We're getting out of here, old boy." Frank Waters was already on his feet, oblivious to the rifle bullets pinging through the ruins and the periodic crash of the nearby Centurions' L7 105-millimetre cannons. "If we don't get to the bridge across the Karun River before the engineers blow it we'll be done for!"

In retrospect coming across the river a second time had been an unbelievably stupid thing to do. That thus far none of them had sustained so much as a scratch was a miracle. However, this was not the time to make an admission of that kind in front of 'the men'.

"Just follow me! Don't stop for anything unless I go to ground!"

The very first tinge of grey was beginning to rise above the eastern horizon as the dishevelled and shell-shocked BBC men stumbled after their leader. They headed south, each man falling over rubble, cursing, picking themselves up and carrying on.

When Brian Harris fell he was instantly jerked to his feet by Frank Waters, who slapped him on the back.

"If we have to run, chaps," the old soldier declared, "drop your kit and keep your heads down!"

Frank Waters had snatched the leaden weight of the film box from the cameraman and slung the sound man's haversack over his shoulder. This latter was full of all manner of widgets and tools that the SAS man could not have named or identified for love or money. However, to a man accustomed to carrying a fifty pound pack on his back and an armful of automatic weaponry in his arms, he carried his lighter, somewhat unwieldy burdens relatively easily despite having lost condition during his recent confinement and starvation. Soon, he was halting every minute or so to chivvy along his other, less fit and hardy colleagues.

Brian Harris collapsed on a sprained ankle.

"Put your arm around my shoulder, old man," Frank Waters commanded and they limped onward, surrounded now by the defenders of Khorramshahr walking and trotting, in remarkably good order south towards the river.

"Where the blazes do you think you fellows are going!" Shouted a man who jumped down from a Land Rover which had crunched to a halt nearby; the motley BBC crew had just emerged from the rubble into the pre-dawn twilight.

"Across the bally bridge!" Frank Waters shouted, gasping for breath.

"Well, well, well," the other man exclaimed, mightily amused, "I confess I honestly and truly thought General Carver was pulling my leg when he said you idiots had come up here!"

That was when the first salvo of the renewed Soviet barrage fell north of Khorramshahr in and around the crater field which had once been the town's railway station.

"Right! Get in the bloody car, chaps!"

"We won't all fit in," objected one of Frank Waters's charges.

"Just get in, chaps!" The former SAS man barked in his best parade ground bawl.

"Calder," the BBC men's saviour introduced himself to Frank Waters's colleagues as the bombardment fell on Khorramshahr proper a few hundred yards away. "Julian Calder. I've been running messages back and forth to our Iranian allies. Fine chaps, all of them. They're positively itching to come to grips with the *infidels*. 3rd Imperial Armoured Division was raised in the area around Tehran, a lot of the chaps regard the coming battle as a chance to exact God's justice on the invaders!"

"Damned good to bump into you again, Julian," Frank Waters bellowed above the roar of the Land Rover's labouring engine and the spinning of its wheels in the sand. He was half-sitting on Brian Harris's lap, the rest of the crew were clinging on for dear life in the back of the Land Rover, painfully perched on their equipment boxes.

Calder, the younger man by a few years was one of the Regiment's – 22nd Special Air Service Regiment's – coming men. He and Frank Waters had had as little to do with each other as possible before the October War and since, notwithstanding that Calder had been his deputy in Iran at the time of the Soviet invasion in April. It spoke volumes for the mess he had got his 'BBC team' into that he was so inordinately glad to see the other man.

"The anti-tank boys were extricating themselves from the ruins," he explained. "I took that as our cue to make a run for it. I hope all our chaps get back across the river..."

"The engineers have orders to blow the south bank pontoons when the first T-62 is half-way across!"

"That's the spirit!"

In the darkness columns of men were trudging and shuffling down to the river.

"We've got all our Conquerors hull down a couple of hundred yards back from the south bank," Julian Calder explained in the gloom as he braked the Land Rover to a slow crawl. His passengers assumed he had braked to negotiate the slope down to the first pontoon. The structure bridging the slow moving river was robust enough to support the weight of a couple of Centurion Mk IIs, and at a pinch, a pair of T-62s but a lighter vehicle could easily run out of control when it encountered the undulating steel roadway.

The Land Rover stopped short of the bank.

"You fellows can walk the rest of the way. I'm going to get back to General al-Mamaleki's HQ if I can!"

Chapter 67

04:45 Hours
Friday 3rd July, 1964
HMS Tiger, Arvand River north of Al Seeba

Rear Admiral Nicholas Davey had anticipated that his ships would be in a lot of trouble a lot sooner. However, as the hours had passed and the gun line of the ABNZ Persian Gulf Squadron – from the vanguard to the rear; HMAS Anzac, HMS Tiger, HMS Diamond, HMAS Tobruk and HMNZS Royalist – had strained at their anchors on the northern side of the main channel of the Arvand River less than a hundred yards from the shore of Abadan Island, their crews had been no more than distant, passive witnesses to the battle going on around distant Khorramshahr.

The four 6-inch guns of the Tiger, the eight 5.25-inch guns of the Royalist and the fourteen 4.5-inch guns of the three destroyers were elevated to deliver long-range plunging fire on the first of a dozen pre-ordained one mile square boxes north of Khorramshahr.

Like everybody else Nick Davey had confidently expected the Red Army to have invested and fortified the west bank of the Arvand River; that it appeared the Russians had neglected to so do frankly boggled his imagination. By rights the gun line ought to have had to fight its way up river, instead it had arrived in prime position to join the land battle without a shot having been fired in anger.

What were the Russians thinking?

Were they really that confident the war was over bar the shouting?

Not that Davey was in any way complacent to have been the grateful beneficiary of such an unexpected lapse on the enemy's part. His ships would be sitting ducks if and when the Russians got their act together; horribly vulnerable to long-range artillery fire and attacks by fast jets. Given that either eventuality would be an extremely bad development he could not for the life of him work out why the Soviets had not yet done...*something*.

To have allowed the squadron to get so far up river unchallenged was criminal. Right now if any of his ships got hit they would ground on the Abadan shore and carry on fighting; if need be the destroyers, and probably Tiger rather and Royalist might advance up river. The destroyers were shallow enough in the water to get all the way up to Basra if the worst came to the worst.

First light was only minutes away.

For the last three hours the fire fight north of the Karun River had blazed; each time the Red Army was repulsed it gathered itself anew and flung fresh blood and iron at the defenders. On Abadan Island fuel tanks were burning and the smoke from the huge, uncontrollable infernos was slowly spreading across the entire battlefield. High above the ships in the gun line air search radars and gunnery ranging sets showed a sky bereft of aircraft.

Captain Hardress Llewellyn 'Harpy' Lloyd, Tiger's commanding officer joined Davey on the open, completely exposed upper, flying bridge. Lookouts scanned the western river bank with powerful binoculars and two squads of Royal Marines had mounted 50-calibre heavy machine guns on the port bridge rail.

The continual distant thunder of exploding shells rumbled across the Minushahr Peninsula, the great bulge of land formed by the meander of the Arvand Rover below Khorramshahr.

"I'd have thought the Yanks would have made an appearance by now," Harpy Lloyd observed, his tone one of mild disappointment. "Perhaps, they don't have the stomach for a man to man fight?"

Nick Davey sniffed the fire-tainted air.

"Yes," he sighed. "Well, hopefully as soon as we're finished with the Russians we'll go back down river and deal with *those* bastards!"

He deliberately said it loudly enough for everybody on the bridge to hear what he said. He wanted everybody on the flagship to know that *their* Admiral was not about to take a single backward step.

The Tannoy blared.

"EXECUTE WORKERS PLAYTIME!"

Nick Davey chortled.

The waiting was over.

"Repeat EXECUTE WORKERS PLAYTIME in sixty seconds from this...MARK!"

HMS Tiger's CIC had maintained a live communications uplink with Michael Carver's Royal Artillery Command Centre, the latter situated in a bunker near the abandoned airstrip. Tiger's and Royalist's guns remained independent but Anzac, Diamond and Tobruk's main batteries were slaved to Anzac's gun director table, an old-fashioned mechanical computer but none the less efficacious for it.

"*Workers Playtime,* indeed!" Tiger's Captain guffawed in the stillness before the storm.

Both men were stuffing pads of cotton wool into their ears, and around the bridge others were compacting wads of material or donning clumsy ear defenders. Nick Davey was already half deaf in his right ear from his time in the Mediterranean in 1941 and 1942; none of the guns his squadron was shooting were real 'deafeners' like the ones he had been too close to in the forties, but they were going to be loud enough!

Loud enough to wake Lucifer himself!

"I was beginning to think the Army had forgotten all about us," Davey remarked ruefully.

"I think everybody will know we're here in a few seconds, sir!"

The salvo bell clanged loudly throughout the ship.

The whole ship – all eleven thousand tons of her – flinched.

As one the battle line disappeared behind a wall of muzzle flashes and grey cordite smoke as twenty-six naval rifles unleashed a crushing high explosive rain upon the Queen's enemies over ten miles to the north.

Chapter 68

"There are two things which we must not lose sight of," Field Marshall Sir Richard Hull prefaced, looking around the hastily convened council of war. Senior officers and Cabinet Ministers had been drawn into Hertford College throughout the small hours of the morning, and the 'hot lines' to the Chilmark Command bunker under the Chilterns carried constant updates from Mediterranean and the Persian Gulf.

"One," the soldier prefaced grimly, "the purpose of the land battle for Abadan and the south west of Iran is *not* to throw the Red Army out of Iraq, or even necessarily to hold onto Abadan Island in the longer term. It is to blunt the Red Army's capacity for major aggressive operations in the foreseeable future, and to embroil it in a war of attrition with our forces and those of our Iranian allies."

The Chief of the Defence Staff sucked his teeth.

"Second, while it remains on station in the upper reaches of the Persian Gulf the USS Kitty Hawk and its attendant battle group represents a deadly threat to *all* our forces in the Middle East, continuing to endanger all attempts to forestall Soviet ambitions in the region now, and in the days, weeks and months ahead."

The old soldier had wondered if he actually needed to spell out the reality of the situation in the Persian Gulf. He had opted to be safe rather than sorry on this, if not on any of the other desperate matters demanding his immediate attention.

"Let me be clear," he sighed. "Axiomatically, if at any time the US Navy interdicts *again* our operations in the theatre the likely outcome is our total defeat and the surrender of the strategic initiative to the Soviets, regardless of how badly we have mauled the Red Army and Air Force in the meantime."

The Deputy Prime Minister, James Callaghan had recently arrived and now sat slumped ashen faced in a chair next to Margaret Thatcher. A Westland Wessex helicopter stood ready to whisk him back to Chilmark, where Peter Thorneycroft, the Chancellor of the Exchequer and the last surviving Tory grandee from Harold MacMillan's pre-October War Cabinet, waited to assume the premiership in the event of a new nuclear cataclysm which destroyed Oxford. The ancient Don's common room had become the ad hoc governmental 'situation room' as the crisis became ever more dangerous.

Admiral Sir Varyl Begg the First Sea Lord stepped forward into the small area cleared in front of the big map of the Persian Gulf hurriedly pinned to the wall over the stone hearth. Although it was the middle of the night it was still warm, and growing increasingly humid in the crowded room.

"I have an update on the situation in Malta," he announced, coolly business-like. "There are currently nine major US warships moored in the Grand Harbour and one other in Marsamxett Anchorage. Among the large warships are the aircraft carrier Independence, the battleship Iowa and the nuclear powered guided missile frigate Bainbridge. Submarines of the 2nd Submarine Squadron and destroyers and frigates of the 23rd Escort Group have taken up positions adjacent to the Iowa, Independence, Bainbridge and three other American vessels in the Grand Harbour from which they can train their torpedo tubes on those...*targets*. HMS Alliance, recently returned from her triumphs in the Western Mediterranean is presently *covering* the USS Leahy in Marsamxett. Thus far there have been no untoward *scenes*. C-in-C Mediterranean Fleet has gone onboard the Independence to *consult* with his counterpart, Admiral Clarey. At Gibraltar the situation is less clear cut. Several American ships have been 'detained', but one, the USS Berkeley which had previously raised steam in preparation for a dawn departure ignored instructions to hove to and is currently standing off Algeciras Bay. No shots were fired. The Berkeley, you may recollect, is the vessel whose captain imperilled his command to stand by HMS Talavera after the Battle of Malta and was again, coincidentally, on the scene to offer assistance to HMS Hampshire when she was attacked last month by the French. Units of the US Sixth Fleet currently at sea have been warned not to approach Royal Navy warships, and that all ports and air bases under British sovereign control are denied to them until further notice under pain of being fired upon." He looked around, hesitated in case there were any questions.

Tom Harding-Grayson raised a hand. "Walter Brenckmann is still trying to clarify the situation with the State Department," he explained wearily. "The poor fellow is beside himself..."

Everybody in the room felt nothing but sympathy for the decent, honourable man who had the misfortune to occupy the post of United States Ambassador to the Court of Woodstock. Brenckmann and his charming wife Joanne, were, to the majority of those now gathered to discuss all-out war with America, the absolute epitome, the perfect representation of the nation that they had all wished that they were still dealing with.

Tom Harding-Grayson looked to the Chief of the Defence Staff and then back to Margaret Thatcher.

"Sir Richard is right," he remarked sadly. "We must fight the United States in the Persian Gulf. And we must do it now before the Americans transfer even more powerful forces to the region."

"They've already got the biggest bloody aircraft carrier in the World in the Gulf!" William Whitelaw retorted angrily. "How on earth do we fight a ship like that?"

The First Sea Lord stepped into the fray.

His calm was that of a dead-eyed gunslinger in a movie.

"The Kitty Hawk is just a ship, Minister. Make enough holes in her below the waterline and she will sink. Just like any other ship."

William Whitelaw's deputy, Lord Carington had taken hold of his friend's elbow.

"Willie," he murmured, knowing the other man was at the end of his tether. "Last year when the USS Enterprise was conducting war games in the path of the first of the Operation Manna convoys Sir Varyl's predecessor and the Chiefs of Staff of the other services developed detailed contingency plans for just this kind of sad scenario."

"Yes, sir," the First Sea Lord confirmed urbanely, "I think the Chief of the Air Staff is best qualified to discuss the counter strike that our forces in the Theatre are presently developing ahead of the Government's yea or nay for the final go ahead."

Air Marshall Sir Christopher Hartley was a big man with a presence to match; the sort of bluff, man's man who was always in motion. He was also one of those men able to effortlessly communicate his physical size and effervescent personality down a telephone line. His voice boomed out of the speaker, filling the room.

"There is only one way to tackle one of these American carrier battle groups," he explained cheerfully. "Ideally, I'd like a couple of submarines *tickling* the sonars of some of the Kitty Hawk's escorts, muddying the tactical picture, as it were, but we're going to have to work with what we've got in the Gulf!"

The airman paused to let this minor caveat sink in.

"What we've got is six, perhaps as many as eight V-Bombers, serviceability permitting, seven Canberra medium strike bombers, approximately a score of fighters; a mixture of Hunters, Scimitars and Sea Vixens. And," he quirked an almost self-effacingly, "three turboprop Gannets which somebody thought might be useful because they can each carry two of the US Navy's 10-inch Mark 43 homing torpedoes. The Americans supplied us fifty Mark 43s to play with before the October War; they wanted us to buy them instead of spending the money developing our own version, but that's by the by. The Gannets and the torpedoes are sitting in a hangar at Dammam, so we might as well use them!"

Margaret Thatcher was glacially still.

Waiting, waiting, waiting...

"The Canberras are being collected together at Riyadh. Half of them will be loaded with up to nine five hundred pounders and a couple of thousand pounder general purpose bombs. The rest will carry thousand pounders and rocket pods under each wing. The fighters are mostly at Dammam or at emergency bases in Kuwait. Some of the Sea Vixens and the Scimitars will carry anti-ship missiles, small jobs mostly for nuisance value. We may get a few extra five hundred pounders or small depth charges on the pylons of the Sea Vixens. The Hunters we'll restrict to the dog-fighting role."

The Chief of the Air Staff took a gulp of air.

Still Margaret Thatcher had not moved. In fact while Hartley had been speaking she had not so much as twitched a muscle.

"The V-Bombers," he went on. "One Valiant and one Vulcan will be armed with a single Blue Danube nuclear weapon."

Hiroshima sized atom bombs. The airman waited again.

Nobody fainted or ordered his arrest so he continued.

"One Victor will carry a single Grand Slam. One Victor will carry two Tallboys. A second Vulcan will carry eight two thousand pound general purpose bombs. The two remaining Valiants – I am hoping that two will be available – will carry twenty-one thousand pound general purpose bombs."

"Blue Danube, Sir Christopher?" Margaret Thatcher asked softly.

It was suddenly so silent in the crowded room that distant birdsong might have deafened the men around the Angry Widow.

"Yes, Prime Minister. Both weapons to be set to initiate at three thousand feet once the aircraft carrying it attain operational ceiling."

The woman's eyes narrowed but she said nothing.

"*When* the aircraft carrying the Blue Danubes are shot down the wreck of each aircraft will proscribe a ballistic arc towards the enemy fleet and explode at the appointed altitude..."

There were mutters of dissent, shock, horror.

"In the confusion," the Chief of the Air Staff barrelled on - much in the fashion of a sprinting lock forward dismissively handing off potential tacklers in a rugby match at Twickenham - several of our fighters will approach the surviving units of Carrier Division Seven at sea level, hopefully drawing the *enemy's* CAP down at the moment the other five V-Bombers and the Canberra force attack, each aircraft approaching the *enemy* fleet from a different altitude and from a different point of the compass. While all this is going on the three Gannets will creep in at wave top height and drop their torpedoes at long range. The sound of multiple torpedoes in the water ought to make a fine old mess of the Kitty Hawk's Battle Board!"

William Whitelaw was struggling to maintain his composure.

"All our experience is that attempting to bomb ships with conventional unguided bombs from high altitude is a waste of time, Sir Christopher?"

"Forgive me, sir," the airman apologised, quietening sombrely. There was a moment of hissing static which filled the crowded room. "If I mistakenly gave you the impression that what I had in mind was a flat and level attack from on high, that was the farthest thing in my mind. The object of the exercise in exploding the two Blue Danubes somewhere in the vicinity of Carrier Division Seven, the subsequent attack at sea level, and the dropping of small homing torpedoes in the water is to create a tactical environment in which the enemy is so confused, that he is unable to bring his infinitely superior aerial and ship-based fire power to bear on our V-Bombers."

There was another pause. When the Chief of the Air Staff went on there was deadly purpose in his voice.

"Given the mobility of the target and the vagaries of bombing such a target from high altitude all V-Bomber crews will be instructed to *dive bomb* the USS Kitty Hawk."

Chapter 69

06:40 Hours
Friday 3rd July, 1964
Army Group South Headquarters, Basra

The whole southern eastern horizon had seemed to be on fire as Lieutenant General Viktor Georgiyevich Kulikov's commandeered Mil Mi-6 Red Air Force helicopter raced low across the marshes north of Basra. Back at the Headquarters of his 2nd Siberian Mechanised Army at Al Qurnah practically every piece of the communications equipment which had been 'live' or in any way functioning at the time of the two big air bursts west of Baghdad was dead, and enemy artillery had subsequently cut all the land lines to Basra. Now he was cursing the idiotic last minute 'fucking about' with the command structure of Army Group South which had left him impotently sitting on his hands when everything south of Al Qurnah had so obviously, gone wrong.

Khorramshahr was burning, splashes of fire tore up the desert and the ruins either side of the Iraqi-Iranian border opposite Basra, and rippled across Abadan Island thirty miles away. Meanwhile, beyond Basra the sky was dark with huge pillars of smoke; something bad had happened down around Umm Qasr.

Kulikov had known Marshal of the Soviet Union Hamazasp Khachaturi Babadzhanian for over twenty years. He had never liked the Army Group Commander; but liking and respecting were two entirely different things. Babadzhanian had managed the Red Army's invasion of Iran and Iraq with cool professional mastery. Despite having been given less than half the tanks and men he needed to do the job until a day ago Operation Nakazyvat had been – in the round, the normal military setbacks and foul ups notwithstanding – a truly brilliant feat of arms. Or rather, it had *almost* been a brilliant feat of arms; Kulikov had always counselled against a headlong assault on Abadan Island.

There was no military necessity to attempt to 'take Abadan' on the run; that was just a line Babadzhanian's Staff had inserted in the original plan to appease the old women in the Politburo. If the morons back in Russian wanted the Red Army to 'storm' the most heavily defended 'island' – that is, a place surrounded by 'serious water barriers' – they ought to have given the Red Army the tools to do fucking the job! For example, a couple of brigades of properly equipped combat engineers to bridge the Karun River; or for example several regiments of airborne troops to seize a bridgehead! But no, everything had had to be done on a shoestring, and *this* year long before the Red Army might actually have been restored to something more than a shadow of its former glory!

Worse, the frittering away of the Army Group's airborne component – first in the diversion at Malta, later in the Tehran operation and the speculative 'leap forward' to seize Urmia – was always going come back to haunt Army Group South and somebody, somewhere ought to have listened to *him* when he said it! Without those irreplaceable assault troops there was no way to seize a bridgehead on Abadan Island without first forcing a contested river crossing. Operations of that kind were always ruinously costly; which was precisely why wise commanders normally husbanded their airborne troops with such exaggerated care. When you needed *those* boys you *really, really* needed them and not having them now was going to hurt like Hell!

Kulikov was a practical man.

One fought battles with the men one had and he could live with that; fighting men got used to being asked to do stupid things. But twenty-four hours ago Babadzhanian had gone over his head and ordered that every available serviceable tank and *his* best, most carefully held back mechanised assault regiments should be thrown against well-prepared, dug in enemy defence lines around Khorramshahr.

It was madness!

Nobody seemed capable of getting it into their heads that once this force – approximated two tank corps beefed up with the entire Army's mobile artillery component and every available combat ready infantry unit that could be brought forward in time – had been expended then the battle for Iraq was *over*!

Worse than that, once *his* army had been chewed up the last trained, professional cadres of the pre-Cuban Missiles War Red Army would be so depleted that it would take years to train replacements. When *his* boys were gone who would there be left to rebuild the *new* Red Army?

The helicopter flared out, hit the ground and rolled for several seconds before coming to a juddering halt in the murky, smoky half-light in an impenetrable cloud of sandy dust. Instantly Kulikov stepped down to earth he was aware of the corrupt taint of smoke and fire in the air.

One of the Army Group Commander's flunkies had tried to stop him flying down to Basra. Kulikov had demanded to speak to Babadzhanian's deputy, but forty-seven year old Lieutenant General Semyon Konstantinovich Kurkotkin had apparently boarded a plane for Baghdad the previous day and not been heard from since.

Kulikov had asked: 'If Comrade Marshal Babadzhanian cannot speak to me who the fuck can?'

Perversely, it made a kind of sense to send Kurtotkin, a 'party general' to Baghdad to keep the newly appointed Commissar General of Iraq from meddling in military matters while the fighting continued. Moreover, everybody was going to have to work out what sort of a new broom Vasily Chuikov's successor, Gorshkov, was going to be and in the meantime there was a war to won.

However, sending Kurtotkin away just before the denouement of the Iraq offensive was insane. Babadzhanian must have been out of his mind fucking up the chain of command hours after he cut Kulikov out of the loop and ordered the attack on Abadan to go ahead forty-eight hours *early*.

Kulikov was still roiling with indignation that the Army Group Commander had 'parachuted in' his man, Vladimir Andreyevich Puchkov, the hard-charging commander of the 10th Guards Tank Division to command the 'shock' corps now embroiled in an artless, old-fashioned frontal onslaught on the Khorramshahr Sector of the British and Iranian defences above Abadan island. It was fucking ridiculous! The right thing to have done would have been to preserve Army Group South's fighting power, to saturate the south of the country with anti-aircraft missiles and to wear down the Abadan garrison by blockade, bombing and the employment of the *whole* of *his* 2nd Siberian Mechanised Army's artillery. Some fifty percent of the latter was still strung out along virtually impassable roads ruined by the passage of hundreds of tanks fifty to a hundred kilometres north of Al Qurnah. Kulikov had pleaded with Babadzhanian to give him another week to bring up 'the guns'; then and only then, could the operation to 'strangle' the Abadan 'pocket' commence. What was going on now was...*madness*.

The way things were going if the Iranian Army got its act together it could suddenly become a big problem! His Field Intelligence Staff freely admitted that it had no real 'feel' for the threat posed to 2nd Siberian Mechanised Army's left flank as it advanced down the eastern bank of the Arvand River by 'surviving Iranian armour north and north-east of the Khorramshahr-Abadan defence area'. That idiot Puchkov and that fucking jumped up paratrooper Kurochnik – in Kulikov's experience he had never met a senior paratrooper who had not landed on his head once too often – had launched their attack on Khorramshahr like some kind of suicidal galloping cavalry charge with no real idea what was in front of them. And when this had started to go horribly wrong they had just done exactly the same thing *again*!

The distant thump of guns faded as he strode angrily into the old colonial mansion which Babadzhanian had taken as his headquarters.

"I demand to speak to the Army Group Commander!" He barked, his feet ringing on the marbled floor as he burst into the cloistered coolness of the former Governor's Palace on the banks of the Arvand River.

An exhausted, greyly ill man in the uniform of a Lieutenant-Colonel of the Staff stepped forward, his expression was hangdog. The man seemed...broken.

Kulikov stopped dead in his tracks.

He swallowed hard, feeling sick.

"What the fuck is going on?" He demanded tersely.

"Comrade Marshall Hamazasp Khachaturi died a few minutes ago, Comrade General. We have attempted to inform the Army Commander's deputy, but General Kurkotkin is believed to be in Baghdad..."

"Then who the fuck is in control here?" Kulikov asked, already knowing the answer.

Nobody...

Viktor Kulikov stared at the other man.

He felt sick...

Army Group South, exhausted by three months of continuous campaigning over some of the worst ground on the planet was locked in a major battle that it did not need to fight; and *nobody* was in control of...*anything.*

Chapter 70

Major General Hasan al-Mamaleki smiled broadly in the half-light as the tall, dusty figure of Major Julian Calder emerged out of the dust and smoke. The Red Army had started shelling the desert north of the Karun River some miles east of Khorramshahr where, presumably, it suspected some kind of threat might be brewing. The bombardment was ineffectual, other than it had created a drifting haze which completely obscured al-Mamaleki's southern positions from aerial observation. More important the shelling told him that the Red Army had no idea whatsoever where the bulk of his forces waited, hull down and heavily camouflaged, dispersed across some dozen square miles of undulating, gully-broken desert and scrub land to the north of his headquarters positioned eight miles east of Khorramshahr.

"I'd given you up for a bad deal, Julian," the commander of the 3rd Imperial Iranian Armoured Division guffawed.

Calder was the younger of the two men by seven years, a man who had seen battalion and SAS service in Cyprus, Malaysia, Kenya and Iran before the October War. Officially, he was Lieutenant General Michael Carver's personal liaison officer to al-Mamaleki. Calder was, in fact, rather more than just a humble 'liaison' staffer. He ran al-Mamaleki's 'field intelligence' company and commanded No 7 Squadron of the Special Air Service Regiment. His men had infiltrated both Basra city and the industrial sprawl on the eastern bank of the Arvand River, fought a couple of sharp actions with Spetsnaz troops probing the Allied defences south of the Iraq-Iranian border, and had been in no small way responsible for the Red Army's apparent 'blindness' ahead of its current offensive.

"I confess I had a couple of moderately *sticky* moments on the way back," the Englishman confessed ruefully. "The C-in-C asked me to find out what had happened to a mutual acquaintance of ours. Frank Waters, he works for the BBC now but he's still just as accident prone as always!"

"I thought the Russians had had him shot until I bumped into him a few days ago at the C-in-C's headquarters," the Iranian guffawed. The two men had not spoken face to face for several days, Calder having been 'out and about' in the field and al-Mamaleki having had the common sense not to interfere in 'SAS business'. Throughout the Englishman's absence he had sent back a string of situation reports keeping him fully abreast of the extraordinary, somewhat eccentric and rushed preparations for battle of the 2nd Siberian Mechanised Army, and the veritable *dog's breakfast* mess the Russians were making of co-ordinating the activities of their western and eastern armies.

"No such luck, I'm afraid," Julian Calder smiled ruefully. "Frank Waters is indestructible!"

Neither main reacted as a rain of Katyusha rockets carpeted a half-mile long stretch of the Ahvaz-Khorramshahr road to the west.

"Anyway, I did the decent thing. I took him and his colleagues back to the river and told them to make themselves scarce."

The ground shivered as new shells landed a mile or so to the north-west.

"The blighters still haven't got a clue where we are," Calder observed dryly. He might have been discussing the state of play at a cricket match at Lord's.

"What news?" The Iranian inquired politely. Al-Mamaleki's only outward sign of nervous tension was the distracted way in which the forefinger of his right hand involuntarily stroked his magnificent bushy black moustache in moments of contemplation. His Staff had gathered around him and the newcomer. "Do you think the Russians have really swallowed the bait hook, line and sinker?"

Julian Calder grimaced and shook his head.

"If we'd written them a prompt sheet they couldn't have been more obliging. Somebody must have put a red hot poker to this chap Kurochnik's nether regions. Babadzhanian or Kulikov, or whoever's responsible for putting an airborne commander in command of so much armour must have had a brainstorm. We think the Russians must have lost sixty or seventy tanks in and around Khorramshahr in the first couple of attacks. We took several prisoners; I didn't have much time to talk to them but it seems that the spearhead units were under the impression they were about to breeze straight down to the Karun River, clear the southern bank with tank and artillery fire and call down the bridging units they've got moored all along the river at Basra. Our chaps were still withdrawing from Khorramshahr about an hour ago. If and when the first T-62s make an appearance on the north bank of the Karun they're going to find themselves in the sights of a score of Centurion 105 and Conqueror 120-millimetre rifles at pretty much point blank range!"

It was all Hasan al-Mamaleki could do to suppress a shiver of angst. He had spent most of his adult life attempting to master the art of armoured warfare. Emerging from or around the ruins of Khorramshahr Soviet tanks would be confronted with nightmarishly accurate massed fire at ranges of significantly less than a thousand yards. Anything under two miles was 'point blank' for the 105-millimetre L7 L/52 cannons of Michael Carver's Centurions, and the 120-millimetre L7A1s of his dug in heavy tanks.

"Because of the success of the Khorramshahr blocking action," Julian Calder explained, making eye contacts around the crowded compartment. It was still cool in the claustrophobic communications truck; in a couple of hours the rising sun would make it intolerably hot, a real pressure cooker beneath its camouflage nets. "*Excalibur*," he went on," has been put back."

Excalibur was the execution signal for Hasan al-Mamaleki to unleash his entire force of Centurions, M-60 and M-48 Patton tanks against the flank and rear echelons of the enemy above the Karun River; ideally at the moment the enemy's much depleted and hopefully exhausted spearhead was running into Michael Carver's 'stand and deliver' defence lines several miles south on Abadan Island.

This prompted a narrowing of eyes, and muttered discontent among the staffers surrounding the two men. Hasan al-Mamaleki instantly stilled this with an abbreviated waving away motion with his left hand.

"Jumping a couple of steps forward," Calder explained as he and al-Mamaleki automatically bent over the map on the bench table. Others respectfully craned their necks to get a better look. "The C-in-C guesses that the enemy will treat his reverse at Khorramshahr overnight as a personal insult. We think this because he's kept pushing armour into the desert north and north east of the town on a fairly narrow front. The naval bombardment has forced him to lengthen his lines, and no doubt, somewhat inconvenienced him..."

There were muted chortles of amusement around the map.

"In any event we're going to give the Red Army an even bloodier nose when it tries to move us back from our positions on the southern bank of the Karun River above Abadan. We have no intention of holding indefinitely but we do plan to kill as many of the enemy's tanks as we can before we pull back to the prepared defence lines around the air base and within the refinery complex. My best guess is that the enemy will either pause to lick his wounds at that stage, or basically," Calder shrugged and grinned mischievously, "put his head in the noose as fast as he can later today and this evening."

It was almost too incredible.

The Red Army was Hell-bent on hurling itself into the carefully prepared meat grinder that Michael Carver had so lovingly prepared for it. Things had gone so well that there was actually an argument for letting the Russians bridge the Karun River virtually unopposed, and for permitting 2nd Siberian Mechanised Army pour its armour onto Abadan Island en masse before launching a counter attack.

But no, that would be being greedy.

First the Centurions and Conquerors of the 4th Royal Tank Regiment would be allowed to have their 'fun'. Besides, it was vital that the enemy *believed* that he had dislodged the 4th 'Tanks' from their positions on the southern backs of the Karun River, if he was to be persuaded to carry on plunging south to his doom with the same blind determination he had shown thus far.

"Do we know what's going on down around Umm Qasr?" Hasan al-Mamaleki inquired.

Calder shook his head.

"No. Not really. Sorry."

The plan in the west was for Major Thomas Daly's small Anzac and British armoured brigade and a regimental-size force of Saudi tanks – some seventy Centurions and M-48 Pattons in total – to move around the flank of the Soviet units laagered in and around the port city of Umm Qasr west of Safwan while gunners south of the Kuwaiti border 'pinned' the Russians against that border. The operations had gone ahead despite the absence of intelligence about the extent of the damage, confusion and dislocation caused by the overnight RAF bombing raids in the area. If the Red Army formations around Umm Qasr had survived relatively unscathed then Tom Daly's armour would be engaged, encircled and destroyed in detail within hours.

However, the imponderables were what they were; there was no point crying over spilt milk or the potentially disastrous naval situation in the Persian Gulf. Sooner or later the Red Air Force would inevitably appear over the southern battlefield and discover that it owned the skies; and nobody knew how quickly that would turn the tactical situation east of the Arvand River on its head. Or for that matter, how long the ABNZ gun line moored north of Al Seeba could survive when it came under sustained attack from both the shore and the air.

Chapter 71

Commander Stephen Turnbull was grateful for the pall of smoke from the burning oil tanks of the huge refinery complex. The wind at higher levels had moved around two points since dawn, carrying the worst of the smoke off to the north and north-east; but down below one to two thousand feet the smog had created a haze under which he suspected the ships of the ABNZ gun line would be virtually invisible to high flying enemy aircraft.

Given the deteriorating 'seeing' conditions after the long night's fighting had slowly petered out – the 'front' was quiet apart from desultory half-hearted counter battery fire – the captain of HMAS Anzac was not that surprised when Rear Admiral Nicholas Davey's barge came alongside the destroyer.

The two men shook hands at the rail and the newcomer smiled broadly at the hastily convened reception committee.

"Let's have no ceremony, Stephen," he suggested.

Turnbull had despatched the others back to their duty stations and the two men made their way up to Anzac's open bridge.

"Things seem to have gone better than we could possibly have hoped last night," the commander of what was left of the ABNZ Persian Gulf Squadron told Turnbull loudly, clearly not bothered who overheard their exchange.

The destroyer's captain and the portly Englishman were of an age, give or take a few years. They shared comparable combat experience and a streak of obstinacy a mile wide. They were also two aging warriors who had a fine eye for taking advantage of their foe's every mistake.

We assumed the Red Air Force would have been all over us by now," Nick Davey pronounced. "The Yanks would have been here by now if they had the guts for it!"

This latter was boomed with such volume that men on the amidships 40-millimetre Bofors cannons probably heard it.

"Clearly the bastards don't!" He added for good measure. "I have spoken to General Carver and he has invited me to 'reposition' several of our ships upstream. We can just about reach parts of southern Basra but we can't actually see what we are doing from down here. With your permission, Stephen," he went on, his tone very much that of a friend asking a brother officer a favour, rather than a superior officer issuing an order to a subordinate, "I propose to take Anzac and Diamond up river with Tiger."

Taking big ships farther up the Arvand River, perhaps as far as Basra, was of course *suicidal*.

"The RAF have still got over thirty Bloodhounds spooled up

waiting for *trade*," Davey continued, rubbing his hands together in anticipation. "They can knock down anything that comes within thirty miles of these parts."

Stephen Turnbull did not need long to think about Nick Davey's invitation to place his command in even greater harm's way.

"When do we weigh anchor, sir?"

"The moment my barge casts off. Tiger and Diamond will follow directly." Davey turned away, resting his hands on the bridge rail. In a quieter, somewhat sober voice he explained: "If it comes to it I plan to take Tiger, Anzac and Diamond as far upstream as the southern point of Om-al-Rasas Island. There we shall moor up again on the western side of the main channel. If we moor up to the east the proximity of the river bank may obstruct direct fire into the enemy's flank and rear. If necessary, I will take Tiger all the way up to Basra."

Turnbull absorbed this.

If the worst came to the worst Davey meant to sink the cruiser in the main channel. But that was looking too far ahead, in the meantime the object of the exercise was to get up river to enable the Tiger and the two destroyers to pour fire into the enemy at what, for the Tiger's 6-inch and Anzac and Diamond's 4.5-inch main batteries was point blank range.

"Permission to lead the squadron, sir?"

"Granted, sir," Nick Davey chuckled.

As the smog of burning oil tanks and battle drifted north the day had broken crystal clear over the desert and marshes of the Faw Peninsula to the west. A little south of west great plumes of black smoke rose like pillars salt over some long lost mythical condemned biblical city. No man could have lived through the last twenty-four hours and not suspected that he was living through times around which latter generations would weave endless new mythologies. There had been three 'wars to end all wars' in the twentieth century and none of them had done anything other than to make the next war inevitable.

For the two men briefly looking each other in the eye on the bridge of the Australian destroyer 'the future' was a thing that neither of them was likely to have to confront. At least, not any future beyond the next few hours because they and most, if not all of their men, were steaming towards their fate; for them this was the last battle, one final trial by fire.

It was as he was leaving Anzac that Nick Davey turned and in a low, confidential tone turned to Stephen Turnbull.

"Whatever happens," he murmured, "It has been my honour to serve with you. God be with you and your brave ship, Stephen."

Then he was gone, clambering clumsily down the rope ladder, dropping into the strong arms of the men in his barge.

Stephen Turnbull watched the boat drift away from Anzac, turn ponderously and head back to the flagship.

Anzac's stern began to swing towards to shore as her aft anchor clanked up out of the muddy waters of the Arvand River.

"SLOW ASTERN PORT!"

The destroyer dragged back on her forward chains.

"ALL STOP!"

"SLOW AHEAD STARBOARD!"

The bow anchor came out of the water.

"SLOW AHEAD BOTH!"

"WHEEL AMIDSHIPS!"

Astern HMS Diamond was emerging into the main channel behind the bulk of the flagship, and grey, wispy smoke was rising from both of Tiger's funnels.

"RUDDER! FIVE DEGREES STARBOARD!"

HMAS Anzac, by the grace of God the bearer of the most honoured name in Australasian history, glided into the swirling two to three knot current of the great waterway of the Mesopotamian cradle of human civilisation.

"Tiger's cut her chains, sir!"

Stephen Turnbull smiled a wolfish smile.

Without a tug nudging, or pre-positioned warps there was no way a big ship – Tiger was over eleven thousand tons and a lot deeper in the water than either Anzac or Diamond – like the flagship could elegantly, or safely, manoeuvre off a lee shore that was literally feet away when the current was pushing against her five hundred and fifty feet long hull as if it was a giant sail. Turnbull's counterpart, Harpy Lloyd, had done the pragmatic thing. Dropped two of his anchors in the mud, gone half-astern on his port outer shaft, and half-ahead on his starboard outer shafts; and presumably, prayed the current would not beach his ship on the western mudflats when he cut his stern anchors adrift.

Turnbull glanced around in time to see the cruiser's bow swinging into the stream and then he focussed on finding the centre of the deep water channel.

"AIR CONTACTS BEARING TWO-NINE-FIVE!"

There was a short delay.

"NO IFF!"

The Red Air Force had made a belated but extremely unwelcome appearance.

"FIVE! NO, BELAY THAT! EIGHT BOGEYS AT ANGELS THREE-ZERO! RANGE SIX-EIGHT NAUTICAL MILES!"

Stephen Turnbull did some ad hoc geometry in his head.

The enemy was coming in from over the Syrian Desert of Iraq on a heading which would carry it over Basra on the way to Abadan.

Why fly a roundabout course over the desert?

"NEW AIR CONTACTS BEARING ZERO-ONE-ZERO! MULTIPLE CONTACTS AT ANGELS FOUR-ZERO..."

Over the bridge speakers the amplified voice of the CIC speaker betrayed a momentary spasm of...*panic.*

"AIR ATTACK! AIR ATTACK! NEW AIR CONTACTS BEARING THREE-FIVE-ZERO! VERY LOW LEVEL! CBDR! REPEAT CBDR! AIR ATTACK IMMINENT!"

CBDR: constant bearing, decreasing range.

Collision course; or more prosaically stated there were several aircraft heading towards the gun line at very high speed.

The Anzac's Bofors cannons started pumping shells into the space the CIC guessed the approaching Red Air Force aircraft would *probably* be whistling through in excess of five hundred knots within seconds.

Anzac had no precision surface-to-air missiles systems; just the latest versions of old-fashioned World War II 'pom-pom' guns.

It was at times like this Stephen Turnbull had always found the rhythmical pumping of the Bofors oddly comforting...

Chapter 72

Squadron Leader Guy French watched the CO's aircraft *Waltzing Matilda* lift off two-thirds of the way down the desert runway and climb steeply into the early morning haze. Beneath his hands *The Angry Widow* strained like a greyhound in the traps.

All the aircraft which had landed at Riyadh earlier that morning had been re-tasked. The original plan had been to take on a new mixed cargo of death, HE, general purpose and cluster munitions to cart straight back up to Iraq to carry on the good work. However, revised orders had awaited 100 Squadron's Victors when they landed in Saudi Arabia. Every aircraft was to top off its tanks and make the fastest possible passage back to Akrotiri with empty bomb bays. The new orders had caught the RAF's Saudi hosts completely unprepared, and presently while the three remaining 100 Squadron Victors queued to take off, a 617 Squadron Vulcan and two 207 Squadron Valiants were parked waiting to be 'filled up'.

Before, during and after last night's raid *The Angry Widow's* EWO had picked up a huge volume of US Navy chatter and detected heavy multi-frequency jamming across the most commonly employed Royal Navy channels. Something had happened out in the Gulf south of Kharg Island but nobody was saying anything.

Whatever had happened was *big* because in the last hour navigators had been warned not to 'trespass' over Israeli air space; all previous overflying permissions having been suddenly rescinded. Given that the Israelis had only just started 'playing ball', this and the US Navy's ECM – electronic counter measures – activities over the Gulf last night would have been *eccentric* at the best of times. This morning it was anybody's guess what it signified.

Waltzing Matilda, *The Angry Widow* and the other two Victors had been held idling on their hardstands twenty minutes while a flight of five 3 Squadron English Electric Canberra medium bombers landed. The newcomers had taxied directly over to the bomb dump.

Trying to understand what was going on Guy French idly ran through the options.

Riyadh was more than a refuelling stop; it was the RAF's desert bomb dump. Back in Cyprus the bunkers had been emptied of all but a couple of bomb loads of the middle-sized flavours of high explosive and general purpose 'eggs'. Other than a few palettes of these 'standard' munitions, all that was left on Cyprus were ten-ton Grand Slams, six-ton Tallboys and a couple of Blue Danube Hiroshima yield old-fashioned fission bombs. Both these latter weapons had been partially dismantled and retained in storage, with 'radiological safety' grounds being cited for not sending them back to England on HMS

Hampshire's second high speed 'bomb run'.

So what did that mean?

Was a return trip to Chelyabinsk with 'big' bombs, Grand Slams, Tallboys, or perhaps even the two Blue Danubes on the agenda? Or did the powers that be have something else in mind? And what the Devil had gone so wrong last night that the follow up operations scheduled for today had been scratched?

"Control to TAW-ONE!"

Guy French was instantly focused on the job in hand.

"TAW-ONE to Control. Ready to roll! Out!"

The controller was a middle-aged Squadron Leader who had been on the reserve list over a decade before being recalled to the service after the October War. His voice was a laconic drawl.

"Control to TAW-ONE.   Permission to roll.   SCRAMBLE! SCRAMBLE! SCRAMBLE!"

Guy French slowly advanced *The Angry Widow's* throttles against the brakes.

"Roger, Control. SCRAMBLE! SCRAMBLE! SCRAMBLE!"

He waited as the Victor's great Rolls-Royce turbofans cycled up towards full power.

"Release brakes!"

The Angry Widow thundered forward.

With her bomb bay empty the bomber bounded down the centreline of the runway and soared into the sky, climbing like a seventy ton fighter.

Chapter 73

07:30 Hours
Friday 3rd July, 1964
Army Group South Headquarters, Governor's Palace, Basra

Lieutenant General Viktor Georgiyevich Kulikov had been struck dumb for some moments when he was informed by the Commissar General of Iraq – whom it seemed had retreated to back into his bunker after Minister of Defence Comrade Admiral of the Fleet Sergey Georgiyevich Gorshkov had flown south from Baghdad – that the 'Basra Sector' was, quote 'to be a no fly zone'. The Collective Leadership were worried that allowing the Red Air Force to operate 'south of the 32nd Parallel 'risked an incident with the aircraft of the United States Navy'. This apparently, would be in breach of 'the protocols agreed' between the Troika and the Americans.

'We've been talking to the Yanks?' Kulikov had asked, dumbfounded.

"Of course we have!" The Commissar General had retorted angrily.

Kulikov had only ever met Yuri Vladimirovich Andropov, the First Deputy Secretary of the KGB a couple of times. On both occasions the KGB man had treated him as if he was a witless Kulak and Andropov's manner had been no less condescending or patronising over the scrambler link to Baghdad.

Minister Gorshkov had decided to come to Basra to 'personally assess the situation' upon being notified of the death of the Commander of Army Group South. It was now assumed that the aircraft in which Marshal of the Soviet Union Hamazasp Khachaturi Babadzhanian's deputy had been flying had been destroyed by one of the two megaton-sized air bursts west of Baghdad. Hearing this Kulikov had not unnaturally, demanded full authority to act as Army Group Commander 'in the current emergency'.

Andropov had slapped him down.

'You will attempt to stabilise the front. No major tactical changes to the plans already in hand may be effected before the arrival of Minister Gorshkov.'

It was as if Andropov had not heard a single work he had said to him.

'Comrade Commissar,' Kulikov had attempted to explain, or rather pleaded, 'our forces around Umm Qasr have been subjected to massive air attacks and are under attack by large formations of enemy tanks. If the enemy succeeds in cutting the road from Umm Qasr to Basra, elements of four mechanised divisions and upwards of forty thousand men will be encircled!'

Commissar General Andropov had not thought this was very likely.

'We command the entire Faw Peninsula,' he had reminded the

soldier.

'The Faw Peninsular is a low-lying delta area, a marshland without roads. If the road to Basra is cut the only way our people can get out is by swimming, Comrade Commissar!'

'Don't be hysterical, man!'

It was a conversation in which two deaf men shouted at each other.

'Issue a command directive that every man is to stand and fight where he is!' Andropov had added, probably genuinely thinking that he was being helpful.

Notwithstanding, Kulikov had tried to reason with the KGB man.

'As if the situation in the west around Umm Qasr is not bad enough,' he had reasoned as his angst constricted his chest and throat, 'we are facing a potential disaster on the front of 2nd Siberian Mechanised Army. The enemy has embroiled us in an attritional battle for Khorramshahr which has delayed, possibly ruled out, the planned amphibious assault across the Karun River on Abadan Island. Our losses have been very heavy...'

'The attack on Abadan must proceed according to schedule!'

'The enemy has sent warships up the Shatt al-Arab to bombard our assembly areas...'

'Why haven't you sunk them?'

'Because apart from a couple of dozen sorties earlier this morning the fucking Red Air Force has been grounded, Comrade Commissar!'

'As I said, that is a political matter, Comrade General!' That was when Andropov had relented and dropped a ground-shaking new bombshell. "Minister Gorshkov has *spoken*. The Air Force has been assigned new operational responsibilities. The Americans are supposed to be *dealing* with the British Fleet.'

Kulikov had stared at the handset, his jaw agape.

'Are you still there, Kulikov?'

'Er, yes...' The Red Army man swiftly recovered a little of his equilibrium even though he felt a little like he had just been hit in the face with the stock of an AK-47. 'They haven't,' he muttered. 'The Americans certainly haven't attacked the British ships in the Arvand River.'

'What?'

Kulikov lost his temper.

'To the best of my knowledge the Americans have not attacked the British ships bombarding my men north of Khorramshahr and if something isn't done about it soon I will have no alternative but to halt all offensive actions east of the Arvand River, Comrade Commissar!'

'That's not your decision...'

'If we go on taking casualties the way we have in the last twenty-four hours we won't have an Army in southern Iraq in a couple of days' time, Comrade Commissar!'

Kulikov was also sorely tempted to inform the Commissar General that the attack on Khorramshahr-Abadan had been put in the hands of a Corps Commander who thought war was a question of knocking holes in walls with one's head, and a paratrooper who knew virtually nothing about armoured warfare.

Babadzhanian must have been delirious by then; he probably had not known what he was doing...

Andropov had terminated the exchange.

In the Soviet Union it was occasionally permissible to ask for a clarification of one's orders; and sometimes – albeit very occasionally - acceptable for subordinates to have some small, usually insignificant part, in planning the execution of those orders. That was the limit of discussion and dissent was never tolerated. Orders were orders and the penalty for disobeying an order was well understood.

Kulikov marched into the operations room of Army Group South and began to bark orders.

"Command Directive Three-One." It was the third day of the month and it was his first command to all ground forces. "All units are to hold their ground. Positions will be defended to the last man."

Several of Babadzhanian's staffers blanched at this.

Kulikov ignored the frowns and narrowed eyes.

"Command Directive Three-two. Organise a blocking force on the Basra-Umm Qasr road at the first major water obstacle south of the city. Command Directive Three-three. Any man fleeing from the enemy will be summarily executed for desertion."

Kulikov stepped over to the map table.

"Command Directive Three-four. Operations ongoing on the eastern bank of the Arvand River will continue. The assault on the Karun River front will proceed as soon as possible according to the existing plan. Command Directive Three-five. The movement of artillery and rocket batteries into the Faw Peninsula south of Basra will go ahead to support anti-ship operations and ground forces across the Arvand River. These units are authorised to operate without regard to the expenditure of available ammunitions stocks."

The distant reverberations of very large explosions filtered into the operations room.

A youthful lieutenant ran into the room.

"There are many, many aircraft over the Abadan Sector!" He gasped breathlessly.

Recollecting his surreal conversation with Commissar General Andropov, Kulikov found himself wondering whose aircraft where bombing whom. If it had not been so galling the situation would have been laughable.

Beneath his feet the ground reverberated softly.

In the heat of battle nobody knew what anybody else was doing.

War is chaos; chaos is war...

Chapter 74

Frank Waters was trying to remember the last time he had had so much fun. It would either have been that time he was caught in flagrante delicto with the wife of that French diplomat in 1955 – the blaggard who had burst into the bedroom brandishing a pistol that went off an inch from his head – or that time he emptied his Thompson sub-machine gun into the command car he had honestly believed that Erwin Rommel was sitting in back in 1942. On both occasions he had thought, for a couple of minutes, that he would die a happy man.

Ever since he had learned his fate on the night of Airey and Diana Neave's dinner party in Oxford when the Prime Minister had given him his new marching orders, his life had been a marvellous rollercoaster. Although he doubted if his fellow BBC 'comrades' felt the same way that was their problem not his. For him the last couple of weeks had been like being born again. Everything was fresh and new, more important, he felt like a completely changed and reinvigorated man. In retrospect he had been treading water for far too many years; shamelessly living off past glories and *that* extraordinary woman had unknowingly given him back the vital spark that had been slowly dimming to nothing ever since the end of his time in the Western Desert in 1943.

He had chivvied his 'crew' off the bridge to Abadan Island before it was fully light. They were all tired and grubby, some more irritable than others especially when he had thrown them trenching implements and told them to make the old communications trench adjacent to the 4th Royal Tanks forward HQ 'deeper', just as the blazing sun rose above the horizon and began to peep through the smoke from the oil fires.

'Look, chaps," he had explained patiently. 'You can either stay here and witness the best Army in Christendom, or anywhere else that I'm aware of, show you how it deals with the Red menace or you can skedaddle. I really don't care what you decide. One of the decisive battles in World history is being fought all around us and if you can't be bothered to film it well...more fool you!'

Presently, the sound engineer was holding a microphone on a periscope-like boom above the parapet, the cameraman had pointed his 16-millimetre film camera at where the pontoon bridge had been before the Royal Engineers blew it up, and Frank Waters was standing on a makeshift firing step viewing the first T-62s creeping out of the ruins of Khorramshahr on the opposite bank of the Karun River.

The 4th Royal Tanks had over a dozen Conquerors and Centurions hull down with unobstructed fields of fire covering the northern curve of the river around the top of Abadan Island. In revetments all along the line squads with L2 BAT (Battalion, Anti-Tank) 120-millimetre recoilless rifles plugged the gaps in the line. The killing ground could not have been better prepared, or the battlefield more expertly *salted*.

'If we were stupid enough to throw all our tanks at the Russians in a fair fight they'd roll over us and hardly know they'd been in a battle afterwards,' he had explained to the others. 'So what we're doing is trying to *bleed* the bastards. We only accept battle if we have to, or if we can dictate the conditions. Khorramshahr was a trap. So is *this*!'

The only thing that surprised the former SAS man was that the Red Army was meekly, almost obediently conforming to Michael Carver's master plan. It was as if whoever was in charge had run out of ideas; or worse, was simply following – by rote – a set of orders designed to get the maximum number of his tanks 'brewed up' in the shortest possible time!

Only one question nagged at the back of his mind: what had happened to the famous Red Army artillery? Standard Red Army doctrine was that the moment it bumped into any kind of fixed or prepared defences armour was supposed to advance behind an overwhelming storm of rocket and shell fire. Last night the Russians had merely peppered the desert ahead of the attack on Khorramshahr, and today there had been only a half-hearted shelling of several targets on Abadan Island after the dust and smoke from the early morning high-level bombing raid had finished. The air raid had been a bit hairy, not least because the Red Air Force had not seemed to be aiming at anything in particular. RAF Abadan – what little remained of it – had been thoroughly plastered from end to end, as had the northern section of the already wrecked and burning refinery complex. In comparison the sporadic Red Army shelling was of was of little more than nuisance value. Somebody had said that bombers had gone after ships in the river too, but nobody knew much about that.

"Make sure you get this!" He exhorted his colleagues. "After a few minutes it will be too smoky to get any real sense of what is going on across the river!"

Fifty yards away a Conqueror's L7A1 fifty-two calibre 120-millimetre rifled gun barked. Almost instantaneously a T-62 the best part of a mile away exploded, its circular dome-shaped turret shooting a hundred feet in the air as the tank's ammunition 'lit off'.

Other British tanks opened fire.

A dozen Soviet tanks were burning in seconds, several of them hit simultaneously by two or three rounds.

A single T-62 managed to fire back across the river before it erupted in a pillar of fire as a round from one of the Conquerors, or a 105-millimetre armour piercing solid shot from a Centurion's L7 gun sliced through its armour like a scalpel through the skin of an apple.

Belatedly, sporadic mortar rounds fired from inside the ruins of Khorramshahr started falling on the southern bank of the Karun River.

Too little too late.

Or so Frank Waters devoutly hoped.

What was that screeching sound?

A screeching sound like Lucifer's henchmen dragging tormented souls down into the pit of Hell coming closer, and closer, and...

"GET DOWN ON FLOOR!"

The first salvo of Katyushas – famously dubbed *Stalin's Organ* by the Germans – screamed down about a quarter of a mile to the east. A Katyusha launcher had anywhere from fourteen to forty-eight rails, capable of firing rockets with warheads of up to twenty kilograms in weight around three miles. It was not a precision weapon; it was designed to saturate whole areas and its capacity to rain terror out of a clear blue sky perfectly accorded with Soviet 'blitz' or 'shock', all-arms offensive doctrine.

The first Katyusha salvo straddled the Karun River. The second slashed through the line of hull down tanks and wiped out several anti-tank revetments. Unless a tank like the Centurion of Conqueror was hit in a vulnerable spot – neither machine had many of those – it was relatively immune from Katyusha fire. Not so the tanks' screening infantry or the men manning the 120-millimetre L2 BAT recoilless rifles, or the telephone land lines linking the 4th Royal Tanks' with Brigade Headquarters.

The sky was torn to shreds by another salvo.

Far away the ground was convulsing, as if from an earthquake.

Now 115-millimetres rounds from the surviving T-62s – several of which were partially screened by other knocked out tanks - were whistling overhead. A loud 'CLANG' nearby registered a hit on a Conqueror. This time the round ricocheted away.

Within a minute two British tanks had *brewed up*.

Frank Waters cowered in the bottom of the trench with the others.

The 4th Royal Tanks had made the Russians bleed again.

Now there would be a price to pay.

Chapter 75

"NOW HEAR THIS! NOW HEAR THIS!"

Flying operations had been suspended temporarily approximately sixty seconds before the public address had demanded attention throughout the flagship of Carrier Division Seven.

"THE FLEET COMMANDER WILL ADDRESS THE SHIP'S COMPANY!"

Like the majority of the USS Kitty Hawk's five-and-a-half thousand crewmen Lieutenant-Commander Walter Brenckmann had been on duty twenty hours straight by then. Down in the carrier's CIC exhausted men manned their consuls and updated plots, more than once the Fleet Anti-Submarine Officer had had to pat a man's shoulder to ensure that he was awake.

Nobody was talking about it but one did not need to be any kind of clairvoyant or mind reader to know that a lot of the men in the CIC, and many of the airmen who had taken part in last night's operations against the Centaur Battle Group – a grand name for an obsolete old World War II British carrier, a New Zealand frigate and a couple of small ASW escorts – felt sick to their hearts. Walter Brenckmann suspected that he was not the only man who was ashamed of the actions the Navy he had loved and served his whole adult life. Away from the cloistered, 'in the know' men in the CIC or those whose duty stations were on the bridge, it was anybody's guess what percentage of the Kitty Hawk's complement honestly believed last night's action had been anything other than an act of gross, unforgivable betrayal.

Pure bloody murder by any other description...

"THIS IS ADMIRAL BRINGLE," the gruffly confident voice declaimed. The words reverberated down corridors, echoed in the bowels of the ship; seemingly falling upon a man's ears from several places at once.

In the CIC fans whirred, multi-coloured lights blinked, men conversed in low, hushed tones, comms links beeped for attention, operators acknowledged in low tones, spoke softly ignoring the ship wide broadcast.

"A LOT OF YOU WILL HAVE QUESTIONS ABOUT YESTERDAY'S *SELF-DEFENCE* OPERATIONS AND WHAT THEY MEAN FOR CARRIER DIVISION SEVEN'S ONGOING MISSION IN THIS THEATRE."

Walter Brenckmann fought to keep his expression neutral.

"AT SEVENTEEN HUNDRED HOURS – LOCAL TIME – YESTERDAY CARRIER DIVISION SEVEN ACTED TO ENFORCE A MARITIME DE-MILITARIZED ZONE, A DMZ, COVERING THE ENTIRE PERSIAN GULF WEST OF LONGITUDE 50 DEGREES EAST."

Men in the CIC were looking up from their desks; the yeoman

standing at the Battle Board had turned around and glanced to their officers. There was no 'DMZ' demarcated or delineated on the Battle Board, nor any large area marked in red labelled with the legend *'bomb everything in this box'*.

"What the fuck is a DMZ?" Somebody muttered in the gloom from behind Walter Brenckmann's left shoulder.

Obligingly, Rear Admiral William Bringle elucidated further.

"THE EXTENT OF THE DE-MILITARIZED ZONE WAS AGREED WITH THE LEADERSHIP OF THE SOVIET UNION AS PART OF A BROADER AGREEMENT TO AVERT THE POSSIBILITY OF FRICTION IN THE MIDDLE EAST INVOLVING THE UNITED STATES IN A NEW GLOBAL WAR WITH RUSSIA."

In that moment there was a horrible, sepulchral silence in the CIC. It was as if time stood still for a second before normal sights and sounds took over again.

"THE PRESIDENT AND THE TROIKA, THE COLLECTIVE LEADERSHIP OF THE SOVIET UNION HAVE, IN THE INTERESTS OF WORLD PEACE AGREED A FIVE YEAR BI-LATERAL ARMISTICE BETWEEN OUR NATIONS."

Walter Brenckmann thought his head was on fire.

Had the US Sixth Fleet launched another sneak attack on the British Mediterranean Fleet?

When, not if, the British retaliated would it be with nukes...

My Mom and Pa are in England...

As his mind roiled frantically through the horrifying possibilities of this new *madness* something happened to him that had never happened before. He rushed to the edge of, and teetered for some moments on the precipice of unreasoning, blind...*panic*.

"AT THIS TIME THE US AMBASSADOR IN OXFORD, ENGLAND IS DELIVERING A DIPLOMATIC NOTE TO THE BRITISH GOVERNMENT MANDATING A CESSATION OF ALL HOSTILITIES IN THE MIDDLE EAST NOT LATER THAN ONE HUNDRED HOURS LOCAL TIME TOMORROW, THE 4TH OF JULY. I AM AUTHORISED TO INFORM YOU THAT PROVIDING BRITISH AND COMMONWEALTH FORCES OBSERVE A POSTURE OF STRICT NEUTRALITY AND NON-AGGRESSION AGAINST US FORCES ELSEWHERE IN THE WORLD, THAT US FORCES WILL ADOPT A PASSIVE OPERATIONAL STATUS..."

Until the next time the President orders us to murder another one of our 'friends'!

Having dealt with the greatest and most shameful volte face in US history William Bringle moved on, his manner that of a man who was keen to resume 'business as normal'.

However, Walter Brenckmann knew that business as usual with the British was not going to be unlikely again in his lifetime.

"KITTY HAWK WILL SHORTLY REDUCE SPEED TO PERMIT ESSENTIAL DAMAGE CONTROL CHECKS TO THE STARBOARD TURBINE ROOM, AND FOR DAMAGE CONTROL TEAMS TO ASSESS IF ADDITIONAL MEASURES NEED TO BE PUT IN HAND TO PREVENT

FURTHER FLOODING. FIXED WING AIR OPERATIONS WILL CEASE BETWEEN FOURTEEN HUNDRED AND SEVENTEEN HUNDRED HOURS. HELICOPTER OPERATIONS WILL CONTINUE AS SCHEDULED."

Walter Brenckmann had felt nowhere near this bad on the morning after the USS Theodore Roosevelt had flushed her Polaris missiles and almost certainly killed hundreds of thousands of Russian men, women and children, old and young, the infirm and babies in arms alike. On the night of the October War he had done his duty; or at least that was what he had honestly believed he was doing at the time.

Now he was no better than an accessory to murder.

"CARRIER DIVISION SEVEN WILL REMAIN AT AIR DEFENCE CONDITION TWO UNTIL FURTHER NOTICE. STAY ALERT. STAND TO YOUR STATIONS. DO YOU DUTY AND UPHOLD THE HIGHEST TRADITIONS OF THE SERVICE."

Walter thought the fleet commander had finished.

"AIR OPERATIONS WILL COMMENCE AGAINST TARGETS IN SOUTHERN IRAQ AND IRAN AT 18:30 HOURS."

Men were looking at each other with widening eyes all around the CIC.

"THAT IS ALL!"

That was the moment Walter realised his naval career was over and that he had taken his last order from anybody on board the flagship. As if in a trance he stepped across to the Commander (Operations) of Carrier Division Seven.

He stood to attention.

"Sir, I request permission to be relieved of my duty station."

The other man, a fifty year old veteran who had been onboard the USS Tennessee at Pearl Harbour nearly half a lifetime ago had blinked at him before he understood what had been said to him.

"Are you certain of this, Mister Brenckmann?"

"Yes, sir."

The older man had sighed a very weary sigh.

"In that case, you are relieved. Report to the Captain at your earliest convenience."

By the time Walter had climbed up to the bridge of the Kitty Hawk he had to stand in line and Captain Horace Epes was visibly agitated, angry-eyed and struggling to keep his emotions in check.

Notwithstanding the likelihood of severe repercussions, in time of war a request to be relieved of one's duties onboard a US Navy ship at sea remained the right of any officer. In extremity such a request might be construed as cowardice in the face of the enemy, gross dereliction of duty, conduct unbecoming an officer and so on, ad infinitum. But Walter's country was not at war with anybody; or rather, it had not to his knowledge formally declared war on another country and the murder of all those brave men on the Centaur and its escorts had not been any kind of act of 'legitimate self-defence on the high seas'. The fleet had attacked friendly ships without warning in international waters; he could not and would not obey the orders of men who were prepared to commit that kind of atrocity in the name of *duty*.

"Dammit, Brenckmann!" Horace Epes raged, pacing behind his desk in his small sea cabin. "I thought you'd be the last man to associate yourself with mutiny!"

"Mutiny, sir? I have associated myself with no such thing, sir!"

The older man had stopped pacing, shocked to be contradicted.

"I have requested, as is my right as a commissioned officer in the United States Navy," Walter protested resignedly, "to be relieved of my duties for reasons of conscience specifically so as not to become in any way a mutinous presence onboard Kitty Hawk, sir."

"You'll be stripped of all rank and privileges and probably do jail time for this, Brenckmann!"

"Possibly, sir," Walter conceded, feeling stronger by the second. "But at least this way I've got a shot at being able to look myself in the eye most mornings for the rest of my life, sir."

Chapter 76

After the first attack Anzac, Tiger and Diamond had anchored a few hundred yards up river. A clutch of bombs had fallen in the Arvand some distance from the Tobruk and the Royalist, still anchored above El Seeba. Then it had gone quiet until eventually, just as Anzac manoeuvred to 'break track' up river, the Red Air Force had returned.

The men manning the Bristol Bloodhound batteries had waited until the approaching high altitude Red Air Force bombers trespassed deep into their engagement envelopes. And then, in ones and twos the twenty-five feet long two ton missiles had thundered into the air. Propelled by two Bristol Thor ramjets and four Gosling solid fuel boosters each Bloodhound was travelling at nearly four hundred miles per hour by the time it left its launcher. Within the next thirty feet of its climb it went supersonic, accelerating through seven hundred and fifty miles an hour. Three to four seconds after launch its four boosters detached; by then the rocket had reached Mach 2.2 and had already identified its target.

Rear Admiral Nicholas Davey had watched the grey rocket plumes of the Bloodhounds climbing at impossible speeds towards the invisible approaching bombers with dreadful awe. Nothing had really prepared him for how quickly and how violently war was conducted in the modern age. The power and the accuracy of weapons was horribly magnified by technological advances; he just felt very old, a relic from another bygone age. In comparison with the mayhem being wrought in Southern Iraq – thousands of people, possibly tens, or scores of thousands must have died in the last twenty-four hours – Peter Christopher's death run in the Talavera now seemed like the last hurrah of an older, somehow more chivalrous World. This war in the Gulf was being fought with radar controlled gunnery, guided weapons capable of smiting an enemy at thirty miles at the flick of switch; or by tanks with guns so big that targets two to three miles away were sitting ducks.

The Centaur and her escorts had been like lambs to the slaughter; World War II type ships with modern radar but with everything else against them. The aircraft flying off the decks of the Kitty Hawk were 'space age' marvels to the men of Davey's generation; the deadly surface-to-air missile systems carried by all the big American ships like something out of a Flash Gordon movie. *His* ships had had no chance, to run, to surrender, let alone to fight back.

It must have been pure bloody murder...

The first MiG-21s had rocketed across the Arvand River like raging silvery wraiths too fast for any gun to bear on them. Tiger's quick firing automatic twin 3-inch mounts had cranked around belatedly trying to acquire a target. The Bofors guns of the destroyers had put up a largely ineffectual 'wall' of fire; and the MiGs screamed through it untouched.

Huge geysers of water erupted ahead and on the shoreward, starboard side of HMNZS Royalist.

Davey ran to the side of the bridge to look back as Tiger groped slowly west, nearly a mile distant from the other ship. Royalist was still moored fore and aft, broadside on to the river bank.

Momentarily the six thousand ton five hundred feet long cruiser disappeared behind a wall of white water. There was a flash, a louder, ear-splittingly sharper two-stage explosion which rumbled across the muddy water easily distinguishable from the dozen near misses.

The spray slowly cleared, the water around Royalist churned.

The ship seemed to be rolling from the punches; aft of her second stack black smoke and ripples of crimson fire walked across her superstructure; ready use 2-pound 40-millimetre reloads exploding.

Royalist's two forward twin 5.25-inch high angle turrets had trained a point east of due north. All four guns discharged in an oddly ragged salvo.

Nick Davey groaned inwardly.

One bomb run and Royalist was already reduced to working her main battery under local control.

Tiger's forward and starboard 3-inch turrets had begun hurling rounds into the northern sky at a rate of one per barrel every three seconds. The cruiser's 'state of the art' automatic main and secondary batteries were notoriously prone to breakdowns but by some miracle everything was still working, albeit at less than optimal rates of fire. The 3-inch mounts were allegedly capable of throwing thirty rounds per barrel per minute into the air, rather than the twenty Tiger's Gunnery Officer was *hoping* to sustain. The fact that Tiger's guns had never really worked properly had always clouded another issue; the ship's relatively limited magazine capacity. In the unlikely event the big guns could ever be persuaded to fire for any length of time without a jam, or a major mechanical or electrical failure, the ship would shoot herself 'dry' in twenty minutes.

Presently, that was not a thing Nick Davey had the time or the wherewithal to think about.

Three more MiGs hurtled in from the west at six hundred plus knots. They were flying so low their afterburners kicked up great rooster plumes of sand and dust as they crested the bank on the Faw side of the Arvand and their iron bombs hit the water.

The splash from one bomb kicked high, flicked up and over the port wing of one jet. The aircraft went straight into the water and disintegrated into tens of thousands of pieces of disarticulated, twisted, splintered metal before the pilot knew what had killed him. But Nick Davey was not watching the wreckage of the supersonic fighter cart wheeling to destruction; he was following the malevolent dark forms of the Russian bombs as they skipped across the water towards Royalist.

Two bombs bounced straight over her.

Another detonated in the water near her stern, or perhaps just under it.

And then the final bomb, probably a thousand pounder crashed into her port side just ahead of her bridge.

The old cruiser shuddered.

Nothing seemed to happen for some seconds.

And then the whole amidships section of the ship crumbled inward and instantly, with mind-numbing swiftness, Her Majesty's New Zealand Ship Royalist blew up.

Chapter 77

Joanne Brenckmann had insisted on accompanying her husband to his *interview* with the British Foreign Secretary. Superficially, Oxford seemed unnaturally calm given the enormity of the events in the Middle East but of course nobody outside government and military circles yet knew of her country's unspeakable perfidy. Things would be very different when the magnitude of the betrayal became more widely known.

Joanne's husband had shown her the latest telegrams from Philadelphia. He had spoken twice to Secretary of State Fulbright overnight and then, an hour ago to the President.

A month ago Jack Kennedy had concluded a secret compact with the British Prime Minister; now he had reneged upon it – as apparently he had planned to do from the start - because he thought that was the only way he was going to get re-elected.

Things had gone from bad to worse. It seemed that overnight there has been a battle in the Persian Gulf in which the US Navy had sunk three British and one New Zealand warship with heavy loss of life.

Joanne's husband had not been prepared to accept Secretary of State Fulbright's account of that action, or of the news of the 'draft peace treaty' with the USSR on trust and had demanded, politely and respectfully – because Walter was the most courteous and civil man she had ever met – to speak to the President. His conversation with Jack Kennedy had been short, less than two minutes and afterwards her husband had just shaken his head when she tried to speak to him about it.

It was only now as they waited in the reception room on an idyllic, sunny Oxford morning looking out over the manicured lawn of the Old Quad of Hertford College that Walter Brenckmann could bring himself to confide all to his wife.

"The President thinks the British are Hell bent on dragging us into a another war with the Russians," he had told Joanne, "he says the Providence was sunk by a British submarine in a quote 'obvious act of provocation' and that Admiral Bringle, the CO of Carrier Division Seven, met with his counterpart, Admiral Davey of the Australian, British and New Zealand Persian Gulf Squadron to give him prior warning that he intended to maintain a 'maritime neutrality zone' in the Gulf. Apparently Davey ignored him. Last night we attacked and sank the British carrier Centaur and three of her escorts. It would have been no contest even if we hadn't attacked them without warning..."

"Walter," she whispered in horror. "That's impossible!"

"Kitty Hawk was damaged in the battle. Not badly, but badly enough to delay planned air operations against British targets in the Gulf today. I am to communicate to the British that if they do not undertake to cease all operations in the region by one o'clock tomorrow morning local Gulf time that Carrier Division Seven will mount 'massive' attacks against the surviving units of the ABNZ Squadron, Abadan and *other* targets in the Gulf."

Joanne's confusion must have seemed perversely comical.

"The President is planning to fly to India in the next few days to sign a non-aggression treaty with the Russians in New Delhi. Special Emissary Thompson of the State Department and Soviet Foreign Minister Kuznetsov have already initialled draft copies detailing the terms of the five-year agreement..."

"For God's sake!" Joanne protested. "Don't those idiots in Philadelphia understand the British at all?"

The United States Ambassador to the Court of Woodstock shook his head.

"No, my dear," he sighed, "they don't..."

The Brenckmann's turned as the door at their back opened.

Tom Harding-Grayson and his wife Patricia entered the room.

There was a bizarre, uncomfortable interregnum while the couples, firm personal friends, exchanged handshakes and shadow kisses with the respective wives.

"I suggested we meet here at Hertford College because the Prime Minister has asked to be present at our tête-à-tête, Walter," the Foreign Secretary explained a little sheepishly.

"Oh, shall I," Joanne began, thinking to excuse herself.

"No, no," Pat Harding-Grayson said immediately. "This must be awful for you. You and I are both invited to attend the Prime Minister's rooms, Jo."

Seven months ago Joanne Brenckmann had still been a Boston housewife. Twenty months ago she and Walter had been talking about whether they could afford to retire down to the Florida Keys. In retrospect that had been a pipe dream but it had been a warm, reassuring notion to entertain as they faced their late middle age together now that all the kids had flown the nest. Seven months on she was in Oxford, England among friends her President had betrayed.

"I'm so glad you accompanied the Ambassador, Mrs Brenckmann," Margaret Thatcher said sombrely, rising to shake the older woman's hand. "We've not really had much of a chance to speak in your time in England but I know from what Pat has told me that you have been a tower of strength at Walter's side throughout these troubled times."

Joanne Brenckmann was struck by the Prime Minister's dignity; and that she seemed fresh, unwearied and utterly unbowed by the events of the last few hours. The younger woman's clear blue eyes held her a moment.

"Sit next to me," Margaret Thatcher directed, drawing Joanne towards one of the threadbare chairs that seemed to be the hallmark of English domesticity. "We're just waiting for Mr Callaghan to arrive and then we shall begin."

There was a tea service on a low table.

"Shall I be mother?" The Prime Minister suggested.

Nobody demurred.

Joanne Brenckmann was starting to think she was dreaming; either that or she had mistakenly walked into the Mad Hatter's tea party.

The Right Honourable Member of Parliament for Cardiff South, the leader of the Labour and Co-operative Party and Deputy Prime Minister in the Unity Administration of the United Kingdom arrived, escorted by his son-in-law, Peter Jay, who made himself scarce once he had safely delivered his charge to the hurriedly called counsel.

"Forgive my lateness," the big, lugubrious man apologised. He was ashen and exhausted in exactly the way Margaret Thatcher was not. Jim Callaghan was late because he had warned her that he needed to consult 'with others' – his own Party's inner circle - before attending Hertford College.

Suddenly, everybody was looking at Walter Brenckmann.

"Jo and I appreciate your personal kindness," the US Ambassador said to the room at large. "It makes what I must say to you all the more," he hesitated, forced himself not to say 'wrong' and instead said, "unpalatable and unfortunate. However, I am here at my country's bidding not as a private citizen."

Jim Callaghan had taken the seat to Margaret Thatcher's left, clockwise around the room were Patricia Harding-Grayson, the Foreign Secretary, Walter Brenckmann and Joanne who had reached out and squeezed her husband's hand.

"The President has instructed me to communicate the following to the UAUK, Prime Minister," the Ambassador said, adopting the air of detached courtroom formality he had cultivated over the years.

"The President believes that is in the interests of all the parties to cease hostilities in the Persian Gulf immediately and for representatives of the said parties to convene at a time and a place to be agreed where our mutual grievances may be discussed."

Walter Brenckmann halted, half-expecting a question.

When there was none he continued.

"The President is determined not to allow the war in the Gulf to escalate into a new global nuclear conflict with the Soviet Union. He asked me to make it clear to you that following the incident in which the USS Providence was lost..."

"The Providence was sunk by a Russian submarine!" Jim Callaghan grunted. "Even *your* Navy must know that, Ambassador?"

Walter Brenckmann did not reply.

"Pray carry on, Ambassador," Margaret Thatcher requested softly.

"The President is profoundly unhappy that two thermonuclear devices were deployed over Central Iraq without prior consultation with the Administration. He considers that this breaks formal and informal undertakings made by the UAUK to the American government."

The quietness had grown icy.

"This and the UAUK's continuing aggression in the Gulf convinces President Kennedy that, at this time, the UAUK is not amenable to seeking a peaceful outcome to the conflict in that region. It is therefore, President Kennedy's conviction that the United States has no other option but to act bilaterally with the Soviet Union to avert a new thermonuclear disaster."

Margaret Thatcher raised her tea cup to her lips and sipped daintily.

"I'm tempted to observe," she said sadly, "that it would have saved everybody a lot of trouble if President Kennedy had adopted this approach in October 1962." She smiled a glacial smile. "Before, rather than after he blew up half the World."

The Prime Minister sat back, looked to her Foreign Minister.

"About now," Tom Harding-Grayson, "Lord Franks, our man in Philadelphia will be delivering a note to Secretary of State Fulbright," he grimaced, "or more likely to one of his flunkies. United States Navy ships at Malta and Gibraltar have been arrested and in due course their crews will be interned as prisoners of war. United States Navy ships still at large in the Mediterranean will be required in due course to surrender, either at Malta or Gibraltar. United States Navy surface ships, submarines and aircraft currently in the Mediterranean Theatre will not be permitted to leave that sea. We have taken this action because since the Cuban Missiles War US forces have launched a series of cowardly sneak attacks on *our* people. We were prepared to accept that previous *atrocities* were attributable to breakdowns in the proper chain of command; but what happened in the Persian Gulf yesterday was a deliberate, unprovoked act of aggression sanctioned at the highest levels of the US Federal Government. Heretofore, the United Kingdom and the United States are, de facto, at war in the Persian Gulf; the matter of whether that war spreads will depend entirely on the actions of the US Government. Lord Franks has been instructed to remind your State Department in the most unambiguous terms that if the United States employs nuclear weapons against the British Isles, British Crown Dependencies or British and Commonwealth Forces anywhere in the World *we* will retaliate. That is all."

Walter Brenckmann blinked worriedly.

There ought to have been more.

"We have to talk about the situation in the Gulf?" He asked, looking to Margaret Thatcher. "We have to stop this..."

Her topaz blue eyes burned with quiet rage.

"I'm deeply sorry, Walter. But *we* have nothing further to say to your Government about the *situation* in the Persian Gulf."

Chapter 78

12:50 Hours
Friday 3rd July 1964
HMS Alliance, Lazaretto Creek, Malta

Lieutenant-Commander Francis Barrington pushed back his cap and leaned forward to cautiously rest his forearms on the relatively cool steel of the cockpit rail atop the submarine's tall sail. It was an atypically overcast, balmy day. Fittingly, dark clouds periodically rolled over Malta from the north. He stifled a yawn. The World had gone completely, stark, raving bonkers again and he had got to the point where he had given up trying to make sense of it.

The intercom beeped for attention.

"Captain," he intoned automatically into the handset.

"Number four is now loaded, sir," reported Lieutenant Michael Philpott, the boat's executive officer from down in the control room some thirty feet below.

"Very good, Number One."

Barrington's gaze fell on the grey murderous silhouette of the seven thousand ton brand new guided missile destroyer USS Leahy (DLG-16) moored across the other side of Marsamxett Anchorage at the oiling wharf, directly opposite the broad mouth of Lazaretto Creek.

The big number '16' was clearly visible under her bow.

For the moment the destroyer's Terrier surface-to-air missile pylons were trained fore and aft, likewise her two twin 3-inch gun turrets. Members of her crew stood at her port rail and stared at the Alliance; Barrington presumed with unbridled incredulity not unlike his own.

His orders were unambiguous: if the Leahy attempted to cast off or made any attempt to activate, or to train her weapons systems off the centreline of the ship he was to launch *all* the fish in his forward 21-inch torpedo tubes into her side.

No ifs, no buts!

If the destroyer made a false move he was to sink her.

It was official; the World had gone stark raving bonkers!

"There's a barge approaching, sir!"

Barrington had posted a detail of four armed men on the casing.

"Ask Mr Philpott to take over from me up here."

Alliance's visitor was a fresh-faced lieutenant from the C-in-C Mediterranean Fleet's staff. Barrington took him to the claustrophobic privacy of his cabin.

"What the Devil is going on?" He demanded wearily. Alliance had been in dry dock the last three days; only returning to her moorings in Lazaretto Creek late last night. "We'd hardly had time to tie up to the emergency buoys this morning and suddenly I'm being ordered to point the boat at that bloody Yank battleship over on the other side of Marsamxett!"

"I'm dreadfully sorry, sir," the other man apologised. "I don't know if anybody actually knows what's going on. All I know is that Admiral Grenville is sending chaps like me out to all the ships and subs we've got guarding the Sixth Fleet ships in harbour. Telling them what *he knows*, if you see what I mean, sir."

The older man waited patiently.

"We don't know all the details but there has been some serious *unpleasantness* in the Persian Gulf. We think American ships and aircraft attacked HMS Centaur and her escorts..."

Francis Barrington's jaw must have very nearly hit the deck because the boy officer – he could not have been more than nineteen or twenty – gave him a very odd look.

"Nobody knows why," the report continued. "Anyway, the order came from Fleet Command to 'arrest' all US Navy ships. The same order went out to Cyprus and Gibraltar. The Marne..."

"The Marne?" The commanding officer of HMS Alliance asked in bewilderment.

"Yes, sir. That's what we renamed that Turkish destroyer Alliance captured after the Battle of Malta. Admiral Grenville said she ought to have her 'proper name' back. Anyway, she's got her torpedo tubes trained on the Independence. Lion was alongside Corradino heights making ready to re-ammunition when the balloon went up; she's got her guns trained on the Independence, too. We've got the Andrew, the other 2nd Submarine Squadron boat in port lined up in Kalkara Creek with her bow tubes bearing on the USS Iowa. Obviously, we're a bit outnumbered but we've got patrol boats close alongside most of the other Yank ships ready to roll depth charges into the water underneath them. The Army have got three or four tanks they're going to drive up onto high ground overlooking the Grand Harbour and the Royal Artillery are emplacing twenty-five pounders along the Valletta ramparts. The only place there's been any fisticuffs so far was at RAF Luqa. Independence flew off about half her air group before she docked. I gather that the Royal Marines have now 'pacified' the troublemakers."

Francis Barrington ran a hand through his thinning hair.

"So we've what," he hesitated, not believing he was asking it, "arrested? *Interned* the whole Sixth Fleet?"

"Yes, something like that, sir."

"And if the Leahy," Barrington waved at the American warship, "so much as blinks I'm *really* supposed to sink her?"

"Oh, absolutely, sir! Admiral Grenville was most categorical about that!"

Chapter 79

"My chaps told me you'd got yourself killed, Frank," Lieutenant General Michael Carver observed as the dusty, bandaged scarecrow figure limped into his forward command trench.

Both sides had stepped back, as if to take a metaphorical deep breath in the mid-day heat. Distantly, guns barked sporadically, otherwise it was almost eerily quiet after the Bedlam of earlier hours.

'Trench' was something of a misnomer in the context of the interconnected anti-tank ditches, tunnels and bunkers dug as deep as the water table would permit which, had the complex been visible from space would have resembled a giant rabbit warren. The 'command trench' was a zigzagging segment of the spider's web of earthworks and maze-like dead ends containing several shallow bunkers half concealed within the wrecked and burning refinery sprawl. Walking wounded from the nearby casualty clearing station were being guided past it and accommodated within it.

Wounded and exhausted men were sitting, lying, and standing everywhere. The air stank of burning and of cordite, even though the shelling of the area had abruptly halted over two hours ago. The relative quietness of the battlefield was unsettling, horribly unnerving in ways the dreadfulness of the barrage, the hammering of the guns, the constant crunching, thudding impact of bombs and shells on the nearby airfield had not been. It was a thing old soldiers understood; that sometimes in war both sides wore themselves out and by default, a kind of unholy mutual unspoken agreement, pulled back to get a second wind.

"No, no, no," the newcomer chortled. The top of his head was swathed in a gory rag bandage and his left trouser leg was caked with dried blood. "I'm fine. God, isn't this a thing!"

"What did you do with your colleagues?"

"I found them a nice deep hole to hide in a about half-a-mile south before I made my way over here, sir."

A medical orderly had appeared from behind the C-in-C's shoulder.

He started unwinding the dressing on the visitor's head wound.

Frank Waters ignored him.

"The 4th Tanks put up a heck of a good show before they pulled back from the Karun River line!"

Carver nodded.

"Yes, they did." Only two Conquerors and six Centurions had made it back into the lines bisecting what was left of RAF Abadan. A man stepping above ground might easily imagine he was standing on a moonscape of craters and blasted concrete. "What did you make of the Red Army's performance last night and this morning?"

Frank Waters thought about this.

Whatever had torn up his scalp had briefly knocked him out. The rest of his 'crew' had had to carry him to an aide station to get his head cleaned up and stitched back together.

"Either they didn't think we were waiting for them or they didn't care, sir," he decided. "I'd have expected them to throw everything at us at once, not in waves. I got the impression their armour isn't talking to their artillery, or vice versa. Perhaps, all their good tankers got killed in October sixty-two?"

Frank Waters flinched as the medical orderly started to re-clean his head wound.

"We could have held the south bank of the Karun for a while longer?" He remarked.

"Yes."

The younger man grinned broadly.

"Is it true that we really do have tanks out in the eastern desert!" He concluded rhetorically. "Just like that cove Julian Calder said!"

Michael Carver smiled.

"Yes," he said again. "Perhaps, as many as a hundred or so. Their time will come but first I need my opposite number to put his head well and truly into the noose."

Frank Waters forgot about the pain.

"What I really want him to do," Caver went on didactically, "is to bridge the Karun, preferably with heavy casualties, assault the south shore and to brush aside the pickets still guarding the road down to Abadan, and," he shrugged, "to get his spearhead embroiled with our defences down here before the 3rd Imperial Iranian Armoured Division crashes into his flank and rear echelon troops north of the river above and to the east of Khorramshahr."

"Stand still, sir," the medical orderly told Frank Waters. "This man needs to go to a dressing station, sir," he informed Carver.

The tall, patrician General nodded sternly.

"The big fly in the ointment is that we don't have any air cover," he said to the former SAS man, matter of factly. "The Americans sank HMS Centaur last night."

Frank Waters involuntarily stuck out a hand to steady himself against the earthen wall of the trench. He was obviously concussed, delirious; Michael Carver had just told him the Yanks had sunk a British aircraft carrier!

Or at least he thought what the C-in-C had said...

Realising the wounded man was having trouble swallowing the news Michael Carver elucidated.

"They sank Centaur, her three close escorts and shot down all her aircraft. We fired off twenty-three Bloodhounds beating off the Red Air Force this morning. That leaves us half-a-dozen to fight off the rest of the Red Air Force and, presumably, the Yanks sometime later today." Michael Carver waved to the west. "One of Admiral Davey's ships blew up this morning; the other four were all damaged in the bombing. The latest news from England is that the Yanks have given *us* an ultimatum to stop military operations by zero-one hundred hours tomorrow," he sighed wearily, '*or else.* Or else we'll all be sorry, I presume."

Carver smiled wanly.

"Oh, and twenty minutes ago my opposite number in Basra radioed me terms demanding the immediate unconditional surrender of Abadan Island."

Chapter 80

14:35 Hours
Friday 3rd July 1964
HMAS Anzac, Arvand River

Commander Stephen Turnbull returned to his partially wrecked bridge after his latest 'around the ship' tour.

In the heat of the day the upper decks of the Battle class destroyer were a cauldron. A man so unwise as to brush exposed metal against bare flesh recoiled in pain, seared. The haze shimmered off the muddy waters of the river as the ship's pumps vomited dirty water over the side.

After the Royalist had blown up the MiGs had concentrated on the flagship.

Although HMS Tiger's fires were out wisps of grey smoke still curled away from her aft superstructure and scorched lattice mainmast. The cruiser was down by the stern, and listing two to three degrees to starboard.

Anzac's sister the Tobruk had had to beach herself on the Abadan shore after sustaining severe splinter damage, and likely several sprung keel plates, from half-a-dozen near misses. She had settled with her decks above water and her main battery still operable, albeit with a much reduced rate of fire. Her forward magazines had flooded slowly; permitting most of her remaining high explosive reloads to be brought up to the main deck. However, with her boilers off line and most of her generators submerged other than firing occasional blind salvoes, she was pretty much out of the fight.

A big bomb had gone off alongside Tiger's starboard engine room. The compartment had flooded in minutes and only desperate counter flooding had kept the ship from capsizing. The MiGs had barrelled in shooting rockets, with cannons blazing. After the fourth or fifth strafing run – it was hard to keep count – the cruiser had been enveloped in smoke.

High-level bombers had saturated great tracts of the river and the banks with bombs; few had come close to the ships in the deep channel and mercifully, the drifting dust, sand and smoke from the carpet bombing had eventually obscured the ships from the aircraft approaching at low level later in the attack. By then it was likely that the first sight the pilots of the attacking MiGs got of their targets was in the split second after they crossed from desert to the river before rocketing past.

There was a 250-kilogram unexploded Red Air Force general purpose bomb lodged in the Anzac's engine room bilge. Another bomb had struck her stern a glancing blow and exploded as it hit the water. Only God alone knew how the blast had failed to set off the Squid anti-submarine mortar rounds stored in the shrapnel-torn ready lockers under the stern deck house. One strafing run had turned the destroyer's funnel into a sieve; another had seen the ship's main mast carried away by contact with the leading edge of a MiG-21's wing. The attacking jet had slammed into the desert in a ball of flame a second later.

The most terrifying thing was how fast things went wrong.

Several twenty or thirty millimetre cannon shells had killed half the bridge watch and severed every electrical connection to the foremast air search and gunnery control radars. It had happened in the blink of an eye in the fractions of a single second it took the attacking MiG to 'look up' over the western bank of the Arvand River, acquire its target and for its pilot's hand to close around the firing trigger. The water around the ship had become a maelstrom of spray and exploding shells, the ship had quivered and rung like a cracked bell as rounds crashed inboard; and then the attack was over.

Those who had survived had blinked, looked around and discovered the carnage...*everywhere.*

No time to be afraid.

No time to panic.

No time to register what was going on until later.

And afterwards...always the blood splashed across the deck and washing away through the new holes, the acrid smell of burning wiring and the moans and the curses of the living and the dying.

Stephen Turnbull accepted a pair of binoculars.

He scanned Tiger through the haze; and then looked beyond the cruiser to where the Diamond was moored, almost aground close to the Abadan shore in a sinking condition. Rocket strikes had disabled the destroyer's forward turrets and a hit by a bomb like the one wedged in Anzac's boiler room bilge had detonated on her stern. Diamond had no rudder control and she was down four feet aft.

Of the original five ship gun line only Anzac and Tiger, both badly damaged, remained capable of moving under their own steam.

Thus far Anzac's butcher's bill was eight dead and eleven seriously wounded.

Tiger had over a hundred dead and injured.

Things could have been worse; the Red Air Force had not been back for over three hours.

Turning his glasses to the north and north-west the smoke shrouded everything.

"The flagship is signalling, sir!"

Turnbull watched the winking Aldis Lamp on the cruiser's bridge.

DAVEY TO ANZAC STOP TIGER WILL ADVANCE UP RIVER BEFORE SUNSET STOP WILL YOU JOIN ME SIR MESSAGE ENDS.

Chapter 81

The offer of 'terms' had been Lieutenant General Viktor Kulikov's idea. The Acting Commander of Army Group South; what was left of the exhausted invasion force which, in the last three months, had driven over fifteen hundred kilometres from the Caucasus to the shores of the Persian Gulf, had understood the moment he walked into the Governor's Palace that the British meant to bleed his army white. Even if things had not looked so disastrous in the west around Umm Qasr, to his mind the burning ruins of the refineries on Abadan Island were not worth the death of a single Red Army conscript. The Persian Gulf was an American Sea; the British could be shelled, bombed and blockaded into submission with minimal further casualties.

"Continuing the assault is madness, Comrade Defence Minister," Kulikov protested as soon as he was alone behind closed doors with Admiral of the Fleet Sergey Georgiyevich Gorshkov. Gorshkov had walked into the headquarters like Christ come to cleanse the Temple, a man on a mission who viewed the battlefield chaos in the western Faw and in the eastern Khorramshahr-Abadan Sectors as 'messes' he was going to personally 'clean up'.

Gorshkov had demanded tactical briefings on all developments in the last twenty-four hours, listened angrily and ordered the amphibious assault on the Abadan bank of the Karun River to go ahead 'without delay'. That was over two hours ago; around the time the Red Air Force had finally got the message that the High Command meant it when it said 'cease operations south of Basra'.

Even as Kulikov tried to reason with Marshal Chuikov's successor fresh Marines and Naval infantry held back for precisely this moment were piling into pontoons and anything that would float down the Arvand River. Moving forward covered by the smoke pall hanging over the Khorramshahr battleground, two companies of combat engineers supported by the remnants of the tank regiments decimated overnight were to bridge the Karun River as soon as the southern shore was secured. In less than ninety minutes the 2nd Siberian Mechanised Army would commence the biggest artillery bombardment of the entire war; with the gunners having orders to carry on firing until they ran out of ammunition.

"We offered the British *honourable* 'terms'," Gorshkov snapped irascibly. "Have they responded?"

"Well, no, not exactly..."

"We should have driven on into Kuwait," Gorshkov went on. "Calling a halt around Umm Qasr was inviting a counter attack. I don't know what Babadzhanian was thinking!"

Kulikov scowled. Whatever his personal and professional

differences with the late Hamazasp Khachaturi Babadzhanian, the man had been a gifted and competent field commander who had worked miracles in the last three months. To have got this far south with both his armies more or less intact – although inevitably worn out, weakened as much by the hostile terrain and sickness as by enemy action – ought to have been the crowning glory of Babadzhanian's career.

The setback at Umm Qasr and the brainless repeated frontal assaults on the Khorramshahr-Abadan Sector where it was suspected, if not actually known, that the British had had several months to prepare a 'defence in depth' had been entirely self-inflicted catastrophes. Twenty-four hours ago the Red Army was the master of the battlefield, now an enemy armoured force of unknown strength had cut the Basra to Um Qasr road and was threatening the southern approaches to the city, and 2nd Siberian Mechanised Army had become embroiled in a dreadful World War II type battle which had already consumed one in three of its tanks.

To compound the worsening 'tactical' situation one of the last two squadrons of Red Air Force Tupolev Tu-95s strategic bombers had been virtually wiped out by British surface-to-air missiles that morning. Moreover, operating from bases in Central Iraq at ranges known to be well beyond their operational endurance, two in three of the MiG-21s sent in at low level to attack enemy armour in the desert north of Umm Qasr, British warships in the Arvand River, and targets of opportunity on Abadan Island had failed to return.

Much as the Red Air Force in Iraq was complaining at the injunction to cease operations south of Basra; frankly, if it kept losing aircraft at the rate it had that morning it would shortly cease to exist as a fighting force.

Ground operations on the eastern bank of the Arvand River would continue; Gorshkov planned to leave what was left of the British Navy in the Persian Gulf to the tender mercies of the Americans.

"With respect, Comrade Minister," Kulikov objected. "There is no guarantee that the promised American air support will materialise. Air support is useless if we can't co-ordinate it with our ground forces!"

Gorshkov viewed the Red Army general with hard, cold eyes.

He would have been lying if he was not uneasy about allowing the United States to 'inflict peace' on the region. He was especially unhappy about the prospect of allowing US Air Force B-52s to overfly newly acquired Soviet territory, or to have to rely on tactical air support from aircraft flying off the USS Kitty Hawk. Strategic Air Command heavy bombers would already be in the air, a corridor having been designated for the eight B-52 and their KC-135 tankers all the way from the Arctic to the Persian Gulf.

He was in a race against time. He needed Red Army tanks 'on the ground' on Abadan Island before the Yankees inflicted their *Pax Americana* on their former British allies. Whatever had been negotiated in Sverdlovsk the map of Iraq and the Middle East was going to be redrawn according to where the front line was at one o'clock tomorrow morning. Possession was *the* law and he was going to grab as much ground as he could in the hours remaining.

Expending every available Tu-95 and MiG-21 in that morning's operations had been countenanced because the Troika – the collective leadership of which he was the military member – did not trust the Americans to fulfil their *obligations* under the five-year US-USSR Non-Aggression Pact. Supposedly, if the British fought on the US bombers would administer the coup de grace in the Abadan sector in the early hours of tomorrow morning; carpet bombing the enemy armour bottling up Umm Qasr and threatening Basra in the south west, before annihilating the surviving garrison of Abadan Island. In the meantime the US Navy would 'mop up' the survivors of the so-called ABNZ Persian Gulf Squadron at first light. But Gorshkov did not believe it; the Americans were too squeamish. At any time between now and the scheduled 'end of hostilities' the America Eagle might retract its claws.

Gorshkov shut his eyes, took several stentorian breaths.

Until a few hours ago Operation Nakazyvat had succeeded beyond the Politburo's wildest expectations. The West's stranglehold on the oil of the Middle East had seemingly been broken forever, the Motherland had seized warm water ports, and the Red Army had humiliated the murderers of October 1962. And then that idiot Babadzhanian had weakened his hold on the Faw Peninsula so that he could dash what remained of his armies against the rock of the fortress of Abadan!

Now the Soviet Union was locked in a battle it could not afford to lose, a battle it had only hours to win before the Americans flew in to steal the Red Army's glory!

"We must fight on, Kulikov," Gorshkov growled, fixing the other man in his coldly phlegmatic gaze. "We will take Abadan. We will expel the enemy from the desert around Um Qasr. Afterwards, we will rebuild our armies, our air force and our navy. One day we will be the equal of the Americans again. Mistakes have been made for which you are blameless. You will be rewarded for your loyalty this night, Comrade General."

There was a respectful rapping at the closed door.

A sweating Major of the staff marched in. "The British have replied to our earlier message, Comrade Minister!"

Gorshkov stared at the sheet of paper.

"I don't speak English. What does it say?"

The junior officer swallowed nervously, taking back the sheet.

He hesitated momentarily and then translated at a rush.

"Ya sozhaleyu, chto eto ne praktichno dlya menya, chtoby prinyat sdachu vsekh sovetskikh voysk na vostochnom beregu reki Arvand. Podpis, Mikhail Carver, General-leytenant."

I regret that it is not practical for me to accept the surrender of all Soviet forces on the eastern bank of the Arvand River. Signed, Michael Carver, Lieutenant General.

Chapter 82

17:52 Hours
Friday 3rd July 1964
The Angry Widow, 90 miles West of Haifa, Eastern Mediterranean

Squadron Leader Guy French ought by rights to have been very afraid; instead he was wholly at peace with himself in a way he had not been since that dreadful night in late October 1962. But for the war he and Greta would have been married very a nearly a year. Their first anniversary would have been in a week or so, in fact; their first boy or girl – they had planned to have a brood of three or four of the little rascals – might already have seen the light of day. But it had not been meant to be and now he was at the controls of a Handley Page Victor B.2 cruising at forty-eight thousand feet towards a destiny unimaginable and unthinkable twenty months ago.

Ground stations in Saudi Arabia, Kuwait and Oman had been tracking Carrier Division Seven - the Yanks were noisy beggars – by simple radio direction triangulation, ensuring that at any given time the RAF knew exactly where to find the murderers.

The idea was to 'swarm' the USS Kitty Hawk and her protectors.

Or more correctly, the scheme was to blind the giant carrier and then 'swarm' it; for Goliath needed to be brought to his knees by nuclear slingshots before he could be stoned to death.

The briefing officer and his team had been grimly honest pulling no punches even though to a man they knew the score. This was a one way mission and nobody was actually being ordered to do anything.

Notwithstanding, squadron and aircraft commanders had been ordered to remind their men that this was a 'volunteers only' show and that no questions would be asked, or any man thought any the less of if he decided that it was 'not for him'.

It was a peculiarity of V-Bomber design that on each aircraft type only the two pilots had ejector seats; the other three 'back seat' crewmen basically being left to their own devices in an emergency. On this mission Guy French had ordered *The Angry Widow*'s ground crew to disconnect the explosive 'ejection charge' beneath his seat. Previously such requests had always been vetoed by higher authority; today nobody had batted an eyelid.

Tonight's order of battle included everything the RAF had to hand capable of operating against the US fleet in the Persian Gulf at twelve hours' notice.

Two Vickers Valiants of No 148 Squadron; 'Fox and Hounds' carrying a single 15-kiloton yield fission bomb, and 'City of York' carrying twenty one-thousand pound general purpose bombs.

"One Avro Vulcan, 'Baghdad Express', of No 9 Squadron carrying a second Blue Danube device; and two Vulcans of No 617 Squadron, 'Jolly Farmer' and 'Show a Leg', each carrying a mixed nine-ton cargo

of one and two thousand pound general purpose bombs.

Four Handley Page Victors; two No 57 Squadron B.1s, 'Merry Widow' and 'Burma Star' each carrying a single six-ton Tallboy and four one-thousand pounders, and the two No 100 Squadron B.2s 'Waltzing Matilda' and Guy French's 'The Angry Widow', the former carrying a single 10-ton Grand Slam and the latter two Tallboys.

Five English Electric Canberra medium bombers of No 81 Squadron – which would be refuelled over Sinai by two No 214 Squadron Valiants – were loaded with six one-thousand pound bombs carried internally, and externally with two rocket pods containing thirty-seven 2-inch unguided missiles.

Depending upon serviceability somewhere between eighteen and twenty-five fighters; RAF Hawker Hunters, and possibly several US-supplied Saudi F-86 Sabre and F-100 Super Sabre interceptors, and a handful of Fleet Air Arm Sea Vixens and Scimitar fighters operating from Kuwaiti airstrips would do their best to distract the Kitty Hawk's combat air patrol and to confuse 'the battle environment' that the US Navy liked to 'understand' at all times.

Almost as an afterthought, three turbo prop Royal Fleet Air Arm Gannets each equipped with two US-supplied 10-inch Mark 43 homing torpedoes had been added to the order of battle.

The operations staff at Akrotiri which was co-ordinating operations with the RAF's command centre in Dammam had christened the exercise Operation Roundup.

Everything had to happen before sunset in the Persian Gulf.

South of Kharg Island, the chosen patrol area of Carrier Division Seven dusk was between 19:30 and 20:00 hours; if the aircraft carting the big bombs to the Gulf were to 'dive bomb' their moving targets they had to see what they were doing courtesy of their pilots' Mark I human eyeballs.

Initially, the Canberras had been going to come screaming down from altitude but in the final plan they were tasked to come in at maximum thrust at wave top height, skipping their bombs towards the big carrier's escorts and loosing off rockets. Any fighters that got past the Kitty Hawk's F-4 Phantoms and her gate-keeping cruisers' long-range Talos and Terrier surface-to-air missile batteries would make strafing and mock dive bombing attacks on targets of opportunity.

All of which was to occur with minutes – ideally immediately after – the two Blue Danubes lit up, hopefully within as little as fifteen to twenty miles of the Kitty Hawk. It was taken as read that the two nuclear bombers roaring in on arrow straight tracks would be easy meat for the US Navy's missile defences; hence both aircraft would activate their Blue Danubes over Sinai set to initiate at an altitude of three thousand feet. The theory was that the longer the Yanks waited to get a 'clean kill' the worse it would be for them!

Guy French still had not really worked out what was likely to happen when he dropped the port wing tip of The Angry Widow and pointed her needle sharp nose at the Kitty Hawk. The best advice available was that extending the air brakes just before 'kicking off' the evolution might delay the moment when the wings came off.

The operations officer had also speculated that releasing bombs at around seven or eight thousand feet might give *The Angry Widow* a 'fighting chance' of pulling up before she went into 'the drink'; but since nobody had ever been so insane as to do anything like this in 'a beast' his diffidence on this subject was entirely understandable.

Guy French had concluded that all in all the best thing seemed to be to make sure the flight deck of the Kitty Hawk was filing the windscreen in front of him by the time the wings 'came off'.

Chapter 83

The Red Army artillery barrage had walked all the way down Abadan Island and all the way back up it again three times before finally, it slackened, and after nearly two-and-a-half hours petered away. By then the whole eastern shoreline was shrouded by an impenetrable cloud of smoke, ash, rubble dust, sand and the vile stench of the great oil tanks burning out of control.

While the wrath of Hell was ploughing up what had once been the jewel in Great Britain's post 1945-war Imperial Crown, HMS Tiger and her smaller consort, HMAS Anzac had been making copious amounts of smoke and 'playing dead' in the fog of battle.

"It is time, sir," Captain Hardress 'Harpy' Lloyd, the cruiser's commanding officer observed, standing at Rear Admiral Nicholas Davey's shoulder.

"Signal Anzac to cut her chains and follow Tiger up river please."

Stephen Turnbull and his brave Australians would not like that but Tiger – even in her presently somewhat careworn condition – was a significantly tougher nut to crack than a thin-skinned fleet destroyer. Tiger had over three inches of side armour protecting her vitals from shell fire, a couple of inches of hardened plate strengthening her main bulkheads, one to two inches of armour on her turrets, and the same on the roofs of her magazines. Although her armament and electronic systems were very modern, her construction was classic Second World War vintage, her hull stiff, a tad over-engineered in an attempt to ensure structural integrity in the event of major battle damage. She was built to take punishment, a lot of punishment, before she went down; Anzac was not and the destroyer's speed and manoeuvrability were no use to her thirty or forty miles up a river in enemy held territory.

"Anzac has acknowledged, sir."

"Very good. Take us up river please, Captain."

The two warships had moored several hundred yards below the point where the Arvand River began to turn to the north around the great flat promontory of Minushahr 'island' which jutted out of the eastern side of Abadan. In times past the river had flowed directly to the sea where now, only a narrow stream separated the two 'islands', before some cataclysmic event, possibly an earthquake or simply one of the periodic great floods of the Euphrates and the Tigris upstream had carved another path through the deserts and marshlands. Everything south of Basra and for twenty or thirty miles to the east and west was the same vast delta formed by the outflow of the rivers of ancient Mesopotamia. Even at Basra the Arvand was tidal, and the land all the way north to Al Qurnah was only a thirteen to fourteen feet above notional 'sea level' in the Gulf.

Tiger slowly drew abreast of the Anzac.

Hats were waved as the men on each ship studied the damage to the other with sombre reflection.

Nick Davey raised a speaking trumpet to his lips.

The ships were so close he could have bellowed across the distance between them without assistance.

"ALL THE WAY TO OM-AL-RASAS, ANZACS!"

Stephen Turnbull stood at the starboard bridge rail of the destroyer and saluted.

"WHEN TIGER OPENS FIRE DON'T STOP FOR ANYTHING, STEPHEN!"

The last two ships of the ABNZ gun line had been charged with filling the Karun River with Russian dead. If necessary Nick Davey was prepared to steam Tiger into the mouth of the river and hold the enemy back with his ceremonial sword...

Which reminded him!

He turned and bellowed over his right shoulder.

"Would somebody go to my sea cabin and find my bloody sword please?"

The sword was unlikely to be much utility in a fight in which the cruiser's 6-inch guns were firing over open sights at an enemy at point blank range.

But one never knew!

And it was always prudent to be prepared.

Chapter 84

19:02 Hours
Friday 3rd July 1964
Karun River, Abadan

The British had blown up their pontoon bridge across the river in such a hurry that they had left their robustly engineered anchoring posts in position on both banks. The bulldozers had had to push the wrecked T-62s, BTR-40s and 80s out of the way but now the first tanks were crossing the river. Already over a thousand infantrymen had been ferried onto the southern back and were advancing, with squads of combat engineers through the shattered defence lines.

From where he stood Major General Konstantin Yakovlevich Kurochnik could see half-a-dozen knocked out British tanks, and all the nearby trench lines caved in. There were bits and pieces of bodies all around him, already the dead meat was bloating and festering, and flies swarmed. The artillery barrage had knocked the stuffing out of the British and Australian troops holding the southern bank of the Karun River. After putting up a token resistance the defenders had melted away and much of the bridging operation had gone ahead at breakneck speed inconvenienced only by occasional mortar rounds and long-range sniping.

Kurochnik was no tanker but he could tell that the enemy had gone to a lot of trouble to dig in their armour and zero in their artillery, and much as he was loath to admit it he was still a little unnerved by last night's nightmare. Any Army on earth other than the Red Army would have broken and run when it ran into the firestorm around Khorramshahr Station; and when the fight was over the enemy had withdrawn in good order, like wraiths in the night. His boys had rooted out the British Centurions in the end; but by God that had been dirty business. At least two of the six brewed up tanks they had examined in the ruins had only been knocked out only *after* they had run out of ammunition!

He surveyed the battlefield. Hopefully, the British had done their worst. Very little was moving in the south. The enemy's desultory counter-battery shelling had stopped an hour or so ago. The haze and the smoke made it seem as if it was already dusk, although sunset was still over an hour off. He planned to send his armour forward to probe what was left of the British defence line three kilometres south of the Karun River; overnight he would build a brigade strength battle group south of the river, that ought to be easily capable of finishing the job in the morning.

His orders to halt at the British main line of defence chaffed somewhat. Now was the time to press home the advantage, to get the job done. He had discounted his intelligence staff's concern about rogue Iranian Army units out in the eastern desert; Kurochnik was not going to waste time worrying about a few rag heads and bandits roaming around the foothills of the Zagros Mountains. If the last twenty-four hours had taught him anything it was that his main enemy was in front of him.

His Corps Commander, Vladimir Andreyevich Puchkov, a typical thick-headed tanker who had obviously bashed his head once too many times on the roof of a turret – he was tall man with a much scarred head which strongly supported this thesis – had been similarly scathing about the 'Iranian intelligence'.

Kurochnik had not spoken to Puchkov for several hours and things had been so fucked up last night and earlier that day that for all he knew the man was dead. Kurochnik himself had only come down to the Karun River ahead of the bridging operation because most of his spearhead commanders were dead or wounded, and in their absence it was vital that somebody got a grip. Reassuringly, by the time he arrived things were under control and preparations were well in hand, the British armour and anti-tank guns having pulled back before the creeping barrage wiped them out. Since then anything caught above ground on Abadan Island was dead.

The shell-cratered ground would make for slow going tomorrow.

That was war; a messy affair.

"I want that bloody communications cable laid back to the forward communications exchange!" Kurochnik yelled at a passing staffer. Down on the pontoon bridge he watched two men trailing lines along the side of the roadway. He needed to talk to Army HQ; the fucking plan kept changing and something had happened to Marshal Babadzhanian because Kulikov, the commander of 2nd Siberian Mechanised was suddenly calling all the shots.

"A couple more Centurions got caught in the open when the last barrage came in," he was informed by a man with KGB tabs on his battledress lapels. "With the tanks we've found knocked out here and the ones in Khorramshahr that means the enemy has lost at least sixteen. We don't think the British had more than thirty or so to start with, Comrade General."

Kurochnik scowled at the other, much younger man. From what he had seen so far one British tank was worth five or six of his. It was not that the T-62 was in any way defective, it was just that the British hardly ever got into a straight fight with his armour. Always, they fought hull down on ground of their choosing and design.

"Do we know what happened to the big ships the British steamed up the fucking river yet?" Kurochnik demanded.

The naval shelling from the Arvand River had decimated several rear echelon units south of the Basra industrial area. A couple of small ammunition dumps had blown up and the tracks down to Khorramshahr – the dirt roads hardly dignified any other description – had had to be cleared by bulldozers. By now the hundreds of grotesquely mutilated bodies piled in the sand by the roadside would be alive with the flies.

"The Air Force claim they sank them all, sir!"

Chapter 85

19:17 Hours
Friday 3rd July 1964
Carrier Division Seven, 29 miles south east of Kharg Island, Persian Gulf

Two McDonnell Douglas F-4 Phantoms were being hauled forward onto the bow catapults as the Kitty Hawk worked up to twenty-five knots on her three undamaged shafts. The great ship had an odd feel, as if she was in a slight cross sea and wind as her giant rudders corrected for the lateral drift caused by the massive power differential of her two port screws against the surviving starboard screw.

Not that the frenetic activity on the flight deck made a great impression on Lieutenant Commander Walter Brenckmann, the former Fleet ASW Officer, as he followed the other dissenters from the carrier's wardroom towards the waiting Sikorsky SH-3 Sea King.

Rear Admiral Bringle had ordered the officers and men who had requested to be relieved of duty be quarantined, removed from his flagship lest they spread the contagion. Of the men transferring off the Kitty Hawk to the fast transport Paul Revere (APA-248), Walter was the most senior man and therefore, it seemed, the man most likely to be made an example of when he got home. He had been summoned before Bringle less than ten minutes ago and informed that he was 'going to regret *this* for the rest of his life', and that 'the Navy will never forgive you'.

Walter had refused to dignify the threat with an acknowledgement.

"You need to put this on, sir," the loadmaster growled respectfully, holding out a Mae West. "Before I can allow you to board the aircraft, sir."

This broke Walter out of his brooding.

"Thank you."

A man behind him helped him don the lifejacket, patted it down and checked it was securely fastened.

"You may board the aircraft, sir."

As he put his foot on the bottom rung of the ladder the man who had adjusted his Mae West spoke lowly.

"Good luck, sir."

Walter was in a daze, staring out of the open main fuselage hatch as the helicopter lifted off the deck. Below him the biggest warship in the World was resuming flying operations, having been wallowing at a dead stop for over four hours that afternoon while clearance divers inspected her underwater damage. Over forty aircraft had been brought up on deck; F-4 Phantom supersonic interceptors, A-4 Skyhawks and A-6 Intruders strike aircraft, a second E-2 Hawkeye to relieve Hawkeye Zero-One which had been continuously on patrol over Southern Iran monitoring the battle for Abadan Island. As he watched a North-American A-5 Vigilante nuclear strike bomber rolled off the

Kitty Hawk's starboard aft elevator.

Having been confined to his quarters since his initial interview with Captain Epes, Walter had no specific knowledge of the operations planned for the coming night; he had just known that in all good conscience he could be no part of whatever fresh atrocity was planned. To have acted otherwise would have been to dishonour the uniform he had worn with pride his whole adult life.

"Shit!" Somebody cried out.

Walter blinked, looked around.

"Albany just cleared her Talos rails!"

Although the cabin door was dogged open, normal practice for a short 'hop' between ships in good weather, Walter's field of vision was restricted to what was visible directly in front of him. The Sea King banked, its pilot seeking to get down low enough to disappear off the Kitty Hawk's anti-aircraft escorts' radars. Walter suddenly saw the grey smoke drifting away from the ungainly looking missile cruiser. Before he could assimilate what he was seeing a thousand yards beyond the Albany the five thousand ton Coontz class guided missile destroyer William V. Pratt, flushed a pair of Terrier surface-to-air birds from her stern rails.

Walter started doing the basic math.

There was no other way to make sense of what he was watching.

The Bendix Rim-8 Talos missile system had a theoretical rage of approximately a hundred miles. Although initially designed to combat Kamikaze style attacks or World War II guided munitions like the German Henschel Hs 293 glider bomb and the deadly Fritz X, it was capable of hitting targets above seventy thousand feet at ranges unthinkable back in 1945. However, given that it was a beam-riding weapon that only switched to onboard semi-active radar target acquisition mode for terminal guidance it was impractical to use the weapon effectively at anything like its maximum range. Talos was launched with a solid fuel booster that fired up a ramjet capable of powering the three-and-a-half ton thirty-eight feet long missile to speeds of up to Mach 2.5. Its three hundred pound warhead was proximity fused to destroy anything flying within a hundred yards of it when it detonated...

Walter went on doing the math.

He assumed the Albany had flushed its Talos launchers under local control; the nearest Hawkeye was a hundred and fifty miles away, and the effective reach of the cruiser's AN/SPW-2 missile guidance radar and the AN/SPG-49 tracking system was around fifty nautical miles. No, belay that, maybe up to sixty assuming the British had only limited ECM coverage of the northern Gulf.

Okay, assume the target is incoming at around five hundred plus knots; that would be closing the range at eight or nine miles per minute. Target lock takes what? Sixty seconds, so the target is fifty miles out by that time. Assume Albany had two Talos reloads hot and ready to go on the rails. How long does a Rim-8's internal guidance box take to spool up? Thirty seconds? Go with that. The target is nearer forty that fifty miles out by then. Talos hits maximum acceleration and intercept speed three to four seconds after launch; from that moment it and the target are closing at around Mach 3, give or take a couple of hundred knots an hour, an intercept rate of more than two thousand miles an hour in layman's language. That's a closing speed of thirty-three or four miles per minute and the target is forty plus miles out. Therefore, impact is in seventy to eighty seconds. The target could be a lot less than thirty miles away by then...

The cabin of the Sea King lit up as if a destroyer's searchlight had been beamed directly into it.

Walter Brenckmann had never been near a nuclear explosion.

But he knew what that light signified.

He had calculated thirty miles; if he was right the blast overpressure wave would hit the helicopter in between three and four minutes time.

He started counting.

At the time it never occurred to him that any aircraft could fly within a lot less than twenty miles of Carrier Division Seven without being challenged and engaged.

One thousand and one.

One thousand and two.

One thousand and three...

The cabin lit up a second time.

The Sea King lurched sidelong; its main rotors dipping into the iron grey waters.

Chapter 86

19:18 Hours
Friday 3rd July 1964
Field Command Truck, 3rd Imperial Iranian Armoured Division, Ahvaz-Khorramshahr Road

Major General Hasan al-Mamaleki and Major Julian Calder had been enjoying – well, drinking anyway – what purported to be 'tea' when an excitable runner brought the news of the two 'bomb flashes' far to the south. The Iranian tanker and the English SAS-man had looked to each other and nodded, taken one more cautious sip at the vile, muddy brew they had been attempting to ingest, put down their mugs and stood up.

There was around another hour of 'usable' daylight.

The time was propitious.

The Centurions, M-60s and M-48s of the 3rd Imperial Iranian Armoured Division would emerge out of the darkness of the eastern deserts and fall upon the flank, and hopefully, the rear echelons of the Red Army divisions racing down to the Karun River. Hasan al-Mamaleki's tanks would be coming out of the darkness, with the enemy silhouetted by the light of the setting sun.

With or without the nuclear flashes in the southern sky Hasan al-Mamaleki would have given the signal to move within the next few minutes. Michael Carver had sent no word from Abadan; hardly surprising after that afternoon's artillery bombardment. The C-in-C might be dead.

"Excalibur!" The tall, handsome man with the magnificent dark moustache barked through the door of the command truck. "EXECUTE EXCALIBUR!"

Julian Calder followed the Iranian out into the dusk.

The smoke and dust of Abadan Island was blowing north across Khorramshahr and the desert near the Iraqi border opposite Basra.

Hasan al-Mamaleki, a tall man, had momentarily added several inches to his stature in the moment of decision. The plan; his plan and Michael Carver's plan was an exercise in crystal clear thinking. The 3rd Imperial Iranian Armoured Division and several battalions of mechanised infantry would drive for the Arvand River, trapping the enemy forces in Khorramshahr and south of the Karun River.

Stop for nothing! Drive to the west! Kill any man who stands between you and the Arvand River! If you run out of ammunition roll over the enemy! Grind him beneath the tracks of our tanks! Death to the enemy!

Ideally, Admiral Davey's ships would have sailed all the way up to Basra to administer the coup de grace to the enemy; but for all the two men knew al-Mamaleki's force was alone.

It mattered not.

Al-Mamaleki meant to drive the invaders off the holy soil of Persia or die.

Out in the desert to the north the sound of scores of tank engines firing up rumbled through the gathering gloom. In the west the sky was still bright. The setting sun threw great long shadows, as if his men were giants and the enemy, pygmies.

Neither Hasan al-Mamaleki nor Julian Calder knew what had happened at sea the previous day, or what had happened in the Faw Peninsula. They guessed the Anzac tankers around Umm Qasr had had some success in 'pinning' enemy formations in the Faw. They had been a little surprised that after the big attacks of the morning the Red Air Force had made itself scarce. Tacitly, they accepted that the Navy's big ships would have been sitting ducks in the confines of the river; and that the Abadan garrison would have been 'dreadfully knocked about' during the day. It had been painful waiting, waiting, waiting while other brave men had fought and died...

The two flashes in the southern sky signified nothing so much as that all was most likely lost.

Out in the desert the first tanks charged west.

Al-Mamaleki and his English friend walked purposefully to where staffers had pulled the camouflage netting off Calder's Land Rover.

It was time to follow the tanks into action.

Chapter 87

19:19 Hours
Friday 3rd July 1964
Carrier Division Seven, 29 miles south east of Kharg Island, Persian Gulf

Walter Brenckmann came to retching and fighting for breath, coughing water out of his lungs, utterly disorientated. Each frigid wave that broke over his face reeked of aviation fuel. Guns were firing in the distance and as he bobbed up and down, his eyes slowly focussed on the unmistakable trails of rockets crisscrossing the darkening skies.

None of it made any sense.

In a moment so surreal that some part of his shocked consciousness knew it was wrong; he attempted, in a jumbled, muddled way to work out how he had gotten from the Polaris compartment of the USS Theodore Roosevelt listening to the big birds flush, one after the other on the night of the October War to here. Wherever *here* was? And then he remembered that he had been pulled off the Theodore Roosevelt last December. He was supposed to be posted to Groton ahead of the nuclear boat command course due to start in March; but no, that was wrong too...

Where was this?

He swallowed avgas-laced salt water.

Coughed, gagged, vomited in between swallowing more water.

His head cleared, he was confused now by a new, vaguely irritating sound. A sort of thrumming, droning noise like a swarm of angry hornets coming closer and closer; his bewilderment suddenly shot through with stabbing terror.

Instantly he was thrashing around in the cold water searching for the angry hornets and kicking away from the deeper, rumbling reverberations of the engines and churning propellers of what could only be a very big ship.

The heavy cruiser USS Boston's towering grey stem loomed above him. Even though he knew it was useless he kicked and flailed with his arms to try and move away from the oncoming ship. The fifteen thousand ton warship was already on top of him and before he had a chance to take a deep breath her bow wave, creaming white like a surfer's dream fell on him and he was rolling and drowning in its crest like a human cork.

All he could think of was getting away from the cruisers giant, racing screws.

It was not until he bobbed to the surface in the Boston's wake that he finally figured out what the 'angry hornets' noise that he had heard - before he was run down by the fifteen thousand ton behemoth – actually was.

There were two...

No, three odd but vaguely familiar dark silhouettes skimming above the wave tops beyond the Boston. The cruiser's anti-aircraft guns were firing but her stern mounted Terrier twin launcher was locked upright – reload position – and therefore not tracking the nearby targets.

The silhouettes of the approaching aircraft foreshortened.

Gannets!

Fairey Gannets; British anti-submarine and early-warning aircraft and the angry hornets' noise was being generated by the Gannets' Armstrong Siddeley Double Mamba turboprop engines driving their contra-rotating propellers.

The first of the Gannets – which had a passing, more streamlined and modern resemblance to old World War II era Grumman TBF Avenger torpedo bombers – passed so close and so low astern of the Boston that its port wing tip almost hit the cruiser's taffrail jackstay. Another flew literally under the cruiser's bow. The Boston had to have been steaming at better than twenty-five knots but it was obvious to Walter that the Gannets had deliberately braved her formidable, bristling gun batteries to use her bulk as a shield against the rest of the fleet's deadly arsenal of guided weapons. A third Gannet zoomed over the bridge of the cruiser and dove down to the wave tops.

Coughing, spluttering, retching Walter watched in horrified fascination as belatedly he started to piece together what he was actually seeing.

Missile trails in the sky; the crash and rattle of distant guns all around the horizon in the last full light of the setting sun, and the Kitty Hawk was turning, the lengthening outline of the huge carrier a lot less than two miles away.

The bomb bay doors of the three old-fashioned Gannets were opening.

The Boston's 3-inch guns kicked up the sea between the aircraft and the flagship; the Gannets levelled out fifteen to twenty feet above the waves, boring in on the Kitty Hawk.

Two black shapes dropped from the southernmost aircraft, and then from the others before Walter lost sight of the attackers. Instinctively he attempted to duck his head under water as the banshee scream of two diving F-4 Phantoms fell on the Gannets.

In some battered corner of his brain there was a quiet corner now.

If the F-4s were down here at sea level who was flying top cover?

Chapter 88

19:20 Hours
Friday 3rd July 1964
RAF Abadan, Iran

Being buried had not been a lot of fun. However, Frank Waters had been so grateful to be dug out in more or less one piece that he had put the unpleasantness behind him in short order. Providing there was somebody left alive to dig a chap out a well-constructed trench system was not the worse place a man could be when things got sticky. Direct hits notwithstanding, getting buried was often the big killer in trench warfare. Old soldiers told tall stories about always hearing a shell with one's name on it; Frank Waters thought that was lot of tosh. If you heard the shell with your name on it who on earth would you be able to tell about it afterwards? He had certainly not heard the one that collapsed the communications trench around him as he was making his way back to his timorous BBC 'comrades'. One minute he was trotting along without a care in the world and the next he was under several tons of bloody sand!

It was the sand that made the job so infernally hard for the Russian gunners. It absorbed and localised the impacts of even the biggest shells; unless a shell landed in a trench or right next to it – literally within inches of it – all that was achieved was to blow more sand into the air.

The split-second flash of the first RAF Blue Danube high in the sky scores of miles away to the south had halted the SAS-man in his tracks.

In a second the rules of engagement had changed again.

There was a second flash as he stumbled into his lost sheep.

"Was that..."

"Probably," he declared, half answering the obvious question. As if it mattered! "Do any of you chaps know which end of a gun to hold?"

Brian Harris nodded in the gloom of the crater in which the crew had been cowering for the last few hours.

Frank Waters and the other man had turned and headed north towards the front lines at about the time big guns started firing off to the northwest. They crouched down, waiting for the incoming rounds but nothing happened.

"That must be our boys," Brian Harris suggested.

Frank Waters listened to the cannonade.

"It sounds like the Navy are getting in on the act," he observed, unwilling to give the Senior Service credit for anything unless there was no other possible explanation for the renewed cannonade somewhere to the north.

The two men picked up weapons – a Sten gun and an SLR, spare magazines and pocketful's of loose rounds - from bodies lying in a gully.

Frank Waters took the Sten gun, Brian Harris the SLR.

"I got a marksman badge with a Lee Enfield," the latter frowned as Frank Waters arched an eyebrow, and he hefted the rifle. "That was over twenty years ago; in comparison this ought to be a breeze!"

The SAS man shrugged.

He preferred the Sten gun but then he was the sort of cove who had been asked to kill all the people in the room more than once; and a long-barrelled infantry SLR had never been anybody's weapon of choice for work like that.

The big guns had reached a crescendo.

Periodically, tank rounds whistled across the lines but most of the firing was outgoing, not incoming. The distinctive bark of L7 105-millimetre cannons all along the front line contrasted with the thump of crash of bigger guns to the north. Mortars were popping, and the revving engines of many, many tanks filled the air as the two men stumbled into the chaotic casualty clearing station where Lieutenant General Michael Carver and his bloodied, dwindling staff now held court.

Michael Carver was brandishing a Webley revolver in his right hand.

He looked up.

"Colonel Waters and Mr Harris of the BBC reporting for duty, sir!"

The C-in-C eyed the two ragged figures.

"That's the spirit," he remarked, calmly. "The ground in front of us is rotten with Russian grenadiers," he went on unhurriedly. "We've got the bastards where we want them but this is going to be a very close run thing. Carry on."

Chapter 89

19:20 Hours
Friday 3rd July 1964
South bank of the Karun River, Iran

Konstantin Kurochnik imagined he felt the heat of the flash in the southern sky. Everything around him had stopped for a heartbeat, movement, sound, *everything*. He had been looking to the north where T-62s, armoured personnel carriers and trucks carrying ammunition, were queued nose to tail all the way back into the ruins of Khorramshahr, waiting to be called forward to ford the Karun River on the second of the two pontoon bridges under construction. The combat engineer companies had worked at reckless speed and several men had drowned in the muddy slow moving waters. Already Kurochnik's spearhead was in contact with what was left of the enemy's defence line north of the wrecked air base and burning refinery complex. A mile to the south Spetsnaz and the best of his surviving infantry units were infiltrating the refinery sprawl.

The indications were that the final artillery barrage had pulverised the enemy, and that the Red Air Force had smashed the British ships in the Arvand River.

In less than an hour it would be dark and soon after that the first American air strikes would fall on the rear of the lines his tanks were probing. Kurochnik still did not believe *that*; he had thought somebody at HQ in Basra was taking the piss when the signal came through. He had insisted on talking to General Kulikov; who had accused him of insubordination.

It was a funny old World when one was relying on the bloody Yankees to finish off the British because the Red Air Force in Iraq had been so beaten up in the last twenty-four hours it hardly existed anymore!

What was it the British said about the Yanks?

Something about how they always seemed to turn up when the fight was almost over?

Kurochnik turned, expecting to see a mushroom cloud rising on the southern horizon. All he actually saw was the haze and dusk merging. Okay, it must have been a relatively small bomb a long way away. Somewhere out to sea...

He blinked as a momentarily unutterably brilliant white light lit up and winked out in a second seemingly almost at the point where the land and sea met the heavens. The flash lingered on his retinas, he blinked.

'Fuck!" He muttered, knowing that by some ill chance he must have been looking straight at the distant nuclear detonation. "Fuck!"

Kurochnik squeezed his eyes shut.

Opened them cautiously; he discovered he had spots in front of his eyes but he was not blind, and sighed a huge sigh of relief. Other men around him were doing likewise.

Two nukes somewhere out at sea?

Maybe the Yanks were finishing off the British navy?

Sweeping the seas clear of foreign competitors!

The spots in his eyes were fading as Kurochnik returned to watching the traffic jam on the northern bank of the Karun River. The sooner the second pontoon bridge was opened the better. The British had fought like lions and the battle was far from over. He could do nothing about the nuclear bombs out in the Persian Gulf; his battle was here on the sands of Abadan Island.

"Sir!" A breathless runner from the communications truck down by the river gasped.

Kurochnik relaxed a little. If somebody was bringing him bad news it meant the telephone line he had watched being strung across the bridge was finally connected to his forward headquarters on the south bank.

"What is it?" Kurochnik demanded irritably.

Whoever allowed all those tanks and APCs to bunch up like that on the north bank ought to be shot!

"There are reports from 12th Urals Brigade, sir!"

Kurochnik's humour dipped another degree.

The 12th Urals Brigade was one of the lines of communication units which had been stretched out most of the way north to Amarah until a week ago. Strengthened with several poorly equipped and untrained penal battalions and stiffened by a cadre of KGB troopers it was deployed north east of Khorramshahr along the theoretically expose flank between the foothills of the Zagros Mountains and an 'anchor point' four or five kilometres above the Karun River. The brigade only had a dozen T-54 tanks and a couple of companies of mechanised infantry; it was commanded by one of Kulikov's favourites, Grigory Vasilyevich Romanov, another political soldier whose only previous 'combat experience' dated back to the great Patriotic War.

Something must have panicked the useless prick!

"Well, let's hear it," he grunted irritably. There were times he honestly thought he had spent his whole fucking career clearing up other people's shit!

"Comrade Colonel Romanov reports contact with strong enemy armoured forces on his left hand flank, Comrade General!"

Kurochnik cocked an ear to the east.

It was the quietest quadrant of the whole sector.

"Send to 12th Urals Brigade," he dictated with a shake of the head. "EXTEND LEFT FLANK TO THE EAST AND FIND OUT WHAT IS OUT THERE STOP REPORT AGAIN WHEN SITUATION CLARIFIED MESSAGE ENDS."

The runner should have been dashing his instructions onto his pad for Kurochnik to sign the signal. Instead, he was staring wide-eyed past his commanding officers right shoulder.

The older man bit off a savage rebuke.

The fear in the boy's eyes told him he was not listening.

Kurochnik swung around to find out what had spooked the kid.

In a moment he too was staring; his mouth agape.

Emerging out of the great pall of roiling grey-black smoke drifting across the north of Abadan Island, the Arvand River and the southern tip of Om-al-Rasas Island in the mid-stream was the terrifyingly scorched and bomb-splintered superstructure of the biggest warship Kurochnik had ever seen in his entire life. Below the ship's bridge the numerals C20 came into sharp focus as the ship glided out of the mist and murk. Smoke seemed to leech from her superstructure and tall masts. The ship was so big, the river so narrow, impossibly shallow for such a tall, frightening vessel. The apparition moved soundlessly, ethereally cloaked in wraiths of mist as she slowly pressed up river against the current and the tide.

Kurochnik noted the fore-shortened main battery turrets fore and aft, the smaller secondary turret below the bridge. The gun barrels were invisible, their muzzles levelled.

Uncannily, he sensed that if he reached out his hand he could touch the muzzles of those guns; the guns that would be the death of him and the last Red Army striking force in Iraq.

In those moments before he died Major General Konstantin Yakovlevich Kurochnik knew exactly what was about to happen and realised – too late - that Abadan Island was a giant bear trap.

His forces on the south bank of the Karun River were doomed to encirclement and destruction in detail; the men and machines trapped against the ruins of Khorramshahr on the north back were equally doomed.

Those men who somehow escaped the exposed north bank of the river would inevitably retreat straight into the arms of the force which had panicked Romanov's 12th Urals Brigade beyond the town.

The last thing Kurochnik saw before he died was the whole side of the cruiser disappear behind a wall of fire and smoke as HMS Tiger unleashed her first broadside.

Chapter 90

19:22 Hours
Friday 3rd July 1964
The Angry Widow, above Kharg Island, Persian Gulf

In the aftermath of the two Blue Danube air bursts the projected 'engagement window is six to seven minutes'. Any longer and the 'swarm' will be too enfeebled by losses and the surviving aircraft would be 'easily' picked off by the radar directed gunnery and precision guided missiles of Carrier Division Seven. Everything depended on utilising the confusion and – hopefully – the initial EMP damage inflicted upon the enemy's advanced electronics by the Blue Danubes to ensure that several of the attacking bombers actually 'got through'.

"Kitty Hawk is slowing!"

Squadron Leader Guy French did not immediately register what this signified.

"Everybody else is rushing about like they've got ants in their pants but Kitty Hawk is slowing down!"

"Roger, understood," the pilot acknowledged. The automated bombing system was feeding him constant small course adjustments as if *The Angry Widow* was on a standard run in to the target from a fixed initial point.

The mixed fighter force of Hunters, Sea Vixens and Scimitars had piled into the fray two minutes ago. Several had already been hacked down by surface-to-air missiles; the others were dog fighting above Carrier Division Seven. Sometime in the next sixty seconds the Canberra's would go in a sea level.

Guy French had no idea how many of *The Angry Widow's* 'big friends' were still in the air. The 'missile lock' panel was constantly ablaze; the Victor ought by rights to have been shot down several times by now.

The voice of the V-Bomber's navigator/radio operator broke over the intercom.

"I think the second Blue Danube went off within about ten miles of the Kitty Hawk. Too far away to do much harm but it must have given the Yanks a dreadful wake up call, skipper!"

How on earth had the Americans allowed a V-Bomber to get that close?

Anywhere close to twenty miles would have been a bonus; but ten miles!

That really was sleeping on the job!

"Kitty Hawk is dead in the water! REPEAT, KITTY HAWK IS DEAD IN THE WATER!"

Guy French was tempted to make a facetious remark.

Something along the lines of: *'Perhaps, she's surrendered?'*

However, that would have been crass, so he simply acknowledged the report.

Hitting a five acre target – the Kitty Hawk's flight deck was over a thousand feet long and at its widest point over two hundred and eighty feet broad – that was travelling and presumably, manoeuvring at high speed, was going to have been an interesting proposition. However, something that big which was 'dead in the water' was an altogether juicier prospect, assuming *The Angry Widow* somehow avoided getting blown to bits by a Talos or Terrier missile before she got within miles of the blasted thing!

Why am I worrying about shipboard missiles?

It was much more likely one of the F-4s would settle their hash with a Sidewinder heat-seeking air-to-air munition or good, old-fashioned cannon fire.

Too many ways to die; best not to think about any of them!

"Dive point in six-zero seconds!"

The best advice on the subject of using a Victor as a dive bomber was...*you must be insane!* Up until yesterday nobody had ever questioned this proposition. It was after all, a self-evident *fact*; although, in the circumstances less than very helpful, and positively inconvenient. Basically, if a pilot flipped the kite over and pointed it at the target as one might in an aircraft designed for *that* kind of work – dive bombing - the wings were liable to come off, more or less straight away. This being the case it was a thing people tended to avoid. Nevertheless, talking among themselves the pilots at Akrotiri had come to the conclusion that the only way to 'get the job done' was to 'dive by increments', and to see what happened. The theory was that if one got close enough to the target then it really would not matter if the wings came off, the physics of momentum, inertia and so forth could then be relied upon to take care of the rest. In any event even if the wings had not already parted company with the fuselage, there was absolutely no way a Victor or a Vulcan was going to pull out of a near vertical dive below ten thousand feet, with or without its wings still being attached to the rest of the aircraft!

Guy French planned to extend the air brakes, chop back on the throttles, point *The Angry Widow*'s nose down twenty-five degrees and gently steepen the angle of the dive as he got closer to the target. It was a thing best done without worrying about being shot down; so he had stopped thinking about the 'being shot down' side of the equation.

There had been a heated debate after the main crew briefing whether the tail would come off if the air brakes were fully extended at supersonic speeds. It was a moot point, since if a pilot pitched a Victor into a steep dive without the brakes 'out' the aircraft would go supersonic almost immediately and the kite would probably be uncontrollable anyway.

"THIRTY SECONDS!"

"Open the bomb bay doors!" Guy French ordered.

The Victor shook as the newly exposed surfaces dragged against the near supersonic air flow.

Both of *The Angry Widow*'s six-ton Tallboys were fused to explode 0.25 seconds after impact. The fusing calculations were complicated in one sense, horribly simple in another. If – and it was a big 'if' – one of the Victor's Tallboys hit the deck of the Kitty Hawk it was liable to be travelling at Mach 1.2, or 1.3 or 1.4, or something of that order; at any rate, for the sake of argument say, in excess of around eight hundred miles an hour. At that speed if its progress was unmitigated by an impact it would detonate approximately three hundred feet beyond its point of contact. However, Kitty Hawk's flight deck was in the parlance of naval architecture, an 'armoured strength deck'. Not only was the flight deck built extremely robustly but it structurally incorporated a one to two inch layer of cemented armour plate, likely to retard, moderately but significantly none the less even a projectile the size and weight of a Tallboy, sufficiently to ensure that the six ton bomb's two-and-a-half ton Torpex warhead exploded at the bottom of, or just below the keel of the carrier as it exited the hull.

The ten-ton Grand Slam on the CO's kite, *Waltzing Matilda*, had been fused to detonate on impact on the grounds that no amount of gerrymandering with the fuse would otherwise stop the bomb going straight through the target and exploding hundreds of feet below it.

For any ship ever built a weapon like a Tallboy or Grand Slam was an unsurvivable nightmare. The Tirpitz, sister ship of the virtually unsinkable Bismarck, had been hit by a single Tallboy in September 1944 which had sliced through her bow and exploded in the water beside the battleship; Tirpitz had stayed afloat but shock damage had wrecked most of her machinery to such an extent that thereafter the Germans regarded the great ship as no more than a static, floating artillery platform. In a later raid Tirpitz had been hit by two Tallboys and capsized in minutes. Any bomb dropped on the Kitty Hawk's flight deck would probably disable her; a single Tallboy would cripple her if it did not sink her, a Grand Slam would certainly wreck her.

"TEN SECONDS!"

"Air brakes to maximum extension!" Guy French drawled. On a day like this a pilot owed it to his crew to sound as laconic as a man on a country drive in high summer. Like a man looking forward to a picnic with a pretty girl...

The bomber shuddered and air speed fell off.

The throttles pulled back.

"FIVE SECONDS!"

"FOUR...THREE...TWO...ONE!"

Guy French's hands moved on the controls.

"Tally-ho, chaps," he declared cheerfully.

The Angry Widow's port wing tip dropped away into space and the bomber's needle-nose tipped down into her final dive.

Chapter 91

19:23 Hours
Friday 3rd July 1964
South of Kharg Island, Persian Gulf

Walter Brenckmann was seeing things with his eyes that his mind was having a great deal of trouble rationalising in his head. He was seeing things he did not, could not, would not believe and yet; they *were* happening all around him. The evidence of his eyes was incontrovertible. Carrier Division Seven was fighting for its life in a battle in which its technological wizardry and incomparable space age weaponry was suddenly horribly fallible. Not since the latter stages of the Pacific War when it had been confronted with massed Kamikaze attacks had the US Navy fought a foe that, whatever it threw at him, *just kept coming.* In the Pacific War Japanese Kamikazes had attacked at two or three hundred miles an hour, often much, much slower speeds; the British aircraft were coming in two or three times faster dragging thundering supersonic booms behind them. Most of the *men* in the Kamikazes had been kids and trainees; the men attacking Carrier Division Seven were veteran professionals.

The Kitty Hawk had been two thousand yards away from Walter, almost directly stern on to him when the torpedoes dropped by the turboprop Gannets had started to hit the carrier. The fish must have been small, lightweight devices with relatively diminutive fifty or sixty pound warheads but that was no consolation. At least two of them had exploded under the stern of the flagship, others had gone off against or under her engine rooms; these latter would have caused local shock damage but been very unlikely to have breached the carrier's double hull. However, the torpedoes which had detonated against or in close proximity to the ship's propellers and rudders...

Although water still churned under her port transom, proving that at least one prop was still turning the Kitty Hawk was as good as dead in the water.

She could not launch or land her fixed wing birds without wind over her decks.

She was helpless, her massive flight deck a giant target.

The cruiser Boston was manoeuvring to place herself on the flagship's port beam. Walter assumed that the Albany would be steering to do likewise to starboard. The Boston had ranged ahead of the Kitty Hawk, now she was racing back into position.

Walter risked a glance skyward.

Five miles above the stricken Kitty Hawk vapour trails crisscrossed the heavens. Already in the east the sky was darkening to black and the first stars glittered. It would be night soon.

The approaching scream of jets drew Walter's eyes down to the ocean.

Two English Electric Canberras; both heading straight for the

Kitty Hawk so low that their jet tailpipes were ripping up the waves behind them. The Boston, every gun firing was racing to put herself between the bombers and the carrier with a great bone in her teeth, cleaving through the water. The cruiser's Terriers streamed smoke and fire as they sped towards the nearest Canberra at impossible speeds.

Walter had not imagined that a close range line of sight wave-skimming shot was viable with a Terrier launcher. Nonetheless the missiles dashed the bomber into the sea half-a-mile short of the Kitty Hawk.

Even in ideal conditions it took at least thirty seconds to reload the launcher rails, and longer to spool up the internal guidance systems.

Walter waited for the surviving Canberra to pull up.

It never happened.

The bomber flew straight into the starboard side of the Boston.

Moments later the its bombs, two thousand pounders and as many as four thousand pounders it had dropped unseen - probably by anybody on the Boston because the aircraft was so low and everybody on the cruiser was diving for cover - skipped once, twice across the water and crashed into the Boston's starboard side.

First there was a big explosion and a crimson bloom of igniting aviation fuel as the bomber instantly disintegrated on impact with the amidships superstructure of the cruiser.

And then a terrible, devastating drum roll of heavy, booming explosions as the bombs hit.

In the space of a handful of seconds the fifteen thousand ton, six hundred and seventy feet long cruiser was a burning wreck. The wreck forged ahead several hundred yards before her engines fell silent and a series of huge secondary explosions began to wrack her shattered hulk.

The cruiser's Terrier magazine lit off engulfing the previously untouched stern in a roiling fireball. A boiler imploded deep in the ship as water flooded into one of the fire rooms. Ready use ammunition for the Boston's five inch secondary battery began to cook off.

Walter shut his eyes.

Men were throwing themselves over the side of the doomed ship to escape the flames. For most there was no hope as the cruiser, her flank torn open to the sea rolled over onto her starboard side where, for long moments she lingered on her beam ends, her red-leaded hull dull in the failing light, before turning turtle and staring to go down by the stern.

Walter watched her go, bobbing in the water a little over five hundred yards away.

Even as he had been witnessing the fate of the Boston he had heard other, heavy explosions – in fact, he had felt them through the water, punching him in the guts and reverberating in his chest – and now he saw a new pillar of smoke rising from somewhere beyond the

Kitty Hawk.

As he watched the carrier flushed both her twin-Terrier launchers.

Walter tried to follow the track of the missiles.

And that what when he saw the silver specs diving towards the Kitty Hawk from on high; like three dark falling avengers, the evil delta bat-like wing of a Vulcan, and the two arrowhead silhouettes of Victors swooping on the helpless carcass of their victim.

The Terriers climbed almost vertically to meet the V-Bombers.

Two missiles found their target; the others slashed past.

Walter almost but not quite breathed a sigh of relief.

But...

One of the deadly killer arrowhead silhouettes was still lancing down towards the stationary Kitty Hawk; and in her slipstream a cluster of tiny black shadows, and one ever larger and larger killer bomb.

It could only be a Grand Slam; twenty years after it was designed still the biggest conventional bomb ever made. It was capable of drilling through thirty feet of reinforced concrete or fifteen inches of armour plate like a knife through butter, before detonating its four ton Torpex warhead.

It was too surreal; a clutch of smaller bombs and one massive, ship-killing missile was following the surviving Victor down onto the Kitty Hawk.

Walter had seen enough in the last few minutes to know that even if all the bombs somehow missed the carrier's five acre flight deck that the bomber would not.

He watched that descending arrowhead with numb incredulity.

Chapter 92

19:24 Hours
Friday 3rd July
The Angry Widow, South of Kharg Island, Persian Gulf

Squadron Leader Guy French had wondered if – when this moment came – he would have the chance to fill his mind's eye with Greta's face. She had been the love of his life. The October War had taken her from him and with her all the futures they might have lived together.

But actually he had no time for reflection and besides his senses, every single nerve in his body and his whole waking mind was overloaded with the demands and the sensations of 'the moment'. He had no idea if he was still actually flying *The Angry Widow*, or if in this terminal dive she was in any way still 'flyable'. Something had hit the aircraft when the Terriers had rocketed past; for all he knew the tail had come off. Apart from anything else there was too much vibration and it was far too noisy to hear himself think.

Down below him the deck of the Kitty Hawk was growing larger in the windscreen. The carrier probably hoped to shoot off another salvo of Terriers but he was more worried about the wall of tracer that several ships beyond his field of vision had started to hose into the sky above the flagship.

Bizarrely, the exploding shells, harmless looking clusters of small black pock marks in the air and the tracery of cannon fire lacing the lower atmosphere prompted him to ask if the Americans' fancy rocketry had proved, in some way, *cranky* the first time it had been tested in a real battle.

It was one thing to reload the launcher rails in half-a-minute and to get a new salvo in the air in no time flat in an exercise when nobody was shooting at you; but what was it like doing it over and over again in a real fight onboard ships that were twisting and turning like scalded cats?

Was it really as easy as he had heard some US Air Force men claim to hold or re-acquire radar target locks when somebody had his hands around your throat and his knee in your groin?

How great were all those marvels of space age gadgetry the Yanks built into their ships these days when it actually came to a real fight?

He had not expected there to be so much smoke down at sea level.

Why is the Kitty Hawk dead in the water?

"We've got her, chaps!" He called over the intercom. "I've got her dead centre..."

The whole airframe juddered, the controls froze.

Suddenly Guy smelled burning through his oxygen mask.

He turned to his right, blinked a couple of times in confusion. His co-pilot, a thoroughly decent fellow from Chippenham in Wiltshire whose parents were life-long doyens of the Wilton Hunt – or had been before the October War – was not there. Or rather, he was not there from the navel upwards and neither was most of the right hand side of the cockpit.

Guy felt the slipstream attempting to rip him out of his seat.

He was hanging on his straps.

Still *The Angry Widow* arrowed down towards the Kitty Hawk.

Physics, aerodynamics, ballistics had a lot to be blamed for, he thought idly. His mind was suddenly quiet as the flight deck of the great ship filled his windscreen.

Only one more decision to make, old fellow...

Guy French shut his eyes as the Victor plunged through the curtain of anti-aircraft fire above the doomed flagship of Carrier Division Seven.

Chapter 93

19:45 Hours
Friday 3rd July 1964
HMAS Anzac, Arvand River

The hull of the destroyer clanged like a bell every time a 115-millimetre round from one of the handful of surviving T-62s sheltering in the ruins of Khorramshahr struck her. The tanks' armour piercing shells went in one side – the starboard – and out of the other, port side, even the high explosive hits seemed to explode as they exited the ship unless they chanced to encounter something solid, like a bulkhead or a boiler.

Commander Stephen Turnbull had grounded the Battle class destroyer in the mud at the mouth of the Karun River after HMS Tiger had been beaten into submission. Rear Admiral Nicholas Davey had taken the big ship east of the tip of Om-al-Rasas Island before she ran onto a sand bank; by then the cruiser's 6-inch main battery and Anzac's four 4.5-inch guns had cleared the banks of the Karun River and both north and south like giant scythes reaping a crop of blood and iron. In the minutes before the enemy realised what was going on, firing unopposed over open sights, the two surviving ships of the ABNZ Persian Gulf Squadron gun line had destroyed whatever hopes the Russians might still have had of any kind of victory. In those minutes they had made hay in the failing light; but as always, there was a reckoning.

If Tiger and Anzac had wrought terrible execution at ranges of a few hundred yards; each was equally as vulnerable to the point blank fire of the surviving Red Army tanks. Soon mortar rounds began dropping around and on the ships, and heavy machine gun fire tore up the waters of the Arvand River as dug in gunners on shore duelled with Anzac's 40-millimetre Bofors and Tiger's last operable quick-firing automatic 3-inch turret.

The enemy had concentrated on Tiger.

The water around her had boiled with shell splashes, and time and again the big ship had rocked with new hits as fires began to go untended. In the end her magazines were shot 'dry'; and she was no more than an unmissable sitting target in the river. Even as Anzac – slowly sinking - had steamed past her Tiger was dying. Fire blackened and riddled with splinter and shell hits everything above the main deck was smashed, only her ragged battle flag still flew, blown hither and thither by the heat rising from the fires below.

"That's the last of the HE, sir!"

Stephen Turnbull heard the shouted report as if through ears stuffed with cotton wool. He was half deaf from the concussion of the big guns, weak from the cumulative effects of several bloody splinter wounds.

"Shoot star shell if that's all we've got!" He yelled above the bedlam.

Only one of the Anzac's twin Bofors mounts was still in action; the destroyer had very nearly emptied her magazines. Under his feet Turnbull could feel the ship settling deeper into the muddy bottom.

The bastards would never sink the Anzac!

What he would not have given to have seen the look on the faces of the Red Army men on the banks of the Karun River when Tiger and Anzac glided out of the fog of war!

Anzac's 'A' turret had been disabled by a direct hit from a big shell, either a 115-millimetre from a T-62 or a 100-millimetre from a T-54. The armour piercing round had penetrated it and killed everybody inside.

'B' turret's twin 4.5-inch guns were still firing, the barrels of both probably very nearly red hot. Every flake of paint had sloughed off the overheated rifles, now in the half-light they looked almost...*rusty*.

Stephen Turnbull surveyed the darkling eastern horizon.

Gun flashes sparkled evilly from the north to the south, from the desert above Khorramshahr to the conflagration consuming the smashed refineries of Abadan.

"Permission to fire the Squid, sir?"

Turnbull tried not to grin too widely. He failed. The notion of shooting salvoes of four hundred pound Squid anti-submarine mortars at shore targets appealed to the mordant streak in his nature. The shore was easily within the two hundred-and-seventy-five yard range of the stern launcher.

"Yes. Carry on!"

The messenger scampered aft.

Ignoring the deck flinching beneath his feet as more hits slammed into the starboard side of the destroyer, Turnbull went to the twisted shambles of the bridge wing and looked aft down the length of his once handsome command. Anzac was being systematically wrecked and there was absolutely nothing he could do about it.

The Squid mortar thumped three times, the big bombs arched across the muddy water between the ship and the northern shore, splashing into the detritus scattered along the northern bank of the Karun River.

Nothing happened for some seconds.

Each round was time-fused.

Two hundred pounds of Amatol made a satisfyingly impressive bang when it went off. The blast from the three explosions wafted across the Anzac's bridge and afterwards, there was an odd quietness. It was the quietness of exhaustion and despair, that moment that comes sooner or later in all battles when the living collectively acknowledge that to fight on a second longer is pointless.

The fighting went on elsewhere; in the Arvand River the Tiger and the Anzac burned and the tide of human misery slackened, as if the flood tide of war had turned.

"Cease firing!" Turnbull ordered, hoarsely. "Cease firing!"

Chapter 94

19:45 Hours
Friday 3rd July 1964
South of Kharg Island, Persian Gulf

It was like a bad dream in which things seemed to be happening out of sequence, each scene tumbling over the next until all that remained was a melange of feverish impressions, any one of which in isolation would have beggared a sane man's sanity.

Big grey warships were stopped in the water and burning; and there were great palls of drifting smoke, and smoke rising like Biblical pillars of salt all around the compass in the fast dwindling last gleaming of the day. And still guns hammered distantly and the trails of missiles still sporadically crisscrossed the sky like messengers of the gods.

The air above and around the flagship had become a killing ground.

The bombs of shattered aircraft still plummeted downward in unstoppable ballistic arcs; and still the USS Kitty Hawk had lain dead in the water. From over a mile away Walter Brenckmann had watched the swarm of smaller bombs, specs like motes in the corner of his eye but each one a five hundred or a thousand pound agent of death begin to fall around the flagship. Tall geysers of water erupted and walked towards the great ship's bow.

One, two yellow-red flashes spoke of hits on the flight deck as the distant thunder of multiple explosions rolled across the iron grey seas. Kitty Hawk might have shrugged off such 'gnat bites' as these hits but her travails had hardly yet begun.

Walter watched the great black dart of the ten-ton Grand Slam falling impossibly fast. The huge bomb seemed to be falling vertically; except it was not. Relative to the Kitty Hawk the missile was still travelling in the direction of flight of the bomber which had released it, drifting, drifting ahead of the carrier. For a split second Walter believed it would miss the carrier's bow.

When it came the explosion seemed to envelope the entire forward half of the massive ship; and Walter thought the Kitty Hawk must sink. A mile away from the detonation of the bomb's four ton Torpex warhead the shock wave hit him like Rocky Marciano had just punched him in the guts. He was astonished when as the water settled the flagship was still...*there*.

He looked up at the screaming in the sky.

The silvery arrowhead silhouette of the diving bomber looked...*wrong*. In the time it took him to work out the most of the V-Bomber's tail and sections of both wings were gone, the aircraft, a Victor had burst through the umbrella of light anti-aircraft fire the surviving escorts had thrown up above the flagship.

Large parts of the bomber peeled away, there were two small

explosions seemingly just behind the nose of the falling aircraft and then the wreck was underneath the deadly mile-thick layer of detonating anti-aircraft rounds. Kitty Hawk cleared her Terrier rails again but by then it was too late, the Victor was too close, too fast and no guidance system known to man could 'lock up' a missile falling from the heavens at twice the speed of a rifle bullet.

Unlike the bombs which had very nearly fallen 'long' the Victor had to have been under some kind of control almost until the end, correcting for drift, its nose pointed at the middle of the Kitty Hawk's flight deck like an assassin's dagger to the heart of his next victim.

There were two explosions.

The first marked the impact of the bomber just aft of the carrier's bridge; it was as if a small bomb had gone off on the deck.

A fraction of a second later the entire mid-third of the biggest warship in the World was consumed by a massive double detonation.

The bomber must have still had her bombs onboard...

Walter stared.

He had just stared, transfixed, hardly aware of the debris, large and small thrown hundreds, thousands of feet in the air tumbling randomly down into the sea between him and the doomed ship. Shrapnel splashed the grey waters nearby while, a mile distant the wreck of the Kitty Hawk began to settle, her bow and stern lifting slowly, brokenly as she lay ever deeper in the water beneath a rising dirty grey mushroom cloud.

Beyond Kitty Hawk a Coontz class destroyer, either the William V. Pratt or the Dewey, was stopped in the water, her stern enveloped in flames. Closer to the sinking flagship the guided missile cruiser Albany was listing to port and smoking from damage forward. Farther away there was another pillar of smoke, another unknown ship on fire in a sea that was suddenly, sickeningly friendless. A lone Sikorsky SH-3 Sea King forlornly approached the broken stern of the Kitty Hawk.

The helicopter began to circle.

It was as if, like Walter Brenckmann, its pilot could not believe the evidence of his eyes and had not the first idea what was going to happen next.

[The End]

Author's Endnote

Thank you for reading this book; and secondly, please remember that this is a work of fiction. I made it up in my own head. None of the fictional characters in 'The Mountains of the Moon: The Gulf War of 1964 – Part 2' – Book 8 of the 'Timeline 10/27/62 Series' - is based on real people I know of, or have ever met. Nor do the specific events described in 'The Mountains of the Moon: The Gulf War of 1964 – Part 2' – Book 8 of the 'Timeline 10/27/62 Series' - have, to my knowledge, any basis in real events I know to have taken place. Any resemblance to real life people or events is, therefore, unintended and entirely coincidental.

The *'Timeline 10/27/62 Series'* is an alternative history of the modern World and because of this real historical characters are referenced and in many cases their words and actions form significant parts of the narrative. I have no way of knowing if these real, historical figures would have spoken thus, or acted in the ways I depict them acting. Any word I place in the mouth of a real historical figure, and any action which I attribute to them *after* 27th October 1962 *never* actually happened. As I always state – unequivocally - in my Author's Notes to my readers, *I made it all up in my own head.*

The books of the *Timeline 10/27/62 series* are written as episodes; they are instalments in a contiguous narrative arc. The individual 'episodes' each explore a number of plot branches while developing themes continuously from book to book. Inevitably, in any series some exposition and extemporization is unavoidable but I try – honestly, I do – to keep this to a minimum as it tends to slow down the flow of the stories I am telling.

In writing each successive addition to the *Timeline 10/27/62 'verse'* it is my implicit assumption that my readers will have read the previous books in the series, and that my readers do not want their reading experience to be overly impacted by excessive re-hashing of the events in those previous books.

Humbly, I suggest that if you are 'hooked' by the *Timeline 10/27/62 Series* that reading the books in sequence will – most likely - enhance your enjoyment of the experience.

––––––––

Thank you again for reading *Mountains of the Moon.*

Other Books by James Philip

The Guy Winter Mysteries

Prologue: Winter's Pearl
Book 1: Winter's War
Book 2: Winter's Revenge
Book 3: Winter's Exile
Book 4: Winter's Return
Book 5: Winter's Spy
Book 6: Winter's Nemesis

The Bomber War Series

Book 1: Until the Night
Book 2: The Painter
Book 3: The Cloud Walkers

Until the Night Series

Part 1: Main Force Country – September 1943
Part 2: The Road to Berlin – October 1943
Part 3: The Big City – November 1943
Part 4: When Winter Comes – December 1943
Part 5: After Midnight – January 1944

The Harry Waters Series

Book 1: Islands of No Return
Book 2: Heroes
Book 3: Brothers in Arms

The Frankie Ransom Series

Book 1: A Ransom for Two Roses
Book 2: The Plains of Waterloo
Book 3: The Nantucket Sleighride

The Strangers Bureau Series

Book 1: Interlopers
Book 2: Pictures of Lily

NON-FICTION CRICKET BOOKS

FS Jackson
Lord Hawke

Audio Books of the following Titles
are available (or are in production) now

Aftermath
After Midnight
A Ransom for Two Roses
Brothers in Arms
California Dreaming
Heroes
Islands of No Return
Love is Strange
Main Force Country
Operation Anadyr
The Big City
The Cloud Walkers
The Nantucket Sleighride
The Painter
The Pillars of Hercules
The Plains of Waterloo
The Road to Berlin
Until the Night
When Winter Comes
Winter's Exile
Winter's Nemesis
Winter's Pearl
Winter's Return
Winter's Revenge
Winter's Spy
Winter's War

Cricket Books edited by James Philip

The James D. Coldham Series
[Edited by James Philip]

Books
Northamptonshire Cricket: A History [1741-1958]
Lord Harris

Anthologies
Volume 1: Notes & Articles
Volume 2: Monographs No. 1 to 8

Monographs
No. 1 - William Brockwell
No. 2 - German Cricket
No. 3 - Devon Cricket
No. 4 - R.S. Holmes
No. 5 - Collectors & Collecting
No. 6 - Early Cricket Reporters
No. 7 – Northamptonshire
No. 8 - Cricket & Authors

––––––––

Details of all James Philip's published books and
forthcoming publications can be found on his website
at www.jamesphilip.co.uk

––––––––

Cover artwork concepts by James Philip
Graphic Design by Beastleigh Web Design

Made in the USA
Lexington, KY
21 May 2019